THE PRINCESS
HE MUST MARRY

JADESOLA JAMES

MILLS & BOON

To my little ones, who make the writing process
both a challenge and a joy!
I love you dearly, and I look forward to
seeing your own happy endings someday.

THE PRINCESS HE MUST MARRY

JADESOLA JAMES

UNDONE BY HER ULTRA-RICH BOSS

LUCY KING

MILLS & BOON

First Published in Great Britain 2022
by Mills & Boon, an imprint of HarperCollins*Publishers* Ltd,
1 London Bridge Street, London, SE1 9GF

www.harpercollins.co.uk

HarperCollins*Publishers*
1st Floor, Watermarque Building,
Ringsend Road, Dublin 4, Ireland

The Princess He Must Marry © 2022 Jadesola James

Undone by Her Ultra-Rich Boss © 2022 Lucy King

ISBN: 978-0-263-30088-8

06/22

MIX
Paper from
responsible sources
FSC® C007454

CHAPTER ONE

Badagry, Nigeria

IT WAS TIME for the bride to dance in, and despite the ruby-encrusted stilettos she was very precariously balanced on, Princess Tobilola Obatola felt as if she were floating. Her vision was partially obscured by a gossamer-light veil, shot through with threads of actual gold.

She had no worry in stepping forward; her attendants were all there, perfumed in a custom blend of rosewater and lemon that made them a fragrant, powdered, gold-draped mass of moving bodies. There were two at her back and one at each elbow, ready to guide the former princess of Gbale—and future princess of the royal principality of Djoboro—to her place at her husband's side. The *álágás,* traditional emcees who were also there to playfully hustle money for the bride from her husband's family, who had come prepared with full purses, were making quite the show of it, and their voices boomed directly into Tobi's ear from a too-loud speaker.

"Our bride, the daughter of His Majesty the Oba of Gbale, His Esteemed Greatness, is here to honor our gathering—"

Tobi barely managed to suppress a giggle. Even on his daughter's wedding day, her father ensured he was recognized. Through the veil, her eyes connected to the warm brown ones of her older sister, Kemi, who shot her a warning look, though it was tempered by a smile.

Behave, she mouthed. Tobi lifted her chin and tossed her head in answer, setting the heavy rubies set in gold dancing in her ears. Oh, she would behave today. That was for certain.

The *bàtá* musicians held their hourglass-shaped *dùndún* drums tight beneath their arms and began to play an enticing rhythm, intended to draw her and her bridesmaids forward. Tobi mixed the shy mincing steps of a modest bride with the swaying hips and waist of a seasoned woman, moving forward lightly, flicking her wide fan open so that it glittered and ruby-studded streamers fell neatly to the ground.

The head *álágá,* sweating beneath her impressive *gele* headdress, announced Tobi's arrival in playful Yoruba, entreating the guests to welcome her, and her husband's family to shower her with gold. Beside her, her translator swayed, interpreting her words for the foreign guests.

"Dance, our bride, dance well—"

The room was awash in laughter and applause and the slightly giddy sounds of champagne-soaked celebration, and as Tobi danced, there was only one thought in her head.

I've pulled this off! I'm free!

Free from her domineering father. Free from a life under virtual lock and key, interrupted only by whatever acts of rebellion she'd been able to manage, brib-

ing guards with jewelry, sneaking out to dance the
night away...

Memories faded into reality as she made her way
across the massive hall. Somewhere in the corners of
her consciousness, she took in the details that featured
in any traditional Yoruba high society wedding: round
tables, laden with centerpieces of rubies, roses and gold-
leaf-plated flatware; the elegantly hand-embroidered
aso ebe worn as uniform by the members of the royal
family; the cell phones and tablets held aloft to capture
a glimpse of the royal bride; and finally her princely
husband and his entourage, waiting for her, draped in
glossy robes of the deepest ruby red.

The only one that mattered, really, Prince Akil Al-
Hamri, her husband, led the pack, flanked at the elbow
by his brother, Prince Malik.

They were both softer casts of their father, King
Al-Hamri the Third, who sat imperiously on a min-
iature version of the great throne he used in Djoboro.
The tiny North African principality hugged the coast of
Morocco. It was created, legend had it, by descendants
of Mansa Musa who had defected from his hajj cara-
van centuries ago, made it slowly and perilously across
the desert in search of the sea, and set up a settlement.
You could see the mark of their Malian ancestors in the
proud tilt of their chins, full mouths, and gently tinted
skin, a shade or two deeper than their Moroccan neigh-
bors, although centuries of intermarriage had created a
diversity that was nothing short of stunning.

Akil, Tobi thought, mouth suddenly growing dry,
was a perfect representation. Then she shook herself
severely. You'd think at nearly twenty-one years, she'd
be able to relegate childhood crushes to where they

belonged—between the locked covers of old Disney princess diaries.

She finally reached the dais with the men.

Tobi knew her part without any prompting from either her sister or the *alaga ikoro*, who was eager to move the ceremony along. She knelt before her father, closed her eyes as he murmured prayers over her. Her stepmother was next, the woman's voice low and cultured, as she'd tried without success for years to replicate in Tobi.

The king of Djoboro's prayers were concise but heartfelt, and at the end he lifted her chin, peering at her through the veil.

"I am thrilled," he said, in a voice loud enough to carry through the hall, "that our homes will be so united. The oba of Gbale has been a friend since we were schoolboys, and to have our children find happiness together is one of the great joys of my old age."

Then it was over, and Tobi lowered herself before her husband. The marble floor of the dais burned hard and cold through the fine beaded fabric of her *iro*.

She glanced up through the veil, only for a second. The look on Akil's face was stoic, although there was a glimpse of conspiracy there that danced round his mouth in the form of a smile. His long fingers moved to grasp the edge of her veil, lifting it gently over her head.

The assembly sighed as one.

"We pulled it off," he said through his teeth, then cleared his throat and launched into his own blessing. Wishes for health, longevity, children—

Her face burned. Things that were not to be for them, as they'd be divorced as soon as they could manage. Her husband had married her to get an inheritance; she'd married him to gain her freedom. There was to be no marital bliss, no happy ending at the end of this fairy tale. There would be no point in looking upon her husband with favor; they would never be together, not in that way. It didn't matter that he was tall and sinewy, with broad shoulders and a tapered, dimpled chin that would have looked utterly absurd had he not been so... large, capable, assured. There was no reason to picture what those arms around her might feel like, or—

There was no time to think; Akil had finished speaking. She took the ceremonial cap of marriage in her hand, placed it on his head with trembling hands. Then there were exchanges of books of faith, of rings, and they stood and turned to face a cheering crowd, thrilled because at last they could dance, and eat.

She was married.

More importantly, she was free.

"Hell of a way to spend a wedding night, little brother."

Akil blinked, startled out of the reverie he'd been in for the past hour or so. The massive suite of the villa rented and renovated for the express purpose of housing the king of Djoboro and his guests was virtually empty; most of his groomsmen, Djoboran mates from school and otherwise, had taken a chartered plane to Lagos to get drunk and prowl the nightclubs for women, he supposed.

Akil had other plans.

"Why aren't you with the boys?" he countered, turning his back on his older brother and placing two shirts into an overnight case. Normally a servant would do the packing, but he needed to be as discreet as possible tonight. A covert flight would be leaving Lagos in the morning, and he needed to be in the airport well before then. Only he and the generously paid pilot of the Djoboran Royal Flyer knew his true destination.

"You know Jamila would end my life if I dared." Malik came up behind Akil, peered over his shoulder; his big brother's extra two inches served him well here. "And you're…planning a runner."

"My plans for the evening are my business."

"Where's your bride?"

He glanced down at his watch. Tobi, presumably in her own chambers, was doing a similar packing job. Their cover story tonight was that they were running away to Lagos under the cover of darkness to leave for a secret honeymoon. In reality, Tobi had purchased her own ticket to Dubai, where she had friends, she said. No one knew that the "lovestruck bride and groom" would be headed to separate destinations.

Akil lifted his head, turned and faced Malik. His brother's face was good-humored, but also slightly suspicious. He'd been confused by Akil's sudden wish to marry, unconvinced by his claim of infatuation with Tobi, and had been trying to connect the dots since then.

Akil, frankly, didn't really care if he did or not.

What his family did meant little to him. His life was finally beginning. He'd planned this escape carefully for the past few years. Exciting new business ventures awaited him, where he'd be able to operate as his own man, not the spare to the throne of Djoboro, his movements not examined through the lens of a throne that would never be his. Spending years under the exasperated gaze of Malik and the king hadn't helped, either. Among other things…some too dark for him to ever utter to Malik. He'd tried once, and he would not reflect tonight on how miserably that had turned out.

Djoboro's gleaming palace hid many dark secrets, including the treatment of its second royal son. And as much as he loved his country—as much as that love for it had kept him there long after it was healthy—the time was finally right, and the thought made his lips twitch as he spoke, deadened his expression.

"She's in her room," he drawled, "packing as well. I think we're entitled to a private getaway after all that drama, yes?"

Malik had the grace to look embarrassed. "Oh."

"Don't worry, the renegade prince has no intent of bolting this time. I won't embarrass you."

"Akil…"

"You know, I think you'd lay off on at least my wedding day." He shot his brother a sardonic smile, then shouldered his bag and headed out into the hall.

He didn't look back.

When Akil finally exited the villa, eager to get some fresh air before being confined for the ride to Lagos, the massive compound was quiet. Even the mosquitoes and other night insects seemed to be exhausted from the night's festivities, and the white stone garden was almost eerily quiet. Akil started when the door behind him opened, and Tobi crept out, only a few feet from where he stood.

"The driver's pulled up outside the gate," she said, but she hesitated. "You're going."

"You are, too." His mouth curved upward. "Dubai, right?"

"Right." Her fingers moved self-consciously to the elaborate wedding coiffure still on her head.

"How are you getting there?"

"Etihad."

"First class, I hope."

Even in the darkness he saw a flash of milk-white teeth. "Thanks to your generosity."

That's right. He cleared his throat. The payout he'd given her was hefty but would be nothing compared to the trust he was to receive. And why, he wondered, did this feel suddenly awkward?

Akil knew her as the daughter of his father's friend, of course. He'd watched her grow up in bursts at events they'd both attended over the years, and his memories of her were mostly as a bewitchingly pretty little girl, one who never stopped talking. He'd been a boy himself and taken little notice of her except for that one fact.

Her rebelliousness had come to light when his father and older brother were discussing her after a visit from the old king, who had complained when asked about his children, who sat with their stepmother, presumably gossiping with the women at their own entertainment that evening.

"Kemi is a good girl, but Tobilola is a trial," he'd said grimly. "I can't wait till she's another man's problem."

The men had laughed good-naturedly, but Akil saw it firsthand when he ran into his underage guest later that night, dressed clearly for Djoboro's rather vibrant nightlife. He'd been eighteen then, so Tobi must have been—fifteen or so? She'd been wearing far too much makeup, a dress he supposed she fancied made her look older, and a scowl that was meant to frighten him off.

"Aren't you supposed to be at the veterans dinner?" she'd demanded before he could ask any questions.

"Aren't you supposed to be in bed with a glass of

milk?" He'd been amused, despite himself. Blowing off his princely duties for the evening possibly wasn't the classiest move of the night, but no one ever missed him when Malik was there. Not that this slip of a girl needed to know those details. It was embarrassing enough to have to sneak out of *anywhere* at his age. Tobi, at least, would understand the nuances of respect in African culture; outright defiance was something to be carefully considered, especially for a royal son.

Again, he wasn't going to explain that to *her.*

She narrowed her gaze, and the two eyed each other for a moment, then she slung an obnoxiously bright designer bag over one slim shoulder. "I won't tell if you won't," she announced, clearly pleased with her notion of mutually assured destruction.

Akil's first impulse had been to laugh in her face, but something about her earnestness held him back. He bit back the snort instead. "How do you plan to get out?"

"Taxi. Called it already." She waved a rhinestone-studded phone under his nose.

"Have fun." He'd pushed his hands into his pockets and pushed off, then paused to look over his shoulder. "Oh, and Tobi?"

"Eh?"

"When you get back, have them drop you off at the north gate. Ahmed's the night guard, and he isn't a tattletale."

He'd saluted her half mockingly before leaving.

Now the party princess was his wife, and they were both still running away. Him to be his own man, no longer tethered by the crown, and Tobi? What did she want? Her own freedom, she'd said, with a trace of desperation in her voice. The seed had been planted in his

mind only a few years ago, at her older sister Kemi's
wedding; the two had been seated near each other and
fell into conversation. Tobi's face was especially mo-
rose for a bridesmaid, and he'd been just tipsy enough
to ask her why.

"I'll miss her," she'd confessed. "It isn't easy, living
at the palace."

"Isn't it?"

"My father is very strict." Her lovely face had been
troubled, and in that moment, he'd sensed a kindred
spirit.

"You'll have to marry then yourself, and get out,"
he'd said lightly, and her eyes flashed.

"Trust me, I would if I had the chance!" she declared.
"It's stupid to even have this conversation in the twenty-
first century—"

"Your reality isn't the same as everyone else's," he'd
said mildly. "And neither is mine." He'd heard the rumors about her father's strictness with his daughters;
everyone had. Conversation had drifted to other matters, but an idea had taken root. And the moment he'd
decided to take his wedding inheritance and use it to
fund his new life, he'd needed a coconspirator, and Tobi
was who he thought of immediately.

So here they were.

There was something very companionable about
standing there in the muggy gray darkness with her:
there were details he hadn't had the time, or the inclination, to notice before. Unlike the heavy woven fab-
rics of her bridal set, she now wore a slinky dress that
dipped low in the front and barely skimmed her thighs;
the way it clung to the soft points of her body was especially distracting.

He felt his body stir, half turned to face her and looked at her, really looked at her, for what felt like the first time.

She's lovely. Large dark eyes, a full mouth, perfect skin, and soft curves that manifested in full breasts and lush hips. She shifted a little and his throat tightened as he caught a glimpse of the dusky points of her nipples, visible through the dress.

Where the hell was she going, dressed like that?

He was startled when Tobi cleared her throat and took a step forward. Her face was unreadable, steeled into a light expression.

"Thank you," she said, and her arms went round him briefly. He heard her clear her throat. She was muttering something else, but Akil was startled by a frisson of lust so powerful he nearly took a step back.

Had he done that he would have completely missed the soft slide of her breasts on his chest, the sweet musk that rose from her skin. She was all warmth and softness, and he was suddenly dizzy, affected by a physical pull so strong it disoriented him for a moment. Yes, he'd seen women in the past and wanted them, almost immediately. Yes, in some ways, the entire night had been set up for this, with all that close, heated contact while dancing, while holding his new bride tight for intimate photos. But this—

Tobi stepped back. He could hear a car pulling up. Instinctively—possessively—his hand slid down to capture her left, drew it up to look at the large cluster of rubies and gold beads on her ring finger.

Embarrassed, she tugged her hand back. "Should I give it—"

He shook his head quickly. "Not until we decide to divorce."

She drew in breath. "I suppose we should talk about that."

She was right, but he didn't want to talk about that. He didn't want to do anything besides indulge the completely unpredicted, irrational want that was making his blood run warm. It was, he realized, affecting her as well. Her breathing had quickened, and she hadn't made a move to step out of the circle of his arms. His fingers inched down to cup her hip and she shivered, then softened against him.

She wants you. He was experienced enough to know it, and she wasn't schooled enough to hide it. He'd seduced a stranger more than once, and yes, in many ways Tobi was a stranger. But she was also his wife, and they had a bargain.

He'd made a vow to let nothing hold him back from this new life, and an entanglement with the young woman who was now tipping full berry-stained lips up in a clear invitation for a kiss…

You haven't enough self-control to be successful at anything. Thank God Malik was born first.

Harsh words, only a few of many, and they hadn't even been the worst of it.

Akil's arms became like iron. Tobi stepped back, looking embarrassed and more than a little confused. She crossed arms over nipples that now protruded clearly from the dress, even in the darkness—

"I'll give you a lift," he found himself saying, and cleared his voice to eliminate the huskiness that threatened to squeeze it tight.

"A lift?"

"To Dubai." He took another, cleansing breath. "I've got the royal jet, you know. They think you're on it anyway. It makes sense."

"It's out of your way."

He allowed his mouth to curve up slightly, and then slowly, deliberately, he allowed his eyes to flicker over her.

"It's probably a terrible idea," he admitted, "but I feel like celebrating, and you're the only one who could… understand that. Will you come?"

Confusion flashed over her face. But in answer, she gracefully reached down into the designer bag at her feet, pulled out a light sleeveless jacket and tugged it on over her dress.

"Okay," she said, smiling.

CHAPTER TWO

"So, what do you want to do?"

Tobi blinked.

"It's a fair question," Akil said in that dry voice she'd come to associate with him. He lifted his heavy brows up and down. In the dimmed light of the Djoboran Royal Flyer, they looked almost too dark for his angular face. "We could eat, watch a film or sleep. There are accommodations for all three on board."

"I know." She'd also known that her new husband was fabulously wealthy, in a way her own father could not boast, and this method of transport was a clear indication. The jet itself was like nothing she'd never seen before. It was all fragrant leather and gold-trimmed paneling. "It's certainly extravagant."

"I'm looking forward to purchasing my own."

"Purchasing your own…jet?"

"Of course. A businessman of my standing needs reliable transport."

Tobi gaped at him. "Just how much is your inheritance, anyway?"

He frowned slightly. "It's ill-bred to talk about money."

"Even with your own wife?" The awkwardness was

dispelling with the lightness of the conversation; Akil had never been so friendly to her before. She supposed it had less to do with her charms and more to do with the fact that he'd gotten his way, but considering they were holed up together for six hours, she'd take what she could get.

Akil began to laugh, a low rumble in his chest that felt strangely intimate. "It's not my inheritance. It's a prince's trust that comes to me—*us*—automatically on marriage to a fellow African of royal blood." His eyes skimmed her face. "There's a bonus if you bear me a son, but I think we can make do with what we have now."

Oh. Heat raced to her face. The kiss that she was almost sure they would have shared earlier still hung between them; it had dissipated with the matter-of-factness of boarding and with their banter, but it seemed her husband could summon the energy with barely a tilt of his smile, and Tobi was many things all of a sudden: too warm, too cold and very aware of how close she was sitting to Akil.

"What do you plan on doing with it?" Tobi asked, her voice barely a squeak.

Akil picked up the remote control of the massive entertainment system and fiddled with it, but he didn't attempt to turn it on. He eyed her as if wanting to gauge her sincerity, then took a breath. The moment of clear self-awareness, almost uncertainty, surprised Tobi as much as it touched her, but when he spoke his voice was clear and confident.

"I'd like to sell the sun." He smiled a little bit at her confusion. "Ra Enterprises, to steal a name from our Egyptian brothers." He cleared his throat, sat up a little straighter. "It's an investment company, specifically in solar power. Some years ago, Morocco began an initiative to switch to and advocate for solar power through the country. It's seen some progress, but..." He trailed off. "I think that myself and my investment will make a huge difference. Just—look at the continent, Tobi. We should be the richest in the world, but the power situation in some countries—"

"You don't have to tell *me*," Tobi responded drily. Nigeria was notorious for its electricity outages and poor supply. There were barely any families, regardless of status or income, who did not find it necessary to have a generator. Mismanagement, of course, was the main culprit, but if what Akil was saying was true—

"People won't have to rely on electricity as much," she said softly.

Akil nodded eagerly. "If Morocco is successful, it can be patented in other countries. You know Djoborans have Malian roots, so that is a huge interest for me. And—"

"Nigeria next, *abeg*," Tobi said, mouth twitching. "I'd love to live somewhere without the smell of diesel choking the air at night."

"You might have to wait a bit. Ideally neighborhoods with little or no access to electricity, whether generator or state-made, would get panels first. It's..." Akil's voice trailed off again, and suddenly Tobi felt quite alone, for he looked so far away.

She felt a stab of longing that had little to do with the crush she'd been nursing for so long, or with his closeness, or with the intimacy of the moment. Akil was leaving, just as she was, but he had—purpose. A plan. She was leaving for—what? Freedom? What would that mean, exactly? Being able to party when she wanted? Moving freely without a guard?

Somehow, the luxury celebratory vacation she'd planned for herself in Dubai with some of the money she was getting paled in comparison and seemed more than a little silly. Ambition had been thwarted completely by her experiences, in a way. All her years under lock and key, she'd lived for the thrill of the moment, for the little pleasures she could steal away. Akil, on the other hand, was leaving with a plan, a *mission.*

What could she possibly offer to the world now that she was free? What was she to do with herself? She almost opened her mouth to share this with Akil, but she closed it against the words. It felt remarkably immature and silly, as if she were indulging in a fit of self-pity brought on by a realization of how self-absorbed she was. And in a quick, determined flash, she thought, *There's no one who's ever been proud of me, but when I get to Dubai, I'm going to make sure I'm proud of myself once this is over.*

Akil lounged back against the sofa, closing his eyes; his thick dark lashes made shadows over his cheekbones.

She swallowed before speaking, plucking at the folds of her skirt. She didn't want the conversation to be over, even after her pause to think. "Surely you could do this without leaving, though?"

When he opened his eyes and looked at her, the gentle camaraderie that had been there was completely gone. "No."

"Surely, the king would want—"

"You know nothing about my father and what he might want." The first flash of anger that had crossed his face was now well controlled, but it burned beneath the surface, and with an intensity that made her swallow. "Djoboro has other interests. And none of them include me."

Tobi pressed her hands to burning cheeks, trying to regain her composure. "Do you hate it very much, then?" she asked, softly.

Akil looked away as if embarrassed by his reaction. When he turned back to her his face was like stone but determinedly light.

"No, I don't, but it is not for me anymore, unfortunately." He glanced away darkly, then shook his head as if clearing the thoughts. He turned back to her and smiled tightly. "Film?" he asked, the earlier moment of intimacy well and truly gone. Tobi crossed her arms over her chest, feeling curiously bereft.

"Fine."

"Are you cold?"

"Not really." She caught her lower lip between her teeth and leaned back, then winced as the elaborate chignon on the back of her head sent hairpins digging into her scalp. Akil noticed at once.

"I don't know how you've been carrying that thing around on your head all day. Can I help you get it off?"

"It is heavy." The chignon was fastened by a large comb of rubies and gold, a gift from Akil's family, and ruby-tipped hairpins were arranged artfully to supplement the heavy knot of braids at the base of her neck. She'd been paranoid about losing any of the precious jewels in the villa, and so had kept the coiffure, but she supposed that on the royal jet…

Taking her admission as assent, Akil gestured for her to move closer. There was one breathless moment where she felt the warmth of his chest at her back, and then those long, slim fingers were gentle at the base of her neck, in her hair.

"I'll go slowly," he said very low by her ear, and though the words surely were not meant to be as sensual as they sounded, she felt a quiver collect low in her stomach. Akil made little noise as he worked; just a grunt here or there as he pulled one heavy pin out, let it drop to the ebony table in front of them with a clatter, then another, and another.

Tobi closed her eyes for a moment and tried to breathe. Akil regarded a pin between his fingers with some curiosity before putting it down.

"Djoboro," he said mildly, "was founded on rubies. That's why it's in everything. Have you ever heard the story?"

"No," she managed. His warm lips were still far too close to her ear, and his voice had dropped to a low rasp. Was he doing this on *purpose?*

"Mali, as you probably know, was an empire built on gold. When the nomads who founded Djoboro left Mansa Musa and traveled to the shores of Morocco, they prayed to Allah for a fruitful resting place. When they settled, at last, it was at the foot of the mountains—now the Djoboran range—that borders the country, taking shelter there.

"The first few years were arduous." He'd finished removing all the ruby pins, and a small pile of them sat glimmering on the table. "You know how legends go—starvation, despair, prayer for a miracle, some enterprising pilgrim stumbles across something that saves the day. Well, ours stumbled across a cluster of rubies, laid bare by a storm he'd taken shelter from. Mining started in the region, and—well. The wealth of the country was built on it, and it's still the only place in Morocco with even a sign of a ruby. We mine other things as well, a few amethysts and loads of copper, phosphate, other less sexy things. But the rubies are where the story is." There was one moment of hesitation, and when he spoke his voice was tinged with regret for the first time since they'd started the conversation. "It's a beautiful place, Tobi. Don't ever let my experiences make you think less of it. I will miss it very much."

He set down the comb on the table, and Tobi let out a sigh of relief as the long thin braids she'd dressed her hair in for the wedding unraveled, falling nearly to her waist. Normally she wore her thick jet-black hair in an Afro blown round her head like a halo, but she'd wanted something she didn't have to think about in her first few days of freedom. She'd barely noticed Akil's fingers in her hair; his heat, the pleasantly spicy sweetness cling-ing to his skin and the hypnotic timbre of his voice were as soothing as it was.

His fingers were still in her hair, and had he moved closer? She bit her lip hard, then took a breath, leaned back against his chest. She felt him stiffen for a mo-ment, then loosen completely as he exhaled.

That thing that had hung between them earlier was back, and frankly crackled at the edges.

"I didn't intend to seduce you tonight, Tobilola," he said with a frankness that surprised her, and at the word, there was that familiar quiver, low in her belly. Oh, she wouldn't mind if he tried, and she reckoned they both knew it. She wouldn't mind at all. She could not say this in words, of course, even with her trademark bold-ness, but she did half turn her head to see if he'd take the invitation he'd rejected before. A pause, and then he captured her lips with his…

She registered softness, a gentle warmth that engulfed her senses. He kissed with the same confidence he did everything else, but it was the unexpected softness that startled her into melting against him. She didn't even bother hiding it; she turned round and pressed herself full against him. The thin dress she wore was worse than wearing nothing at all; it was only a barrier to the feel of him on skin that was suddenly tingling. She knew instinctively that he'd handle her body as gently as his mouth moved against hers, and she wanted it more in this moment than—

He was kissing her more urgently now, and she had to bite back the *please* that was threatening to break forth from her mouth. Arching against him was one thing, begging would be another. His lips skimmed a place on her neck she didn't even know was as tender as it was and—

"Akil," she whispered, knotting her fingers in the fine linen of his shirt, as if he'd vanish if she didn't. The sliver of skin where his shirttail met his trousers was far too tempting, and she slipped her fingers upward, felt the muscles tense. His skin was warm and taut and she just knew, even as her face burned at the thought, that he would taste as good as he smelled. He kissed her almost reverently, and she'd never felt more like a princess in her life…

His princess.

Akil's hands slipped upward to grip her thighs, and Tobi retreated into the softness of the cushions with a half sigh. Despite his gentleness, her mouth felt very swollen now, almost bruised; she had no idea how long they'd been kissing. It wasn't just all lust haze, either; her heart was racing. In this setting, the soft lighting, on her wedding night, surrounded by the sort of riches that most people only dreamed of—it was all so romantic, a manifestation of what had started out as a teenage fancy.

"It's okay," she whispered, and the inhalation of breath that followed lifted her breasts, swollen and aching beneath the thin fabric of her dress. His eyes focused on them for one moment, and they darkened. Then he hardened his jaw.

"Tobi," he said, and his voice was not unkind. "Sit up. I'm sorry, this isn't a good idea at all."

Tobi didn't move. "I—what?"

In answer, he released her thighs and cleared his throat, moving backward himself. He extended a hand to help her up and dumbly, she took it. As soon as she was properly upright Akil was on his feet, that half-pleasant, inscrutable look from the wedding back on his face.

"I'm sorry," he said simply. "That was wrong."

Tobi opened her mouth to answer—with what she didn't know—but Akil was speaking still.

"We're headed in opposite directions, Tobi. You're my wife, and in a way my partner in this, not some pleasant distraction to celebrate a successful night. This isn't fair to you."

Pleasant distraction? She felt as if she'd been kicked in the gut. "Akil—"

He shook his head. "You'll thank me for not…well, you'll thank me. I'm sure you've got your own plans, as well. A liaison would only complicate things."

Complicate your noble vision, Tobi thought a little bitterly, even knowing she had absolutely no right to think like that, no claims to Akil at all. After hearing his grand scheme Tobi still had not managed to shake off that feeling of aimlessness, and, as open as he'd been, he hadn't even asked her specifically about her own plans, had he? And the kisses they'd just shared, he hadn't been particularly attracted to *her*, other than physically. Tobi was no fool; she'd seen how his eyes had lingered on her breasts earlier. He was content to kiss and touch her, but he'd locked her out the moment any sort of intimacy had entered the conversation.

He doesn't care. Why would he? She'd forgotten what he was to her—the means to an end. Tobi had never registered as anything else. That was all, and a few ill-advised kisses in the soft, secluded light was not enough to change that. She wasn't enough to change that. She'd never been worthy of much attention. Her father had made sure of that, and her favored older sister, kind as she was, hadn't helped.

Again came that surge of determination. She would prove to her father, to Akil, to everyone, that she was more. That she had more to offer. This was the beginning of that. "Sorry," she managed. She was trying for a nonchalant voice, but it came out rather strangled.

"There's nothing to be sorry about." Akil cleared his throat. "I'm going to instruct staff to bring us a meal, and you pick something to watch." He looked down at his watch. "Congratulations, Tobi. Freedom in four hours."

Tobi managed a rather sickly smile, but it slid off her face as soon as he was out of sight.

Freedom, yes. Money, yes. But what on earth was she to do with it?

CHAPTER THREE

Three years later

"I'M *BANNED*?"

The sound of her voice reached a pitch that made heads turn in the arrivals line at Dubai International Airport, but Princess Oluwatobilola Obatola Al-Hamri didn't care one bit. Her adversary, a bearded officer dressed in a snug-fitting khaki uniform, looked bored at her outburst. Bored!

"No entry," he barked, sliding her passport back to her and waving the next person over.

This infuriated Tobi even more.

"Come," the officer directed, but Tobi ignored him.

"Let me see," she demanded, leaning over the counter to where she'd just had her eyes scanned. Her rhinestone-encrusted Gucci sunglasses clattered to the floor, but she barely noticed. The white-robed immigration officer leaned back in alarm, then looked to make sure the officer was still there.

"Madam, you cannot come over here—"

"And why not? How is this even *happening*?" Tobi's mind raced through every possibility, still coming up short. Her residence permit was still valid. It had been ar-

ranged by the mobility team of *African Society*, the reality show she was set to film in three days. For one month
she and other prominent society women from the continent would take up residence in the finest suites at the
Chantilly Hotel to be wined and dined by the handsom-
est, richest men in the Emirates, and hopefully, generate
enough drama to become the summer's blockbuster hit.

Tobi was feeling more optimistic than she had in a
long time—it had been such a rocky road for her. The
first eighteen months of her freedom had been fueled
by enthusiasm and adrenaline; she'd enrolled in a business program, worked night and day on a business plan,
invested heavily and lost spectacularly. It was so bad
that she'd actually contacted Akil on impulse. After all,
he was her husband, wasn't he?

She hadn't been able to reach him.

She tried official channels—email, a message through
his secretary. She was promised extra funds in a carefully worded letter, and the next moment a large amount
of money, wired from Morocco, had shown up in her account, still with no message, no acknowledgment at all.

That was enough for her to burn with humiliation;
Tobi could take a hint, and this one had been applied
with all the subtlety of a hand grenade. She'd swallowed
her pride, paid her debts, buried the real hurt she felt
beneath a fit of industry and turned to the one com-
modity she had—her face, and her name.

Cultivating a socialite persona in Dubai wasn't difficult at all; the culture was ripe for it, and she already
had quite a reputation from the social media accounts
she'd kept running during her years of captivity, mostly
for her own amusement. This show promised a quarter of a million dirhams in her pocket, and grimly Tobi

told herself she would never be ashamed of the path she had taken. It was honestly earned money, and some of the socialites and influencers she met were the most elegant, well-educated women she'd ever known. They certainly weren't stupid enough to lose a veritable fortune in a year.

A quarter of a million, she reminded herself as she signed the contract with a flourish.

Per episode.

Sometimes being married to a prince, regardless of how big an ass he was, paid off. Literally. And if she felt like she was selling off a little of her soul, well then—so be it.

Now Tobi noted through her shock that the nasty little man was speaking rapidly into a black headset. Two female police officers, swathed in a skirted version of his uniform, came over rapidly.

"Ma'am, you have to come with us," said the older of the two.

"I most certainly will *not,*" Tobi said haughtily, drawing herself up to her full height. She reached for her mobile. "I'm going to call my hosts, and they will sort out this problem immedi—"

"Call whoever you want, it will not help," called the immigration officer from where he lounged at a safe distance. Now that backup had arrived, he seemed almost to be enjoying himself. "You have a ban everywhere in the Gulf Cooperation Council. Maybe a problem with another country."

What?

"We can arrange a flight for you back to Nigeria, ma'am," the second female officer said.

Back to Nigeria? Only literal *steps f*rom entering Dubai? After a vacation of only a week?

Over my dead body.

"That won't be necessary," she said. Unconsciously the crisp voice her father used to address his staff crept into her vowels; she did not bother to correct it, as her older sister, Kemi, often begged her to do. She gathered her irritation around her as a sustaining force. Someone was going to hear about this, and they weren't going to like it when they did. She fixed her face back into its usual imperious expression and stalked back out for the long walk of shame back through the arrivals terminal, flanked by her new friends.

Were he a man who indulged in any sort of frivolous emotion, Prince Akil Al-Hamri might have actually been nervous.

He glanced down at the handmade ruby-studded watch on his wrist and took a deep breath before taking a sip of the rich, smoky Dalmore that sat in the bottom of the heavy crystal tumbler his attendant had just handed him. He'd need the fortification before facing his sure-to-be-furious wife.

Tobi.

Even the thought of the lengths he'd had to go to get her here tonight was irritating. Why was she so stubborn? He'd sent several politely worded letters—at least, he assumed they were politely worded; he'd had no reason to think his lawyers would be rude—requesting an audience with her. They'd reached out by phone, email, even telegram. No response. The only thing his lawyers had produced was that his messages had been received—and Tobi, from all indications, was deep in debt and flying to Dubai to star in a reality TV show.

Akil forced himself to take a deep breath when he realized he was gripping the glass tight enough to imprint the pattern into his palm. There was a tightening at his temples, too, one that the aspirin he'd taken as a preventative did little to assuage. It wasn't just irritation at the thought of her ignoring him: it was a faint, niggling guilt that was born of what he'd done to her eighteen months ago. She'd reached out for help. He'd ignored her. He'd wanted to drive home the message that their lives were to be completely separate and sent a good chunk of money to get the message across.

You weren't fair to her. And now you want a favor.

It was not the ideal position for him to be in.

He glanced at his watch again; his contact at immigration had confirmed her arrival an hour ago. Plenty of time for his wife to have worked up a good head of steam.

Akil rose to his feet, placed down his glass and headed for the exit.

There was no way in hell he was going to enjoy this, but he had no other choice.

"You *bastard*!"

Akil found Tobi in the lobby of the Dubai International Airport Hotel, a no-frills accommodation with the ugliest striped carpet he'd ever seen in his life. His wife looked completely out of place, shifting from one designer high heel to the other, and he took a long moment to survey her carefully. He hadn't seen her since their wedding night three years ago.

She was dressed in the flamboyant style she'd adopted soon after marriage, no doubt a response to finally escaping from under her conservative father's thumb. The ruched minidress she wore glowed against her smooth dark skin and ended mid-thigh, showcasing strong, slim legs that were perfect stems for the curves above. The neckline was as low as the hem was high, and thin gold chains looped round her slender neck. Despite all her jewelry, she was missing one crucial piece on her left hand, and he raised his brows.

"Where's your ring?" It's not like he could have missed it. The hideous thing had come from the royal vault, and could likely have been seen from space.

She glared, ignoring the question. "I should have known you were behind this," she fumed. The anger on her face did nothing to diminish her beauty. It was the first thing that Akil had noticed about her on their wedding day, to be honest, after all those years apart. The full lips in the round face and heavily lashed, doll-like eyes still gave her a look of innocent prettiness, despite the layers of makeup she wore. He cast his eyes down to the Louis Vuitton carry-on luggage at her feet, as well as the various bags from duty-free, bulging with purchases.

"You really left me no choice, Tobi. I've been trying to reach you, and you didn't reply." He gestured that she should sit in one of the leather chairs in the hotel lobby. She sank down into the nearest one; he suspected she needed to, and fought back a sudden urge to smile. Nothing about this was funny, but seeing Tobi so ruffled was decidedly amusing; she looked like an angry hen.

"*What* is so funny?" she demanded. "What you did is probably illegal."

"Yes, likely," he agreed politely. Thank heaven for

wasta, and the fact that he had plenty. He rarely called in his royal title, but it's clout had been very useful today, not that Tobi would want to hear that story. "Water?"

"You can go to hell."

"Gladly, after I'm done with our business this afternoon." His voice hardened. "Look at me, Tobi."

She glanced up. If looks could kill… He continued, his voice showing a calm he did not feel.

"The fact that you ignored me is completely unacceptable. What if it was an emergency?"

Her chin began to shake, and he could see her cheek dimple inward ever so slightly, as if she'd bit it to hold back tears. "I stayed out of your way," she said, staring down at the small glass table in front of her. "It's what you wanted, isn't it? It's what you *paid for."*

"So you didn't answer this to be petty," he pointed out. It was what he wanted, and he'd told her with no hesitation.

"My motives are none of your business."

She'd changed, he thought. She was just as beautiful as she'd ever been, but some of the spark he remembered had gone out of her eyes. He felt a sudden pang of remorse that surprised him; after all, he'd had his reasons for cutting her off thoroughly. He still remembered the hazy attraction of that night and how intense their kisses had been.

Pull yourself together.

"You'll come with me," he said briskly. "My jet is ready to go. I'll explain everything there."

She drew back. "I'm not going anywhere with you."

He laughed without humor. "You will, or I'll ban you from every country you attempt to enter, including your own. So, choose. Stay in transit hell—" he stood, smoothed his trousers "—or come with your husband and have a nice, *reasonable* chat aboard a private jet. Your choice, *my love.*"

At that, Tobi's face hardened, and she stood. "You must be crazy to think I'll follow you anywhere. No, Akil. I'm not a child to be ordered round by you, and despite whatever you've conjured in that small mind of yours, you're not a despot or anyone with power. You've got my attention. Either speak your piece or get out."

Their eyes met as wills clashed for a moment; then Akil sighed before speaking the words he could barely believe himself were true.

"My brother, Malik, is dead."

Akil relayed the shocking events with as much feeling as if he'd been discussing the weather and for a moment, they didn't register because of that.

"Malik—" she echoed dumbly. She remembered Malik, of course—a taller, harder-edged version of her husband. He'd danced in a perfectly correct but expressionless matter at their wedding, and had kissed her cheek with lips so cold she'd winced a little. Still, he'd seemed rather healthy—

"Blood clot, they say. Completely undetectable and just as unavoidable," Akil said crisply. "Painless, I suppose that's a good thing. Two days ago."

"I—I hadn't heard." Why on earth did he look like that? She knew that Akil tended toward the stoic, but he looked positively unmoved.

"Djoboro is small, and no formal announcement has yet been made. Most people wouldn't be able to name the current ruler, for all their airs."

Tobi didn't know what to react to first—the news,

which was horrific enough, or Akil's cold relaying of the news. "I'm so sorry, Akil," she said weakly.

He gave no other acknowledgment than a brief lift of his shoulders. "You see now," he said, "why I needed to reach you. I'm expected to return to Djoboro tomorrow."

"And?" Tobi's face must have still registered confusion because Akil was staring at her as if he couldn't quite believe she was being so thick.

"Malik has been acting as regent for two and a half years." Akil's voice finally showed some hints of strain. "I am his *brother,* Tobi, and the spare heir to the crown. Malik's wife, Jamila, had no children. And if indeed I am the regent king, that makes you—"

Tobi felt quite faint, and Akil's full mouth curved up into the first genuine smile of the afternoon, rusty as it was. "Sit," he said, almost kindly, and Tobi did, feeling she had to.

"I'm—"

"Yes. You are, as of two days ago, acting queen consort of Djoboro." He paused to let that sink in. "Perhaps we should have commenced with the divorce much earlier."

"It's hard to divorce someone you've convinced yourself doesn't exist," Tobi snapped, forgetting momentarily that he'd lost a brother and she should, at the moment, try to be comforting. Why, anyway, would she bother, when he clearly wasn't bothered himself? She raised her chin. "I'm very sorry for Malik's death, but again, I'm not sure why I'm here. I agreed to marry you so you could get your inheritance, and you've done very well with it. Otherwise, you made it more than clear you want nothing to do with me." Bitterness made her words sharp. "As far as I'm concerned, I've more than fulfilled my part of the bargain."

Akil's eyes glittered, and Tobi lifted her chin, crossing her arms across her chest. The past three years had wrought many changes in the young woman who had trembled in her husband's arms on their wedding night. She'd made her own way in the world, perhaps not as nobly as her stuck-up husband, but she'd done it. She'd made a name for herself, and she'd vowed many times along the way after that dreadful night with Akil that no man would ever make her feel less than worthy again.

That, and the fact that she was married, made for both a quiet and cold bed, but she'd learned to ignore it. She'd rather die a virgin if it kept her self-respect intact. Akil had the power to strip it from her with a few well-chosen words, but only if she let him.

She wasn't going to let him. Then he spoke, his voice casual and calm.

"I know you're angry." He moved in closer, eyes dark with something very much like—triumph, and this made her even angrier. He was so sure he had her. "It's quite a skill, being able to blow through that amount of money in only three years."

Tobi felt as if he'd struck her. "I—"

"I'd make it worth your while if you came back. No—no need to get up in arms, Tobi," he said at her outraged expression. "I have very little curiosity as to how much money you've handed to Hermès, or whomever—"

"I used that money to go to school!" cried Tobi, not even sure why she was defending herself; it was what they all thought of her, wasn't it? "And I made an investment that didn't—"

Akil waved a hand. "Again, not curious. I helped you then. Now I need a queen, and unfortunately for you, we are married. I don't see how you have a choice."

Tobi felt as if she'd been set on fire.

"If you think," she said icily, "that you can come here and bully me into acting as your queen, Akil Al-Hamri, you've another think coming. I'm not a child, and you haven't asked me a single thing—you've *demanded* it. You've made absolutely insulting assumptions about my doings, and you've shown up out of the blue after ghosting me for three years. You haven't even shown one iota of regret that your brother is dead!"

"My only regret," Akil gritted through his teeth, "is the fact that I have to go back."

Tobi made a noise of mock sympathy through her nose. "What a pity, the playboy prince who outwitted the evil royal family has to go back and do his duty. Finally act like a man, instead of a spoiled child—"

Akil visibly recoiled at that, and part of Tobi was horrified at the words speeding from her mouth without any hint of slowing down. It was as if all the hurt and resentments of the past few years had culminated in this single moment, and she was as intent on hurting him as he had her...

It probably shouldn't have hurt this much, she thought, suddenly tired. The problem had been that deep down inside, she'd wanted attention from him, hadn't she?

She could not say much more, however, for Akil turned on his heel and walked out of the lobby of the hotel.

CHAPTER FOUR

HAD HE SPOKEN, he would have cursed her. Not because of her harsh words—the headlines she'd clearly been reading about him over the past three years must have stuck quite firmly in her brain. No, it was her ill-timed accusation about Malik that made the blood throb in his temples!

Akil had never cared what people thought his reasons might be for exiting the royal family—they would think what they wanted anyway, and for months, North Africa had buzzed with rumors. The pet one—and the one that his wife clearly favored—was the one that painted him as a spoiled, entitled royal brat who wanted to spend his life partying on yachts and plowing through beautiful women while his father's health failed.

Now, with the weight of the invisible crown already on his head, how could he get Tobi to do what he wanted…needed? He mentally reviewed what he knew about the young woman—fearless, headstrong, stubborn, nothing like her more docile older sister. *And considerably more attractive.* The odd thought appeared, unbidden, and he frowned, shook his head, returned to his train of thought.

His brother's death must have him more unsettled

than he'd thought. Malik. He closed his eyes briefly.
The last time he'd seen him was on the night of his
wedding. Pain wanted to come and wash over him; he
wanted to both cry out and clench his teeth against
the unfairness of it all. Malik had been born to rule—
he'd thrived on the hope of it since childhood. When
their father's memory started fading over two years ago,
shortly after Akil and Tobi's wedding, Malik had taken
the regency gladly, though the event had been tinged
with sorrow. He'd contacted Akil, asking him to come
home. He hadn't. And he never would have, had this not
happened. Now it wasn't just an individual imploring
him to come home, it was an entire country. And care
little as he might for his family, Akil cared a great deal
for Djoboro. He loved his country with all his heart.
Hell, Djoboro was the reason he'd stayed long after it
was healthy anymore, long after he'd realized there was
no role for him in his family except for that of trouble-
maker. He'd married, he'd left. He'd been the happiest
he'd ever been for the past three years. However, his
past had caught up with him in more ways than one. He
had no brother. His father mentally was no more. And
he had a wife, who by every indication wanted nothing to do with him.

What was wrong with her? Yes, there had been no
communication between them since they'd gone their
separate ways, but hadn't he provided for her finan-
cially, even more than their agreement had stipulated?
He would be lying if he said he hadn't been curious, or
if he said he'd never thought about the undeniable attraction that had led to the brief passion of their wedding night. It hadn't just been lust that night; it'd been a
profound protectiveness that had scared the hell out of

him. There was no way he would ever be able to make her happy; his upbringing had left him with no tools to do so. And that night, even beneath the haze of passion they'd found themselves in—

Tobi had kissed him that night like a woman who needed more than he had the capacity to give. There'd been no artifice there, nothing but an earnest wish to be closer to him. And that had scared the hell out of him. Using each other to escape was one thing—starting something as risky as a relationship with a woman he could hurt was another. He never, ever in his life wanted to give another human being even a fraction of the pain he'd grown up with, and the way she'd looked at him that night—

It scared the hell out of him.

So he'd cut her off as thoroughly as he had his family. His sole concentration had been on Ra Industries—and he had succeeded there, far beyond his wildest dreams. Somewhere, buried in his mind, had been a desire to share his success with Malik when he was ready, give Djoboro the opportunity to invest in *his* business.

Now he'd never have that chance.

Akil squeezed his eyes shut against another wave of distress; if he gave in to it, in to any of it, he'd never be able to do what needed to be done, which was to get his wife and go home. It would be easy enough to force her into doing what needed to be done; for all her bravado, Akil was very schooled in manipulation. After all, his family had been experts, and part of why he'd left. But there was something in the wide set of his wife's eyes and a tremble about her mouth that struck something very much like conscience in Akil's chest.

He didn't have the strength to fight dirty. Not tonight.

Akil took a moment to steady himself, then turned and walked back into the lobby. Tobi hadn't moved; she sat with her knees pressed together, suddenly looking very much like the young woman he'd taken to Dubai that night just a few years ago. She'd been just as beautiful then, and just as distressed, and he'd responded to her just as strongly. Memories came rushing back in bits and pieces, more suggestions than actual scenes. Soft, sweet lips and scented skin. A warm body pressed against his. An exhale of breath and a trembling frame. And not all those reactions had been hers, were he honest.

He'd kissed her in a moment of impulse, a moment of weakness that he refused to dwell on, and she'd responded so very readily. He took it as a mark of pride that he hadn't let things go further than they did. But now, looking at her face…

Akil pushed the thought from his mind. Enough thinking. He had to get Tobi to come back with him, and he realized he might know just how to do it.

The Djoboran royal jet hadn't changed at all since Tobi was last in it. Then, she was a new bride, shaky with adrenaline and having successfully escaped virtual captivity. Now she was a woman wedded but not wanted— until now.

She and Akil sat silent and hollow-eyed in the main cabin, pods swiveled to face each other. A flight attendant had served them tea with a flourish, then bowed deeply and retreated. It sat untouched between them, along with an array of gorgeous pastries, gleaming with honeyed pistachios in layers of thin dough and sprinkled with gold dust. Akil did not seem to want to speak;

his eyes were focused on somewhere just above her left shoulder, and his spirit was far, far away. He'd asked her to come on board after he returned, saying that the quiet and privacy would be better than anything they could produce in the busy airport.

Tobi had agreed. After all, he'd lost his brother, and that was a fact she could not ignore. Now she endured the silence and picked at one of the sweets she'd been served before she couldn't take it anymore.

"Are you all right?" she said.

Akil's eyes flickered over her face, and his mouth twitched, just a little. "Truthfully, no. But I don't want to talk about it." His fingers idled at his own pastry. "I expect I should ask for your forgiveness."

"Don't, unless you mean it," Tobi replied, crossing her arms.

"No, I mean it," he said, and suddenly it was hard to breathe, because his eyes were fixed on her with an intensity that made her blood run hot. "I am sorry for ignoring you. I had my reasons."

"As I had mine for reaching out to you in the first place," Tobi said quietly. "You think very little of me, don't you? Just like everyone else."

Akil winced visibly. "Fair comment. What happened?"

Tobi chewed her lip for a moment, trying to gauge his sincerity. "I think it matters little in the light of what's going on—"

"Earthly things matter little to Malik now," he said drily, "but you and I are still here. I appreciate your concern. Go on."

Not even a sign of traditional grief. She eyed him for a minute before speaking. "I—it was stupid. I had this idea to set up a safe house back home, for women who need help and have no other options. A safe place to go until they're back on their feet, or can fend for themselves, no matter where they're from. Medical care, financial assistance, business loans—"

"I get it." There was a gleam in Akil's eyes. "It's a very good idea."

"Yes, but it was executed quite badly. Investing in Nigeria is risky as it is because of the levels of corruption, and I didn't make the smartest contacts." She'd been colossally ripped off was more like it, but that part of the story was still too painful to explain in detail. "I lost everything. And so—I contacted you."

"Ah."

It was only one word, only the smallest bit of acknowledgment, but the intensity in his eyes was enough to steal her breath away. The indifference was completely gone; for the first time, it felt as if he were looking at her, the real her. The Tobi who sometimes thought so little of herself, and strove so hard to do better.

Then he looked down, and the moment was dissolved.

"Malik and I were estranged at the time of his death," Akil said. His jaw was clenched hard, and there was a new glimmer in his eyes that hadn't been there before. Not tears—that would have been far too much for Akil—but some deep-seated, unspoken emotion. It grabbed Tobi round the throat like some dark force, pulled her in.

"I have to go back," he added, simply. "And I need your help if I'm to pull this off successfully. It isn't a ruse, not this time. I plan to stay."

She swallowed. "And me?"

"It's essential, for many reasons, that I have the woman I married by my side." All rage and arrogance was gone from his face now; he was sunken-eyed, an exhausted apparition that barely resembled the man who'd accosted her in the airport. "In return, I'll help you get your business back up and running. I will make sure it succeeds."

"More quid pro quo?" Tobi asked, a little more acidly than she first intended.

Akil raked his fingers through the thick hair on his head. "No, Tobilola, I'd do it even if you said no to this. It's a splendid idea," he continued. "And you clearly possess the heart of a queen, even though you don't want to take on the role."

Those words, simply spoken, broke something in Tobi that evaporated the anger like the morning mist, and she felt tears spring quick and hot to her eyes. Akil appeared to take no notice; he was turning a teacup over in his hand. It looked absurdly small in his long fingers.

"All right," she whispered. "I'll do it."

There was no triumph in Akil's face; he looked far too exhausted for that. He reached out and took her hand, ran his thumb over where her pulse beat wildly in her wrist; then he gently placed it back in her lap. "I'm going to give orders for the steward to get your things, and we'll be off as soon as we get clearance, if it's all right with you?"

She nodded, wiping furtively at her cheeks with her hands. "All right. And—I'm sorry about your brother."

"Kind of you to say," Akil replied. He stood and was gone in moments.

Now, hours later, and in flight, Tobi wondered if she'd made a mistake. After a deliciously hot savory meal served when they reached cruising altitude, Akil launched into the first of many speeches, all traces of what had been before completely gone.

"We land in a couple of hours," Akil said crisply once their plates had been cleared. "At the border of Djoboro and Morocco, there's a place there where the kings are buried, and Malik…"

"I understand," Tobi said quietly.

"There are protocols for the ceremony, of course, but—" And here, Akil drew a breath. "There will be a memorial back in Djoboro. Open to family and friends, and broadcast to the general public. It will need to be warm. Personable. Relatable."

"All right," Tobi said slowly.

"My sister-in-law, Jamila, will be on hand to answer any major questions, but she's understandably distraught. You'll be doing a lot of the heavy lifting."

It took a moment for this to register; then the tea cart was in danger again, for Tobi sat up straight. "Wait— what? You expect me to plan this?"

His brows lifted. "Not *plan,* exactly, but we need a member of the family to oversee the team that does it. You cannot possibly expect Jamila to subject herself to that kind of work when she's lost her husband so suddenly, and my father—" If his voice faltered a little on that word, he recovered quickly. "The man is mentally inept. I doubt he remembers what he ate for breakfast."

The casual cruelty of the statement stole her breath away. "He's your *father.*"

"So my mother told me."

"What is wrong with you?"

Akil's mouth twisted.

"And you won't have any input?"

He looked at her as if she were crazy. "Of course not."

"But he's your brother!"

"This isn't a line of conversation worth having," he said, and extended his legs. "Are you going to do it or not?"

Tobi gaped. "You don't want any involvement with this at all?"

"I have too much to do, Tobilola."

"But it's your brother! And I only met him once. You can't possibly expect me to—"

"Our team will have you apprised of everything from his education to his usual drink order, and there's thousands of hours of footage of him in our family archives. Give me something to do at the service, if you want, although I'd prefer to not do anything."

Tobi sagged back into her seat, and Akil began to busy himself with post-dinner cocktails, muttering under his breath. "Never so glad to see wine in my life. You should have some more tea, though, Tobi. You look a little faint."

A dumbfounded Tobi allowed him to hand her a glass teacup of an amber brew that smelled deliciously of mint and spice. "Mind, it's hot."

Tobi didn't know how to address this. Running a memorial service as her first act as queen, and for a man who'd proven to be nothing but exacting—and frankly, far more complicated than she remembered?

She sipped.

The tea was sweet and bracing, and the spices seemed to permeate her senses, soothe her churning stomach. She focused on the fine carvings in the glass for as long as she could, and when she looked up Akil's eyes were on her face.

"I thank you for doing this," he said, and though the words were stiff they were not ungracious. "It makes it…easier."

"What happened was tragic," Tobi conceded, and nearly fell off her seat when Akil spoke again. This time his gaze was fixed on the window, on the rectangle of sky that glowed white-blue through the velvet curtains. He looked as if he wanted to take to the skies himself. Tobi knew in a way exactly how he felt; she'd often worn the same expression, flying home from brief diplomatic trips with her parents, short bursts of excitement in a monotonous life.

"…people like you," Akil was saying, startling her from her reverie.

"Excuse me?"

His gaze dropped down to her face, though she had the feeling he still wasn't seeing her, not really. A part of her wanted desperately to follow him wherever he was—somewhere inside there, he must be grieving. But when he spoke, his voice was still steady and impersonal.

"I've followed your…online presence. You're very personable, Tobi. Warm. Funny. People connect with you. My people connect with you." The words were staccato, brief, and said as if they were foreign on his tongue. "My popularity has not been…high since I left."

"You left to do a good thing," Tobi said, confused.

His lips curved into a smile that didn't reach his eyes. "Perhaps, but the press chose to concentrate on other things instead, and my father's PR machine worked overtime to ensure his people thought I wasn't—well. It's a long story."

"You're still the son of the house."

He made a noise under his breath. "You'll see. My return may be rather unpleasant. You, on the other hand, you've already got quite a following. Our wedding generated a great deal of public interest in Djoboro, and there are people who've followed you with fascination. Schoolgirls, naturally, might be the biggest group, with all the princess worship. Women. Families. I've been castigated for abandoning you. It's not an ideal way to begin my rule."

Oh—*why* was Akil this complicated? She'd never known a man who could enrage her, frustrate her, sadden her and drive her to sympathy within a few sentences. What was it her father always said? She licked her lips, trying to remember before she spoke.

"Ilé ọba tójó ẹwà ló bùsi," she said, and smiled a little at the look of confusion on her husband's face. "It means that the king's house burned, and he added beauty to it. You will turn this into something wonderful. You brought the sun to Morocco, after all, didn't you? You'll do better for Djoboro."

She did not know where the words came from, or the confidence with which she uttered them. And for a moment, she thought she'd reached Akil as well. A glimmer of what in a normal person might be hope brightened his eyes for a fraction of a second.

Then his face settled back into its usual jaded caution.

"See? That's why you'll do great with the memorial service," he added brusquely, and cleared his throat. "Come, we've much more to go over."

CHAPTER FIVE

AKIL FULLY EXPECTED an ice-cold reception upon arriving back in Djoboro, and the royal family more than adequately played their parts. He and Tobi landed at the border of Morocco, then were flown by helicopter over the Djoboran range, whose majesty was shrouded in desert twilight. Tobi was fatigued; he could see it in her eyes, though she didn't allow it to show in the set of her shoulders or the angle of her chin. Good. She would need that strength in the coming days. Aside from absolutely necessary courtesies, no one had approached the royal couple, offered any words of consolation. They were too grieved, and Akil fancied he saw a resentment in the dark eyes of the members of the court that they were loath to hide. It only made him set his shoulders higher, lift his chin.

Over the centuries, royal Djoborans were buried in the Valley of the Kings, a shallow dip at the base of the Djoboran range, shrouded from view of the main road by an obligingly craggy landscape. As a child Akil found the place terrifying. Now the site suited his mood perfectly. There were no palaces or fine houses here, only the imposing mausoleum, stretching as if trying to touch the sky, and a pillared, wall-less shelter to accommodate witnesses who were expected to leave that same day. There were never any visitors here, no offerings of fresh flowers or any sentimentalities. The former rulers of Djoboro were left to their own devices here, and now Malik was to join them.

Malik, who'd tried to reach out to him numerous times in the past few years, only to be rejected.

I'm not sorry for it, Akil told himself. He'd made that decision about his brother years ago, and if there was one thing Akil did not permit, it was regret. But standing here in the oppressive heat of the North African sun and listening to the final declarations made over his brother's coffin, he found himself clenching his jaw so hard against roiling emotion it hurt.

They'd been boys once, and best friends, before their differences and their father's attitude tore an irreparable rift between them. Perhaps he should not have blamed Malik? He'd been a child himself, after all; it wasn't his job to protect Akil.

The ceremony was bone-wearyingly long. There was a long recitation for both years of the young king's rule, detailing his accomplishments and his service to the crown. There was a tribute to his widow Jamila, who he knew must be buckling under the silent reproach of having not conceived an heir in their five years of marriage. Akil would have been a tolerable king had there been an end in sight to his rule; now, Djoboro was stuck with a regent king that nobody wanted or respected.

Why am I even here?

As if reacting to his inner turmoil, he felt Tobi stir at his side. In his ruminations, he'd literally forgotten she was there. She glanced up at him, face half shrouded by the heavy veils she wore, and he was startled when she slid a small hand over his, hesitating for the briefest of moments before closing it over his fingers.

She did not look at him again. And despite himself, Akil's heart began to beat a little faster. She felt sorry for him, and if Akil hated anything it was being pitied. But he also could not deny that his heart ached now with an intensity it never had before, and she was the only ally he had, reluctantly or not.

The king's house burned, and he added beauty to it.

He didn't drop her hand.

Thank heaven that's over, Tobi thought, closing her eyes and sitting back in the enormous tiled tub of her suite in the Djoboran royal coach.

Post-ceremony, the royal couple had been escorted to the decidedly old-fashioned form of transport, used for generations to ferry members of the royal family within the country. It would, Akil told her, take them directly to the capital, where Jamila's old apartments were being readied for their new occupant.

"Certainly we can't turn her out so soon," Tobi had protested. Jamila's pretty round face was drawn, and she had barely said a word to Tobi at the ceremony, but perhaps she shouldn't be expected to. "At the very least she should have her home. And I'm assuming the palace is large enough to—"

"You know how these things work, Tobilola," Akil had scoffed. "Royal life is not exactly about sentiment. The king dies, the new king takes his place. Period. And Jamila was hardly there. Malik only ruled for two years."

"Still," murmured Tobi.

"You're headed for failure if you plan on letting your

emotions rule you. Excuse me, I have matters to attend to." Akil had stridden off with one of the many robed advisers that to Tobi had completely interchangeable faces. She was relegated to the care of a silent middle-aged woman who spoke no English; she took Tobi through swaying, drafty corridors to a comfortable suite that consisted of a sleeping car, a lounge and a bathing car.

"Mamlaka?" she asked, a little hesitantly, not sure if she was using the sovereign title correctly.

The woman understood. She pointed to a small door on the north end of the sleeping car, one that presumably led to Akil's suite. She then briskly drew an enormous tub of steaming water, produced a number of fragrant bottles that were sprinkled in and stood imperiously, pointing to Tobi's sandals, dress, veil and overdress until she shed them.

Tobi had done traditional hammams while on vacation, of course, and this bath seemed to be a condensed version. Her attendant scrubbed her vigorously first with soap and soft flannel and then with a preparation that felt a bit grittier than sand-crushed seashells, perhaps, in fragrant paste. Then came oil, rubbed into every crevice, and scraped off with a curved, sickle-shaped tool. The woman was too matter-of-fact for Tobi to be embarrassed, and in moments Tobi was settled in pleasantly hot water that reached her chin, made her skin tingle.

The woman said something to her, patted her on the cheek almost maternally, and was gone, leaving Tobi alone with her thoughts. She closed her eyes, leaned her head back, tried a little idly to identify what the pillow beneath her head was stuffed with. Pine needles? Eucalyptus? Whatever the delicious blend, it was loosening the bands of anxiety and tightness at her temples.

When the door of the car rattled open, she didn't even open her eyes. Doing so might risk how absolutely comfortable she was. "I wish I knew how to ask for a top-up of hot water," she murmured.

"There's a tap for your foot on the lip of the tub," a deep voice said, and Tobi shot upward so violently that a wave of water threatened to cascade over the edge.

"I—what are you—"

"You summoned me?"

"Summoned for where?" Tobi threw an arm over her chest. This sort of bath didn't even have the benefit of bubbles to hide beneath, and her body felt as if it'd been set ablaze. She twisted and looked over her shoulder to see Akil regarding her with decided amusement.

"Turn around!" she shrieked.

"So you didn't call for me?" He did turn, but not before a smirk and a languid skim of the length of her that made her face heat more than the bath.

"I certainly did not!" Her mind raced, and then she groaned, standing up and wrapping the towel round her body. The train was swaying gently now, and she had to clutch the fine brass handrails with all her might before climbing out; the tiles were slippery with oil. In her scramble to get out fast, her feet went out from under her. Akil whirled around in a flash and caught her upper arms.

"No, don't!" she cried, scrambling for the rectangle of luxurious Egyptian cotton that hid her modesty.

"Don't be ridiculous," Akil said roughly. He was at her side, supporting her to sit up. He removed the heavy brocaded dressing gown he was wearing and draped it over her shoulders. It smelled so like him that Tobi felt quite dizzy for a moment. She clutched the fabric around her damp body, and only when it was secure did she turn her head.

"Are you all right?"

"Fine," she mumbled, more embarrassed at her over-reaction than the fall itself. Akil now wore nothing except a pair of white cotton trousers, tied carelessly with a frayed drawstring, and considerably dampened by the water from her bath...

She drew her gaze upward in near panic. She'd never seen Akil in any state of undress before, and the lean hardness of his body was simply too much. He was hairless, and had obviously had a bath of his own; his brown skin gleamed in the soft light as if touched by bronze. Shadows placed every muscle in sharp relief, and his face, softened by amusement, was a fitting crown for it.

She squeezed her eyes shut. Maybe if she wished hard enough she'd find him gone when she opened them.

"Your hands are shaking," Akil said, and the gentleness in his voice made a lump form in her throat. Perhaps she was more tired than she thought. "Come on, Tobi. Up, and let's go. Your lounge car will be much warmer. We might be in the desert, but the nights are very cold."

Tobi opened her eyes and wordlessly took Akil's extended hand.

"You're not talking," he pointed out, and tugged her forward.

"I'm embarrassed," she said through gritted teeth. "I don't know why. I did ask after you, but I have no idea why Hajar would tell you I wanted you!"

"She likely assumed you wished me to catch you in the bath. You did look very fetching," Akil drawled, and the blaze of head-to-toe heat was back.

"I would *never,* even if we were actually—" She swallowed. "We buried your brother today!"

Akil lifted his bare shoulders. They'd reached the sliding door between the cars in her suite, and he shoved them open with perhaps a little more force than was necessary. "All the more reason to comfort your grieving husband, no? It went well. I'm sure you're exhausted."

Akil guided her through the lounge, seemingly unconcerned by his near nakedness. She couldn't take her eyes off the hollow at the base of his back, or the tensing of muscles beneath his skin as he walked. What was wrong with her, ogling him as if—

"Sit down. I'll ring for tea and something to eat," Akil ordered, settling her on a velvet-covered chaise longue.

"Please, some cool water as well," Tobi murmured, squeezing her thighs together as tight as she could. She knew it was exhaustion and nervousness, but she was suddenly terrified she'd cry. Beneath the heavy layer of brocade, her body was beginning to do things utterly outside her permission. It fairly hummed with an odd energy that she knew had very much to do with Akil. Her skin was tingling, and she'd never felt more aware of how heavy her breasts hung beneath the layer of embroidered fabric. It rubbed against nipples that were growing harder and more sensitive by the moment, and she crossed her arms, trying to still their movement. No hopes there. She'd stopped growing taller soon after primary school, much to her annoyance, but her breasts and hips had had a mind of their own and kept going long afterward.

Usually, she considered that an asset. Not today, though. And Akil seemed totally oblivious. When he came close to her, filling her space with that delicious scent, those trousers riding low on his hips… She dropped her eyes and skittered back a bit. She felt incredibly foolish, but she couldn't have stopped herself any more than she could stop breathing.

"What?" he demanded.

"I—just—could you—please put something on?"

Surprise lit his eyes, followed by that vague amusement she never was sure was real or not. "You're wearing my dressing gown," he pointed out.

"Please," she said, and he laughed for the first time since they'd reconnected in Dubai. He left, and in moments returned, tugging a white djellaba down over his stomach. The robe was stiff with newness and nearly touched the floor round his feet.

"Better?" he said a little arrogantly, and settled himself next to her.

"Thank you," Tobi said, and stared down at her hands. She wished it were better. He was covered now, yes—but his half-naked form had been firmly imprinted in her brain, and she knew it wasn't going anywhere anytime soon.

CHAPTER SIX

SO THE PARTY PRINCESS, the socialite of the year, was easily embarrassed by the sight of a half-naked man. *Interesting.*

Tobi hadn't looked at his face since he'd reentered the room, and was guzzling ice water as if she'd just run a marathon. She looked quite fetching in his dressing gown, he had to admit. The brocaded fabric swathed her curves tightly—and what magnificent curves they'd been, soft and supple with water and oil. Oh, yes—he'd seen everything, and the reality was just as enticing as her form-fitting wardrobe had promised.

He'd married a beautiful woman, in body as well as face. And a denser person than either of them would be able to discern the tension in the room. It was no surprise for him; Tobi was very attractive, after all. Any man would be stirred at the sight of her. But her reaction to *him*—

It was a distraction, and a welcome one. It chased out the darkness of the thoughts that had been crowding his head since he'd received the news of his brother's death. It reduced everything to the here and now—the two of them, the seclusion, the soft lighting, the fact that he knew precisely how naked she was beneath his robe. His wife, to take if he wanted, to release some of the tension that had held his body taut for days. It would chase out the memories and the threat of the mental regression to the hurt, angry young man he'd been.

You need this. And from the way Tobi's chest rose and fell, he did not think he'd be unsuccessful if he tried. Her lashes were fluttering rapidly over smooth cheeks; he suddenly was reminded of another night, three years ago, and he knew that in some ways this was a continuation of what he'd left unfinished then.

There were many words of seduction that he knew he could use on Tobi that night, but the memory of their wedding night stole them from him. Instead he extended his hands in silent invitation.

Tobi pressed her fingers to her cheeks. "It's—Akil, I don't know."

"Just allow me to hold you for a moment, *habibti,*" he said smoothly, and then she was there in his arms, pressed full against his chest. It was odd, in a sense, for tenderness was blunting the edges of the lust he expected to feel, and his hands did not go to her body, but to her face.

This was an entirely different type of distraction than he'd intended.

"The coach is beautiful," she said.

"I suppose it's decorated in better taste than the airplane," he conceded. "This is just the beginning. My people love luxury."

She was looking up at him curiously, and her expression was troubled. "I don't understand you," she blurted out. "We buried your older brother today, your father is ill, and you will be made king in a few days. King of an entire country you didn't even want, and you're not speaking about any of it."

"There are much more pleasant topics at hand," he said, a little more sharply than he intended. He trailed his fingers down to the hollow in her neck where rubies and gold had rested on their wedding day; funny, he could remember exactly how she looked. "I'm thinking about our wedding night, for example, and how lovely you looked."

She licked her lips. "You're trying to distract me."

"Indeed I am," he agreed.

"Are we never going to discuss—"

"No, because there is nothing *to* discuss." He managed to temper his voice a little more this time. "All I'm interested in at the moment is you, Tobilola, and how lovely you look in this light."

"Surely you don't think I can be waylaid by—" she said a bit breathlessly.

"I'd like to try."

He dropped his mouth to her neck, kissing the tender skin there, and Tobi actually whimpered. "Akil, this isn't—"

"Would you feel better about this if I admitted I was heartbroken? If I said I loved my brother dearly and will miss him for the rest of my life?" Tobi flinched at his sarcasm, but her soft breaths were coming faster at the sound of his voice, and at the brush of his lips that followed every sentence. He was moving upward now, toward his real target; the full, soft mouth that was parted with want, despite herself. He'd never touched a woman whose body was so delightfully reactive. "I'm not a liar, Tobi."

"But—"

"You know nothing about my family, or me." And it was true. He'd married Tobi as part of a deal, and there was no way she would be the one to draw out what he'd kept hidden for years, even though his body now felt more alive than it had been in months. "If you want me to stop, now is the time to say it," he said, his voice husky.

"You're not yourself," she said a little helplessly, and he laughed against the soft fold of skin at the corner of her mouth.

"I assure you that I've never felt more like myself than I do today." Then, as if falling upon some delicacy he'd been saving for hours to enjoy at his leisure, he kissed her.

Yes. This was exactly what he needed.

After a moment of frozen hesitation, Tobi matched his urgency so intensely it startled him. She kissed him hungrily, as if she'd wanted this forever. Her mouth tasted of honey, spice, cardamom and something vaguely familiar, an essence that hung round her that had stayed with him since that first night. Unfinished business, yes, that's what this was, and their bodies remembered exactly where they'd left off, even if their mouths refused to admit it. And if he managed to do this, managed to get her to a place where nothing mattered but the slide of skin on skin, he might also be able to banish all the ghosts that threatened to disturb his peace tonight.

He was using her. And she was letting him, frankly.

She should be angry, ashamed, horrified! She should be anything but what she was now, softening even more beneath his touch, arching her body up to him in clear invitation.

They were picking up where they'd left off, in a sense, and she wanted it badly.

Tobi shifted, her fingers catching his biceps, her leg sliding between his, and he grunted, slid his hands down for a greedy exploration of her bottom, her hips, palming both through the fabric she was draped in.

Tobi let out a sound that was half whimper, half moan, and in answer his hand curved round where one of her breasts rose soft and full beneath embroidered brocade. He thumbed her nipple through the fabric almost roughly; at this point they were so swollen, so sensitized, it was as if all the sensation in her body was reduced to those aching tips and a steady throb between her legs. He caught one between two of his fingers and tugged.

An oath escaped from her throat, and Akil chuckled. His hands were everywhere: her cheeks, her waist, her breasts. They found the braided belt on the dressing gown, the one she'd tied so securely, and toyed with it almost playfully.

"Akil—"

"Slowly," he said softly, and then he was drawing fabric from her shoulders, baring her breasts to his gaze.

He was so still for a moment she opened her eyes, and the look on his face brought that blaze of heat back, not embarrassed this time, but something far more primal. Whatever her reservations, all which seemed to have flown into the night, the mutual desire was undeniable. The swaying of the train was making her breasts move in a way that would have embarrassed her, but Akil's bold seduction had given her a wantonness that made her lift her chin instead, answering his look with a steady gaze of her own.

His mouth twisted a little, and then all her bravado was gone, for he tugged her close, palmed the heavy weight of her breasts in his hands. He was silent as he caressed her, first with gentle strokes of his fingers, then soft kisses, leaving her nipples untouched till they ached so badly she was virtually thrusting them at his mouth.

You know what I want. Stop teasing me. The teasing was not born of malice, though; it was a wish to draw out her pleasure to the highest point, until it was almost unbearable.

"Akil," she managed, and skittered violently as his thumb finally passed over her left nipple, circling the tight swollen bud slowly. Akil did not speak; instead he lowered his head to her other breast, catching her nipple between his teeth for *just* long enough and then sucking hard. For several moments the only sounds in the room were the few gasps she simply could not hold back and the hum and clack of the coach, hurtling toward its destination.

She might reach the peak of her pleasure just like this, she thought helplessly; her body had never been so tightly wound, so ready for it in her life. Akil's skillful fingers had left her breasts to slip through where the gown covered her thighs, and he was cupping her there now, the slickness she knew would be there surely on his skin. There was the barest brush, and she was gasping as her body tightened, then released, splitting into what felt like fragments of herself.

It'd taken so little.

Akil rocked her forward, and she buried her face in the crook of his neck. They were both breathing hard.

She could feel the hardness of his arousal against her bare thigh, through the layers of clothing he still wore; she shifted against him, and he made a sound deep in his throat.

"Will you let me—" she began, then stopped. Akil shook his head.

"Not tonight," he said gently. "We will, but not tonight. I need all my wits about me tomorrow, and you need to sleep." He tipped her chin up, peered into her face. His eyes were dark as the night speeding past through the red-and-gold velvet curtains. "Tobi—"

A draft came over her bare skin, and she shivered. She made as if to draw the robe closed, and he helped her after the slightest hesitation.

"You are so very beautiful," he said simply, running his hands down the slender length of her, then pulling the material together over her breasts. "There is no reason this time together can't be—pleasant for both of us, Tobi."

Tobi felt her insides chill, and she shifted to full sitting position, ignoring the now-uncomfortable dampness between her thighs. "What are you saying? You wish me to act as your queen in all senses, even though you don't—"

She couldn't finish her sentence. To think of love would be nothing more than absurd. She couldn't even fathom why the word had come to her mind, except she knew in a helpless sort of way that if she let him, Akil could easily work his way into her heart. His gentle words to her about her suitability for queenship had eased open the gates.

"I am grateful for the service you're rendering," Akil said, and that full mouth of his curved up. "We've a lot in common, Tobilola. We left our situations, made something of ourselves. Although duty brings me back, you're under no such obligation, at least not forever." He paused and took a breath. "Plan what you're going to do later, Tobi. I have no intention of bringing you into the hell a rule can be. There is no place for you here. I won't allow it. Enjoy Djoboro, help me conquer public opinion—share my bed, if you desire. But know that you're free at the end of it."

His voice lowered on that last bit, and Tobi felt her insides cramp with unfulfilled want against the aching emptiness that hadn't been filled by him. There was another emptiness there, too, and this one was somewhere deep in the caverns of her heart. She'd married Akil to escape her father's oppression, but she hadn't yet found a home, had she? She'd had noble aspirations. She'd gone to school. She'd failed miserably at her first attempt at business. Since then it'd been a series of hotels, apartments and visits to fellow socialites, parties and schmoozing with the most ridiculous company. Now, looking at her husband, the king, she felt her failures more keenly than she ever had before.

In reality, she wanted to help people and have a place to call her own. And like an idiot, she'd let that want lead her into the kingdom and the arms of a man who would not offer her that, even if he could.

At least he was being honest.

She drew her knees up. Akil was no longer looking at her; he was staring out the window, as if in a trance, initiated by the steady click-clacking of the train. The heat between them had fully dissolved. She waited a full moment before she spoke.

"So what am I to do afterward, then?"

Either he did not note the catch in her voice, or he chose not to recognize it.

"You have plenty of time to figure that out," he said in a voice that she supposed was meant to be comforting, and eased to his feet. He hesitated for a moment, then bent and kissed her cheek. His own was like sandpaper against her soft skin.

"Get some rest, Tobilola," he said, not unkindly. "We arrive at the capital at dawn."

CHAPTER SEVEN

THE AFRICAN PRINCIPALITY of Djoboro, named for its ancient ties to Mali, hugged the coast of Morocco. It was small, exquisite, and it was her new home—for the time being, anyway. Hajar woke her with the dawn, opening the curtains of the royal coach wide, humming low to herself as she laid out toiletries and items to refresh her mouth, hair and skin that filled her chambers with a rich scent.

With the aid of a translator app on Tobi's phone, she explained they would pull into the capital in less than two hours. Akil was awake and with his advisers, and she was asked to kindly join him as soon as she was ready.

Tobi thoroughly enjoyed a solitary breakfast of eggs, fruit and creamy, sour *labneh* with cheese and fresh-baked bread, looking out to the soft oranges and purples of the early morning. In a way, she was glad that Akil didn't appear; after all the emotion of last night, he'd have ruined the serenity of the morning. She was treated to a hazy sun rendered in brilliant reds and oranges, rising over the red-brown hue of Djoboran mountains, all flanked by desert that seemed to stretch to infinity. In front of them she could make out the gray outlines

of the sea, so far away it seemed to blend into the sky.
When she finished eating, Hajar bustled her over to
where her clothing was set out on the bed.

There was nothing there from her own wardrobe;
it was all brand-new and exquisitely tailored, down to
undergarments of some slippery, gauzy fabric so soft it
felt like she wore nothing at all. The dress itself was a
simple slip of corded cream silk that touched the ground
round her feet, followed by a gauzy overdress embroidered heavily at the neck, hem and wrists with fine gold
thread. She'd never seen such careful finishing; there
wasn't a loose thread to be seen. There were beaded
sandals and a matching belt; Hajar pulled and prodded
until it encircled Tobi's slim waist to her satisfaction.
Then, face pleased, she retreated from the room.

Only a few moments went by before there was a
knock and the door slid open.

"Oh, good. You're ready. Almost."

It took Tobi a few moments to place the petite woman
standing in the doorway. She was dressed similarly to
Tobi, except her gown and overdress were of the deepest
obsidian black. She carried a small mahogany chest in
one hand, and a long black ribbon draped over the other.

"National dress suits you, I think," she said briskly.
"There was a time when I would have killed for your
height; long skirts absolutely swallow me up. Do you
like it?"

"Very much." Tobi felt more than a little awkward.
She hadn't seen Jamila since the funeral; she hadn't
even known she was on the train! Akil hadn't deigned
to give her that information the night before. "I—how
are you doing?" she asked, reaching out an impulsive
hand. She could still remember the death of one of the

royal princes in her own father's house years before, and the devastated mood that had taken over the entire palace for days.

Jamila did not look displeased by her gesture, but she did look surprised. "Heavens, how good of you to ask, I'm fine. I'm here to help you prep for this morning. There will be a processional, and now that I am relegated by my husband's death to princess royal—" she said this with no apparent distress "—you must learn all my protocols."

Tobi kept from gaping, barely. What a family! Jamila's unlined face was perfectly serene; she didn't look distressed at all. In her smooth accented English she detailed the processional that would begin in an open car, followed by a walk across the country square, to the main palace.

"Then they'll ceremony you to death, with nary a cup of tea in sight," she wrapped up drily. "Your attendant will have water and cinnamon candy, so do signal for either if you ever feel faint. Keep your chin up, and never look directly at any camera, or some idiot blogger will accuse you of seeking them out. Pleasant half smile at all times, and one half pace behind the king."

Tobi nodded, wondering if she should be taking notes. "Where is he?" she asked falteringly, then immediately felt like an idiot for doing so.

"He'll be along shortly before we disembark. Sit down."

Tobi did promptly, and Jamila summoned Hajar, who brought in glasses of tea and a formidable-looking glass box of makeup brushes. As she worked on Tobi's face, Jamila drilled her charge.

"I know you've been married for three years. Have you learned Djoboran at all?"

"A few greetings," Tobi said hesitantly. *How could I when we weren't even together?*

"Say them."

Tobi did so, feeling rather foolish. Jamila nodded and corrected her pronunciation. "Your accent is rather pretty, though. Use them—it will be well spoken of. Any French? Arabic?"

"Only schoolgirl French, and I assure you that no one wants to hear that."

"We'll have to get you a tutor, then." Jamila sighed and drained the cup of Moroccan tea. "Yet another thing for us to do."

What kind of thing was this, expecting a widow of only a few days' time to shadow her? "Jamila, I'm sure you're preoccupied with much. I would hate to impose—"

"Impose on what?" her sister-in-law snorted. "I'm childless, I've lost most of my appointments, and I need to prove myself useful in something. This isn't an imposition, dear, it's duty. And duty isn't your husband's strong suit, so as usual, we women need to compensate."

"I think that Akil has very much proven his dedication to the crown," Tobi replied. "After all, he—"

"Don't talk, you'll spoil Hajar's work. And of course he hasn't." Jamila was maddeningly calm. "He's treating us all as if he's doing us a favor, and hasn't yet said a word to his poor father—"

You're wrong, Tobi wanted to retort. But she couldn't; what evidence did she have? After all, Akil himself had warned her about his own lack of popularity.

"I feel quite sorry for you, actually," Jamila finished. Hajar stepped back, finally pleased with her work, and Jamila wrapped a length of black satin ribbon round her sleeve.

"Mourning band," she informed her. "*I* will have to look like a crow for the next year, but the throne is above things as commonplace as human emotion. Full black on you and Akil is considered unseemly. Oh, there are dozens of rules. But you're starting with the advantage of not having a poor reputation, Tobi. Use it well, and your husband will give you whatever you want."

Jamila smiled, just a little, running her fingers through the locks of glossy hair not covered by her black mourning veil.

"Now you look like one of us," she said, her voice tinged with satisfaction.

Tobi looked and was quite startled at her reflection. Hajar had done wonders with all her pots and brushes; somehow Tobi's skin looked brighter, clearer. The *kajal* round her eyes and the false lashes she added made them look twice as large, liquid-dark against a clear background of white; her lips were full and touched with a gloss of berry-brown. She looked exactly like herself, only a greatly enhanced version.

"You really should wear no color other than white," Jamila remarked as if she were the author of her sister-in-law's beauty herself. "It brings out all the tints in your skin. No question why Akil married *you,* even though he had to go all the way to Nigeria to do it. Nothing to your older sister, of course, she was born with style, but you'll do. Now come, let me help you with this headdress, and coach you in the management of that skirt. The last thing we need is the new queen tumbling down during her first appearance."

The closer they got to the capital, the more stony-faced Akil became, and Tobi had no idea what to do about it. After her drilling by Jamila, she was led to the car used by the royal couple for entering and disembarking. It was outfitted simply with a thick silk rug so plush it muffled all sound and fat velvet-upholstered seating that ran round three out of four walls of the car. It was empty except for Akil, who had earbuds in, with a look of intense concentration on his face.

"I expect that Jamila has informed you of everything?" he said, glancing her way.

Tobi felt an odd thrill at the sound of his voice; her body immediately chose to associate it with other things, the husky way it'd sounded only the night before, saying all manner of things while his hands teased her breasts. She forced herself back to the present with some effort. Whatever Akil was thinking of, it clearly wasn't close to that: he was staring at her as blankly as if she'd been... Jamila.

"I'm ready," Tobi assured him. "But—Akil, I thought it—I mean, she's just lost her husband. I don't want to burden her with—"

Akil shook his head. "Burden her? It is her responsibility as monarch to share her knowledge. You don't shirk your responsibilities just because someone died, do you? What if you'd been her daughter?"

But what about time to grieve? Tobi thought. No one in the house of Al-Hamri seemed to have ever heard of the word; their hyper-focus on their rule was the only thing she'd seen spark any real emotion. Jamila was just as haughty as Akil was being now, and she'd seen no evidence that Malik had been any different. And the closer they moved to their destination, the stiffer, less animated her husband became. His face had darkened, become stormy. There was absolutely no hint of the humor, however slight, that had softened his mouth the night before. She cleared her throat. "I like the national dress," she said for the sake of saying something to lighten that awful silence. She smoothed her beringed hands over the embroidery.

"Good, because you'll be wearing a hell of a lot of it in the days to come," Akil said grimly.

"Jamila brought me some choice pieces from the vault," she continued, reaching up to touch the enormous rubied jewels dangling from her ears. They were fastened with a hook of gold that slid behind each ear; they were far too heavy, Jamila explained, to be worn the normal way.

Akil's responses became limited to grunts deep in his chest.

"Are you nervous?" she asked.

He shot her a contemptuous look. "No."

Well, excuse me. She wanted to ask if the old king was somewhere on this coach as well, if he was to make an appearance. No one had really referred to him at all in the time she'd been here, and she was curious; where was he? Surely he wasn't so ill that he needed to be hidden away?

She could recall the stern-faced man with deep grooves in his forehead and round his mouth. He and her father thoroughly enjoyed each other's company, and there was always a handful of sweets in his pocket for the children in the house whenever he visited.

"Will your father be there?" she asked after a moment.

Akil's face tightened even more; goodness, she hadn't thought it possible. "His presence is as irrelevant to this ceremony as his existence is to the crown."

Tobi gasped at the harshness of his words. "Akil—"

"It's true."

"But he's the former king!" Tobi protested. This cold, almost dismissive treatment, was it because he was ill? "Surely he can watch from somewhere quiet? He was well-loved, was he not? The people will want to see him."

"He may in his private apartments. I don't know his setup." Akil lifted and lowered his shoulders. "And if you are quite finished, Tobilola, I'd like to keep listening to this." He pointed to his earbuds.

Tobi was horrified, a horror that pushed away her anger at being so summarily dismissed. That poor old man! Inwardly she vowed that she would visit him as soon as she could, ensure that he was being treated well, at the very least, and maybe get some answers as to why Akil was being so cold.

CHAPTER EIGHT

THE ONLY GOOD thing about the processional, Akil thought grimly, was that Tobi had no idea what was going on.

He'd expected some degree of coolness from a crowd that had been coached for years to think him the worst sort of cad, but the people that lined the streets of Djoboro's main city square to watch the arrival of the new king greeted him with near silence. Not a reverent silence, but the type of silence produced by a group that is too polite to jeer. He knew he'd only escaped that because of Jamila; the small erect figure in her fluttering black robes drew roars of appreciation, as well as piles of the vivid star-shaped flowers that were the only real things of beauty agriculturists managed to coax from Djoboro's desert soil.

Tobi was greeted with a garland of them by three wide-eyed schoolgirls who giggled when she bent to greet them hesitantly, the words in traditional Djoboran awkward on her tongue. She followed up with some of the phrases she'd mastered on the way over, and the girls answered, clearly delighted that this new princess could speak to them, awkwardly as she managed. She spoke in soft, dulcet tones to everyone she met, personalizing the conversation for each of them: courtiers, the prime minister, representatives from other royal families.

The crowds were curious with Tobi, as well they might be; there was much craning of necks, enthusiastic applause and murmured conversation when she passed. Teenage girls seemed most excited to see her. Tobi stopped once, twice, three, four times to crouch and pose for cell phones held aloft. The new king received the customary bows of the head, but not a single person on that busy avenue made eye contact with him.

It stung Akil more than he'd ever admit.

After the processional came an extensive tour for Tobi's benefit, bolstered by a fat guidebook. Churches, mosques, casinos, historic sites and national parks all blurred together in a two-hour tour of the capital city. Akil made up for the churning low in his stomach by interrupting her official guide, adding a comment here, an anecdote there; he recalled official visits and events with encyclopedic accuracy. It was unnerving how much came back to him and how quickly, and the odd ache he felt at the sight of his old home.

Perhaps he'd missed it more than he thought. He knew his issues stemmed from the family he'd clashed with, not the land itself. And now, he was to enter the enormous palace of Djoboro as ruling monarch. An unpopular one at the moment, yes, and one who'd been self-exiled until a few days ago, but he was king. King!

At the end of the processional, the little band was placed inside a large black car and driven the last couple of miles to the palace. Akil had traveled this route many times before in many other processionals; he could clearly remember sitting in the back of the black limousines that were in style at the time, looking at his brother and his father. The two always sat side by side, knees brushing, talking in low tones about matters of state, future plans. Akil was not expected to participate, and was regarded by his father with astonishment when he did try...

It'll take you years to catch up, boy. Don't bother trying.

Now those words were haunting him. Since Malik's death there had been parliamentary letters. Thousands of notes from meetings he hadn't known existed. Recordings. Conversations with heads of state. Not to mention the constant stream of updates from the condescending advisers he'd inherited from Malik and from his father, advisers who resented taking orders from the resident ne'er-do-well.

He wished he could fire them all, start anew. But such would be impossible in Djoboro. They were divinely appointed, products of a long line of tradition. Even his ancestors seemed to want to set him up to fail.

Why am I even doing this? He'd asked himself this question every single day. He'd barely slept since Malik's death; there was simply no time. If he was to conduct himself with any modicum of competence at all, he had to plan his day down to the millisecond. His advisers, though helpful, lacked the sympathy that would truly make their contribution meaningful.

And it was as if his brother hovered over his shoulder, along with the man his father had been, sneering at him. Willing him to fail. It made his breathing shallow at the oddest times, made him break into a cold sweat when he did manage to sleep.

He told no one of this. Ghosts weren't real; weakness was. And he had to crush this weakness beneath the heavy boot of achievement.

A curse on all of them, he thought, his jaw tightening. Soon as he found his feet, he'd replace them all. And he'd move his wife and himself to the private residence he'd used years ago; it was only a twenty-minute ride from the main palace.

There was no way he could pull this off under the accusing eyes of the past, and all the kings that had walked the corridors before him.

After the processional, and a banquet to welcome the royal couple that lasted till midnight, Tobi was shown to lush quarters that barely registered, given the hour. Then she was up at six again; that morning was her first official meeting of court, where she was formally introduced as Akil's wife to the members of the royal family. There were four besides Akil's: the Houses of Malik, Akram, Zaki, Yousef. Faces blurred, but she kept her back straight, kept that pleasant half smile fixed on her face.

Despite the long journey, Akil seemed to only grow stronger as the hours passed, with a freakish gleam in his eyes that worried her; she'd seen it in her father in years past, when the older man was working on a project and refused to take a break. He'd crack if he wasn't careful. For now, her husband seemed to sustain his energy with a steady stream of golden-brown Arabic coffee, candied pistachios and an ice-cold energy drink. His composure only seemed to waver in one meeting: a PR team had been flown in from the UK, specifically tasked with the new king's reputation and public perception. Here she learned precisely why Akil had needed her so badly.

"You're the lowest-rated monarch, by public poll," the leader of the team said bluntly. "Issues we've identified include leaving your position as a working royal three years ago—"

"I'm here now, am I not?" Akil said coldly.

"—abandoning your young wife, who is quite popular across the entire female demographic—"

Tobi felt herself flush, sat up a little straighter.

"—and most importantly, your relationship with the former king. There are rumors of a rift—"

"Not rumors. All true."

"Whether it is or not, it needs to be repaired in the public eye." The consultant's eyes were as calm as Akil's were stormy. "In short, Your Majesty, the public has been led to believe you're inconsiderate at best, mulish at worst, with no regard for tradition."

Akil's dark eyes had taken on a glitter she recognized. "Traditions change."

The man cleared his throat. "A public reconciliation—"

"Not going to happen," Akil said, and rudely.

That meeting ended abruptly. And after several more Tobi found it hard to keep her eyes open. She would not ask Akil when she could take a rest, she was determined, but after six hours on the house floor with the scantest of water breaks, she stretched her eyes so wide open they burned. She blinked and reopened them one, two, three times, and—

"Wake up," her husband said, prodding her.

She flushed so hard beneath her skin she had to remove the linen jacket that Jamila had bullied her into wearing that morning, fanning herself with her notes. No one seemed to have taken notice.

Finally, blessedly, it was over, and she and Akil were in the back of yet another dark car, cinnamon-and-orange-scented air-conditioning wafting over them. She closed her eyes, too tired to even stress over the awkwardness of being alone with him, and in such close proximity. It felt like barely a second before Akil spoke into her ear.

"Tobi, we're here."

She blinked. They were in the driveway of an enormous stone-gray villa; she could not see much of it, as the compound was dark.

"This isn't the palace," she said, and a yawn nearly cracked her jaw into two. She opened her mouth to apologize for falling asleep again, but the words died on her lips when he smiled. The driver came round and opened the door for her; they eased out into the driveway and stood facing the house.

"You must be exhausted," he said, and his voice was the gentlest she'd ever heard it. Something inside her constricted at his tone. She would not admit it, but she was hungry for that kindness, and she hated herself a little for it. She could not afford to want this from Akil, she reminded herself, and lifted her chin.

"I can't believe you're not," she murmured. She opened her mouth to say something else, but another of the jaw-splitting yawns she'd been stifling for two hours appeared, and Akil chuckled.

"Like you Nigerians say, 'you really tired.' Let's go."

"I'm not sure I can even walk," she groaned, then yelped as Akil took a step forward, scooped her up into his arms with one seamless motion.

"Akil!" She looked round, scandalized. "You can't—"

"Don't you realize how romantic this makes me look?" he teased. "Hold still. I'm not as coordinated as I look."

That was an unlikely claim. She'd never felt as light as she did now, borne so easily in her husband's arms. His muscles were tensed and felt so incredibly solid that she relaxed into him despite herself, resting her head on his chest. His heart was thudding; the beat was steady, strong.

"Eyes are everywhere on Djoboro," he said into her ear. "And believe it or not, there was already a story this morning about our sleeping in separate rooms—as if my parents ever stayed together! Queens and kings never do."

Oh. She fought back her disappointment, then chastised herself for being disappointed in the first place. So this was all for the benefit of the cameras, then?

Don't be a fool. Why do you think you're here in the first place? She cleared her throat.

"What do you think of our little country?" he murmured, somewhere in her hair. She licked her lips.

"For a place that stresses modesty and taste, there are an awful lot of casinos."

He half snorted, half laughed, then walked through a massive carved door into a foyer. A line of staff dressed in black and white stood, but Akil shook his head.

"Hello, everyone. She's exhausted. Introductions to-morrow," was all he said, and the staff scattered. Tobi took the opportunity to half hide her face in his neck, closed her eyes. Her senses were overwhelmed by that now-familiar sweet spiciness of his skin, completely unaffected by the twelve-hour day. If anything, it had only become headier, more complex.

"You smell good," she whispered, and she felt rather than saw him smile. Fake or not, this was awfully nice and there weren't any cameras here, were there? "Thank you for sending them away."

"You wouldn't have remembered a single one, the way you are now." His voice was rumbling low in her ear. She sensed them crossing a large space, then walking into a lift; he was still carrying her as if she weighed little.

"I think I did all right," she said sleepily.

"Your accent is abysmal, and you kept galloping ahead of me. But, yes," he admitted, the mocking leaving his voice. "You did *splendidly,* not just 'all right.' I was very impressed."

Warmth sparked deep in her chest at his praise; she'd never had any from her father, regardless of how well or how badly she'd behaved. "Thank you."

He grunted in response. They were now moving rapidly down a long hallway; he paused and made a turn, said a command in Djoboran. Tobi, sensing the light changing behind her lids, opened her eyes and peered out.

They were in a large, quiet bedchamber. Enormous windows stretched from ceiling to floor, heavily curtained. The room was decorated in the same opulent style as most of the buildings she'd seen since her arrival, but avoided most of the rusts and reds that were popular. This room's tiling and arched doorways were rendered in cool shades of blue and green, shades that reminded her of the landscape she'd seen when she arrived, the way the mountains touched the sky, and the lush green of the land that brushed the sea. Djoboro, she thought, was as complex as the man who held her now—in equal parts barren and rich, and all unsettlingly beautiful.

Akil eased her from his arms atop the coverlet of the massive bed; she actually whimpered as she sank in. The mattress was made of some material that immediately yielded to her frame, hugging her body, yet supporting it. Akil's hands were gentle at her feet, tugging off her shoes, dropping them to the floor.

"I'm going to get makeup all over the coverlet," she protested drowsily.

"No matter. They'll change it." He looked tired for the first time since they'd arrived, new lines about his mouth. He shucked off his jacket, muscles straining against the snow-white shirt underneath, and then he was unbuttoning his shirt, and Tobi was suddenly wide awake.

"What are you doing?" she whispered.

"I'm getting this damned uniform off so I can sleep." His voice was calm. "And yes, I'll be sleeping with you. Staff gossip like old market women, and it won't kill either of us to cohabit for the time being, regardless of…"

*Regardless of if we're sleeping together or no*t. All thoughts of slumber fled as Tobi half sat up in bed. Her mouth went dry as he pulled his shirt off his shoulders.

In the hazy confusion that came from exhaustion, she registered bronzed dark skin that stretched tight over those heavy muscles; he was leaner without clothes, less stocky, but even more powerful-looking. The little light in the room played over his chest, down his stomach, disappeared into the waist of his trousers; he shucked them next, revealing tight black shorts, legs that were as lean with muscle as the rest of him. Tiredness could not explain why her mouth was dry and why her body was suddenly so tense it hurt.

"Akil..."

He wasn't looking at her; instead he was sighing through his nose, drawing back the coverlet. Tobi's stomach tightened at the prospect of being so close to him. Suddenly, this was too intimate, too much and yet...

"Sleep well, Tobilola," he said, and rolled onto his side, his back to her. It was a wide and formidable back, corded, full of knots under that flawless skin. She wanted desperately to touch it, to press against him, to indulge in his warmth as if she were a cat. She waited ten minutes, watching the breaths lift and lower his back. When they grew slow and regular, when he'd relaxed, she reached out tentatively, touched his shoulder. "Akil."

"Eh?"

"Are you sleeping?"

"I *was.*" The lilt in his voice indicated that he'd been very happily occupied doing so.

"Thank you," she said. That tension had filled her chest, threatened to break out in something as undignified as tears, or something ridiculously sentimental. If he rejected her now she might actually die, she thought, feeling close to hysteria.

She was shocked when he rolled full over, pulling her against him.

"Sleep," he commanded.

"Akil—"

"I remember what happened on the train," he said roughly. It was his first allusion to their kisses that night, and Tobi felt oddly relieved that he said it—so he'd been thinking of it, too! "I won't pretend I don't. I don't want to be alone, all right? But we are *not* dealing with that tonight."

She nodded, and the flash of warmth through her extended from her head down to her toes.

I don't want to be alone.

So this was more than just about those cameras, after all.

The feel of him should have been overwhelming, but instead it was reassuring. Warm. Safe. Despite his arrogance and their squabbling, she'd never felt safer in her life. It was strange; Akil was the first person she'd shared any intimacy with that she didn't feel the need to run from.

Tobi swallowed, then adjusted so that she better fit the cradle of his arms. Her bottom pressed between the apex of his thighs, and she was startled to feel—

"Oh," she breathed, and Akil growled.

"Yes, it's you. I'm only human, after all."

She laughed, and the sound was breathy and unnatural, even to her. "Is it uncomfortable?"

"Quite pleasantly so. Stop moving."

"Why?" She shifted again, and Akil's fingers snaked down lightning-fast to capture her wrists. She made a sound deep in her throat. It was as if someone else had taken over her body. It was part lust, and part fascination at the fact that, well, in *this,* at least, she could make him react.

"Akil…" She lowered her voice, turned her head. She could not see his face, of course, from this angle, and there was something very sexy about being trapped here, against his smooth, hot skin. He muttered something that could have been a curse and she laughed. It felt so odd to be in such a clear position of power over Akil, but curiously heady as well.

"You're a lot more naked than I am," she whispered.

Everything stilled, reduced to them, close together on that bed; then, he sighed as if defeated and released her wrists. "I should have known this was a terrible idea."

"And yet you brought me here," she pointed out.

"Yes." His mouth tipped up a little. It made this all a little easier, this tacit acknowledgment of what had been burning between them since the very beginning. "You want to be naked, you do it."

Tobi half sat up on the bed; her stomach was churning, and sleepiness was completely gone. She forced herself to meet his eyes, then, before she lost the courage, she pulled her top over her head, her skirt down her hips. The bra came next, and— God, the clasp *stuck*. She fumbled with it like a teenager before finally, impatiently, yanking it over her head. She felt horribly awkward. This had to be the most unsexy striptease ever. Her fingers skimmed the waistband of the thong she was wearing with the first bit of hesitation.

"Stop," he said. "And open your eyes, Tobi."

"I don't want to," she mumbled.

"Ojo," he mocked.

Her eyes flew open indignantly. "You finally learn some Yoruba only to call me a scaredy-cat?"

"It also means 'reign.' I could be calling you a queen."

"Not the way you pronounced it!" She sat up all the way and looked at him, and then she couldn't breathe for a moment because he was looking at her, directly into her eyes, and the look on his *face—*

She scuttled backward, and he laughed. *Laughed.* "Don't back out now. You started this."

She was hyperconscious of her breasts bouncing on her chest as she scooted back, on the way his eyes rested on them and then on her face, and finally—of the way he was now straining against those black boxers. If he were as large as the shape of him there suggested—

She moved backward again and then there was nowhere to go; she was pressed against the plushness of the velvet headboard and he was kissing her. Hard. It was not an initial kiss; it was a continuation of what they'd started on the train. It was a bruising kiss that told her he was in deadly earnest, and she, Tobi Obatola, was definitely in over her head.

Then his hand curved possessively round one of her breasts, and she lost all coherent thought. It was startling, the way her body surged up to meet his, as if they'd both ceased to be themselves, as if they'd been taken over by some passion both were loath to admit. He made her look at him as his thumbs skimmed her nipples; he spoke low and husky in her ear, and she could not stop the shuddering that went through her body. Unexpectedly, as good as it felt, she felt overwhelmed by emotion. Akil wanted her, yes, and he hadn't wanted to be alone, but there was no tenderness here; she could be any woman with a lush body and warm scented skin. He was enjoying—*this.* He wasn't enjoying *her.*

Unbidden, tears sprang to her eyes; she shut them tightly.

Akil's mouth was making a slow, careful descent down her body, leaving a heated trail where his lips touched. He made a rough sound of appreciation when they grazed her thighs, when he found her warm and sweet and—

"So ready," he breathed out soft against her skin, and he was kissing her there, drawing back when she cried out. "Watch me," he instructed.

No. She'd see nothing but this in her dreams and waking hours and she supposed he knew it. But she bit her lip till it bruised, looked down at the curly dark head hovering between her thighs and let out a shaky breath. Her body was buzzing with want; her nipples were swollen and so tight it was painful at this point. Slowly she lifted her hands to cover the stiff points. It felt good, and would keep her from touching Akil's head, his gleaming bronzed back, tense with muscle.

When his mouth lowered to her again, she vented the breath she was holding on a moan. Minutes faded to nothingness; she concentrated on the ripples of pleasure beginning low at her spine, spreading upward to where her fingers teased her swelling breasts. Akil's full mouth was gentle, languid; his tongue skimmed where she was swollen and wet so precisely that breath cramped in her lungs. Just as the ripples were cresting over into something both new and intensely familiar, Akil lifted his head, pressed his forehead to hers, replaced his mouth with a featherlight pass of his fingers.

"So sweet," he said, and there was a new huskiness in his voice. Tobi tipped her mouth against his hesitantly, tasting the odd sensation of herself on his tongue, and she sighed, then gasped as he slid a finger inside her.

"I want you to tell me what you want," he commanded.

"I—" Tobi's body felt as if it were on fire. *Impossible.* Besides what she wanted, what her heart was beginning to whisper to her in quiet moments since they'd arrived was something she could never say aloud. Not to him. Not after such a short acquaintance, and not after the terms of their deal. She hadn't even dared to say it to herself. But the truth was—even in their tensest moments, she thought of him. And he'd said—he'd said—

She terminated the thought swiftly. That was too dangerous to pursue. What her body cried out for now was much, much safer.

Or was it?

"Akil…"

"Tell me." There were two fingers now, stretching her, applying soft pressure to where she pulsed inside, and Tobi could not talk at all. Instead she bit her lip against the moan that wanted to escape, began to roll her hips against his fingers. Hesitantly at first, but then harder—

He swallowed the broken cry of her pleasure with his mouth, withdrew his fingers slowly as she shook, trying to regain her composure. In the haze she could feel his hands drift slowly up to her breasts, thumbing her still-swollen nipples almost absently. She forced her eyes open.

He was looking directly at her, and she swallowed. Then she reached out herself, placed her hands on his chest.

"I want to touch you," she said quietly, and a muscle jumped in his cheek. The next few moments were an exploration of taut skin, hard muscles, long limbs—all so different from the rounded softness of her own curves. Tobi explored with fingers and lips, noting where his breath caught in his chest, where he held back a sound behind gritted teeth.

"I know I'm not hurting you," she said with a fraction of her old spirit.

He forced out a short laugh. "No, you're not. But I have not done this in some time, Tobilola, and—"

His words trailed to nothing then, for she dipped her hand in the waistband of his shorts, finding him straining, hot, hard, heavy in her hand. He cursed low under his breath, and Tobi arched against him as much as she could, laughing softly against his mouth. Instinct dictated her slow caresses, the pass of her thumb over the tip of him, and when he groaned—

"Not done this in some time?" she said innocently.

That brightness was back in his eyes, eclipsing them, making them as dark as coal. "No. I'm married," he said shortly. Tobi had little time to register this, for in an instant he'd flipped her to her knees and applied a gentle slap to her rear end that made her squeal with shock and excitement.

"Minx," he said, low and hot into her ear, and she could feel him, bare now, nudging against her entrance, which was hot and aching again. "This is entirely your fault."

Tobi responded with a husky sound of her own; she'd never made such a noise in her life, but embarrassment was dissolved by want. His fingers went to the tiny bundle of nerves he'd teased so expertly before and Tobi found herself pushing back against him. Hard.

"Please," she whispered. "Now, Akil." She couldn't think. She couldn't remember that it was her first time with any man, she couldn't remember protection, she couldn't process anything except the fact that she wanted him to fill her. Desperately.

He said something quiet and low as he adjusted himself behind her; then he entered her with one quick thrust.

She gasped as the sting came first, and it was enough to buckle her knees with shock. He hadn't been rough; on the contrary, but it was startling, that sudden feeling of fullness, the swift discarding of the barrier there. She could not help but cry out, a much different cry from the ones she'd uttered before—and Akil froze completely. She whimpered a little as she felt her walls contract, lock him in. Her body definitely wanted this, no matter how shocked it was by the abruptness.

"Are you all right?"

She was all right—she'd never been so well in her life. But she was also very aware of the pain from that initial thrust, and if it continued—

"I'm—I'm so sorry, Akil, it hurts."

His hands loosened at her hips, and the oath he uttered reverberated through the bedchamber. Her body, so shockingly, deliciously full a moment ago, now empty.

CHAPTER NINE

THE DAWN FOUND Akil wide awake, troubled and looking at his young wife. Despite the fact that he felt completely drained, he couldn't have slept even if he wanted to. The pure terror that coursed through his veins every time he gazed at Tobi's face, gentle and sweet in slumber, would not allow him to. Neither did the memory of the night they'd shared.

She'd been a virgin. A *virgin*. And he'd thrust into her that first time like an absolute brute. She'd been so wet, and swollen, and ready, whimpering his name and begging him, in the most becoming matter, after he'd teased her to near madness. He'd positioned her gently on her hands and knees, lightly skimming skillful fingers between her thighs, increasing gentle pressure and parting her downy softness till she arched in a gloriously wanton way, pushed back against him, cried out his name in a soft, broken voice—

He'd done it that way because he didn't want to look at her. He didn't want her to see him, and could not risk the tenderness that made his whole body ache showing in his eyes. And then he'd *hurt* her, thrusting into her like some kind of—

He swallowed. There had been *some* resistance, but

he'd been so swift—and she'd barely made a sound, not until she couldn't take it anymore. And then the sound she had made—

"I'm—I'm so sorry, Akil, it hurts."

He'd turned her over rapidly then, seen the tears on her lovely face, the bright red indent where she'd bitten her lip raw. And the arousal had drained from him like water from a sieve.

"Why the hell didn't you tell me!" he'd yelled before realizing that reaction was equally bad; she'd curled up on the bed, absolutely humiliated. And he'd *still* berated her.

"A virgin? That is not information you withhold!"

"I'm sorry—I didn't want you to think that I was—"

"That you were what? That you needed to be treated gently? Tobi, what the hell?"

Panic had seized him, made his words harsh, his voice hard. Tobi had tried to escape, but he wouldn't let her, and after a struggle that involved a hot bath he'd forced her into, she'd cried on his chest before falling asleep in his arms.

A disaster. That's what this had been. And morning was here, soft dancing light on her beautiful face, and he had no idea what the hell he would tell her. He closed his eyes, stomach roiling, and wondered for a moment if he'd be sick. He had spent years cultivating and maintaining hard-edged control. To what end? Manhandling his wife and taking her with all the finesse of a bull in heat?

The self-loathing made his mouth feel bitter. He began easing himself off the bed—and then he froze, because Tobi's eyes were open, and fixed on him. Her lips trembled, a little; she pulled the thin sheet that covered her still-naked body a little tighter to her, and something coiled tight in his stomach.

He didn't look her in the eye. He *couldn't.*

"Good morning," he said, and the timbre of his voice was odd, even to him.

"Akil—"

He shook his head. He didn't want to hear her say anything, not because she didn't deserve to speak, but because he actually felt sick on the inside—and everything depended on his holding himself together. "I owe you an apology. The fact that I had no idea that you were—that you'd never—"

"How could you possibly know that?" Her voice was quiet. "You don't know me."

"No." She was right. He didn't. He'd married a stranger, he'd dared to indulge in sex as—what? Stress relief?—and now he was paying for it.

"I was completely out of bounds."

Tobi laughed incredulously. "If I remember correctly, I begged you to…well, you did exactly what I asked you to! If I couldn't handle it—"

"That isn't the point!" Akil realized just a bit too late exactly how loud he was; the sound of his anguish reverberated in the massive bedchamber. "I lost control," he said after a pause. And by his ancestors, he still hadn't regained it in the presence of this maddening woman.

"Akil. It was the heat of the moment."

"I do not have heated moments." His voice was clipped, brusque.

"I don't understand," she said softly, and sat up in bed.

He closed his eyes against the headache that was forming, and partly against the sight of that damned sheet sliding down again, the firm heaviness of her breasts.

"Do you know why we're here, Tobi?" he said.

"Because you are king." Her voice was soft. "And you're doing an amazing job so far."

Akil squeezed his eyes shut; this could not possibly get any worse. It seemed that every encounter he had with Tobi uncovered another layer of intimacy that he could not afford to have. Not with her. Were it someone he cared for less...

He pushed away the thought with all his strength. "Listen. I've never done this."

"Never had sex, you mean?"

He glared at her.

"Well, what else was I supposed to infer?"

"This is not the time to get *cute,* Tobilola." Akil closed his eyes again. He was no longer warding off a headache; he couldn't ward off something that had arrived and apparently, intended to stay. How could he make her understand? "I have had a few discreet relationships, mostly abroad. But I always knew I would marry. Preferably someone with experience—"

"But you got me, didn't you?"

"Yes," he agreed before he considered how it sounded, then cursed inwardly and opened his eyes. A hurt look had crossed her face.

"I'm sorry about your tragic backstory, but I'm not a child, Akil. If I neglected to tell you about this it was because..." Her voice trailed off.

"Because what?"

"I didn't want you to stop," she said, and her voice was a near whisper.

The two sat together on their large marriage bed, in a silence that was only broken by faint outdoor noises: birds, the wind rustling the leaves.

"You *cried*," he said roughly.

"Because you were angry. And I was embarrassed."
Her face was tight with it now, and unbidden, an image
of her came back to him, in vivid, living color. She'd
been in that incredibly provocative position, bottom
high, thighs apart, and she'd looked back at him, and
the hunger on her *face*—

He forced his thoughts to halt because if he could
keep his mind from wandering, his body was a little
easier to get into line. And he was feeling it stir at the
memory, even after all this—

Wordlessly, he slid from the bed. He should be able
to avoid this vivid, alluring woman, find plenty to keep
her busy.

And at night, when the danger was in them being
alone, here in this massive bedchamber, he'd find plenty
to keep him busy.

Tobi's mouth tightened, and he realized too late that
she'd probably read his mind. This was too much; he
was too vulnerable now, too emotional.

"I am your wife," she repeated.

"Yes." He didn't argue with her. It was true, after
all—and the more he argued, the more he ran a risk of
saying what he'd kept hidden all these years. He needed
her to help him become a respected king, and then he
needed her to go. Then, and only then, he'd resume control. He stretched, winced when he heard something
pop. "My back is a mess of knots."

"That's because you're tense," Tobi snapped. The
emotion on her face, thank goodness, was hidden now;
this would make it easier.

"I'm going to call for a masseuse. For you. Then
we'll have breakfast and I'll show you round the house."

"Fine." If she sounded sulky, she managed to hide enough of it to make him hopeful.

Perhaps he could pull this off after all.

Akil was as good as his word, and ten minutes after he exited, an iron-faced woman with a portable table walked briskly into the bedchamber, hustled a still-naked Tobi off the bed, prodded and kneaded at her muscles until Tobi felt like a pile of goo. The bedchamber had two massive bathrooms on either side; Akil was presumably shut into one. Hers was decorated in soft shades of lilac and blue, and was already stocked with her favorite Jo Malone products. How Akil's staff had discovered these details, she had no idea.

When she emerged from her ministrations, fragrant and calm, Akil stood impatiently in front of a rack of clothing, fully dressed in a simpler version of the linen tunic and trousers that were staples here. "Did you fall in the drain? We're behind schedule."

"I'm not going to let you spoil my mood," she countered. "I've just enjoyed a massage, and I'm so relaxed right now I think I could do a split."

He fought back a smile.

"Day two. Everything has to be perfect." He looked at her, and Tobi's heart sank, despite herself. The man she'd shared a bed with the night before, the man who'd been so absolutely desolate this morning, was completely gone. In his place was the insufferable Akil from the Dubai International Airport, his eyes carefully shuttered of all emotion. "Jamila will be here shortly to dine with us."

"Oh, Jamila," she sighed without thinking, and Akil's mouth twitched.

"Is she giving you a hard time?"

"No, the contrary, actually." Tobi paused. "She's incredibly kind and very helpful. But I simply don't understand how...she just lost her husband. I think I'd be completely nonfunctional if anything happened to you—"

She realized what she was saying much too late, and aborted her sentence, feeling her skin burn in a way that had nothing to do with hot water or exfoliation. Akil was looking at her, a curious softness in his eyes.

"You're a very good person," he said after a long moment. "And so is Jamila. But it hasn't been easy for her. I'm glad you like her."

"I really do."

"Good. Now get dressed," he ordered, a hint of bossiness coming back. "I can't tell you how tired I am already, and the day hasn't even started," he added as if to himself.

Something about his drawn face gave Tobi courage, and she chewed the inside of her lip before stepping up to him, wrapping her arms round him without a word. She did it quickly, with no thought of consequence; he stiffened in surprise, but he *let* her.

"Never mind your hugging nonsense," he said gruffly, but his voice sounded just constricted enough to make her own throat tighten.

"I think you're doing a splendid job," she whispered into his skin. It was easier when she wasn't looking at his face.

"I have no choice." He was pulling away from her now, but his hand lingered at the small of her back. "Thank you," he added, after a moment. "And please, go get *dressed.*"

Tobi appeared ten minutes later, dressed in a soft day dress of brightly patterned *Ankara* that belted at the waist, left her arms bare. He looked at her, nodded approvingly, and headed off without a word.

She said nothing as she walked alongside her husband, nodding politely at the lines of staff awaiting her in the foyer, handed the head housekeeper and butler the gifts she'd brought them—fine chocolate, nuts.

A tour of the house and grounds was next, and Tobi found it impossible not to let her eyes widen with delight, much as she wanted to remain cold, distant. Her new home sat just outside the city, on one of its highest hills, and its construction was like nothing she'd ever seen before. Everything about it seemed to want to embrace the sun: massive windows that let in light from floor to ceiling, skylights, verandas and porches. A balcony the size of a small bedroom with a glass floor was at the highest point of the house, and the view was astounding: the city spread out below them.

There was pride in Akil's handsome face that completely overtook the tension of that morning; he placed a hand on Tobi's back in a gesture that was quickly becoming familiar, pointed to four hills that flanked the city. "Those are the other royal houses." He hesitated for a moment. "Technically, we should be staying at the palace. But I don't—like it. It feels as if I can never have a rest."

"That I definitely understand. But it's beautiful, all of it," Tobi said, a lump coming to her throat. She was queen of all of this? *Temporary queen.* She had to remind herself that this wasn't permanent.

"It is," Akil said matter-of-factly. "It's not a giant like Nigeria, of course. But there are certain problems we've avoided by staying so isolated. And the country's reputation as a tourist paradise is enough incentive to keep it in good shape." He tilted his head. "Of course, you know what our main export is."

"Rubies," Tobi said promptly, and she actually laughed at his expression, despite herself. "And don't praise me for knowing. My sister is a jewelry collector, and she's thrown quite a bit of money your way."

"I'll have her sent some of our finest." He looked at her for a long moment, considering, it seemed; then he reached out and grabbed her hand.

"Come."

Tobi was so startled that she allowed him to tow her down the hall, into the lifts, and back to the main foyer. He led her outside the main entrance, then gestured to one of the two massive pillars in the front of the house. "See that brick?"

She peered at it. Unlike the concrete villas that were more commonplace, the stones of Akil's house were gray and white swirls, almost like marble, with pinkish-red stones of varying size.

She gasped and pressed her hand to her mouth. "Those aren't—"

"Uncut rubies. Yes." A smile played round the corners of his mouth. "The king's house has them in every single stone. That's how plentiful rubies are in our little mines. However..."

His voice trailed off, and he looked at the horizon, his dark eyes hazing over.

"What is it?"

"There's quite a bit of illegal mining. We try to regulate it, but..." He lifted his shoulders. "I don't want this to be a country that exports riches at the expense of its citizens. There's so much of that on the continent already."

The passion in his voice made it deeper, richer. "You intend to reform, then."

"I do."

They were quiet then, but the silence wasn't uncomfortable; it was reflective, heavy with thoughts shared and unshared.

Tobi rested a hand on the pillar. The heavy stone was warm with the heat of a thousand blazing mornings like this one, and seemed to have possessed the spirit of the house's resident: proud. Upstanding. Immovable. She stepped forward and pressed her cheek to the pillar, closing her eyes. Akil would not let her do this, would not let her lean on him.

She didn't want to lean on him, she reminded herself. This was about getting resources and finding what she was supposed to do. She could not afford to fall in love with this beautiful piece of the world and definitely could not afford to develop feelings for its king, no matter how hard her stomach turned over whenever he fixed those eyes on her face.

"Tobi." Akil's voice held its usual sharpness, but she knew instinctively that it was from concern this time, not irritation. "Are you all right?"

She shook her head, then nodded, knowing full well she must look confused, at best. "I—no. Yes. I mean—" She stared out over the landscape till the blue of the sky and vivid green of the hills began to blur into one. She was inspired by his words; she was touched by the beauty of the landscape, and in some ways, she was envious. Akil so clearly belonged here, whatever the challenges of his position. And she—

"Tobi?"

She looked up.

"I want you to know how essential you are to this process," he said firmly. "You are going to do well."

Oh. How was it that Akil always managed to steer to the heart of the matter, whatever it was? She swallowed, and was grateful when he seemed not to expect a reply.

"I've also made a decision," he said after a moment. "I'd like you to handle my PR with the team from London."

She stared for a moment, uncomprehending. "What?"

"I have very little patience, which I'm sure you've noticed. You'll deal with them better than I. The briefs, the recommendations—all of it. I'll hear about it once things are finalized, of course, and have the final say, but you did really well in Dubai—"

"I hated what I was doing in Dubai," she countered softly. "It was for the money."

"Nevertheless, you did it well." Akil hesitated, then peered down into her face. "You are my wife, and my partner in this. I believe that you can do it the best. I don't have many people here in my corner yet, Tobi. That will change, of course, but it will take time. This is something I know you'll do well. I believe this sincerely."

There was silence for a moment, then Tobi nodded. "All right."

"Would you like to see the grounds?" he asked, as if nothing had happened.

Tobi took a breath. She wanted a lot of things, but this wasn't the place or the time to mention them. "Very much."

CHAPTER TEN

AKIL DISAPPEARED SOON after the tour, bidding his wife farewell with a kiss—for the benefit of the staff, Tobi told herself sternly. The thought did not stop her from nestling into the crook of his neck for one self-indulgent minute.

This is the last time, she told herself. She needed to concentrate less on him and more on the fact that she was queen and had a memorial service to plan, not to mention her new responsibility to brief the PR team, and the official coronation ceremony, the public-facing one that would celebrate the new administration, set to happen in a month.

She broke out in veritable chills when it came to that. And what sort of a life was she locking herself into by agreeing to do this? She'd married Akil to run from a life devoid of freedom; now she was picturing a future with him because it was impossible not to. He was fast growing tied to the woman she was becoming. Oh, she wasn't stupid. With every encounter, every kiss, every touch, every conversation, she felt herself wanting him more. But if there was nothing permanent for her here...

Her thoughts were interrupted by David Ashton, the tall whey-faced man who served as head of Akil's PR team. Their briefing that morning was a breakfast meeting, and they sat at the conference table with coffee, fresh fruit and a bewildering assortment of pastries that nobody touched. David smiled at her, a little sardonically, she thought.

"We appreciate your time, Your Majesty."

"It's fine. What is this about?"

It was just as well Akil wasn't there, Tobi thought when the man opened his manila envelope. They were very concerned, David said, about public perception over Akil's estrangement with his father. The former king had been extremely popular, and Akil was being accused in the press of everything from simple callousness to elder abuse.

"Is the public really so blindly devoted to the former king?" Tobi wondered.

"They're more concerned with the fact that Akil doesn't deserve the throne, and he has no regard for tradition or for family," David said blandly. "There have been worse rows behind the scenes, and all have been neatly covered up in the past. It would do the king well to at least attempt the appearance of a reconciliation."

"He's too honest for that."

"Yes. Or too stubborn, it might be interpreted."

Tobi ignored that, even though a part of her secretly agreed. "What do you want him to do?" she asked simply.

"Be seen visiting the old king, perhaps, and making sure he's a part of the coronation celebration. King Al-Hamri knows these things, but is refusing to take the necessary steps. Perhaps you can be of help in persuading him?"

Perhaps I could lose my head, Tobi thought sarcastically. But perhaps she was here for the direct purpose of doing what Akil wouldn't or couldn't do? She chewed her lip for a moment before speaking.

"What if I were to see the old king myself? Spin it that it was arranged at the behest of the king. You could even imply he was there himself, if you wanted." She certainly had done that herself, more than once in Dubai. She particularly remembered a blog that had been written as a result of seeing her in a rooftop garden with one of the ruling sheikh's sons—although the truth was, he'd been leaving as she was arriving. If her socialite life had taught her anything, any story could be created from hearsay and a blurry photo. Akil wouldn't like this, but she'd explain. And it would buy them all some time.

He'd put his trust in her. She had to do this well. And if she could use the skills she'd picked up over the past couple of years, silly as they sometimes seemed, to help him...

David was looking at her thoughtfully. "It's a start," he said grudgingly, pushing back his chair. "I can arrange something for this afternoon, Your Majesty."

"Jamila can come as well," she decided.

"Very well, ma'am."

Akil would understand, she told herself as she broke up the meeting and stood, preparing to go find him. He might even be grateful she'd found a way to solve his problem without involving him at all. And the former king, could he really be that terrible? The old man had been an uncle to her of sorts in the days when her father used to visit, and this was the least she could do to honor the man he'd been, even though his vengeful son seemed determined to wipe every trace of his legacy.

Perhaps fate had brought her here for this reason, to do what Akil could not?

PR has decided it might be a good idea for me to be seen visiting your father. All right? We're setting up something for this afternoon, just a brief lunch. Jamila's coming, and we'll be photographed going in and out. Good press.

Akil wouldn't have even seen Tobi's text message were it not for a covert bathroom break. Standing in the sitting area of the gentleman's lounge, he felt his body break out into a sweat.

She did *what?* What the hell was she doing?

Without hesitation, Akil headed back to the main room and abruptly suspended all meetings for three hours, citing pressing business. He ignored the looks on their faces; this was much more important. Yes, he knew that Tobi wanted to help, and yes, he knew that they'd developed an odd closeness in the past few days, and yes, he had given her the reins on this, but she had no right, no right at all.

Adrenaline had him breathing shallowly, and he forced himself to calm down. It'd been different, years ago, when the only role his father had played was a seat at his wedding. Now, he ruled, and if he wanted to keep his sanity, his father must be kept completely separate from everything. *Especially* his queen.

The former king was kept in a sprawling estate formerly used as a summer home by his parents, a secluded place by the sea that was about an hour out of the city. It represented happier times, and that was why, in a way, Akil had chosen it for his father's convalescence, if that was the word he wanted. They had spent most of their summer vacations there as boys, and his father was much more relaxed when out of the public eye. He'd drunk less. Spoken to his wife with actual kindness. Looked at Akil once or twice as if he weren't a complete disappointment, and his more violent tendencies…

Akil shoved the thoughts from his mind. He couldn't let them affect him, not if he was to face his father today. Part of him hoped he could grab his wife and make a quick exit, but he knew in his heart that wasn't likely to be the case.

The manservant who met him at the door regarded Akil with a flash of astonishment that was quickly buried under a mantle of professionalism. He bowed low.

"Where is my wife?" Akil said impatiently.

"They are in the moon garden, Your Majesty. If I may announce you."

"No need," Akil said crisply, and walked into the house.

From what he could tell, the place was airy, spotlessly clean, well-kept. Built in a traditional Moroccan style, with open corridors and rooms, high arched entryways for air to pass through, decorated in shades of peach and a brilliant blue that reflected every ray of the sun. He remembered his mother's voice, trailing sweet and clear through the halls, her tinkling laugh. He remembered the way he and his brother's feet had sounded, drumming loud on the tiled floor, of the way they chased each other and slid into the walls.

He walked a little faster.

As had been for years, Akil smelled the garden before he saw it. The moon garden was the house's main showpiece, and he found himself pausing a little to take a breath before entering. The cool green oasis was littered with benches and little stone tables; trees heavy with foliage shrouded parts of it in shadow, welcome pools of coolness in the scorching sun. There were flowers everywhere, all of them white, from all over Africa, heavy with sweet tropical scent. It was in front of a cluster of enormous peonies that Akil found his wife, his sister-in-law and his father.

The years had shrunk him. Out of his royal robes and in a simple striped djellaba worn by many men his age, he hardly looked like the king Akil remembered. He was talking animatedly to Tobi, and Jamila, who'd clearly elected to leave off mourning for the visit, was adjusting the sleeve of her pale green dress and nodding as well.

Akil did not blink; he did not swallow, and he did not allow himself the comfort of wiping his palms on his hands. Instead he lifted his chin and started forward. He didn't know what was louder, the angry throbbing in his head at the thought of Tobi's actions today or the thudding of his own heart.

More than anything, he was discomfited at the idea the man could still affect him so much. His father hadn't touched him for years by hand, and hadn't spoken a word to him in years, either.

The old man no longer had power over him! Akil squared his shoulders and moved forward with all the arrogance he'd learned from the former king.

"—tell your father he must visit me sometime, it's been too long," he heard him say comfortably. "You were a good girl to come and see me, Tobilola. You'll come to Jamila's wedding, I hope?"

On Tobi's left, Jamila's face gave little away. "Of

course she'll come," she said smoothly. "I wouldn't have it any other way, *baba.*"

"Excellent, my daughter—excellent. We just need your mother back, and Akil—"

You're going to get Akil back sooner than you thought, Akil thought drily before pushing aside a delicate fern and stepping into full view of the party.

Silence fell. Tobi's face was equal parts scared and defiant, and Jamila looked resigned to whatever would come from this, but it was his father who spoke.

"Can I help you, young man?"

Shock, almost visible in its intensity, rippled through the group. Tobi opened her mouth, but Jamila shook her head and placed a warm hand on Tobi's arm, warning her to be silent. "Don't you know who this is, *baba?*" she asked cheerfully.

The visit so far had gone very well, although it had been startling to realize that the old king thought her still a teenager, the impulsive daughter of one of his childhood friends. He'd greeted her as such, spoke fondly of Malik, reprimanded Jamila for not bringing him.

"He's been very busy, though, since I took ill," her father-in-law explained. "And with Akil away…" He would not expand on where Akil supposedly was, regardless the amount of gentle prodding she attempted. Jamila shot her an "I'll explain later" look that Tobi found maddening at best.

Akil away *where?*

"I wouldn't have asked if I knew who he was, would I?" The slightest bit of impatience had entered the old king's voice. "And its's a bit irregular, I think, to show up unannounced."

"Oh, I invited him, *baba*. He's a—friend." Tobi choked a little on the words, and for one wild moment it felt as if Akil would choke right along with her. Jamila looked as if she were holding her breath, and the old king peered into his son's face.

"Ah. I know what that's code for. Welcome, son." And he reached out, took Akil's hand. His face was frozen in disbelief, and partly fury.

"It's an honor to meet you, Your Majesty," he said, more than a little stiffly, and gave one jerk of his head. "I've come to collect Tobi and Jamila."

"Oh, so playing chauffeur, then?" his father chuckled. "If you'd like to—"

Akil did not wait to see what his father would offer; he spun on his heel and left the garden abruptly. Tobi felt the chill down to her toes; Akil was *furious.*

"I'll come another day, sir," she said to the former king, and stood, feeling a fresh wave of pity wash over her. She wasn't even sure he knew how sick he was, but she did know one thing—the man was incredibly lonely. She'd been lonely so much herself she recognized the signs. Sequestered here, with no one but his staff to keep him company, and no visits at all from his only remaining child…

In one last bit of defiance, she bent and kissed the warm wrinkled cheek quickly, then turned. Akil was already gone, presumably heading for the front door with all speed.

"I'll stay to give him lunch and take the next train," Jamila said quickly, and Tobi suspected the older woman wanted no part of whatever it was Akil would lay on her. She couldn't blame her, either. She reached her husband and waited breathlessly for the explosion, but he didn't say a word. Not when they were in a car on the way to the station, not when they had boarded the royal coach, not when they were served pastries and tea, and not when Tobi brought forth timidly shared nuggets of conversation. It wasn't until they'd left the shore well behind that Akil deigned to lay eyes on her, and when he did his own were as cold and remote as the pebbles on the shore.

"I'm going to assume you were led astray by the PR team and they convinced you to see that man out of goodwill," Akil said, and his voice was as cold as his eyes.

Tobi steeled herself not to flinch. "Actually, Akil, it was my idea. They wanted you involved, and I left you out of it. This would be a great story. He's your *father.*"

Akil snorted without changing expression. "Not that it made much difference, he didn't recognize me. He thinks Malik is still alive, and he thinks you're a teenager. He's been told he's recovering from an illness and will return to the capital soon. Which is true enough. He'll eventually go back, in a box."

"But—"

"Don't let sentiment make you a fool, Tobi," Akil said coldly, and that was too much.

"And you shouldn't let your complete and utter lack of it make it hurt you in the long run!" she retorted. "He's an old man, Akil. He's sick. He doesn't have all his facilities, and you've got him shut up in that place, secluded from everyone else—"

"He's in his favorite summer home, where he had happy memories for years, and he's in the care of staff he's known for decades!" Akil's voice rose. "I moved him because us coexisting at the main palace would be completely destabilizing! His mind is gone, Tobi. Do you really think it would be better to break the news of the death of his pride and joy to him? To let him know that he's unfit to rule, and that the son he's despised for years has taken the throne? Do you think it would be good for him to relive that, every day? Your argument is completely refutable and silly."

Silly? Tobi was beginning to see red, and her voice was beginning to shake. "He's a king—"

"A former king," Akil interrupted, his eyes beginning to glitter dangerously.

"—and I stand by the choice I made. It was a small concession that will do you a lot of good, Akil. It will show that, in some way, you do care. That there is some love there, despite your separation."

"Everyone is worthy of care, but love shouldn't be reserved for everyone. He certainly hadn't much for me," Akil added, half under his breath, and more than a little bitterly.

Her throat was thickening with a sudden need to cry. She didn't know why she was so very emotional about this; an impersonal, very rational part of her realized that Akil was right, in some ways. But what bothered her about it, she supposed, was the utter lack of care her husband had for his father. Was he truly so cold, so unforgiving? Could he put those he loved out of sight as well as out of mind so effectively?

After all, he'd cut her off rather effectively before. And though it had no right to, though he'd promised her nothing, the old hurt resurfaced and brimmed.

Akil was peering at her half furiously, half warily,

as if he were trying to choose between verbally flogging her or trying to investigate the source of his wife's distress. "I know you did it to help," he said after a long moment. The anger was still in his voice, but it had dissipated somewhat.

"Right." To Tobi's distress, a tear escaped her left eye, and she wiped at it furtively. Akil silently produced a square of spotless white linen from his pocket and she shook her head. "I don't need it."

"Take it."

She did, dabbed at her eyes.

Akil leaned back in his seat and crossed his arms. His face was formidable. "I don't want you to waste tears on that person."

"I was fond of him as a child, Akil," she whispered, voice muffled by the layer of white fabric. It smelled of him, and she closed her eyes briefly, feeling something in her chest constrict. What was wrong with her? Why was she so emotional lately? "And that memory is all I have to go on. Won't you tell me what happened? I can't make informed decisions unless I know the whole story."

Akil looked trapped and angry and resentful all at the same time for a moment; then he took a breath.

"Maybe. Yes. But not today," he said crisply. "And you will not go back there," Akil said after a moment. His voice was calm; all the concern had gone out of it.

At that Tobi stiffened. "Is that an order?"

"It's a fact." Akil stood to his feet. "We will not discuss this unpalatable subject again as it seems to distress you, but *you will not go back to see him*. Is that understood, Tobilola?"

Tobi gaped. "You are forbidding me to go?"

"You've other things to do, like the pleasant, *simple* task of planning my brother's memorial service, which I'm sure you've neglected in favor of chasing a senile old man. Find a way to solve the problem that doesn't involve him. Or, even better, trust me to turn things around without having to pander to such nonsense!" Akil pivoted and left the car without a further word.

CHAPTER ELEVEN

TWO DAYS. IT took two days before Tobi said a word to him outside of general politeness. Akil told himself he didn't care, stifling the uncomfortable feeling that surfaced whenever he replayed their argument in his head. After all, he had plenty to do.

After the initial ceremonial bits of kingship, there was debriefing. Loads of debriefing. Akil hadn't felt so inadequate at anything since he was in school, the dunce to Malik's genius. He spent nights in his enormous study, where he could be alone, and that was what he wanted the most.

Malik hadn't changed a thing during his brief rule, and just as they'd done upon his arrival, ghosts of who they'd been seemed to hover, mockingly, ready to assess every single thing he did, ready to chant the old man's words directly into his ear.

Who are you trying to deceive?

You can't do this.

You'll fail—as you always did.

He blocked out the voices with every bit of strength, therapy and discipline he'd curated over the past three years. Since leaving, he hadn't failed. Without his family tearing him down, he'd been a success.

He had to be meticulous and thorough in a way he'd never been before he left. As he had in Morocco with his own business, he listened to recordings of that day's sessions, taking his own notes, ensuring he understood every concept before moving on to the next, essentially learning the ins and outs of what his father and brother had had years and special training to master. He ignored the coolness of advisers who probably thought what everyone else did—they'd gotten short shrift from him—and concentrated on the information they provided instead. It took discipline. It took endurance. It took time.

He could make no mistakes whatsoever.

He'd been painted as a selfish idiot by the press already, thanks to this father's years-long PR blitz. He wasn't going to give them any more ammunition. He arrived early, left late and acted like a model monarch.

The entire time, his disagreement with Tobi hovered in the back of his mind, an unresolved thing that made his stomach tighten.

Of course there was no way she'd understand why he'd done what he'd done, why he'd isolated his father from himself. There was no way she'd be able to understand why and how their relationship came to be. Even the thought of explaining made him feel tired. He wasn't exactly eager to expose his past weaknesses. Not to *her.* Were he thinking about it objectively, he'd realize that perhaps he blamed himself, if only a little, for what happened, for not being what his father and brother had insisted on.

Abusers often intimidate their victims into blaming themselves.

The words, spoken by one of the many therapists he'd

seen years ago, came to him unbidden now, and he swallowed at the memory. Truth had been hard and long in coming, and he refused to revert. Yes, he'd come back, but to avoid a constitutional crisis, not for either of *them*.

His eye went to a heavy wood-paneled chrome clock as it struck three. The massive thing had been a gift from the queen of England decades ago, and had been here as long as he could remember. Diplomatic trips, that was yet another thing he'd have to navigate. Kingdom issues within the whitewashed walls of the Djoboro palace were one thing; diplomacy was another. And he, as alone as he was now—

Unbidden, an image of Tobi came to his mind during the processional, crouching low to greet the flock of little girls who'd met them there. She'd handled the crowds with such aplomb, and invitations from far and near were pouring in for her. She was pretty, she was photogenic, she said all the right things, even at court.

And he was here, jamming information into the last vestiges of his aching brain, trying his damnedest not to—

There was a soft noise at the door, and Akil looked up sharply. He'd banned everyone from the room hours ago. But the long-legged figure standing in the archway of the royal study was Tobi. She held a tray in her hands.

Akil was more surprised by his bodily reaction than her actual appearance; he started almost violently, and a flush of actual heat captured him from neck to forehead.

"Oh," he said, and got to his feet, feeling remarkably foolish.

Tobi said nothing; instead she walked into the room, placed the tray carefully on the table in front of him, out of reach of the papers he had scattered about. She was dressed more casually than he'd ever seen her, in a pair of cotton sleep shorts that barely reached the tops of her thighs, a blue tank top with a gently scooping neck, and a duster in African style tie-dye that nearly touched the floor round her feet. In the braided rope slippers she wore, her small feet were adorned with small gold rings, and her toenails were polished with a ruby color that matched her fingernails. Her braids were already tucked beneath a turban that matched the duster, and her face was fresh, free of any makeup.

She looked astonishingly beautiful, and he swallowed back a sudden lump in his throat. This was *bad*.

He focused on the tray for a moment; he smelled Djoboran mint tea wafting gently from a glass pot, freshly baked bread, hummus, large dark grapes that looked absolutely bursting with juice, *labneh*, olive oil, creamy garlic sauce sprinkled with chives, and olives.

"I'm not hungry," he said a little gruffly, but Tobi said nothing, only began to decant the tea into the matching glass cups on the tray. "And it's unseemly for you to be trotting about at all hours with trays like a maid."

"Is it simply impossible for you to thank someone decently, without annoyance?" Tobi's voice was sweet and even. "I'm not here to apologize. I've nothing to apologize for. But I have it on good information that you're practically killing yourself these past couple of days."

"And you're here to rescue me from myself then?"

"I do care about you, you know," Tobi said softly. She hunched her shoulders forward as if to protect herself from whatever onslaught was coming, and strangely the sight gave him a pang deep inside. "What you're doing is hard. And I'm your family, whatever our arrangement."

Silence fell while Akil digested that piece of information. Tobi was still focused on the tray, pushing the tea and then a loaded plate of food at him almost shyly. She still wouldn't meet his eyes.

Akil exhaled slowly, then sat.

Tobi nodded, gathered the folds of her duster round her and turned to go, but Akil found himself speaking. The words came out halted and reluctant, but they were sincere.

"Perhaps… I was too harsh. Please—sit. If you want," he amended. He didn't quite know how it'd come about, but Tobi in a single stroke had dissolved the irritation of the past few days. It was disarming. He never seemed to be able to stick to a resolution when it came to his feelings for her.

"I used to do this for my father and his guests when I was a girl," she said, and finally looked at him, offering him a small smile before easing herself into one of the upholstered chairs near the desk. She waved off his offer of anything but tea. "Jamila and I have an engagement at one of her patronages tomorrow morning, and you should see the dress I've got to wedge into." The corners of her mouth lifted. "Jamila seems to be living vicariously through me, since she's got to wear black for the next year."

"You should be sleeping, then."

"It still feels odd, our room. It's so large."

And empty. There was no censure there, at least none that was deliberate, but Akil felt guilty. She was here because of him, and he'd allowed his own anger to get in the way of supporting her. He'd left voluntarily, but Tobi was a true stranger to Djoboro. And impulsively, he'd acted exactly like the people he had issues with. *Not very kingly behavior.*

He looked her full in the face for the first time since she'd come in. It was as drawn and tired as he felt, and there were faint hollows beneath her eyes.

"Eat," he said gently. "If your clothing is too tight tomorrow it'll only spark pregnancy rumors, which, trust me, is a good thing."

"Oh, goodness." She looked rather ill at the thought, pressed a hand to her abdomen.

"Is the thought so repulsive?"

"I'll pass on that one." She shuddered. "And I think I'll take that plate, after all."

Akil filled it silently. It was a companionable silence this time, and one that was oddly comforting. He found himself looking at the young woman in front of him with her head bent over bread and oil, and an image flashed through his mind, unbidden, then another, and then another, like a montage on a movie set.

Tobi, round with his child, soft and warm with love both given and received. A baby, round-cheeked, with her smooth skin and his dark eyes. The three of them in Djoboro, looking out through the enormous palace windows that flanked every corridor, showing their child his country. Their country.

The images faded as quickly as they'd come, and he was back in the dimly lit study, eating quietly with his wife. They would have to remain images, he supposed. There was no bearing on them in real life, and Akil was never one to believe in fairy tales.

Eventually, Tobi's head began to nod. When it nearly hit the table, Akil laughed and suggested they go to bed.

"Come up," he said, and his voice was heavy with compassion. "I promise, no funny stuff tonight. Just sleep." He did not, thank goodness, refer to his father, or to her visit. He kept up a steady stream of one-sided conversation as they walked slowly to the lift, and took her up to their floor.

Sensation was reduced to the feel of his large, warm hands on her body, stripping her gown and jewelry from her, rubbing her feet, tucking her into a bed with fresh sheets that smelled of lavender and lemon. He pulled off his own clothes, slid in bed beside her, pulled her into the warm wall of his chest.

"Tobi, thank you," he said, and his voice was quiet. Humble, almost. "Everything you have done has been in my support. I recognize that."

Tobi shut her eyes tight, fighting against the roil of emotion that came without fail whenever Akil was being close to gentle with her, and forced a smile that she hoped was casual. "It has been fine. It's…interesting, interacting with everyone. Kingmaking is quite different in Nigeria, and yet some things are exactly the same."

"All the diplomatic sycophancy, I suppose."

"It's more than that." She looked down at her hand, where it splayed on the snow-white sheets. "I was seven, perhaps, when the old oba of our town died. I remember my father's ascension clearly."

"Tell me about it." Akil's voice was mellow, but it was alert. He shifted so that his chest made a warm muscled bed for Tobi to lie on; she closed her eyes, speaking round the slow, steady beat of his heart.

"When the old king dies," she said softly, "the first thing they'll do is deny it. There are a lot of rituals involved, mysteries, they aren't public knowledge. No one, aside from those privy to such things, lays their eyes on the king's body, not even his wife or children. The oba is buried in a secret place, and then, well. There's a lot of bidding, behind the scenes, sometimes."

"Kings aren't put there by birth?"

"Sometimes they are, and it's very straightforward. But there are always other royal families, someone else who can make a claim. And the kingmakers, who are appointed by our old deities to name the new king, they hold supreme power. They are the ones who can hear the voice of the oracle, can tell us what the gods want."

"I thought you went to Catholic school," Akil said, but his voice was interested. It was new for Tobi, this sort of quiet conversation. Her father, sister, stepmother and brothers had never been ones to have serious conversations with her; she'd always been Tobi the trouble-maker, Tobi the trickster. Since she'd come to Djoboro, it was the first time she'd ever been given any great responsibility. Akil had recognized her ability as well as her longing to be taken seriously.

It felt amazing, to be honest.

Tobi laughed. "This has nothing to do with Catholicism. It's tradition."

"Well, it's put you in good stead." Akil's voice rumbled in the dark. "Were I the jealous type, I'd be very much so. You've charmed the country, Tobi—we make a formidable team. And I haven't forgotten what you said—we're rebuilding what was burned, to make it more beautiful."

We make a formidable team. I haven't forgotten what you said. Had she ever received that sort of praise from anyone in her life, even Kemi? In just a few short days, she'd found a place where she was important, where what she did mattered. She was somewhere where her past had no bearing on what people thought she was capable of. And, despite his ill temper and myriad issues, Akil had given all of this to her. Part of her felt truly pathetic for her thoughts veering toward this direction in the first place, but it was true.

Tobi blinked hard against tears that welled suddenly. It was funny, she'd never cried in all her years of captivity at home, never at all, but she seemed to do little else lately. She stiffened when Akil half turned her and impulsively nosed her face, not wanting him to discover, but he'd already tasted the wet, the salt.

"Oh, Tobi," he said, and the compassion in his voice made her heart hurt. "You must be tired out of your mind. Why are you crying?"

Good question. She was crying because all of this ultimately had an expiry date; she was only useful to Akil in establishing his kingship, and once that was over, once he'd won over his people...

"I'm trying to get used to the idea that you soon won't need me anymore," she whispered. She might as well be honest, as long as she was in this situation.

Akil's arms grew rigid for a fraction of a second, then he sighed. "Tobi—"

"Don't worry, I'm not in love with you." Possibly another lie, if she were honest with herself, but she could not afford that, not now. "I'll take the money and go."

He grunted. "It sounds rather crass to say it like that, Tobi."

"But that's what it is, isn't it?" She swallowed, hard. "I agreed to this bargain, and you're going to get what you want—"

"You will as well," Akil said, a note of warning entering his voice.

"I know. Trust me, I know. But—all this…"

"All what?"

"All this." Tobi pushed back against him, then sat up. She couldn't see him in the darkness of their bedroom, and that made her feel safer somehow. "You acknowledging me, and praising me, and holding me, and kissing me—"

"Tobi."

"We're here in bed, and we're both naked, and we're not having sex," she said, her voice breaking a little. "Don't you see what that means?"

"That's because you're tired. And besides, we've only had sex once—"

She shook her head. "I—no, Akil. What we're doing now—that's what lovers do. But I know this isn't about anything but the kingship, and I know you'd have nothing to do with me if it weren't for it. I keep telling myself this, over and over. And yes, I'm tired, and I never stop hearing Jamila's chattering in my head, but I just don't know—"

It was too overwhelming suddenly, and she wrapped her arms round herself, trying to contain the unexpected wave of pain that rushed in. Days of ignoring her own vulnerabilities, her own desires, had culminated in this: a veritable breakdown in front of the man who was responsible for it all.

No, she corrected herself. *He's not responsible. I am.* She'd come here of her own free will, Akil's demands aside. She'd allowed him to kiss her, to touch her, to take the virginity she'd maintained for—what reason?

The passion between them was more than lust, at least on her side.

"You should have left me in Dubai," she mumbled, and lay back down, curling herself up in a ball so tight her limbs ached. She heard Akil sigh and lower himself next to her.

"Perhaps I should have. I don't know what to say," he admitted finally.

Where the hell is this going to end up? She wanted to cry out, but she pressed a fist to her mouth instead. She'd given up enough of her dignity tonight. But she needed to know. So she could protect herself, if nothing else.

"Tobi," he said after a moment. "Please try to understand." He took a breath; she felt it, warm and gentle, caressing her shoulder. "I do care for you on some level—how can I not? You're brilliant, bright, absolutely fearless. In some ways I wish I were more like you. But, Tobi, I know my own shortcomings. I know where I come from and how I was raised. And there's no way I can be anything to you but a disappointment in the long run. This job—it takes people, steals their souls. You weren't born to it. I'm trying to protect you."

Tobi closed her eyes. Yet another man who'd denied her what she needed the most by trying to protect her. Were they all like this? And yet he was still talking. He moved forward, drawing her back into the circle of his arms, his front to her back, speaking in those same oddly dispassionate yet gentle tones.

"If this is too hard, if it helps, we can try and separate sooner—"

"No," Tobi whispered. Separation at this point would

only hurt worse. He already knew every inch of her body, and she craved him like a drug.

If she didn't have anything else, she'd still have that.

She turned around, identified the bit of shadow that must be his face, leaned forward. Her kiss landed on his cheekbone; she found her way to his mouth, made a soft sound deep in her throat as she kissed him.

"I'm tired," she said after they drew apart, "and possibly hormonal."

"I understand," he said simply, and that was all he said. He was frowning, as if he were trying to decide something—and then, in a split second, he opened his mouth.

"I'm not trying to provide excuses," he said. "But you're a good person, and I just want to explain."

"Explain?"

"Yes. This is all tied to my past, Tobi—there is much you don't know. It's complicated, at best. I know you want to make peace. I appreciate it. But what I've done is the extent of what I can do. I'll allow the visits, at any rate. But that is all."

Tobi nodded at the concession, something tightening in her throat. "You can tell me about it, you know."

Akil's grip tightened on her, and his voice came, gentle in the saffron-scented darkness.

"I know. And I will, perhaps. But—not tonight, Tobi."

She didn't answer; there was nothing in the room but her quiet breathing, and Akil spoke after several beats. "So, what was it like for you after?"

"After…?"

"After your father took the throne."

Oh. Tobi was so surprised by the question she turned

her head. Akil had never shown a more than rudimentary interest in her past before, and it was startling. "It was odd," she said after a moment, "knowing he was so important. It was fun at first. We lived in the palace, went to the best schools. He married again, and we were fortunate, his second wife was very kind to us."

Akil grunted.

"Then, after my sister Kemi became a teenager, things were a little harder. She was—kidnapped while out with friends, held for ransom." Tobi licked her lips. She still remembered that day, the palpable terror in the air, the way her stepmother kept running to the bathroom, her delicate stomach disturbed by fear, the family clustered round her father's phone, listening to the demands of the kidnappers over speakerphone, to the man's rough voice describing with glee exactly what he planned to do with the teenage princess, should his demands not be met. "It was awful. When they did get her back, there was an—altercation—and a man was shot and killed. Kemi was shot, too, and it crippled her arm."

Akil said nothing, but she could feel the tension in his body; he was listening to every word.

"We were virtually on lockdown after that. My father took us out of school, kept us in the house, except for mandated outings where we had to take a full security escort. My sister actually met her husband on a state trip—I made her sneak out with me to a nightclub, and there he was."

Akil chuckled. "You didn't meet anyone that night?"

"I ditched Kemi to go to a party at the local university. I don't think she's forgiven me to this day." She smiled at the memory. Kemi had gotten pregnant that night as well with her little nephew, Ayodele, a bit of information she decided to keep to herself for now. "My father was so horrified at that state of affairs, he sought to make me 'another man's problem,' as he put it, as soon as he could—that's where you came in. He thought a great deal of your father."

"And mine of yours," Akil admitted. His lids were lowering; his face was growing slack with impending sleep. Tobi wrapped her arms round him, laid her head on his chest and closed her own eyes, reveling in the tenuous bond that they'd formed, at least for tonight. She could see the dawn pinkening the sky in the large window opposite the bed; they would have to be up in a few hours, anyway.

It was time to rest, for there would be much to do tomorrow, and even more in the days to come.

They had a royal house to rebuild, and she would put her heart into it for as long as he needed her.

Finding herself was a nice bonus.

CHAPTER TWELVE

"YOU'RE READY FOR the memorial service? You're *sure?*" Akil clarified, looking suspiciously at his wife where she sat opposite him at the breakfast table, dressed demurely in a pale green dressing gown, embroidered with white around the hem and sleeves. He hadn't placed any restrictions on her nightwear, but since that first disastrous night in their suite, Tobi had quietly switched to nightwear that was pretty, but the opposite of sexy: long-sleeved pajama tops and loose bottoms, dressing gowns, nightgowns with matching robes. He supposed she was trying to dress for the new role she'd taken upon herself.

Too bad it didn't work. On the worst nights when he closed his eyes he could see her full mouth curved up into a mocking smile, the gleam of her skin against the white of the pillows on his bed, her breasts thrust upward, nipples jutting out, puckered and ready for his mouth. It would have been easier, as well, had he not known exactly how tight and hot she'd been, pulsing hard around the length of him...

"Akil?"

He blinked. There it was again, that soft and dulcet voice she'd been using lately. They hadn't argued once since that night in his study; she'd been acting like the ideal wife. She spent a great deal of time with Jamila, shopping, attending affairs of state in his stead, even going as far as to help his sister-in-law move her extensive holdings to her new royal home at the edge of the city, and unpacking things with her own hands.

"She's a good girl," Jamila said in her weekly reports to Akil, and he knew that was high praise from the former queen. When Akil mentioned it she tucked her braids behind her ear and looked up at him with an expression that was *almost* shy.

"She's important to the royal family, so she is to me as well," she said quietly.

The words hung between them, heavy, loaded with a meaning that he was unwilling to explore. Then Tobi cleared her throat and scuttled from the room, and the moment was lost.

Thank goodness.

At night, he'd find Tobi bent over a language book at the old-fashioned secretary in the sitting area of their bedchamber, head wrapped in enormous headphones, sounding out greetings and pleasantries in Djoboran that were awkward on her tongue. There were flash cards with the members of parliament written in her bold hand that tumbled out of her purse.

In the evenings, he found himself eager to spend time with her, speaking about his work and his hopes and dreams for future projects. Tobi was bright and innovative, he found, and an avid listener. She had a talent for identifying the heart of a matter and pulling out objectives; her mind was like a heat-seeking missile, worming straight to the source and identifying solutions. It was she who mentioned a project that her father had successfully run in Nigeria years ago, providing grants to local drillers who wanted government backing to start their own businesses. It greatly reduced unregulated drilling and black- market sales in that area, because the government had handed the locals the means to success, and created a ready-made workforce at the same time.

"It might work here, too," she'd said simply, toying with the end of her braids in a gesture he'd grown used to as one of her tics. They'd been lunching on the veranda, and Tobi had been staring out at the landscape. "This is a monarchy—it's getting older. It's maturing. Changing."

She had his interest. "Tell me more."

"My father is a king. He gave me everything I wanted, except freedom to be my own person, and I finally started sneaking around to do it. That might be what's happening here. If people get support from you, if you let them know that you *trust* them to be independent—"

"Then we win in the long run," Akil said slowly. "Talent stays in the country. It's a thoroughly modern model, Tobi."

"I wanted to help." She couldn't look at him, and Akil suddenly wanted her to. Desperately.

"Tobi?"

Reluctantly, as if pulled by some unseen force, she turned her face. When her eyes met his they flickered to his mouth, then back up as if she'd caught herself doing something wrong. He took a moment to drink her all in: full lips, long lashes, all the loveliness he tried to forget existed, most of the time.

"It seems odd, not to be arguing with you," he murmured.

She did smile then, a little sarcastic twist of the lips.

"I'm trying to be good. I've got a great deal of money riding on it, after all."

Akil had no idea why that statement affected him the way it did, but he found himself drawing back. "Indeed you do."

Tobi's fingers returned to the end of her braids. "I was thinking, I'd like to throw a party. Not what you're thinking," she said, before he opened his mouth. "It'd be a formal banquet, for the Royal Council. I think it would be a nice gesture before the coronation. I also thought it might be nice—to tie your brother's memorial with it."

She was right. "I'd intended to send them some gifts," he admitted, leaning back. *To celebrate hell freezing over.*

Tobi shook her head. "That's nothing compared to entertaining them in your own home."

"They may not come," he said darkly.

"An invitation from their monarch? All of them? I seriously doubt it. They're snobbish, but they're not crazy."

He grunted. He wasn't so sure, and really hadn't given a toss until then—what were they going to do, take the crown from the only living heir because they resented his exit three years before?

"They know they need to make peace, it's for the good of the Crown, after all. Let them see how you've grown up and how much you're willing to entertain statecraft," Tobi entreated.

She was right. He didn't want to admit it, but she was right.

"I think, perhaps, a week from today." She tilted her head, and his fingers itched to touch the soft arch of her neck. He knew from experience that she'd tense deliciously and begin softening against him. He reached out, brushed the backs of his fingers on that tempting patch of skin, and yes—she tensed with a gentle intake of breath.

"You're just full of good ideas, aren't you?"

"It's hardly a good idea. You know what to do. You're just too stubborn to do it."

"That is true." Akil allowed a rueful smile while still stroking her skin. He could see the rapid rise and fall of her chest. He knew it was a terrible idea, but he couldn't help himself. He could not have stopped himself from drawing his wife to him any more than he could have stopped the earth's rotation. It was want, pure and simple, and the soft curse she uttered before lifting her arms up to his neck was one of response, not denial.

"Akil, *please*," she said, and he cradled her face in his hands, kissing her deeply. All that mattered in that moment was how soft her lips were, the sweet slide of her tongue against his, and pleasing her.

They kissed like lovers, with all the sweet hesitation of something new, heady, real. Any reservations in Tobi seemed to have melted away completely in those first few moments, and she was mewling soft and desperate against his lips, his neck. He hadn't even touched her beyond cupping her face, but the way she was *squirming*—

They'd reached a point, he thought a little hazily, where they could freely admit how much they wanted each other, and the throb beginning in his lower regions was beginning to surpass everything else in importance.

"Do you want this?" he found himself rasping out in a voice that sounded *nothing* like his.

She laughed, and for the first time in weeks she sounded like her old self, arrogance mixed with incredulity. "Of course I do. But—" She squeezed her eyes shut, paused to whimper when his lips connected with a particularly sensitive spot on her neck.

"But what?"

She forced her eyes open, and lust began to erode at the edges of the tenderness; her pupils were blown wide with arousal. "Not here," she said, and pulled away from him, biting her lip so hard he was sure she'd leave a mark. He took a ragged breath of his own.

"Lead the way," he said.

They weren't going to make it, Tobi thought almost wildly.

She and Akil were somewhere in the deserted hallway that led to their bedchamber, and his big, hot hands were everywhere. He'd completely dispensed with control, and that unleashed something in Tobi she'd been suppressing in all these weeks of being his wife, the wife he wanted. He'd stopped her at least three times to kiss her hard, eat up her whimpers and moans with the softness of his mouth, divest her of various articles of clothing; her dress there, buttons scattering across polished tile. Her bra, twisted over her head, left in a stairwell.

The lace underwear she wore took the longest to remove; he pressed her hard against the bedroom door, hooked his fingers in the sides, worked them down inch by inch until she was trembling with need.

"I'm not going to beg," she said through her teeth.

"I think this might happen before we even get inside," he said, his voice raspy and low. Ripples of pleasure went through her even at just the *suggestion*—

"Akil—" she gasped.

"Quiet, for once," he said, laughing low, and before she could protest he was on his knees. He used his fingers, his tongue, nipped and soothed, held her firm, right where he wanted her, until her resolution not to beg was a thing of the past. When their position grew too awkward, when she wanted to arch her back, his strong arms lowered her to the floor. And oh, she begged, threw dignity away with the last of her clothing. She did it in soft little whimpering gasps that ended only when that hot, wicked tongue of his swept *directly* over where she wanted him most—

Explosions. Stars. All the clichés. She was boneless, draped uselessly against the floor, leg dangling over his shoulder. And he was withdrawing from between her legs, looking very pleased with himself.

She was too wrung out to feel irritated; she rolled half over, mostly to shield her face. If he said something sardonic she'd die. But instead he reached out and touched her cheek.

"Are you all right?" he whispered, and then he stretched out beside her, drawing her into his arms. She could feel the length of him on her back, hard and pulsing; in answer to the question she rotated her hips, delighting in the pull, the ache.

"I want you," she whispered.

"Not here," he said with the barest note of laughter in his voice. He was up on his feet in a moment, and when she stood as well he swept her into his arms with as much ease as he'd shown that first night he'd carried her over the threshold. Moments later, when she was sinking into the softness of the mattress and he was slowly, sweetly making love to her with hands and mouth and finally, *finally* filling her aching emptiness with slow, warm thrusts, it was hard to remember how to breathe, or which way was up. And in the midst of it all was something else, something that sparked bright as flame, and yet filled her with complete despair.

She wasn't in love with him yet; she was too pragmatic for that. Or at least she thought she was, and had the self-control to keep her feelings for him from turning into anything else. But this—this wildness, this emotional surge—this was completely out of her hands, something untamed and unexpected. She had no idea how to stop except to stay away from him, and that was impossible.

Air was crushed from her lungs, and she swallowed hard.

She was in trouble.

CHAPTER THIRTEEN

TOBI WORKED HARDER at the party for the Royal Council than anything she'd ever worked at in her life, and felt a heady pleasure at the way it was all coming together. Along with the ever-present Jamila she consulted with party planners, PR people, even her older sister, Kemi, whose parties were written up in Abuja's society pages even more than those of the first lady herself. She reacted with shock at her little sister's first call.

"*Akil* has you doing this? What did he find out about you? Who'd you kill?"

"Whatever." She glanced over her shoulder to where she could hear the sound of the masseuse, pounding her husband's muscles in the privacy of his bathroom after a morning of lovemaking; he was late to parliament, something that was nearly unheard of. She was putting off her own shower and getting dressed. She'd never admit it to Akil, but she loved the pull and burn that came after vigorous sex with him, his salt on her skin, the tang of him on her lips. She cleared her throat and wrapped herself in the coverlet on the bed. "It was my idea."

Kemi's response to that was dumbfounded shock. "You hate those things. You used to sneak out of Daddy's—"

"I've thrown dozens of parties!"

"Not *this* type of party."

"I know. I *know*." Tobi pulled the coverlet completely over her head. "I want to do it. For Akil. I need to know what to do."

Her sister grunted in amazement. "Well—miracles still happen! Simplicity is key. Think about what would be pleasantest for your guests, not yourself. Luxury is felt in the details, pretty surroundings, smiling hosts, excellent food and wine. You've got to make them never want to stop eating."

Tobi obediently took notes on her phone, then made the same call to her stepmother, her father's senior wife. *She* almost fainted at the thought of her stepdaughter willingly hosting a royal event, but by the time she hung up, Tobi felt confident that she'd be able to pull off the event of the season and give her husband a human side that the men and women of the council would appreciate. He was already proving himself to be a faithful leader, serving his country through his economic work.

Now they would see the man, one who despite her fears, she grew closer to every day. She saw him when he was proud, remote and kingly in ceremonial dress, presiding over court; she also saw him when he was sitting huddled over his papers at two in the morning, mouthing the notes for the day, eyes blurry with little sleep. She came to respect both sides and was determined the people would as well.

He would win them over. *They* would win them over.

Akil spent the morning of Tobi's party holed up in his study, doing his best to avoid the virtual army of planners, workers and installers that had swarmed his residence since five that morning. Tobi had crept from the circle of his arms at about three, and presumably was somewhere in the din. Akil plugged in the best noise-canceling headphones he owned, hunched his shoulders down and worked. Since Tobi had mentioned the mining program weeks ago, he hadn't been able to get the idea out of his head. He'd researched similar programs in other countries, and even went as far as to call her father for advice. He'd been surprised and demanded at first to know if his daughter was behaving herself, then reacted with surprise when he'd told him what it was for.

"Tobi told you that?" He laughed. "I had no idea she had anything in her head besides makeup, dresses and raising my blood pressure."

Then you don't know her. Akil had bitten his tongue, taken the information he wanted, and ended the call as quickly as possible. Tobi was an extraordinary young woman, beautiful and intelligent. It nettled him that her upbringing had quite possibly pigeonholed her into thinking she was no better than parties, reality shows. Hell, even being married to a person like *him,* as much as he was enjoying it.

He closed his eyes. He didn't do it often when he thought of Tobi, because the gesture inevitably recalled images of her, taut and damp with perspiration and writhing beneath him. His hunger for her grew every time they had sex, and she shed a little more of her inhibitions with each encounter. Even thinking of it now in this casual way made his body cramp with need.

Akil shifted uncomfortably, then reached for the glass of ice water sitting on his desk. He was unused to this level of want when it came to any woman, and he knew on some level that this was due to intimacy, not lust. He wanted to be close to Tobi, but sex was the only thing he'd allow. Even the thought of letting her in, giving her the type of power he'd never allowed anyone, *ever*—

He couldn't afford it. Especially not if he planned to set her free.

He was drunk off her heady sweetness and his years of self-imposed celibacy, he told himself. Tobi had to go—it was better. He would not have her destroyed by the same system that made him what he was. The deal would be upheld.

He would admit, only here, when he was alone, that perhaps, after all, he'd miss her.

Akil was startled from his musings when his door opened, then irritated when he saw the time. He'd spent a good part of an hour daydreaming about her, for God's sake. His frown intensified when he saw that it was Tobi, but something in his chest leaped up, a little sunburst of warmth. Her braids were gathered into a messy topknot on her head; she was dressed in a T-shirt that showed off a sliver of taut stomach. She was frowning.

"Here you are," she said accusingly. Akil leaned back in his office chair, shooting her his best indolent look.

"Where else would I be?"

"You're supposed to be getting ready!" She glanced down at the small digital tablet she held, expression agitated. "The barber's already here, your masseuse arrives in an hour, and—no. No, don't get up, and do not come over here, unless you're planning to go out the door and meet—"

She was already softening, already sighing, and fell completely quiet when Akil kissed her.

"Calm down," he said simply.

"I can't," she said, and tried to step back, but he held her fast. That delicious floral scent was rising from her skin, and he was already—

"No," she said forcefully, as if she read his mind, and he laughed and released her.

"Sit down and have a drink."

"No." She scowled. "You need to come with me."

"Drink first," he wheedled. "I'll tie up the loose ends on this report, and we can leave together. You need a drink. You look manic."

She faltered, then sighed. "Fine. One drink. Quickly. And you keep your hands to yourself."

He crossed over to the bar, decanted a finger of whiskey into a glass, handed it to her. Tobi made a face and took the tiniest sip, and he laughed. "We've neglected this part of your education."

"I know how to drink it. I just don't like it." Tobi set the offending glass as far from her as she could manage. "Give me rum. Something sweet."

He sighed but filled her request, and the two sat quietly together, sipping their drinks. Tobi's eyes were bright and not quite focused on the wall art she was staring at. Akil cleared his throat after a moment.

"I don't want you to think that all my grumbling means I'm ungrateful," he said after a moment. "This will do much for my profile."

"And if I know how to do anything, it's how to throw a party," Tobi said drily, crossing her legs. "Not that you'd believe it to listen to my stepmom. She simply can't fathom that my socialite lifestyle might relate in any way to the high-society posturing she enjoys so much."

Akil smiled, and they sat in silence for a moment,

cradling their glasses in their palms. "You didn't enjoy it when you were home?"

"I hated it," she said so emphatically that he smiled. "Sneaked out every chance I got from state events. It wasn't the parties themselves, I think—it was the company, and the fact that I was there just to be on display."

"You found your own ways of having fun, though." His mouth tipped upward.

"Oh, yes. I made sneaking out to clubs an art form."

"And you never were caught?"

The smile faltered a bit on Tobi's face. "Oh, I got caught often enough. Usually it was an enterprising housemaid who wanted to get on my father's good side, or the guards I bribed slipped up and forgot to pick me up on time." Her brow grew furrowed as she remembered. "My father had a good firm hand with the *koboko*—"

"*Koboko*?"

"Cane. The type used to drive goats," Tobi said, shaking her head at the memory. "He never hesitated to use it. But I was as stubborn as an old goat—and beatings never stopped me, so he found more creative ways to keep me under his thumb. Punished my maids, punished my older sister." She opened her mouth, then closed it. She didn't really like talking about her father, or those times, but there was something about Akil and his actual interest in her words today that made her want to speak more.

"I'm not defending his…methods," Akil said after a pause, "but I can see why he would want to keep his daughters safe."

"It's a justification for trying to control us," she said briefly. "I'm glad I got out."

Akil grunted, still looking at her with that mixture of curiosity and admiration on his face. "You are an extraordinary young woman," he said briefly.

"I've hardly done anything."

"You've managed to maintain your spirit," Akil said, "which is more than I can say for Malik. His entire personality was built, shaped, curated around the needs of the Crown. I couldn't do that, so I had to leave."

"Do you ever regret the path you've taken?"

He was silent for a long moment before he spoke. "My father abused me for years, Tobi. Mentally, physically, in every way you might imagine. He resented me for my mother's failings, and later, for my own. I'm not sure he ever cared for me. And Malik—" He took a breath. "My break with him will always hurt more than the one with my father. I told him everything on the eve of my seventeenth birthday. I couldn't take it anymore, wanted to kill myself. He laughed, Tobi. Derisively. He didn't believe a word I said, not after how I'd behaved over the years. He accused me of showboating, of seeking attention—"

Tobi covered her mouth with her hand.

"Yes." Akil nodded. "It was then I became determined to leave. My father was a skillful liar, and Malik, unfortunately, was caught in his web fairly early. Neither of them would have been an ideal person to sit on the throne, but I am different." His eyes were suddenly fixed on her, and so fierce that Tobi leaned back. "I am ready to serve my kingdom for as long as it needs me, but it has to be *my* way."

It was such a passionate declaration that Tobi felt a stab of envy—she'd never found anything to care about as fiercely as he cared for his country. Her father had never engaged her with the work that he did, had never thought her thoughts were worth anything.

She glanced at her feet, where the tips of her toes gleamed ruby red. "You shamed me a bit," she said quietly. "I've managed to escape, but I haven't done much for myself—or for anyone else. Until I came here, that is."

"Your tendency toward self-pity is tiresome," Akil said drily. "What do you call the program you were trying to implement? It's going to be successful beyond your wildest dreams—just wait. It's hardly the end of your life," Akil added, and he offered her a smile that was almost kind. "Besides, you're helping me. And as my wife, my queen, you will have access to the world. You will have access to everything you want to learn, and you will be able to take up any cause that you wish. Say the word, Tobi. I will make it happen."

He was offering her the world, and Tobi felt her heartbeat quicken at his words, as well as the intensity that pooled deep in those brandy-dark eyes. He was offering her the world, but he would never offer her himself, and Tobi wasn't sure that it was enough.

Akil's voice broke into her thoughts. "It seems appropriate to tell you now that I'm implementing the program you suggested," Akil said after a moment. "I'd like to give you full credit. And I'd like you to head the committee, if you will?"

Surprise crossed his wife's lovely face. "Me? I'm not an economist."

"Luckily, I am." He allowed the corners of his mouth to tilt up. "And you're something far more important— you know people, and you think about what's good for them from a human standpoint, not just an economical one. You're interested in people, in their needs. And that—well. That will make you a splendid leader, any-where you find yourself."

Tobi was staring at him as if she'd never quite seen him before, and the emotion on her face was something *he'd* never seen before. She set down her glass and crossed her arms over her chest, hunching her shoulders forward, resting her elbows on her thighs. He took a sip, tilted his head, waited. He was a patient man; he could not drag it out of her.

"I don't know what to say." Her voice was quiet.

He lifted his shoulders. "You don't have to say anything. I just wanted you to know that about yourself. You can do something worth more. Don't take that first failure as an indication of inability."

"You're assuming a lot," Tobi said mildly, but she did not correct him; instead her dark eyes fixed on his face as if fascinated.

"I've been through a lot," he countered, "and I've been that person, Tobi. My paternity has always been called into question, and though the palace shielded me from it, it came out. Children can be cruel. I couldn't run away from who I was, so I channeled that energy into making a contribution that no one could deny existed. And I'm glad I was successful. I admit, I started it to prove a point. But now I want to be just as success-ful as king, doing the best for my people—"

He stopped. He hadn't intended to run on for that long, but there was something about having Tobi around that made him want to speak. He cleared his throat. "Well, anyway. That is all."

Something in Tobi's eyes had softened considerably, altering her face completely. It was as if he looked past the woman she presented as on a day-to-day basis, sud-denly saw the one she was. He'd seen her sometimes, late at night, nestled into the curve of his arm after a particularly intense session of lovemaking, when they were too tired to hold up those masks they both clung to so desperately. He'd seen glimpses of a future that they might be able to have, if only—

He pushed the thought out of his mind, because his wife had stood and was approaching him, a determined look on her face. She peered down into his, then she smiled.

"I almost believe you mean that," she said, and he laughed and yanked her down onto his lap. The kiss that followed was eager and sloppy, and both were laughing when they separated. Tobi managed to twist just enough to palm his smartphone from the tabletop and shoved it into her shirt.

"Got it," she said triumphantly, and tried to escape, but Akil held her fast.

"You don't want me digging for it," he warned.

"Maybe I do," she shot back—and then gasped when his fingertips gently scissored the nipple that was already swelling for his touch. She was always ready for him, it seemed, and the way those tight buds felt in his *mouth*—

One stroke and it pebbled, and suddenly he was far more interested in that than he was in his phone.

"*No,*" she said determinedly, and wriggled off his lap. Her face was alive with laughter, and she backed up. "None of that. Maybe later, if you're as nice to our guests as I want you to be. And I'll hold this till then, too. *No more working.*"

He said she'd make a splendid leader, and frankly, tonight, she felt like the queen she was. *His* queen, no matter how dangerous that was. She stood at the entryway of the Al-Hamri Royal House, welcoming the

men and women who were descendants of the oldest
houses of Djoboro. She smiled. She laughed. She used
the lessons her exasperated stepmother had drilled into
her for years to the best effect. She stood, always a half
step behind Akil, his hand firmly at her waist. He hadn't
let go of her for more than a few minutes the entire
evening, and Tobi allowed herself, just for tonight, to
imagine they were actual partners, that this was more
than a marriage of convenience.

Over the past few weeks her feelings for Akil had
blossomed into something else entirely, along with her
growing confidence. The mere sight of him sometimes
made her body ache.

She felt a hot flush begin at her temples, spread
downward. Akil made her aware of her body in ways
she didn't know were possible, and she now had to deal
with the side effect of wanting him, all the time.

She'd dressed in anticipation of that tonight, in a
form-fitting gold gown, and she'd been startled by the
woman who looked back at her once she was ready. She
looked like the finest ebony dipped in gold. The dress
fit so tightly to her curves it was almost indecent, yet
covered so much of her skin it was wholly appropriate
for that evening. She'd paired the dress with jewels from
Akil's family vault—all rubies of course, set in gold so
pure it softened from the heat of her skin. For the first
time she looked like a woman soft and glowing with
affection, wanted and received, not a child longing to
escape her loneliness.

Yes. That was it. She wasn't lonely anymore, and
Akil was the reason. She dared not articulate what
that meant, not with the deal they had on the table,
but tonight—

She let him hold her, dance with her, whisper words that dripped with honey. She let him kiss her in dark corners when guests were occupied with revelry, let those long, sensitive fingers tease the skin of her inner thighs till she couldn't take it anymore, laughed low at the dampness he'd created there.

"Later," was all he said, smoothing her skirt down, and, yes, she was thinking about it. She'd progressed to the point where she was fantasizing about them together, new places, new positions, new ways of pleasuring each other. Akil seemed to know her body at this point as much as she did herself.

But they still had a party to get through. And frankly, she thought as she surveyed the gathering with pride, she was becoming as emotionally invested in Djoboro as she was in its king.

I do love it here.

"Wonderful job, my dear," Jamila said to her about halfway through the party. She had spent most of her time sitting on the overstuffed velvet armchair Tobi had prepared for her, and now she patted the arm of it when Tobi came over.

"Are you having fun?" It certainly looked like it to Tobi, and she'd been careful to ensure Jamila was paid the respect she deserved at the dowager princess. Now she gestured that Tobi should bring the plate of delicacies on the table at her elbow a little closer and take some. "I'll wager you haven't eaten all night. Sit for a moment."

"You're right, I've been busy." Tobi laughed, patted her tummy. "This dress doesn't allow for much food, either."

"When you're pregnant it will be important." Jamila

looked a little wistful, and Tobi was suddenly over-come. *Children—*

She hadn't allowed herself to think about it, not with her situation being as tenuous as it was. She and Akil used protection. Their marriage was temporary, after all. But she couldn't stop herself imagining that maybe one day a little girl or a little boy, with dark eyes like their father, and her deep skin...

Tobi forced herself back to the present when Jamila spoke. Her eyes looked out over the room with her characteristic sharpness, at the people milling about, talking, laughing, enjoying wine and conversation, il-luminated by the gleaming candles and the beauty of the night sky.

"This was a stroke of genius. You are a good part-ner for him," she said, and smiled at Tobi. "You want what's best for him."

"He wants the same for me," Tobi said, remember-ing their conversation earlier.

"I'd hope so."

"He's had a rough start to his reign..." Tobi's voice trailed off, just a little. "I hope that this small contribu-tion makes some difference."

"I know. It's a pity it won't."

Tobi blinked. Out of everything that Jamila could have said, she wasn't expecting that. Not at all. "Ex-cuse me?"

"He'll never be the man his father was. Not really." Jamila reached for a whiskey glass and took a long, meditative sip. "I shouldn't tell you, really, but I'm rather tipsy. It'd be nice if someone besides me is there to console him when it doesn't happen."

Tobi's heart was beating so hard she could hear it

in her ears, a throb, a rush of blood. She stared at her husband, who was currently laughing with a group of older men. His face was animated. Happier than she'd ever seen it, and she knew it was because he thought, he thought—

"He isn't playing the game, Tobi. His relationship with the old king—he simply doesn't realize how much he was loved and the legacy he built. He's allowed his bitterness to get in the way, and believe me, it is noticed."

Tobi's face must have reflected shock, for Jamila laughed, a little kindly. "You're the daughter of an oba yourself, my dear? Surely you know how old kings are revered?"

"The king is ill!"

"Yes, and his son has exiled him. A pleasant exile, but still an exile. The old king hasn't been seen at a single state ceremony since Malik died, and no one is buying the illness excuse. He attended every single state affair of Malik's, with assistants and nurses, of course. People loved it. Djoboran culture is very much about respect for elders and caring for them. Akil knows this, and he's ignoring the one thing that will never allow people to think he's reformed."

Tobi could not speak, could not answer, only fixed her eyes on Akil, on his happy face. It simply couldn't—

"The old king needs to be at the coronation," Jamila said calmly, downing the last drops of whiskey from her glass. "He needs to be there, or all is lost. You need to make sure of that, or the people won't forget. His father's been hand-training the press for decades, Tobi. They are restrained now out of respect for Malik, but it won't last forever. I don't know how you'll do it, but—trust me, Tobi. I wouldn't steer you wrong."

"You can't tell Akil this yourself?" Tobi felt a sudden rush of anger against Jamila and her ever-smooth, ever-bland, blasé face. But she stood, looking down imperiously at Tobi.

"I'm going to the ladies' lounge," she said. "You stay here and wait for your husband. He will need you in the upcoming days."

With that, she turned and swayed off in the direction of the bathrooms, and Tobi was left with a knot in her stomach bigger than any she'd ever felt before.

CHAPTER FOURTEEN

THE ROYAL CORONATION CEREMONY, the official, public-facing recognition of Akil's accession as king, approached, and Akil found himself descending into razor-sharp focus that manifested in little sleep, little food and hyperconcentration at work. He woke long before the sun was up and slept hours after it set, fortifying himself with coffee as he did so. Tobi's mining apprentice idea had taken on a mind of its own, and had been formally presented to parliament with rousing success. The program would officially be launched in a year's time, and the excitement within the kingdom had become a palpable buzz. The Royal Council had thawed noticeably since the party, and the press had been neutral if not gushing. Finally Djoboro seemed ready for a celebration.

Akil was determined to make a good showing at the ceremony. He was sure he'd terrorized poor Tobi with long detailed descriptions of everything that needed to be done; she was so uncharacteristically quiet and distracted that he finally confronted her a few days before.

"Are you," he said sardonically, "planning to kill me at the forum, like Julius Caesar? I know I've been insufferable for the past few weeks, and you haven't said a word."

"That assumption says more about you than it does about me," Tobi said primly. She was poking at bowl of cream and summer berries with little appetite; Akil's brow furrowed.

"Are you pregnant?" he demanded, and *that* got a reaction from her, at least.

"Heavens, no!"

"Are you on your—"

"If you know what's good for you," she said, eyes flashing dangerously, "you will *not* ask that question."

"Then what's wrong with you?"

"Perhaps it's the fact that I've got such a wonderfully *sensitive* husband," she spat out, but there was an oddness about her expression that made him frown. He tossed his napkin onto the table, leaned in and peered into her face.

"Would you stop?" she exclaimed, drawing back.

He knew he was irritating her, but he had to get some reaction out of her. "Are you nervous about the coronation?"

"What is this, twenty questions?"

"I'm not sure what you're referring to."

"It's an expression. This game—" Seeing his face, she gave up. "Why do you care, anyway? It's not like I'm here because my feelings matter."

Akil heaved a sigh. "If by this point, Tobi, you think I don't care about your feelings, you are more disillusioned than you let on."

At that, something in his wife's face tightened; then she looked down at her hands. He waited, taking a sip of the rich Turkish coffee, savoring the bitter taste.

"I don't know what I'm supposed to do after this is all over," she said, gesturing vaguely at the gorgeous sprawl of land that lay before them, bathed in the pale light of the early morning. "I mean, what? Go back to Dubai? Nigeria?"

"You have something to do in Dubai, if I recall, and you will have the full support of the palace behind you." He had to kill this now, before emotion turned it into something unpleasant, something he did not want to deal with at the moment. "Tobi, you can do anything you want to do! Finish your women's housing project, get firmly entrenched in philanthropy. An economics degree. Documentaries, if you're determined to do film. I can set you up on a goodwill tour, and you can talk about the mining program. It was your brainchild, after all, and I've given you full credit. The role of working royal is yours."

"Just not the role of your wife," she said softly.

Did she want that? He dared not ask. "I'm not asking you for a divorce, Tobi, although you certainly can have one, if you want one."

"You'd be surprised," Tobi muttered, pushing back the offending bowl. A server appeared, took it away.

"I can't promise to love you, Tobi. We set this deal in place so we could both walk away."

"And what if I don't want to?"

The silence in the room was so loud it was practically echoing, and Akil felt a sudden rush of half defensiveness, half anger. So she would force his hand, then?

"Tobi, you have to," he said, and his voice held a note of pleading in it.

"Have to…what? Completely ignore the fact that every time I'm in your bed it hurts a little more because

I know I must remember it can't mean anything? Ignore the fact that I have my own projects here now, my own responsibilities—do you intend that I walk away from them? I'm *human*, Akil. And so are you. If you want an adviser, you've plenty of those. I'm your queen. And I want to at least explore the possibility of being that in every sense. I mean we already are, aren't we? You just refuse to acknowledge it, and for someone who prides himself on plain speaking—" She broke off at last and half turned, presumably to hide her face.

Her outburst left Akil's skin tingling and an odd stinging behind his eyes.

"Do you want to stay?" he asked after a moment, taking a breath to ensure his voice would be steady. "Here?"

"Am I allowed to want that?" Her voice sounded choked.

That blossoming warmth that belonged to her, that lived deep in his chest, was sparking at the sound of her words. It was as if she were offering him something cool to drink, something to relieve a thirst he hadn't known he had until it was there, spilling over the edges of her hands.

He'd married Tobi to fill a need he'd had at the time. Now she seemed the answer to other needs he'd allowed to go dormant for a very long time. The most frightening thing was that he could so easily picture what their lives together would look like, and her place in it. It happened every time she sat across from him to have a meal, or spoke with him about matters of state, or drew her scented softness close in their clean white bed.

Her large dark eyes were fixed on his face now, and she'd crept forward, just a little. "Akil…" she whispered.

"Beautiful Tobi," he said quietly, and then followed up with words in his language. They were low and soft and altogether too quickly said for Tobi to even begin to understand them, but the unexpected tenderness behind them was real, and when his lips met hers neither was surprised.

"Akil," Tobi murmured. It felt somehow as if they were breaking a rule, and she wasn't sure whether she should be the one to acknowledge it, or her husband should. All she knew was that if he continued to kiss her like this and then pull away, she would be left feeling so much colder, and so much emptier, than she had before.

"Be quiet," he said in what was perhaps the gentlest voice she'd ever heard from him, and cradled her face in his hands.

This was disconcerting for more reasons than the obvious. Tobi felt desire, but it was nothing like the heady indefinable lust that usually characterized their encounters. This was want, but a want for tenderness. She wanted to be held. She wanted to be cradled in the shelter of his arms, the way he was doing now.

She wanted to be close to Akil. And for just a few seconds, physically at least, he was letting her in. And it felt better than anything else she'd ever experienced.

She should just stop him. She should make a sarcastic comment, or a joke, or brace her hands against that massive chest and push back, push away from the hurt that was sure to come if she stayed here. But she did not. She stepped into the circle of his arms, tucked her head with a sigh and allowed Akil to continue kissing her.

"Please, please—" she whispered, bringing his hands up to palm her breasts, arching against him with a deep-rooted need that there was no point in suppressing. She was surprised when her husband's self-control shattered as quickly as hers. In moments her skirt had been hiked up to her thighs, and before she could scream, before the shudders that tightened her body completed, he was between her legs and finally, *finally* inside her.

He was speaking words against her ear. Rasping out things that made her shake. *I need you, I need you now, just like this—*

This was madness, she thought hazily before everything shattered into a million bursts of color and light and she became a trembling, panting facsimile of herself. They did not speak, only clung wordlessly to each other, having used each other for something absolutely vital.

"Are you all right?" he asked, and when she nodded, he kissed her, closed-mouthed. He looked calmer now, too, she noted as she slid from beneath him, ignoring the wetness between her thighs.

She couldn't stop trembling. Despite the raw, disjointed nature of their union today, it'd been their most intimate yet.

I need you. No, *I need you* now. She'd never forget those words, breathed hotly against the shell of her ear, or the shakiness of his voice as he'd said them. Akil, who'd never needed anyone in his life, had admitted he did. To her. There were marks on her body that were proof of his urgent passion, but they were nothing compared to the marks left on her heart.

She loved him. She loved her tempestuous, arrogant, passionate husband with all her heart. She'd fallen in love with his strength, his dedication, his commitment to the country he loved. He'd humbled her, possessed her, and she reveled in it.

* * *

Tobi headed to her PR committee meeting that afternoon feeling as if she were floating, still feeling Akil's lips on hers, his gentle hands warm and sure on her body. He hadn't pushed her away for the first time. He'd drawn her into the circle of his arms instead, reluctant as it might have been. And for the first time, she had a name for the feelings she'd been trying to fight for weeks.

Not love—she could not presume to think of that, now. But she was beginning to know what she wanted, and where Akil fit in that. And for the first time, those small daydreams seemed tinged with possibility. It was quite a trip back to earth, hearing David's dry voice bringing up his pet subject: Akil's relationship with his father.

"We believe the king should be a part of the coronation ceremony," he told her. "In some way, at least." The execution would be fairly simple. The old king was to watch the coronation ceremony from a secured location, and was to be brought out—briefly—on a balcony to wave to the people, shortly after his son was crowned. He would be flanked by Jamila and Tobi, who would ensure he was whisked away as quickly as he was seen.

"It's the only way," David said crisply. "Remember, Tobi. This is for his good, about creating a narrative. He'll never have to appear in public again after this, if we want."

We're manipulating an old, sick man, Tobi thought, but goodness knew that the former king would probably approve of such manipulations himself, were he lucid enough to hear the plan. However, she wasn't worried about the old king; she was worried about Akil.

"There's no way the king will agree," she said simply. "It's a good idea, but you must find another way."

"This is the best way." David leaned forward, eyes gleaming with conviction. "It will allow the people to see that he doesn't shun tradition, whatever his personal feelings. And he doesn't have to know, Your Majesty. A single moment, and it'll be over. He won't be able to do anything about it after it's done, and he's given you leave to approve every PR move."

She could still taste the spice of him on her lips, and the sensation was made uncomfortable by David's suggestion. "I couldn't not tell him—"

"Surely you see the importance of this," he pressed.

She did. The worst part was that she did. Being a monarch was being slave to tradition; she was part of a royal house herself. But there was something that sparked so new, so vital in Akil that she'd been attracted to since the beginning.

Would it really be folly to support him in finding his own way instead? Was there a medium? A compromise?

What had her husband said about David's team? *They overstep their bounds.* Still, he'd hired them for a reason, hadn't he? And were she being completely honest, Tobi saw nothing but sense in the team's suggestion. She hated the fact that all the good her husband had done in the past few weeks had been brushed away by the sting of public perception.

If she did this, she knew it wasn't just about his father—it was about opposing Akil, for the supposed good of the country. And in light of the encounter they'd just had…she shifted, feeling her body grow ever more tense.

CHAPTER FIFTEEN

HE'D ANSWERED THE question completely wrong, Akil thought, closing his eyes against the memory of that morning with his wife. She'd asked him—outright— if she could stay. And instead of drawing back, of putting up that wall that would keep her at a safe distance from the damaged man he was—he'd drawn her in instead. Kissed her. Touched her. Caressed her. Reveled in the soft warmth of a body that was beginning to feel like…home.

He hadn't had time to panic then, with her nestled in his arms. Now he was. This was not going to plan, not at all, and he didn't know what to do about it.

What do you want, Akil? Would it really be so difficult to let her in? To allow the possibility of something different—something lasting—to take the place of his grand plan?

Akil pushed back from the massive desk in the king's study, stood to his feet and began to pace, as he was wont to do when in deep thought. His reasons for keeping Tobi at arm's length felt flimsier with each encounter, with each kiss.

He was a man who prided himself on honesty. But the thought of facing the truth about Tobi? His stomach knotted so tightly he had to pause for a moment and draw a deep breath.

He started at the soft knock on his door, and at his "Come in!" Tobi appeared, holding a manila folder against her chest. She was clearly coming from a meeting; her braids were twisted into a high knot, and she wore a pencil skirt and button-down. Even in this simple dress and minimal makeup she looked stunning—as much as she did on his arm, in their throne room, in his bed…

Heat suffused his body from head to toe. Was he smitten to the point of ridiculousness, then? His father had been much the same way, and look at what happened to *him*.

Akil cleared his throat.

"Hello," she said in a voice that was quiet, almost deferential. "May I speak to you?"

"Of course." He gestured for her to sit and she did so, crossing her legs. His eyes flickered over the smooth dark expanse of thigh she revealed before he forced his eyes back to her face.

What the hell was he, a teenager? No. He'd never been this ridiculous as a teenager.

Tobi was speaking now, fiddling with the manila envelope as if she were trying to decide whether to speak or not. "Can I ask you something?"

"I don't know, can you?" he said drily.

She ignored the sarcasm and forged ahead. "Why—" She bit her lip. "I never got an answer to what I asked last night. Why don't you want me to stay?"

The air seemed to still as the words hung between them, and Tobi continued.

"Making love to me—it isn't an answer really. You—

we've never had any trouble connecting in bed. And we can't—we have to be honest with ourselves, Akil. There's something."

She was right, and the sincerity of the words were blocking his own from coming out. He set his jaw and looked out toward the wide window, the rugs, the bookshelves—anywhere but at the woman in front of him.

"I'm not expecting some huge declaration, Akil. That'd be stupid. But I do have feelings for you. I won't admit more than that, but they're there. And more than that, I love it here. It's beginning to feel like home. And If I'm expected to go—"

"Tobi—"

"It's better sooner rather than later. Before this gets any deeper," she said simply.

Akil closed his eyes briefly, then stood and crossed the room to an upholstered two-seater in place for visitors. What he had to say couldn't be done across a massive desk, and he wanted to give her that respect at least. "Will you sit with me?"

She assented, and when the two were settled he began to talk, looking down at his hands the entire time.

"My mother," he said, "was young when she married my father, and quite in love with him. I think she resented his dedication to his rule, to his public service and, well, she felt neglected, and she acted out. There was an affair. There were affairs," he corrected, and his mouth was tight.

Tobi let out a breath slowly. "Oh."

"I was born in the midst of all this. You can imagine the drama," he said crisply. "I am my father's son, of course, he verified that years ago, but the effects of his wife's betrayal stayed with him. I think a part of him still believed, despite all the evidence, that I might not be his son, or worse yet, that I was a son conceived out of duty, not loyalty or affection. He drank a great deal. It didn't affect his rule, he was clever enough not to let it, but it was *not* a happy upbringing for me, Tobi. And I rebelled because of it. I can't—I watched that turn my father into what he was—"

Tobi's eyes were glimmering with unshed tears. "Do you think me capable of that sort of betrayal then?"

Akil shook his head so vigorously it seemed in danger of leaving his shoulders. "No—*never.* I don't trust *myself* not to turn into him. I'm completely unequipped to love, Tobi, the way that you deserve. And I believe that to try it—it'd be a costly experiment, Tobi. There's no guarantee—"

She could barely hear what he was saying; there was roaring in her ears. She'd poured her heart out only for him to say this?

"You don't get into a relationship because it's *guaranteed,* Akil!" She had to take a breath before continuing. "I actually feel sorry for you." Her chin was trembling now; she could not stop it even if she wanted to. "You think so little of yourself, when the truth is that you have everything. It's a sad place to be."

"You presume too much," Akil said through his teeth.

"You're one of Africa's top economists. You're rich as Midas." She began ticking off on her fingers. "You literally have the opportunity to change the entire financial outlook of your country, and you have such a capacity for kindness." Her voice broke a little on the last word. "I saw it in so many forms that I almost fell in love with you. And even with all that, you choose instead to cling to the unwanted bastard prince that he made you into—"

"You go too far!" His face was dark with anger and she was glad!

She'd finally, finally broken through the facade, and Akil lunged to his feet. The sudden movement made him throw out an arm for balance, and Tobi automatically ducked, throwing her own arms up to protect her head. A moment later she lowered them to see her husband's horrified face.

"Tobi. I wasn't going to hit you!"

"I know. I—" Tobi began backing up. Akil was still speaking, but she couldn't hear him; there was a rushing in her ears, all humiliation and sadness and finally, an acceptance that this had to end. She turned on her heel and ran. Ran from the confrontation, ran from the mingled shock and anger and regret on his face, ran from everything. It would not take long to pack. She'd never wanted to be back in her old wardrobe more than she did now.

True to form, she stumbled before making it over the threshold and Akil was there, steading her, big hands on her shoulders. She swore and turned, shoving him with all her might.

"Leave me alone!"

"I will not." His voice was low and urgent. "Tobi— I wasn't going to strike you. I would never. Especially not after the way I grew up—"

Tears were falling hard and fast now, and she no longer tried to stop them. "I don't want to talk about this anymore."

"Tobi—"

"No," she said forcefully. "I initially came to talk to you about the coronation. David wanted us to bring your father out, to have him as part of the ceremony, all without telling you. I told them off, Akil. I told them that you'd always been your own person, your own king, and they should give you the respect and the courtesy to win over your people as yourself. I told them that I trusted you, and if they didn't have the wherewithal to find a solution, they weren't the team for you. I believe in you—I believe in what you're doing. But I won't let it extend to this—I simply won't."

She finished her speech and stood, chest heaving, face tense and drawn. When Akil reached for her she shook her head violently, stepped back.

"I'm going to leave," she choked out. "I'm going back to Dubai. Oh—don't worry, I'll be back for the ceremony, and all the state events. But if this is how you want it, I'm not going to wait for you to throw me out."

"Tobi—"

"I'm not going to go any deeper, Akil—it hurts far too much."

He let her go. He let her stumble to the bedchamber they shared, let her throw clothing in a bag, let her charter the Royal Flyer to head back to Dubai. He didn't stop any of it.

The night that Tobi left, Akil did not go home. Tobi would not be there, filling the hallways with her spirit and laughter. Despite his best efforts, Akil could not banish the image of his wife standing before him, tears running down her face, and then, worst of all, cowering as he shouted like he was a—

Akil shook his head to clear it. If he were really

serious about intending to cut Tobi from his life, he couldn't think about any of this; there could be no regrets, no hesitation. He could not think about the fact that his wife, despite his best efforts, had forced out his own secrets—and the two had more in common than he ever could have imagined. Akil had rarely been in the position of caring about someone other than himself, and he found the prospect no more than a little terrifying especially—

His heart was involved. That much was clear; he wasn't that self-delusional. But what was he going to do about it?

Akil prepared for bed that night, stripping down to his undershirt and neatly folding his trousers at the foot of the sofa in his office. His secretary would not blink an eye when she came in the next morning; she was used to the eccentricities of her employer, and Akil often stayed the night when he was working on a particularly complicated problem. This problem had nothing to do with economics or the state of the nation, however. It had everything to do with his heart, and with Tobi's.

He did not love her—he could not love her! But as the hours ticked by with no promise of sleep, he could not deny that he was here, wondering how she was, barely able to hold himself back from texting her, from begging for her forgiveness. He'd treated her with such a callous lack of consideration, and he knew, deep down, that he was completely in the wrong.

She had not acknowledged the money he'd wired to her as soon as his staff confirmed she was off the premises, but she hadn't sent it back, either. Hopefully the realities of life outside the palace would make her do exactly what he wished: take the money, go away.

His guilt kept reconstructing the crumpled figure of his wife as she ran from him hours before, but he whispered back reassuring truths to himself. Tobi was young. She was beautiful. She would eventually find something to do, find another person to love, and she would be absolutely fine.

The thought of her being with anybody but him made his stomach clench so tightly he attempted to get up and run for the restroom, then forced himself to stay exactly where he was. This lurch of his insides was guilt. It had completely crippled him, and he knew he was entirely in the wrong.

So what the hell was he to do, then? What was next?

Akil had never in his life been without a plan, had never been in a place where he wasn't sure what happened next. He lay on his back, stared up at the ceiling of his office and wondered exactly how it had gotten to this point.

Never in all his years had Prince Akil Al-Hamri felt regret, but he did now. It didn't matter, the fact that he'd cleared all physical evidence of her.

She still haunted the corridors in his memory, and those came hard and fast: their white-hot arguments and passionate reconciliations. The way she smelled, all spice and sun. The tangy sweet taste of her skin. The way her smile brightened up her face, and the way she listened to him. Engaged with him.

He hadn't known he was lonely until she left.

Whenever his chest tightened with what felt uncomfortably like regret, he listed the benefits of her leaving, mentally. He'd married Tobi for her royal status, nothing else. His near-violent attraction to her had startled him, but he hadn't let it get in the way of his faculties.

He would not love her; he could not love her. His focus had to be on the throne; he had no room for anything else. A woman would have been a distraction, a diversion away from the plans he had.

What he hadn't expected was that Tobi would have proven herself an equal partner in all this, a force of her own to be reckoned with. He also hadn't expected—

No.

If he let his thoughts run on, who knew where they would end up? He'd made his decision; Tobi was gone. He was alone again. He would go off, find a quiet place to lick his wounds, regroup, return, figure out what to do with the rest of his life.

He was king, and finally—reluctantly, but finally— his people were beginning to accept him as such.

So, what now?

When Akil finally exited the palace, the sun had long sunk in the sky, and a glance at his watch told him it was well after nine thirty. Good. Everyone would be asleep. He wouldn't even be going back to the house were it not for some legal documents he needed; he hated the sight of the place now.

When his driver silently opened the back door of the massive SUV that waited in the parking lot, Akil peered into it, then looked at his driver.

"You're fired," he said with excruciating calm.

"No, he's not. He's been in the family's employ since before you could drive. Get in, Akil. And Elias, be so good as to take a turn around the parking lot. We should be done in ten minutes or so."

The driver disappeared, and Akil set his jaw. It was the last person he expected to see. In the wan light of the back of the car, Jamila looked very tired.

"I cannot believe you made me chase you," she said. "What do you want?"

She sighed. "I want you to know how very disappointed in you I am, Akil."

Disappointed! "I dare say—"

"You don't. And you won't. This is my piece. What I'm talking about is the abominable way you've treated your wife. Your *wife,* Akil."

She stopped talking for a moment, took in a heavy breath. "That girl is in *love* with you, and you allowed it. You took her into your bed—yes, it's obvious by the way she looked at you, don't deny it—and made her think of herself as a valuable part of your life, and then cast her aside. It's actually more despicable than anything your father ever did. He was disgraceful, but his wife? Her feet didn't touch the ground, and he didn't care who knew it."

"We had a deal," Akil ground out.

"That you bullied her into. And then she unfortunately fell in love with you." She shook her head hard. "I'm a widow, Akil, before my time. Malik regretted the breakdown of your relationship so much. He tried his best as a child to make sure you felt loved. But I fear it broke something elemental in you instead. You need to examine yourself. Return to your wife. Divorce her properly if that's what you both want, but this—straddling two lives—this isn't fair, Akil. To either of you."

The two stared at each other for a long moment; then, Jamila sighed, her face returning to its usual inscrutability.

"There's Elias, trying to be discreet," she said, and waved his driver back over. "Drop me off at my own house, Akil. I've said all I wanted to say."

Akil swallowed hard, then waved a hand to Elias in assent. When Jamila was safely back at her home, he sagged back against the leather cushions of the car.

You made her think of herself as a valuable part of your life, and then cast her aside.

He did not want to remember Jamila's words, but the memory of Tobi's stricken face stopped him cold. He hadn't intended to do it. Tobi's sweet stubbornness had crept through his defenses with a strength that had been surprising to both of them. He'd taken advantage of her innocence, whispered sweet words in their intimate moments, gained her trust. The fact that he'd intended no malice mattered little; he'd carry the shattered look on her face with him for a very long time, if not forever.

And she was still his wife.

Somewhere, beneath all the callousness and jadedness beat the heart of a man with a conscience. And in that heart, he knew he'd done her wrong.

He also knew he loved her, beyond anything he thought himself capable of. The seeds had been planted the night of their wedding, when he looked into the eyes of the frightened girl who held herself erect despite her union with a perfect stranger. He'd admired her. Three years later, he'd desired her, possessed her. And now...

This isn't fair...to either of you.

Jamila was right. And he burned with something he could not quite yet name.

Shame, perhaps.

Arriving at the Dubai International Airport felt in some ways like stepping back through a portal in one of those children's fairy tales after the heroine has been asleep. Time seemed to have stood still in some ways. Arrivals was still swarming with tourists, students on break, visitors from every country imaginable and wealthy housewives in fluttery black abayas with their white-robed husbands steering them gently forward, hounding groups of chubby-cheeked children in voices tired from hours of flight. There were women like her, young, spectacularly dressed, fully made up, looking for love and adventure in the desert heat. Tobi felt as if she had been transported to the past, a past where she didn't belong anymore. She realized she belonged in Djoboro, in the ruby- studded house with the windows facing the sea, pressed close in the embrace of a man who even now, in the depths of her hurt, made her heart tighten with longing until the point of pain.

Before she hit the baggage claim, she received an alert that her account had been credited. It was a huge amount and that made Tobi even angrier, a hollow sort of anger that was tempered with self-disgust. A message followed:

We don't have to talk about this now, Tobi. But I'll be in touch.

She'd brought this on herself, selling herself to a man with no human feeling. Tobi wished more than anything that she could return the money immediately, but she was about to head into the great unknown, without any idea where she was going.

She still had the numbers of the producers she was speaking to before Akil had reappeared in her life, but she'd ghosted them for weeks, with no intention of ever going back. She simply wasn't for that world anymore, but what was she supposed to do now? She had truly put her life on hold for a man who had set her aside without a thought. How could anyone possibly be so cold?

And yet she knew she could not have imagined the moments they'd spent together, the intensity of his gaze, the gentleness of his touch, the way he'd considered her, listened to her, held what she said in high regard. Akil didn't hate her, and part of Tobi wondered whether hatred might have been easier. He'd liked her. He respected her but had chosen, once presented with her heart, not to love her.

That rejection hurt more than anything else.

Tobi ignored the fragrant stalls advertising duty-free perfume, chocolates and other delicacies, and instead went directly to a taxicab, taking it to the Chantilly Hotel and asking for a quiet room overlooking the marina. She threw open her suitcase and took a look, then had to blink. The bright, colorful clothing assaulted her eyes for the first few moments. After the life of quiet opulence she'd lived for the past few months, her old garments looked overblown, garish.

Who was she anymore? It was as if the stubborn, strong-minded girl she'd been had transformed into something else under Akil's overbearing hand—but it'd been more than that. Her father had tried to bully her into being something she wasn't, and she'd never capitulated. Even with all his nonsense, Akil had done more than that—he'd shown her new sides of herself, and she'd blossomed under his tutelage as well as his touch, sexually as well as intellectually. He'd shown her possibilities for her own life that she'd never had before.

He'd made her truly feel like she had the ability to be a person of significance, for the first time in her life. And even in her anger, in her grief, she lifted her chin, set her jaw. It didn't have to stop here. She'd had a vision, hadn't she? She wanted to make the world a little bit more hospitable to girls and women who had no other options. She would take the money Akil had sent, and she would *make* it happen!

Broken heart or not.

I'm going to have a shower, get dressed and think this through. Tobi leaped into the enormous marble-tiled shower in her suite, allowing water as hot as she could stand it to beat down on her body until she couldn't tell where her skin began and the stream of water ended. She used the rosewater-scented body wash liberally and stepped out, dripping, on the mat. She rubbed herself briskly, anointed herself with lavender oil, shea butter, and sprayed perfume until the clouds of it made her cough. Then she donned the skimpiest, brightest thing she could find in the wardrobe—a sparkly minidress of marigold yellow—did her makeup, ran her fingers through the tiny braids she'd taken to wearing in Djoboro, and surveyed herself in the mirror.

The girl staring back at her looked like Tobi, perhaps except for the eyes. Those were sunken and sad, but they were also brighter. Wiser.

In some ways, she'd found herself in Djoboro. She'd gained faith in her own abilities. She'd, for the first time, been taken seriously when she came up with an idea, and her husband had treated her with the same consideration as he would any other adviser. The girl Tobi had caught a glimpse of the woman, the queen she might become, and leaving that so quickly was something that weighed heavy on her heart.

But she was still Tobi, wasn't she? She could make this happen anywhere.

She glanced down at her phone. No texts, no calls from Akil. He hadn't even checked in to see that she'd arrived safely, although she knew that his many representatives around the hotel would get that news back to him quickly. And for now, despite her grand revelations, she'd never felt more alone in her life. She navigated to her contacts, scrolled down and called a familiar number.

Her sister picked up on the first ring.

"You are in Dubai," Kemi said, and her gentle voice made tears spring to Tobi's eyes. She blinked them back, hard; she didn't want to cry anymore.

"How on earth did you know?" Tobi sank down into one of the plush armchairs at the window that faced the sea. She could see boats on the water, little dots of gray and white on brilliant blue, while the Dubai skyline loomed over the marina in sharp relief. It was beautiful, everything that she wanted, but something deep inside her longed for the gentle slopes and brilliant green of Djoboro's landscape. She craved the country she'd grown to love, just as much as the man she'd left behind there.

"Akil called me," Kemi said, "and told me to expect your call." There was a pause, and her sister chuckled, a low sound that reverberated over the line. "I'm downstairs."

"You're what?" Tobi sprang to her feet and ran to the door, throwing it open as if her sister could materialize just by her doing that.

"Yes, I flew over as soon as Akil told me." Her sister paused. "Are you all right, little sister?"

Tobi took a great gasp of air that was both laughter and crying at the same time. "I don't know whether to be thrilled or horrified that you're here. I'm such a mess, Kemi. It all is such a *mess*."

"Come downstairs then, and we'll talk."

Tobi was already flying toward the elevators. When she reached the bottom floor, she saw Kemi immediately, looking as round and comforting as she had months ago, when she'd last seen her. Her face and body were still soft with her recent birth, and her eyes, though heavy with lack of sleep, were the happiest Tobi had ever seen them. She rushed straight into Kemi's arms and closed her eyes, allowing herself to be engulfed with the familiar, subtly sweet scent of lilies of the valley.

"Oh, my love, you've been crying," Kemi said softly, and rubbed her sister's back in gentle circles. Tobi didn't even bother denying it.

"I think I might be able to stop, now that you're here," she said in a voice that quavered a bit. She pulled back and kissed her older sister on both cheeks. "You look well," she said, and sniffed. "I hope Luke doesn't hate me for dragging you out here and dumping him with the children."

"Please don't give that man any sympathy," said Kemi. "He's being backed up by an army of nannies and staff, and he has a set schedule for the twins every single day until I'm back."

"Sounds very much like Luke." Tobi laughed a little shakily. Her sister reached out and placed gentle fingers under her chin, raising it up so that she could read her face. "You look sad around the eyes," Kemi said. "But otherwise, you look well. It looks as if he was able to get you to hold still long enough to put on a little weight."

She tilted her head, considering more. "No, actually, it isn't weight at all. You look softer. More womanly."

Tobi felt her face get hot; she knew exactly what it was. It was something that she noticed when she looked in the mirror herself, the fact that she was now soft and radiant with tenderness given and received. During her weeks with Akil, something blossomed, something that had taken the girl that she was, turned her into a woman who *needed*.

"How long can you stay?" she whispered.

Her sister's face grew grave. "As long as you want me to. But I'm hoping that you won't need me, because he'll come and get you."

If only. She closed her mouth against a laugh.

The whole story came out, little by little, amid plates of shawarma and hummus and fried chicken, enjoyed in the privacy of a curtained booth in the hotel restaurant. After, they retreated to Kemi's big airy suite, switched on the television to watch Turkish dramas and leaned on each other on the big bed, much as they used to do years ago, while in their father's house. After speaking at length about Akil, Kemi talked a little about her own marriage, something that Tobi appreciated. It was not in her nature to brood over anything for a considerable amount of time, and she was already tired of crying, although there was a hollowness at her core that she felt nothing would ever fill.

"Don't be afraid of loving him, no matter how much it hurts," Kemi said softly. It was two in the morning, and they sat among the greasy wrappers from their dinner and late-night snacks. Tobi could not sleep and Kemi wouldn't, so her older sister had begun re-braiding her hair for her, using a small container of gel to smooth the soft wooliness of her hair into neat cornrows that framed her face. "It's your right, Tobi. Never feel bad for having feelings for anyone. It shows that you're open to love, even if he's not, and there's nothing wrong with that. Akil—" She took a breath. "Love scares him. But when love blossoms, and is given space to grow, it expands inside you until it pushes out all the fear. It fills your heart until there's no room for anything else, and it's special. It makes us human."

Tobi closed her eyes, listening to her sister's musical voice, ringing with the tenderness that comes from loving and having been loved. She knew that Kemi was right. She also knew that the most painful part of this, and what Kemi hadn't addressed yet, was that it would be Akil's decision, and his alone, when it came to loving her back.

He's already made his decision, hasn't he?

Quietly, head resting deep in the recesses of her sister's soft lap, Tobi reached into her heart, let go of Akil.

If loving him was at the cost of her own self- respect, her own self-worth—

Don't do it. She had to be a queen unto her own self, regardless of what her title was in person.

If Akil was lost to her; she had to move on.

CHAPTER SIXTEEN

ONLY A YEAR AGO, Tobi would've been absolutely delighted to be walking down the hall of the Chantilly Hotel in the company of Samuel Ojo, one of the biggest philanthropists in Ogun State, whom she'd pitched her idea to for the Obatola Safe House for Girls and Women two weeks ago, with her full royal titles signed proudly at the bottom. She'd done her research this time, hiring planners from David Ashton's firm to run the entire project. After days spent brooding, crying, feeling sad and, quite frankly, waiting for Akil to call, Tobi had finally given up and made a few calls of her own.

"I'm thrilled you find this a promising opportunity," she said, shaking the older man's hand smoothly, and walked him down the hall to the main conference room, where her planning team awaited to pitch what she'd worked on night and day. "I'm so keen to work with you."

"I should be saying that to you," the older man said, and smiled. "It's a wonderful initiative, Your Majesty, and much needed."

"It's one very close to my heart." Tobi pushed open the door to the massive conference room, and she blinked and took it in. Sunlight streamed from skylights up above, and the room was decorated with the same sort of opulent style that was so characteristic of this part of the world. The floor was carpeted in cerulean blue and gold, and the massive wood conference table was flanked by luxuriously soft padded chairs. However, none of this registered to Tobi, for her entire planning team was gone, and the lone man seated at the table was none other than—

"So you were the one who's had David's attention divided this entire time," Akil said in his usual soft, accented voice. "I had a hell of a time getting the name of his new client out of him." His eyes fixed on her, her face, her hot-pink manicure, matching skirt and blouse, and the distinguished businessman at her side. Tobi stood frozen, then found her tongue with some effort.

"I've got a presentation right now," she said woodenly.

Samuel's eyes darted between Tobi and Akil. "This is—"

"Her husband, Akil Al-Hamri, king of Djoboro," Akil said smoothly. "Mr. Ojo—sorry, I read the name on the presentation folders—might I borrow my wife for a few moments? A bit of an emergency has come up."

"Why, of course." Samuel cleared his throat and turned to her. "Your Majesty."

"Tobi, please," she managed to say through lips that felt frozen. "And really, Mr. Ojo, there is no need—"

"There's no trouble at all. You've very generously booked me till tomorrow, and I'm happy to have a drink. Just call up when you're ready." He said farewell to them both and was gone, leaving Tobi breathing hard, staring at Akil in a mixture of shock and fury.

"I'm sorry for crashing, but you've kept your movements very covered," Akil said simply. His dark eyes rested on her face with an intensity that froze her inside. "You see, Tobi, I found it quite impossible to get on without you."

She stood very, very still and concentrated all her efforts on breathing in and out. Akil's mouth tipped. He eased out from the conference table and walked over to her, his hands pushed deep in the pockets of the linen trousers he wore.

"Well?" he asked mildly.

Tobi blinked hard, then turned and walked away as rapidly as she could in her high heels. She had no thought except to get away from him, and *now.* Akil's footsteps quickened behind her, and she began to run. It was futile; Akil's hand was at her elbow, and she found herself hustled into a family restroom. Akil closed the door and locked it.

He looked down at Tobi, who was still gaping at him.

"Are you *crazy*?"

"You're beautiful when you're angry," he rasped with a heat in his eyes that made the blood rush to her face. He reached down to touch her chin, but she yanked back.

"Don't touch me. *Don't touch me!*"

"Tobi—"

To her horror, she started to cry, and it wasn't just a few tears, either. It was ugly and loud and wrenching, the culmination of everything that had been building between them for ages. He reached out presumably to calm her, but she shrank away from him.

"I hate you," she said emphatically, and pressed her palms to her eyes. She could not look at him, at that grave expression. She heard him clear his throat, and felt him press a square of clean white fabric into her hands. She took it, mopped blindly at her face.

"I'm sorry I did that, but it was the only way I could think of to get your attention," he said after a moment as Tobi struggled for breath. She had to regain her dignity. She *had* to.

"You couldn't have called? Sent a message?"

"Would you have replied? I wouldn't have."

"Leave," Tobi ordered, her voice shaking. Akil was all she could see, filling the frame of her vision, all broad shoulders and dark eyes, eyes that spoke far too much. She backed up until she couldn't, until the back of her legs touched one of the large soft armchairs in the lounge area, and she sank into the seat. Her heart was hammering so hard she imagined most of the blood in her body had rerouted there, leaving her very lightheaded. Akil looked down at her for a long moment, then sank down so quickly Tobi gasped aloud, and rested his dark head in her lap.

"Oluwatobilola," he said, and her full name never sounded quite as sweet as it did now, rumbling low from his chest. "Tobi. Please. My love, please—"

He was saying words that didn't quite make sense, because she was swallowing hard, trying desperately to keep from crying. Her fingers slid as if on instinct to the dark curls clustered on his head; the smell and feel of him was overwhelming. Her body contracted, softened for him almost involuntarily. It completely ignored her reasoning, her anger, her resentment. It was as if her body was determined to conform to the shape of him, yield to the hands gripping her thighs, surrender completely to his will without her permission. They were not in bed, they were fully clothed, but yearning knifed through her as if they'd never been separated. He did not speak, but the message in his stance was clear.

An entire king, at *her* feet.

"No," she said, but her voice was feeble, and Akil raised his head. A gentle smile lifted the corner of his mouth, and Tobi's heart skipped a beat, even as she grasped mentally for strength. She found some in the anger that had resided low in her gut since she'd left Djoboro.

She struggled to her feet, and in a flash Akil stood, too.

"What the hell are you doing here?" she demanded, and was distressed to hear that her voice did sound exactly as she felt, exhilarated as well as afraid. She was trembling like the limbs of the iroko tree during Harmattan, and allowing Akil to cup her cheek in his hand, to look deep in her eyes.

"Tobi," he said again, his voice tender. "Please—"

That was the last thing she understood completely, for he began speaking in a mix of Djoboran and English, as if the latter was inadequate to express the depth of his feelings. What he said was so accented and so rough she could not catch most of it, but the meaning was clear.

He was begging. For her pardon, for her forgiveness.

She stopped him by bracing a hand on his chest; that was a mistake. She could feel muscle working under the thin fabric of his shirt, and he trapped her hand there with his before she could step sideways, make her escape.

"Tobi?"

She swallowed hard. "You know I didn't understand anything you said."

At that, his lips quirked up, ever so slightly. "I said that I'm sorry," he replied simply. The raw emotion of minutes before was gone, and in its place a steadiness that was no less terrifying in its intensity. "I came to beg your forgiveness. And to come for my wife, if she will have me."

Tobi was appalled at how her heart leaped at those few words; was she really so much a fool, after all? "You didn't want me," she whispered.

Akil's face was grave, but it still had so much tenderness in it that her heart constricted despite herself. "Yes," he agreed.

"Give me one good reason why I should just…" Her voice trailed off, and Akil's heavy brows drew together. He straightened to his full height, and once again, Tobi felt the space grow smaller, as if he were filling the room with his essence. The difference now, though, was that hers seemed to meld with his. He was drawing her in, or trying to. He wasn't crowding her out.

"You shouldn't," he said simply. "I don't know if I would. But I was wrong, Tobi. And I am here to say that without reservation, whether the story ends in my favor or not."

Tobi's heart was drumming in her ears; she closed her eyes for a brief moment.

"Have you ever thought of what we could be, *habibti?*" he said, and the tenderness in his voice cramped low in her stomach. She folded her arms protectively round herself, but he was closing in on her; she could feel his warmth on her skin, smell salt and starch and sandalwood and everything that was undoubtedly Akil.

Had she thought of what they could be? Of course she had.

"We had potential. So much potential. And I failed to see it." The warmth of his lips were a fraction of an inch away from her temple; he would take her in his arms next, she knew, and if he did that all would be lost. She'd no longer hold the cards. Her cursed attraction to Akil was a weakness now, and she was determined not to give in, not to—

His full mouth was so tantalizingly close, and her breath quickened as dull, familiar want began to tighten at her breasts, hot and heavy between her thighs. She licked her lips, and Akil swore softly under his breath, then stepped back.

"I told myself I wasn't here for that," he said as if trying to convince himself, then cleared his throat.

She found her lips tipping up despite herself. "We've never had any issues with that side of things, have we?"

"Certainly not." He tilted his dark head.

Tobi swallowed. He wasn't pressing her for a response, and she supposed that was something. Although a part of her, that deep dark bit she could not let surface, would not have minded at all if he pressed her hard against the tiled wall, lifted her skirt, acted on the possessive glimmer he was doing a poor job of hiding.

Akil had never been quite so afraid in his life, standing there in a freesia-and-vanilla-scented restroom lounge at the Chantilly Hotel, staring at Tobi's lovely face.

She wouldn't accept anything he did or said; why should she?

He'd managed to fall in love with the only person he'd treated terribly, and he had to reconcile that. Akil was not here because he expected Tobi to fall into his arms; that would be ridiculous, given all that he had done. But he wanted to tell her he was wrong, let her know on some level how much she meant to him. So he spoke.

"I think what I regret the most is the fact that I hurt you," he said. "My relationships are far more important than anything I've been chasing. And repairing mine with you is my first priority. I wronged you terribly, and I will spend the rest of my life trying to convince you to have faith in me, Tobi. In *us.*"

"You're not a man of faith."

"No." His eyes skimmed over her face. It looked thinner, and more tired than it had since he'd last seen it, and the thought that he was the one to cause those lines in that smooth skin…

"Tobi," he said. "My family is a study in selfishness and in lack of care. It's all I saw growing up. My duty seemed the only thing worth fighting for, because there simply wasn't anything else." He took a breath. "But all I can think about now is you. You first, Tobi. I want to be precisely what you want. My duty is you, now. Us. And if what you said when we last saw each other is true, if it still stands—"

Here, he broke off. He could not speak any more, could not trust the words that came out of his mouth not to veer into his usual high-handed persuasion.

"I have very much to learn," he said humbly. "I'd just like some time to try."

"Akil, what are you saying?" Tobi asked, unwilling to allow herself to believe what she was hearing.

"I'm sorry," he said simply. "And I'd like you to come home."

Home. The word blurred her vision, just for a moment, and Akil began to speak again, looking deep into her eyes.

"Think about the way this city rose from the sand, how it came to be. Years of investment, decisions, work. Dedication. And if—"

He paused, and she tilted her head. "What?"

"I'm coming to see that love is like that," he said. "I was willing to work for Djoboro, but I wasn't willing to work for love. For you, although my heart was telling me otherwise. I blamed it on my father, and on my hatred for him. But Tobi, don't you see? If I do that, he *wins.* And I lose possibly the best thing I've ever had."

He stopped then, and crimson stained the copper of his skin. His eyes softened to the point that she blushed; the way he looked at her was more intimate than any caress, and she felt it so hard she pressed her hands to her stomach. He rested his forehead against hers.

"Tell me what you're thinking," Akil whispered, almost desperately. And then, sounding like his old self for the first time since he'd arrived, he added, "I insist."

"You can't force people to open up, Akil," she rebuked.

"No," he agreed. "So, then, what is it?"

She had to laugh, and she took a step back. "I want— I think I want you to take me back to my room."

Akil was kissing her now, safe in the innermost recesses of her suite at the Chàntilly, and she could think of nothing else. His kisses were hard and hot and slick and a little brutal, and his breathing was low. Husky.

He kissed her as if there was more of her below the surface of her mouth, and he was trying to reach it by all
means. By the time his lips dropped warm and slow to
that tender place on her neck to nip at the hollow where
sweat already was collecting, Tobi was in danger of losing her footing.

"Please, Akil—I'm dizzy—"

"Good." There was a tense sort of satisfaction in
those words, breathed low against her skin, and Tobi
cried out as she felt herself hoisted upward as if she
weighed nothing. Akil's hands were quick and impatient
with her skirt and blouse, and in a flash, she felt herself
lowered to her bed, and then Akil was looming over
her. In the darkness of her room she could see nothing
but the occasional flash of white that signified teeth or
eyes; his hands seemed to be everywhere.

"I'm not here to force you," Akil said low, in her ear.
The sound of his voice sent a ripple through her body
that tensed it so violently she could not speak for a second. It wasn't fear or anger; it was want, the crippling
sort of want that tightened her nipples to the point of
pain, that caused that soft hidden place between her
thighs to throb. It was Akil that had made her feel these
things first; he was the only man who'd ever touched her
like this. Who'd ever touched her at all, really.

"Akil," she ground out, and the tail end of a whimper
came with it, for he was tracing a line from that hollow in her neck he'd kissed and bitten only moments
ago down between her satin-covered breasts, over the
quivering mound of her stomach, and lower—

He seemed to have gotten whatever confirmation he
wanted, because she heard the soft rustling of clothing
being removed, and he was in her bed. She fumbled for

the bedside lamp, but she felt his grip lock lightly over her wrists, tug them upward.

"No," he said, and his long fingers were on bare skin, skimming over a nipple so engorged and sensitive that she jumped. His fingers twisted hard round one flimsy strap till it broke; she started to protest, then choked instead as his mouth, hot and wet, closed over her breast. His other hand released its iron hold on her wrists and skimmed down between her thighs; they fell open eagerly, and she felt his surprise as he encountered soft skin and nothing else.

The feeling of his hands and mouth on her in the dark of her room was almost unbearably erotic; she was already beginning to shake. Akil withdrew his skillful fingers exactly at that point, and Tobi cramped almost painfully around nothing. She opened her mouth to protest, but was cut off again when the dress was wrenched down completely, and that slow, exploring mouth was descending her body.

Akil was speaking against her skin, low and filthy, a sort of gravelly huskiness in his voice. He said things that made her throat tighten, that made her heartbeat accelerate faster, as if that were possible. She was his, only his. He hadn't been able to sleep because she hadn't been there. He'd dreamed of her, and his body burned. His kisses were bruising, fierce; and Tobi rose to match him, meeting his passion with a fire of her own she had no idea she was capable of. *Mine*, he whispered in those final moments when he was buried deep in her silken heat when he finally let her shatter.

When dawn met them, naked, entwined and weary in the tangled sheets of Egyptian linen that covered the bed, Tobi squinted at her husband in the feeble light.

Their fingers were laced together; his eyes were closed, and his chest rose and fell with each breath. He looked even more handsome in sleep, she thought. Her lips were still tender and bruised from his kisses as well as her own arousal; her breasts were heavy. Full. Swollen. Before she could ease herself from the bed Akil turned full over, reaching for her in his sleep, drawing her close to the warm scented folds of his body.

It felt so familiar, so *right*, that tears sprang to her eyes.

"I'm taking you home," he said, and there was a quiet desperation in his voice. "If you will come? I don't know how to do this, Tobi, how to not hold back."

"We both have a lot to learn." She hesitated. "It's a risk for me as well."

He was quiet for a moment. "Then I promise not to make you regret it. Tobi, I'm grateful I had the opportunity to fall in love with you. Goodness knows I didn't do anything to deserve it. And I will spend the rest of my days making sure you feel more loved and valued than you could have ever dreamed possible. That is, if you'll let me?" he asked.

This time, the tears that sprang to Tobi's eyes were of pure happiness. Akil loved her, truly loved her. And she believed him. The closed-off king had opened his heart to *her*. He'd shown her that she could do anything she set her mind to, and he was right.

"Yes, Akil. I'll let you," Tobi said with a growing smile. She pulled back and looked him in the eyes. "I love you, my king."

Akil smiled back, the biggest smile she'd ever seen. "And I love you, *my* queen."

EPILOGUE

One year later

THE HOUSE OF the king was indeed rebuilt, and it was truly beautiful.

Full of hopes and dreams for the future that quite eclipsed the uncertainty with which their relationship began, Akil and Tobi returned to Djoboro more reflective and a great deal wiser.

"We've much to work on, and some of it will be painful," Akil had said that first evening they were back, sitting shoulder to shoulder on the main balcony of their home. And it was, at first. There were tears. There were misunderstandings. There were tender moments, in which they pressed together so tightly it was difficult to tell where one began and the other ended. They cared for Jamila, who was finally coaxed into showing her grief, if only a little. They cared for the old king, and if Akil never was completely comfortable around him, at least he was back at the palace. He'd suffered, also, and was paying the ultimate price in the ruin of body, mind and spirit. And when the one-year celebration of Akil's ascension to the throne took place, the couple danced in the streets with their people with hearts that were as light as their feet.

Later that evening, arms wrapped round his neck in the quiet of his study, Tobi told Akil of her own dream.

"I haven't been to see anyone yet, but I'm fairly sure," she said softly, and laughed at the look of wonder on her husband's face. They'd talked about children, of course, in a sort of offhand way that indicated they would come eventually, but were not particularly planned for at the moment. To Tobi this felt all the more special; it had come so organically, from many nights of love.

Akil said nothing, and he didn't have to—the joy burning in his eyes was intense enough to consume them both. Instead Tobi bent, pressed her temple to his, and her mouth tipped upward as his hand skimmed the curve of her belly.

The little boy or girl to come in a few months' time would fill the corridors with laughter and gurgles, and give its parents joy for many years to come.

"I'm glad. I'm glad it's happening now," Tobi said after a moment. "We're ready for it now."

"I quite agree," Akil said, and kissed her gently.

The dancing princess and the rebel prince had finally found each other, and their future was as bright as the Djoboran sun.

* * * * *

UNDONE BY HER
ULTRA-RICH
BOSS

LUCY KING

MILLS & BOON

For Charlotte, editor extraordinaire.

CHAPTER ONE

'QUEM ÉS TU e que raios fazes na minha cama?'

In response to the deep, masculine, insanely sexy voice that penetrated the fog of sleep enveloping her, Orla Garrett let out an involuntary but happy little sigh and burrowed deeper into the cocoon of beautifully crisp, cool sheets she'd created for herself.

Duarte de Castro e Bragança usually paid her dreams a visit the night following the day they'd spoken on the phone. Every time his name popped up on the screen her stomach fluttered madly. The ensuing conversation, during which his velvety yet gravelly tones sent shivers racing up and down her spine, unfailingly left every nerve-ending she possessed buzzing.

They'd never met in person and their calls weren't particularly noteworthy—she ran an ultra-exclusive invitation-only concierge business of which he was a member, so they generally involved his telling her what he wanted and her assuring him it would be done—but that didn't seem to matter. Her subconscious inevitably set his voice to the photos that frequently appeared in the press and which she, along with probably every other hot-blooded person on the planet, couldn't help but notice, and went into overdrive.

It was unusual to be dreaming of him now when she hadn't spoken to him in over a month. Even stranger that he was speaking in his native Portuguese when he only ever addressed her in the faintly accented yet flawless English he'd acquired thanks to a British public school education, followed by Oxford.

But she knew from experience that there was little she could do to prevent it, and really, why would she want to even try? The moves he made on her... The way she woke up hot and breathless and trembling from head to toe... It was as close as she got to the real thing these days, not that the real thing had ever been any good in her albeit limited experience, which was why she gave it such a wide berth.

Besides, there was no harm in a dream. It wasn't as if she harboured the secret hope that the things he did to her would ever become reality. The very idea of it was preposterous.

Firstly, quite apart from the fact that she steered well clear of things she wasn't any good at, getting involved that way with a client—any client—would be highly unprofessional.

Secondly, there was no way a staggeringly handsome, fast-living aristocratic billionaire winemaker would ever notice her in the unlikely event they did get round to meeting.

And finally, the entire world knew how devoted reformed playboy Duarte had been to his beautiful wife and how devastated he'd been when she'd died of an overdose six weeks after giving birth to their stillborn son, even if he was now reported to be handling the double tragedy with unbelievable stoicism.

No, her dreams were private, safe and, even better,

unlike reality, completely devoid of the hyper-critical voice that lived in her head, constantly reminding her of how much she had to do and how, if she wanted to feel good about herself, she must not fail at any of it. In the dreams that featured Duarte, perfection wasn't something to strive for; it was a given.

'Hello,' she mumbled into a gorgeous pillow that was neither too hard nor too soft but just right.

'I said, who are you and what the hell are you doing in my bed?'

This time he did speak in English, his spine-tingling voice a fraction closer now, and, as a trace of something deliciously spicy wafted up her nose and into her head, warmth stole through her and curled her toes.

'Waiting for you,' she murmured while wondering with a flicker of excitement what he might do next.

Thanks to a last-minute let-down, she'd been working flat out for the past week, preparing his estate for the annual meeting of the world's top five family-owned wine-producing businesses. Her exhaustion ran deep. Her muscles ached. A massage, even an imaginary one, would be heavenly.

'Get up. Now.'

Well, that wasn't very nice, was it? Unlike those of Dream Duarte, who generally smouldered and purred at her before drawing her into a scorchingly hot clinch, these words were brusque. This Duarte sounded annoyed. Impatient. Where was the smile? Why was the hand on her shoulder shaking her hard instead of kneading and caressing? And, come to think of it, why could she smell him so vividly? His scent had never been part of her dreams before...

Realisation started off as a trickle, which swiftly became a torrent, and then turned into a tsunami, crashing through her like a wrecking ball and smashing the remnants of sleep to smithereens.

With her heart slamming against her ribs, Orla sat bolt upright and cracked her head against something hard. Pain lanced through her skull and she let out a howl of agony that was matched in volume by a thundering volley of angry Portuguese which accompanied a sudden lurch of the mattress.

Ow, ow, *ow*.

God, that hurt.

Jerking back, she clutched her forehead, rubbing away the stars while frantically blinking back the sting of tears, until the pounding in her head finally ebbed to a dull throb and the urge to bawl receded.

If only the same could be said for the shock and mortification pulsating through her. If only she could fling herself back under the covers and pretend this wasn't happening with equal success. But unfortunately she couldn't and it was, so gingerly, with every cell of her being cringing in embarrassment and horror, she opened her eyes.

At the sight of the man sitting hunched on the bed, shaking his head and running his hands through his dark, unruly hair, her breath caught. She went hot, then cold, then hot again. Her stomach flipped and her pulse began to race even faster.

Yes, Duarte was actually here, very much *not* a figment of her imagination, and oh, dear lord, this was *awful*. He'd caught her asleep on the job. She'd all but invited him to join her in bed. And then she'd headbutted him—her most important, wealthiest client—and that was saying something when to even be considered deserving of an invitation their members had to have a minimum net worth of half a billion dollars.

At least she'd kept her clothes on when, energy finally depleted, she'd crashed out, which was a mercy, even if they were on the skimpy side, since it was hot in the Douro Valley in June. But how on *earth* was she going to redeem herself?

That he hadn't been expected back for another three weeks was no excuse. Her company promised perfection on every level. Their clients demanded—and paid outrageously for—the very best. This was the absolute worst, most mortifying situation she could have ever envisaged.

'I'm so sorry,' she breathed shakily, deciding that grovelling would be a good place to start as she pulled up the spaghetti strap of her T-shirt, which had slipped off her shoulder and down her arm.

Duarte snapped his head round, his dark gaze colliding with hers, and the breath was whipped from her lungs all over again. The pictures she'd seen of him in the press didn't do him justice. Not even slightly. They didn't capture the size or presence of the man, let alone his vital masculinity, which hit her like a blow to the chest and instantly fired parts of her body she hadn't even known existed. They didn't accurately reflect the breadth of his shoulders or the power of his jean-clad thighs that, she noticed as her palms began to sweat, were within touching distance. Nor did she recall ever seeing in any photo quite such cold fury blazing in the obsidian depths of his eyes or a jaw so tight it looked as if it were about to shatter.

'Can I get you some ice for your head?' she managed, inwardly wincing at the memory of how hard she'd crashed against him before remembering the emergency first-aid kit that she kept in her bag just in case. 'Pain-killers, perhaps?'

'No,' he growled, his expression as black as night, tension evident in every line of his body. 'You can answer my question.'

Right. Yes. She should do that. Because now was not the time to be getting caught up in his darkly compelling looks that were having such a strangely intense effect on her. Now was the time for damage control.

'My name is Orla Garrett,' she said, praying that despite his evident anger Duarte was nevertheless reasonable enough to see the amusing side of the situation once she explained. With the exception of this lapse in professionalism, the service her company provided him with was excellent and that had to count for something. 'I'm co-owner and joint CEO of Hamilton Garrett. We've spoken on the phone.'

His brows snapped together and she could practically see his reportedly razor-sharp brain spinning as he raked his gaze over her in a way that made her flood with heat.

Should she hold out her hand for him to shake? she wondered, a bit baffled by the electricity that was suddenly sizzling through her. Somehow, with her still beneath the sheets and him still sitting on top of them not even a foot away, it didn't seem appropriate.

Far more urgent was the desire to surge forwards and settle herself on his lap. Then she could sift her fingers through his hair and check his head for bumps. She could run her hands over his face and examine first his impressive bone structure and then the faint stubble adorning his jaw. At that point he could wrap his arms round her and flip her over, set his mouth to her neck and—

Agh.

What was happening? What was she thinking? Was she *nuts*?

Appalled by the wayward direction in which her thoughts were hurtling but deciding to blame it on possible concussion, Orla swallowed hard and pulled herself together. She had to ignore the scorching fire sweeping along her veins and the all too vivid images cascading into her head, the reasons for which she could barely comprehend. There'd be time for analysis later. Right now, she needed to put some space between her and her client, so she scrambled off the bed on the other side and onto her feet.

'As per your instructions,' she said, fighting for dignity, for control, and smoothing shorts that suddenly felt far too tight and uncomfortably itchy, 'I've been preparing the guest accommodation for your conference. So far, all the bedrooms are ready except this one.'

Which was the one that looked to require the least work. The other five had been complete tips. Bed and bath linen had been left awry and crusty wine glasses had been abandoned on surfaces thick with dust. Downstairs had fared no better. Coffee cups overspilling with mould had littered the drawing room and empty wine bottles had filled a crate in the kitchen.

Trying not to gag at the smell, Orla had wondered what on earth had been going on here before reminding herself sternly that it was none of her business. Her job was to see that her clients' wishes were fulfilled and that was it.

'I've agreed the menus for the weekend with Mariana Valdez,' she said, hauling her thoughts back in line and focusing on the tiny stab of triumph she felt at having acquired the only chef in the world to currently hold ten Michelin stars, who was virtually impossible to hire for a private function, 'and all dietary requirements will be catered for. I've instructed Nuno Esteves,' the Quinta's chief vintner, 'to make available the wines you stipulated for dinner on the Friday and Saturday nights. The river cruise has been scheduled for the Sunday afternoon and the crew is prepping the boat as we speak. Everything is on track.'

Duarte shifted round to glower at her, clearly—and unfairly—unimpressed by what she'd accomplished under very trying circumstances. 'And all the while you've been sleeping in my bed.'

'No,' she said with a quick, embarrassed glance at the rumpled sheets, which didn't help her composure at all. 'I haven't. I booked into the hotel in the village, and I've been staying there. The nap was a one-off, I swear. Not that that makes it any better. It's unforgivable, I know.'

Not to mention inexcusable, even though excuses abounded. Duarte wouldn't be remotely interested in the fact that she'd been let down at the last minute by the team she'd put in place to carry out his requests and had had no option but to see to the situation herself, however inconvenient and however long the hours. It wasn't his problem that she'd somehow found herself in possession of the wrong set of keys and had had to break a window to get in so she could unlock the back door from the inside and proceed from there. Like all their clients, he paid a six-figure annual fee to have his every instruction carried out, without question, without issue, free from hassle and the tedious minutiae of implementation.

'I can assure you that it will never happen again,' she finished, mentally crossing her fingers and willing him to overlook the blip. 'You have my word.'

He let out a harsh laugh, as if unable to believe her word counted for anything. Then he gave his head a slow shake, at which her pulse thudded and panic swelled, because as the dragging seconds ticked silently by she got the sickening feeling that he wasn't going to forgive. He wasn't going to forget. The tension in his jaw wasn't easing and his mouth wasn't curving into a smile as she'd hoped. The anger in his dark, magnetic gaze might be fading but the emptiness that remained was possibly even worse. His expression was worryingly unfathomable and his voice, when he spoke, was icy cold.

'You're right,' he said with a steely grimness that made her throat tighten and her heart plunge. 'It *won't* happen again. Because you're fired.'

Duarte barely registered the soft gasp of the woman standing beside the bed, staring down at him with the mesmerising eyes the colour of fifty-year-old tawny port that had sent a jolt rocketing through him when they'd first made contact with his. He hardly noticed the way she tensed and jerked back, her expression revealing shock and dawning dismay.

He couldn't think straight. His head throbbed from the earlier collision. His chest was tight and his muscles were tense to the point of snapping. It was taking every drop of his control to repel the harrowing memories that had been triggered by setting foot in this house for the first time in nearly three years. To contain the savage emotions that were battering him on all sides.

Frustration and surprise that his instructions had not been carried out correctly warred with fury that his fiercely protected privacy had been invaded. Shock on finding a beautiful, golden-haired woman fast asleep in his bed clashed with horror at the desire that had slammed into him out of nowhere at the sight of her. The grief and guilt that he'd buried deep had surged up and smashed through his defences and were now blind-siding him with their raw, unleashed intensity.

None of it was welcome. Not the swirling emotions, not the clamouring memories of his difficult, deceitful wife and tiny, innocent son who had never got to draw a breath, and certainly not the unexpectedly gorgeous Orla Garrett here, in his space, wrecking the status quo and demolishing the equilibrium he strove so hard to maintain.

'I'm sorry?' she said, sounding dazed and breath-less in a way that to his frustration made him suddenly acutely aware of the bed, and had him leaping to his feet.

'You heard,' he snapped, striding to the window and shoving his hands into the pockets of his jeans before whipping round. 'You're fired.'

Her astonishing eyes widened. 'Because I took a nap?'

The reasons were many, complicated and tumultu-ous, and very much not for sharing. 'Because you're clearly incompetent.'

Her chin came up and her jaw tightened. 'I am many things, I will admit, but incompetent is not one of them.'

'Then what would you call this?' he said, yanking a

hand out of his pocket and waving it to encompass the bed, the room, the house.

She flushed. 'A lapse.'

'It's more than that.'

'The circumstances are extenuating.'

'And irrelevant.'

She stared at him for a moment, frowning, as if debating with herself, then she took a deep breath and gave a brief nod.

'You're right,' she said with enviable self-possession. 'I can't apologise enough for all of this. For hitting you in the head and, before that, implying that I was waiting for you. Obviously, I wasn't. I was asleep. Dreaming. About someone else entirely.'

Who? was the question that instantly flew into his thoughts like the sharpest of arrows. A husband? A lover? And what the hell was that thing suddenly stabbing him in the chest? Surely it couldn't be *disappointment*? That would be ridiculous.

Despite having spoken to Orla frequently over the last few years, which had presumably given her an insight into certain aspects of his life, he knew next to nothing about her. But that was fine. He didn't need to. Their relationship, if one could even call it that, was strictly business.

Whether or not she was single was of no interest to him. So what if her voice at the other end of the line had recently begun to stir something inside him he'd thought long dead? Given that he'd sworn off women for the foreseeable future, the wounds caused by his short but ill-fated marriage still savagely raw, it was intrusive and annoying and not to be encouraged.

'You've been working on the wrong place,' he said,

angered by the unacceptable direction of his thoughts when he worked so hard to keep them under control.

'What do you mean?'

'I instructed you to fix up the accommodation at the winery. This is not the winery.'

Her brows snapped together. 'I don't understand.'

'This is Casa do São Romão, not Quinta do São Romão. So you've broken into what was once, briefly, my home. You've been poking your nose into places where you do not belong and sleeping in my bed. And in the meantime, the task I *did* assign you remains unfulfilled.'

She stared at him, confusion written all over her lovely face. 'What?'

'You've made a mistake, Ms Garrett,' he said grimly, although actually, to call Orla's actions 'a mistake' was an understatement. She'd invaded his space. Whether she knew it or not, she'd seen things he'd never intended anyone to see. Not even *he* had ever again wanted to have to confront the evidence of his torment, his grief and his guilt, which he'd indulged at length before locking away for ever. If this house had been left to rack and ruin, taking with it the memories contained within and turning them to dust, that would have been fine with him.

But at least the contract between him and Orla's company had come with an NDA. At least the truth about his supposedly perfect marriage would never emerge. The thought of it brought him out in a cold sweat. He judged himself plenty. He didn't need judgement from anywhere else.

'I can't have,' said Orla, visibly blanching, evidently stunned.

'Are you suggesting it's *I* who's made the mistake?'

'What? N-no. Of course not,' she stammered, the blush hitting her cheeks turning them from deathly pale to a pretty pink. 'There must have been a communication error. I'm so sorry. I'll make this right.'

There was nothing she could do to make anything right. What was done could not be undone. He should know. His son couldn't be reborn with a heartbeat instead of without one. He couldn't rewind time so that he could both erase the argument that had caused that and subsequently see what was happening with Calysta in time to stop her taking her own life. No one could. What he *could* do was get rid of Orla before he lost his grip on his fast-unravelling control.

'You have five minutes to get your things,' he said, his voice low and tight with the effort of holding himself together when inside he was being torn apart, 'and then I want you gone.'

CHAPTER TWO

Rooted to the spot, Orla watched Duarte turn on his heel and stride off, her heart hammering and a cold sweat breaking out all over her skin. The floor beneath her feet seemed to be rocking and the room was spinning.

Oh, God, he was furious. He clearly didn't tolerate mistakes and she couldn't blame him, because neither did she. In fact, she hadn't made a single one since her engagement, which had come to an end four years ago. And even *before* that she'd done her level best to avoid them. Mistakes equalled failure and failure was not an option in her world.

As an overlooked, average middle child squashed between an older sister who sang like an angel and a brilliant athlete of a younger brother, she'd fought hard for her space in the family. She'd worked like a demon to get the best grades at school and siphon off some of the parental attention her more talented, more successful siblings attracted so easily. And it had worked. So well, in fact, that striving for excellence, for perfection, had become embedded in her DNA. Her sense of self-worth depended on it, she knew, and she couldn't imagine ever approaching a task with the expectation of anything less.

But she hadn't allowed her childhood insecurities to surge up and swamp her for years, and she certainly wasn't about to start now. Her blood chilled at the very idea of it. So it didn't matter at this precise moment how the mix-up here had happened when her company went to great lengths to ensure a project ran as smoothly as possible. An analysis of what had gone wrong would have to wait.

Nor was her opinion of Duarte's reaction to the situation of any relevance. She might think that his response was totally over-the-top when firstly, she'd never let him down before, secondly, there was still time to fix things, and finally, he had the unexpected bonus of a freshly gleaming home, but he was the client. He was clearly furious that she'd screwed up—although he couldn't possibly be as angry with her as she was with herself—and it was her job to reverse that. To get herself unfired. And not just because she had two decades' worth of hang-ups to battle. After years of grafting to prove her talent, her worth and her indispensability, of single-mindedly focusing on reaching the top, she'd finally been allowed to buy into the business. She had no intention of giving Sam, co-owner and joint CEO of Hamilton Garrett, any reason to regret that decision. Duarte earned them millions in fees and commissions—almost as much as all their other clients put together—and she would *not* be the one to lose him.

It wouldn't be easy but nor was it impossible. The coldness of his tone—worse than if he'd shouted at her, in fact—wasn't encouraging, but all she'd have to do, surely, was handle him the way she handled anyone who was reluctant to give her what she wanted. People always saw things her way in the end, and he'd be no different.

Taking a deep breath to calm the panic and channelling cool determination instead, Orla grabbed her trainers and strode out of the bedroom. She raced around the balcony that looked over the ground floor on all four sides of the house, until she came to the top of the wide, sweeping stone staircase.

'Wait,' she called, spying Duarte heading along a corridor, and hurrying down the steps. But he didn't stop, he didn't even show any sign he'd heard her, so she tried again. Louder. 'Conde de Castro. Duarte. Please. Stop. I can explain.'

He threw up a dismissive hand. 'No.'

'I'll do anything. Just name it.'

'It's too late.'

It couldn't be. That wasn't an option. 'How can I make this right?'

'You can't.'

She could. She *would*. She just had to figure out what he wanted. A discount, perhaps. Didn't everyone love a bargain, even wildly successful billionaires? 'I'll waive your fees for the next three years. Five. No, *ten*.'

'Your fees are a rounding error to me,' he said bluntly, continuing to power ahead with long, loose strides while she, still barefoot, remained hot on his heels. 'And if you think I'm continuing with my membership of your organisation, you are, once again, very much mistaken.'

Right. Not that, then. 'I'll make a donation to a charity of your choice.'

'You couldn't possibly match the sums I already donate.'

That was undoubtedly true.

Damn.

'I'll have someone else handle your account,' she offered, ignoring the odd sense of resistance that barrelled through her at the thought of it because desperate times called for desperate measures.

'No.'

Well, good. But on the other hand, not good. In the face of such intractability, she had little to work with here and she could feel the panic begin to return, but she banked it down because she wasn't giving up.

'Could you stop for a moment so we can talk about this?' she said, fighting to keep the desperation from her voice and thinking that while his back view—broad shoulders, trim waist—was a fine sight, it would be a whole lot easier to persuade him to see things her way if they were face to face.

'There's nothing to discuss.'

'Have we ever let you down before?'

'You've let me down now.'

'Your conference isn't for another three weeks. There's more than enough time to prepare.' Just about.

'That's not the point.'

Then what *was* the point? None of this made any sense. Yes, she'd made a mistake, and she winced just to think of it, but objectively speaking, it was hardly the end of the world. So what was going on? At no point during the course of their relationship had Duarte come across as in any way eccentric. His requests were by no means as outrageous as some. Quite the opposite in fact. She'd always considered him entirely reasonable.

So could it be that he was just stubborn? Well, so was she. She stood to lose not just his business and her partner's respect and confidence in her but also quite possibly her emotional equilibrium, which relied on her continually succeeding at everything she did, and that wasn't happening.

'There must be *something* I can do to persuade you to change your mind,' she said, breathless with the effort of keeping up with him and adrenalin-fuelled alarm. 'Something you want.'

'There isn't.'

There was. Everyone had at least one weakness, and Duarte wasn't *that* godlike.

Think, she told herself as she continued to hurry after him. She had to think. What did he want that he didn't already have that only she could get him? What would he find irresistible? Impossible to refuse?

Desperately, Orla racked her brains for what she knew about him. She frantically sifted through a mental catalogue of interviews and articles, revisiting the phone conversations they'd had, grasping for titbits of information, for something, for *anything*…

Until—

Aha!

She had it. Thank *God*. The perfect challenge. It wouldn't be easy. In fact, it would most likely be immensely difficult, otherwise he'd already have achieved it. But making the impossible possible was her job. She had her methods. She had her sources. She frequently had to get creative and think flexibly. She'd find a way. She always did.

'How about a bottle of Chateau Lafite 1869?'

* * *

If Duarte had a fully functioning brain or any sense of self-preservation, he'd be sticking with his plan to shut this place back up and get the hell out of here so he could regroup and reset the status quo that had been shattered when he'd been informed that there was activity up at the house.

He'd only been back on the estate half an hour before the news had reached him. He hadn't waited to hear the details. His intention to spend the evening among the vines, which calmed his thoughts and grounded him in a way that nothing else could these days, had evaporated. A dark, swirling mist had descended, wiping his head of reason and accelerating his pulse, and he'd driven straight here, leaving in his wake a cloud of clay-filled dust.

He'd assumed whoever it was had broken in. He'd been fuelled by fury and braced for a fight. Then he'd found her, a golden-haired stranger in his bed, and the mist had thickened. Women had been known to go to great lengths to attract his attention. His wife, who'd gone to the greatest lengths of all by deliberately falling pregnant and effectively trapping him into marriage, had been one of them. So what did this one want?

The discovery of Orla's identity had cleared some of the mist, but it had made no difference whatsoever to his intention to eject her from his existence. He never deviated from a plan once made, whether it be a seduction, a marriage proposal or perpetuating a lie in order to assuage his guilt. Yet now, unhinged and battered, and with the name of the wine he'd been after for years and the whisper of promise hovering in the ether, he came to an abrupt halt and whipped round.

'What are you talking about?'

For a moment Orla just stared at him as if she hadn't a clue either, breathless and flushed, but a second later she folded her arms and squared her shoulders.

'You think I'm incompetent,' she said, her chin up and her eyes lit with a fire that turned them to a dazzling burnished gold and momentarily robbed him of his wits. 'Let me prove to you I'm not. I read in an article a while back that the only material thing you want but don't have is an 1869 bottle of Chateau Lafite. I will get it for you. Give me twenty-four hours.'

Incredulity obliterated the dazzle and the return of his reason slammed him back to earth. Seriously? She thought it was that easy? She had *no* idea. He'd been trying to get his hands on this wine, without success, for years. He'd tried everything. Persuasion, negotiation…he'd even toyed with the idea of bribery. What could she achieve in twenty-four hours? A couple of phone calls. That would be it.

'It's an exceptionally rare vintage,' he said scathingly, unable to keep the disbelief from his voice.

'I wouldn't expect it to be anything less.'

'Only three bottles exist.'

She stared at him for the longest of seconds, blanching faintly. 'Three?'

'Three,' he confirmed with a nod. 'And none of the owners is interested in selling.'

'Well,' she said, straightening her spine in an obvious attempt to recover. 'Not to you, maybe.'

But they would to her? What planet was she on? Delusion? 'You must be mad.'

'I've never felt saner.'

No. The colour had returned to her cheeks and her gaze now was filled with cool determination. She looked very sure of herself. Whereas he'd never felt *less* on solid ground. Spinning round like that had put him too close to her. Every cell of his body quivered with awareness. He could make out a ring of brown at the outer edges of her golden irises. Her scent—something light and floral, gardenia, perhaps, subtly layered with notes of rose and possibly sea salt—was intoxicating. The blood pumping through his veins was thick and sluggish. The need to touch her burned so strongly inside him that he had to shove his hands through his hair and take a quick step back before his already weakened control snapped and he acted on it.

'What makes you so sure you'll succeed where I didn't?' he said, crushing the inappropriate and unwelcome lunacy, and focusing.

'Experience,' she said. 'Tenacity. Plus, I never fail.'

Orla's tone was light but he detected a note of steel in her voice, which suggested a story that would have piqued his curiosity had he been remotely interested in finding out what it might be. But he wasn't. All he wanted was to forget that this afternoon had ever happened and get back to burying the guilt and the regret beneath a Mount Everest of a workload and getting through the days.

And in any case, she wouldn't be around long enough to ask even if he *was*. While he had to admire her confidence—however misguided—she would fail at this challenge and when the twenty-four hours were up she would leave. Which would mean having to find someone else to prepare the winery for the conference, but rare was the problem in business that couldn't be solved with money.

If it came to it, he would pay whatever it took. The conference was too important to screw up. Each year, in the belief that a rising tide lifted all boats, representatives from the world's top five family-owned wine businesses got together to analyse global trends, to solve any viticulture issues that might have arisen and generally to discuss all things oenological. This year it was his turn to host, the first since he'd taken his place as CEO three and a half years ago when the news that he was going to be a father had ignited an unexpected sense of responsibility inside him, which his own father had taken advantage of to retire.

There were those who couldn't see beyond the tabloid headlines and expected him to run the company into the ground by selling off all the assets and blowing the lot on having a good time, despite the twenty per cent increase in profit that had been generated since he'd been in charge. He didn't give a toss about them. He did, however, care about the business that had been going for nearly three hundred years. Its continued success depended on what people thought of his wines, and he was part of that package. He wasn't about to give anyone a reason to trash either his reputation or that of his company.

'So do we have a deal?' she said, jolting him out of his murky thoughts and recapturing his attention. 'Do you agree that if I succeed in acquiring this bottle of wine for you by this time tomorrow, you will recognise how good I am at my job and un-fire me?'

No, was the answer to that particular question. Orla had had her chance and she'd blown it. Duarte had a plan and he intended to stick to it. No allowances. No compromises. He'd been there, done that during his relationship with Calysta, regularly excusing her sometimes outrageous behaviour and ultimately sacrificing his freedom for what he'd believed to be the right thing, and he'd sworn he would never put himself in that position again.

Yet what if she did somehow succeed? he couldn't help wondering somewhere in the depths of his brain where recklessness still lurked. He'd be in possession of a bottle of the wine he'd been after for years. The headache of having to find someone else to finish the job she'd started would vanish. And then there was the sizzling attraction that was heating his blood and firing parts of his body he'd thought long numb and clamoured to be addressed.

Despite the reputation he'd earned in his twenties—which had been wholly deserved, he wasn't ashamed to admit—Duarte had no interest in romance these days. Love was a minefield into which he had no intention of venturing. It was messy and chaotic and could cause untold pain and resentment. In the wrong hands, it could be dangerous and damaging. Unrequited, it could be desperate and destructive.

Not that he'd ever experienced it himself. He'd married Calysta because she was pregnant. A strange sense of duty he'd been totally unaware of previously had compelled him to stand by her and give their child his name. He'd never forget the moment he learned her pregnancy wasn't accidental, as he'd been led to believe. They'd been arguing about their lifestyle. He'd been determined to knuckle down and live up to his new responsibilities, she'd wanted to continue raising hell. In the heat of the moment, she'd yelled that she wished she'd stayed on the pill, and Duarte's world had stopped. He'd demanded an explanation, which she'd given, and at that moment any respect he'd had for her as the mother of his child had been blown to smithereens. He'd been taken for a fool, betrayed, his ability to trust pulverised, and the scars ran deep.

But it had been over three years since he'd slept with anyone, which was a long time for a man whose bedroom had once had a metaphorical revolving door. So perhaps that was why he was so aware of the flush on Orla's cheeks, the fire in her eyes and the way her chest still heaved with the effort of having raced to catch up with him. Maybe that was why he could so easily envisage her in his bed again, only this time with her wavy golden hair spread across his pillow as she gazed up at him, desire shining in her stunning topaz eyes and an encouragingly sultry smile curving her lovely mouth, focusing wholly on him instead of dreaming about someone else. If she was around, he'd have the opportunity to investigate this further and perhaps put an end to the sexual drought he'd been experiencing.

So, all things considered, he thought as the strands of these arguments wove together to form a conclusion, the pros of agreeing to her audacious proposal outweighed the cons. Changing the plan would be strategic, not weak. There'd be no need for compromises or allowances. The power, the control, would all be his.

'We have a deal.'

CHAPTER THREE

ORLA HAD LEFT Duarte's house with a longer to-do list than she'd had going in, but as she'd carted her things to the hire car she'd parked round the back first thing she'd refused to entertain the possibility of not getting through it.

She had to pour all her energy into delivering on her promise, she'd told herself resolutely, firing up the engine and driving away. She had to temporarily forget the fact that her job and all that was attached to it hung in the balance. She couldn't afford to panic. She needed all her wits about her if she was going to achieve what would no doubt turn out to be her toughest challenge to date.

The minute she'd arrived back at her hotel, after paying the site of the old winery a visit to scope out the venue she should have been focusing on, she'd called the office back in London. On learning, to her distress, that the mistake had been entirely hers, she'd doubled down on her efforts to fix it.

She didn't know how or why she'd misread the email that contained the details of Duarte's instructions but she hadn't wasted time dwelling on it. Instead, she'd been spurred into action. Since the Quinta was three times the size of the Casa and time was marching on, she'd sourced and hired a team from a local company to prepare it. A company new to her and an untested team, she'd recognised, but she had no doubt that she would be there to supervise.

Once that had been sorted, she'd set about tracking down the wine, which had been as challenging as she'd assumed. Although she reckoned she'd done a good job of concealing the sheer panic that had surged through her at Duarte's revelation that only three bottles of the wine he wanted existed, her confidence had been knocked for six. But she'd kept her cool, and on learning subsequently that all three bottles had been sold individually at auction fifteen years ago, she'd rallied. She knew the auctioneers well, and a ten-minute phone call had eventually furnished her with details of the sales.

The owners of the bottles she'd traced to Zurich and New York hadn't budged for anything. As for the bottle located in France, well, that had been a tough negotiation too, but ultimately a successful one—thank *God*—and as a result she was back at the top of her game, which was where she intended to stay.

There was no possible way that this evening Duarte would have the same impact on her as he had yesterday, she assured herself as she marched through the former manufacturing section of the winery, passing between rows of oak barrels that reached the roof and breathing in the rich scent of port that permeated the musty air. Those circumstances had been extraordinary, brought on by shock and, when he'd whipped round to face her in the corridor, so fast and unexpectedly she'd nearly crashed into him for the second time, the kind of proximity that punched her hard in the gut and flooded her with heat.

He'd looked at her for the longest of moments, she recalled, feeling a flush wash over her before she could stop it. That dark, hostile gaze of his had fixed to hers as if trying to see into her soul, and weirdly, time had seemed to stop. Her surroundings had receded and her focus had narrowed until all she could see was him. Her breasts had tightened and her mouth had gone dry. She'd felt very peculiar. Sort of on fire, yet shivery at the same time, and it had taken every ounce of strength to haul herself under control.

These circumstances, however, were anything but extraordinary. Given that they'd arranged this meeting an hour ago, there'd be no surprises. No head butts or strange spells of dizziness. No stopping of time, no galloping pulse and certainly no tingling of body parts. Her job was safe. She'd achieved the impossible and proved her value to him—and more importantly, to herself— and that was all that mattered.

Coming to a stop at the threshold of the room in which he'd told her to meet him, Orla pulled her shoulders back and took a deep breath. The anticipation and adrenalin crashing through her were entirely expected. The success of a project was always a rush, and with the added pressure of this one, and the sky-scraping stakes, the high was even higher.

On a slow, steadying exhale, she knocked on the door and at the curt *'Entra'* opened it. The room appeared to be half-office, half-sitting room. She briefly noticed a sofa, a coffee table, a sideboard and a pair of filing cabinets, but then her gaze landed on Duarte and yet again everything except him faded away.

He was sitting behind a desk, all large and shadowy, with the setting sun streaming in through the open window behind him and bathing the room in warm, golden light. If she'd been able to tear her eyes away from him she might have admired the twinkling river that wound through the landscape and the gently undulating hills beyond, their terraces covered with vines that were dense with verdant foliage stretching to the horizon. She might have found serenity in the big, airy room with its cool flagstone floor and rough, whitewashed walls.

But to her bewilderment and distress she couldn't look away. She couldn't focus on anything but him. He was just so magnetic, so compelling, and now she was feeling anything but triumphant, anything but serene. Her skin was prickling and oxygen seemed to be scarce. The linen shift dress she was wearing was by no means tight—in fact, she'd deliberately chosen it because of its loose-fitting nature—yet when the fabric brushed against her body, shivers ran down her spine. She felt strangely on edge, alert and primed, as if waiting for something to happen, although she couldn't for the life of her work out what.

'Do you have it?'

The deep timbre of his voice scraped over her nerve endings, weakening her knees dangerously, and for a moment she wondered, did she have what? Her marbles? Her self-possession? Apparently not. Because despite her hopes and expectations to the contrary, his effect on her was still so intense she could barely recall her own name. The X-rated dreams that had invaded what little sleep she had managed to grab were cascading into her head, so detailed and vivid she was going dizzy, and God, it was stifling in here.

But enough was enough. She couldn't go on like this. It was totally unacceptable. She was a professional. She was here to work. She had to get a grip. And breathe.

'I do,' she said, giving herself a mental shake before stepping forwards into the room and setting her precious cargo on the desk, which unfortunately put her in a position where not only could she see him better, but smell him better too. 'There. Are you impressed?'

Duarte didn't respond. She doubted he'd even heard her. He was wholly focused on the box she'd put in front of him. Staring at it with what looked like barely concealed awe, he leaned forwards, undid the catch and lifted the lid.

Her gaze snagged on his hands as he carefully removed the bottle and slowly twisted it first one way then the other. Strong tanned hands, she noticed, a tingling pulse beginning to throb in the pit of her stomach. Long fingers with a light dusting of dark hair, neat nails. She could envisage them tangled in her hair, on her body, sliding over her skin and—

'Take a seat,' he murmured, popping that little bubble for which she was grateful, yes, *grateful*, not resentful.

Orla sat. She didn't know why. The plan had been to present him with the bottle, remind him of her competence and their deal, at which point he'd un-fire her and she'd get back to the business of preparing his estate for the conference. Sitting had not been part of anything. But then, nor had staring and hungering and magnetism, or indeed, weak, wobbly legs.

'Tell me how you did it.'

Right. So normally she didn't divulge her methods any more than she revealed her sources. Both were her currency, and her little black book of notes and contacts was worth a fortune. But in this case, since Duarte was directly impacted, she should probably disclose at least the bare bones of the transaction.

'I made a few phone calls,' she said, determined to ignore his potent allure and remembering instead the events of the last twenty-four hours. 'I tracked one bottle down to Zurich, another to New York and the third to France. This one came from there. I had it flown directly here from Nice and took delivery of it an hour ago.'

He arched one dark, disbelieving eyebrow. 'Just like that?'

Well, no, but there was no way she was going to go into how stressful it had been. How wildly her emotions had oscillated between panic and relief. How slowly the minutes had dragged as she'd waited first for responses to the approaches she'd made and then for the bottle she'd acquired to actually arrive.

So many things could have gone wrong. The plane could have crashed. The box could have been dropped. It could have been stolen en route. Anything. Her nerves had been shredded right up until the moment she had the wine in her hands. But he didn't need to know about the roller coaster of a ride she'd been on today.

'The logistics and insurance took some working out,' she said coolly, as if it hadn't taken every resource she had or wrung her emotionally dry, 'and it took a while to establish that the bottle had been meticulously stored with temperature and humidity control, but essentially, yes.'

Her explanation did nothing to remove the scepticism from his expression. 'So all you had to do was ask, and Antoine Baudelaire simply handed it over?'

If only. 'Not exactly.'

Duarte's brows snapped together, his eyes narrowing a little, and Orla shifted uneasily on her seat because this was where it possibly got a little awkward.

'Monsieur Baudelaire gifted the bottle to his daughter six months ago as a birthday present,' she said, mentally crossing her fingers that he'd be reasonable about the terms that had been agreed. 'It was her I negotiated with. First over the phone, and then over Zoom.'

'His daughter?'

'That's right. Isabelle.'

'What was the price?'

There was no point in pretending there wasn't one. Money hadn't worked. She'd had to get creative. 'She's organising a charity ball around Christmas time,' she said. 'She's been looking for a guest of honour to boost ticket sales and encourage auction donations. She now has one.'

The temperature in the room dropped a couple of degrees and Orla shivered at the thunderous expression now adorning Duarte's perfect features. He sat back and she wanted to lean in to close the distance and capture his scent again, which was completely ridiculous.

'You pimped me out,' he said, a tiny muscle hammering in his jaw.

'I prefer to think of it as a provision of services in exchange for goods.'

'Of course you do.'

His tone was cold, his words were clipped. He was clearly furious, and her heartstrings twanged because by all accounts he didn't socialise much these days and the idea of a ball in all its gaiety must be deeply unappealing. But it was only an evening of his time. A fair swap, she'd figured, relieved beyond belief to have secured the bottle with relatively little trouble, even if it had taken a while to find out what it was that an heiress who had everything she needed and an overindulgent father might want.

'Believe me, you got off lightly.'

His face darkened even further. 'In what possible way?'

'She also wanted you to be her date.'

Isabelle had waxed lyrical about Duarte. She'd never met him but she'd read everything there was to read about him and pored over every photo. She was under the impression that she was the one to bring love back into his life, if only they could meet. However, if Isabelle could see Duarte's expression at this precise moment, she might have thought differently, because he now looked appalled as well as angry.

'She can't be much more than a teenager,' he all but growled.

'She just turned twenty. And you're thirty. I pointed that out. She eventually saw the better of it.'

It had taken some persuasion, and she'd had to call on every skill she possessed, but there was no way Orla was going to agree to *that*. It was one thing offering up his time and his influence, quite another to act the matchmaker. Her company left that up to others, and for some reason the mere idea of the stunning and no doubt perky Isabelle batting her eyelids at the gorgeous Duarte made her feel like throwing up.

'Am I supposed to be grateful?'

Quite frankly, yes. The infatuated girl had a crush on him the size of Portugal. She'd have clung to him like a limpet and been hard to prise off.

'I could always give the wine back,' she said, with a quick pointed glance at the wonky bottle that predated modern glass-making techniques and was standing on the desk in all its dusty, unassuming glory. 'All you have to do is say the word.'

The scowl on his face deepened. 'No.'

'OK, then.'

And that, she thought, as a deluge of relief and triumph washed over her, was how it was done.

Orla thought she'd won. Duarte could tell by the smug satisfaction on her face and the delight dancing in the depths of her eyes, and on a rational level he knew she deserved her moment of victory. She'd defied the odds. She'd achieved something that had always been out of his reach, and he ought to be impressed by what she'd accomplished because, objectively speaking, she was a genius.

On a deeper, more emotional, more turbulent level, however, the deal she'd struck to secure the wine sat like a rock on his chest, crushing his lungs and fogging his head. She'd involved him in her negotiations and allowed him no say in the matter. She'd used him to get what she wanted, and the feeling that he'd been manipulated—again—burned through him like acid, spinning him back to a time he'd been taken for a fool, a time he strove to forget.

With the memories of Calysta, her calculations and her volatility descending thick and fast, the fog in his head intensified. Emotion roiled around inside him. Every instinct he possessed was rising up to fight it. The need to regain the upper hand and to shift the balance of power back in his favour hammered through him.

It shouldn't be hard, he assured himself darkly. He held all the cards. Or at least he ought to. He was Orla's client. In a way, he was her boss. Yet he got the strange feeling that bending over backwards to please him simply because he paid her to do so was of little importance to her. Intense relief was woven through the triumph in her expression and it struck him now that there'd been a trace of desperation in her voice when she'd been running after him down the corridor yesterday afternoon, begging him to reconsider firing her. Something that hinted there was more at stake for her than the mere loss of a client.

With the arrogance of someone used to calling the shots and having his every order obeyed, he'd assumed uppermost in her mind would be keeping him happy, but what if all she really cared about was rectifying her mistake?

'Your strategy was a risky one,' he said, the odd, unexpected hit to his pride adding to the turmoil churning around his system and lending a chill to his tone.

'In what way?'

'You're counting on me to hold up your side of the deal.'

As the implication of his words registered, Orla's smile vanished. She went very still and wariness and tension gripped her frame. 'Are you saying you won't?'

And *now* he was back in control, he thought with grim satisfaction. 'I'm simply saying assumptions are unwise.'

Anger sparked in her eyes. 'If you renege on the terms I agreed my reputation will be destroyed.'

'You should have thought of that before you decided to use me.'

'It's one evening of your time and I *did* think of that,' she fired back. 'I read you had integrity, Duarte. I read you played fair. Is that not true?'

It was true, dammit. Just as he fought for his reputation to protect his business against the naysayers, he worked hard for his success and did things by the book. 'It's true.'

'I thought as much,' she said with a curt nod. 'So if I did take a risk it was a calculated one. I considered one evening a small price to pay for something you've been after for years. And yes, I suppose you could refuse to support the ball if you wanted to, but there are things at stake for me here that you couldn't even *begin* to understand.'

So he'd been right about the story. 'Like what?'

'My livelihood for starters.'

Which implied there was more. 'What else?'

'Isn't that enough?' she said, her chin and her guard back up. 'I've worked insanely hard for what I have. Don't destroy me simply because you can.'

And now he was even more intrigued. Why was *she* at risk of destruction, rather than her reputation or her job? What was really behind the offer to complete a challenge she must have known had a stratospheric risk of failure? What made her tick? And, come to think of it, what was she was doing here, seeing to his instructions personally? Who had she been dreaming about while asleep in his bed?

These were questions to which he sorely wanted the answers, he realised with a disconcerting jolt. He had no idea why. But then, nor could he work out why the fact that she'd used him as leverage in her negotiations didn't seem to matter quite so much now as it had a moment ago.

Perhaps the angry energy crackling around her, which gave her a stunning, dazzling glow, had short-circuited his brain. Or perhaps it was because, on re-flection, he could see that what Orla had agreed with Isabelle Baudelaire was hardly outrageous. Once upon a time, before he'd met and married Calysta and duty and responsibility had become of primary importance, he'd frequented many a party. More often than not he'd *started* the party. And, as Orla had pointed out, it was only one night and it was for charity, so how tough would it be?

Furthermore, his acceptance of her terms would mean that *their* deal was on and she'd therefore be stay-ing to oversee the preparation of his conference, which would bring benefits beyond mere convenience, because at some point over the last twenty-four hours he'd had to admit to himself that he wanted her. Badly.

What else could account for the change in his be-haviour that had occurred the moment she'd mentioned the wine, when these days he *always* stuck to the plan? Why else would he have crashed out on the sofa in this stifling room last night instead of returning to his airy apartment in Porto that benefited from a sea breeze, as he'd intended?

He'd told himself it was simply a more efficient use of his time and better for the planet if he parked the he-licopter instead of toing and froing between here and the city of his birth, a distance of some two hundred and fifty kilometres. But that didn't explain the height-ened awareness he'd felt all day or the anticipation that had been rocketing through his system ever since he'd received Orla's text asking where they should meet. Or, indeed, the frustration and disappointment that he hadn't run into her today despite making himself wholly available.

No. He wanted to strip off the dress rendered see-through by the evening sun streaming in and tumble her to the sofa so much it was addling his brain, a brain that was already running on empty thanks to a severe lack of sleep. He'd had an uncomfortable night, and not just because his six-foot-three frame was too big for this room's compact two-seater sofa. Enveloped by the warm, velvety darkness, the still silence broken only by the cicadas chirruping in the vines, he'd tossed and turned, his imagination going into overdrive as he'd revisited the events of the day.

What if he'd kissed Orla awake instead of shaking her shoulder? had been the thought rolling around his head even though he was no fairy-tale prince. What if he'd capitalised on the brief flare of desire he'd caught in the depths of her eyes the moment before she'd leapt from the bed as if it were on fire?

His imagination hadn't cared about how inappropriate that would have been. His imagination had embraced hindsight, which recognised that she quite possibly felt the attraction too, and had gone wild, bombarding his head with visions of the two of them setting the sheets alight until he'd had to head to an old disused bathroom to take an ice-cold shower, where finally he'd found relief.

'All right,' he said, his mind teeming with ideas about how he might make the most of the situation that had landed in his lap. 'I'll honour your deal.'

'Thank you,' she said with a brief, confident nod,

as if she'd expected his agreement all along. 'And the one between us?'

The one that meant he wouldn't have to find someone else to finish readying the estate, provided the chance to get the answers to the questions he had and offered him the potential to find out if she was as attracted to him as he was to her and, if so, do something about it? It was a no-brainer.

'That one too.'

CHAPTER FOUR

OH, THANK GOD for that, thought Orla, the tension gripping her body giving way to relief so intense it was almost palpable.

Things had taken an unexpected turn for the worse for a moment back there and the sudden potential reversal of fortune had sent her into an almighty spin, but she'd stayed cool and calm, and disaster had been averted. The mistake she'd made had been fixed. Her job was secure, her reputation was intact and her demons remained buried. Her work here was done. And now, with the adrenalin and stress fast draining away and the monumental effort of controlling her body's wayward response to his taking its toll, all she wanted to do was sleep because she was shattered.

Stifling a yawn, she pushed up on the chair arms and got to her feet, every muscle she possessed aching and sore, and she didn't even pause when he said, 'Where do you think you're going?'

'Bed,' she muttered, envisaging her gorgeously comfortable room at the hotel and almost weeping with need. 'It's been a very long, very eventful twenty-four hours.'

'Don't leave just yet. Stay and have a drink with me.'

Now, that did make her pause mid-turn. Because, despite her desperation to flee consuming every one of her brain cells, something about his voice seemed different. The chill had gone. His tone was smoother, lighter, less antagonistic and more like that of the man in her dreams.

Curious, her pulse skipping, she turned back and glanced down to find that he was looking at her with focus, with intent, and the tiny hairs on the back of her neck shot up. At the sight of the decidedly wicked glint in his eye, and the faint yet devastating smile curving his mouth, she shivered, and heat pooled low in her belly.

What was he up to? Why the glint? Why the smile? Why the abrupt one-eighty personality change?

She didn't want to know, she told herself firmly. She was tired and confused and her defences were weak. She should have ignored him and carried on with her exit. She shouldn't have allowed her curiosity to get the better of her. She didn't need glints and shivers. She needed respite from his effect on her and to recharge her batteries.

'Thank you, but no,' she said, crushing the tiny yet powerful urge to say yes and indulge her curiosity a little while longer because she had a plan to which she intended to stick.

'It doesn't seem right to drink this alone.'

He waved a hand in the direction of the bottle she'd acquired and her eyebrows shot up, shock momentarily wiping out the fatigue and the wariness along with the plan. *'This?'*

He gave a nod. 'Yes.'

'You're planning on *drinking* it?'

'I am.'

For a moment she just stared at him, scarcely able to believe it. Had he lost his mind? Perhaps yesterday's bump to the head had done more damage than had first appeared, because this wasn't just any old bottle of wine. This was special beyond words. Surely it wasn't for drinking.

'But it's over a hundred and fifty years old,' she said, aghast. 'It's worth a quarter of a million dollars. If you drank it, that would be it. History and a fortune blown in a matter of minutes. Shouldn't it be in a museum?'

'It *is* mine, isn't it?' he said reasonably, although she noticed that both the glint and the smile had faded slightly.

'Well, yes, but—'

'I never wanted it simply for the sake of owning it, only to admire it from a distance while it gathered even more dust. I've wanted it for its story, to savour and appreciate it and learn from it. So let Zurich and New York put theirs in a museum. I'll do what I damn well please with mine.'

'Of course,' she said, hastily back-pedalling, since, despite the easy way he'd delivered the explanation, he didn't look at all pleased at having his decision questioned and really she ought not to be antagonising him when she'd only just got her job back. 'It's none of my business what you do with it. But seriously, please save it for your guests at the conference. It would be completely wasted on me. I know nothing about wine. I'm more of a cocktails-with-an-umbrella kind of a girl.'

'Then I'll teach you.'

To her alarm, he surged to his feet in one fluid movement and made for the sideboard on the other side of the room, but she didn't want him to teach her, she thought a bit desperately. She wanted a break from the dizzying breathlessness that she couldn't seem to shake no matter how hard she tried. She wanted space. Sleep. And at some point she really ought to try and figure out why she'd messed up his instructions in the first place. 'What if I don't want to learn?'

'Isn't it your job to see to my every request?'

While the question that wasn't a question hung in the air, Orla narrowed her eyes and shot daggers at his back. Bar the immoral, the illegal or the unethical, it was, damn him, and it occurred to her suddenly that not only was he drop-dead gorgeous, but he was also determined and ruthless and clearly unused to hearing the word 'no'.

Not that that was remotely relevant at the moment. Why he would want her to share the wine was anyone's guess, but she had the feeling that she was still on somewhat shaky ground and he was the client, which meant that he was right. Within reason, what he wanted, he got. So she'd let him do his spiel, have one quick sip of wine and *then* she'd be off. 'Fine.'

'Excellent. Come and join me.'

Armed now with a decanter and a corkscrew, Duarte picked up the quarter of a million dollars that he was about to throw down his very tanned, very attractive throat and strode to a seating area where half a dozen glasses stood upside down on a tray in the centre of a coffee table.

Orla eyed the only seating option warily. The sofa wasn't a big one and he'd take up most of it. Perhaps she could drag the chair she'd been sitting on over. But no.

It was solidly wooden and impossibly heavy. It wasn't budging, no matter how hard she pulled.

Taking a deep, steadying breath and assuring herself that it would be fine, that all they were doing was tasting wine, she moved to the sofa and sat down, wedging herself as tightly into the corner as she could. But, as she'd suspected, it wasn't enough. There was just too much of him. He was stealing her air, dizzying her with his proximity and robbing her of her composure, and she had the feeling that alcohol was only going to make things worse.

Yet she couldn't move. In fact, as she watched him brushing the dust off the neck of the bottle and carefully removing the cap, she wanted to scoot over and lean into him. She wanted to find out exactly how hard and muscled his chest might be. His shirt was unbuttoned at the top to reveal a tantalising wedge of tanned skin and gave her a glimpse of fine dark hair, and her fingers itched to investigate further.

'The grapes that made this wine grew when Queen Victoria was on the British throne,' he said, tilting the decanter and slowly pouring the contents of the bottle into it while she set her jaw and sat on her hands. 'Ulysses S Grant was the US president. Echoes of revolution and Bonaparte still sounded through France. It was a hot, dry summer in Bordeaux that year, a perfect climate for growth and harvest. The vineyard had just been bought by Rothschild. This was the first vintage to be bottled under their ownership. Nothing was mechanised. These grapes were picked by hand and transported by horse and cart. They were trodden by the feet of a hundred locals instead of going into a press as they do nowadays.'

His deep voice was mesmerising. The web he was spinning was lulling her into a sensual trance from which she didn't want to emerge. She was there, in France. She could feel the heat of the sun, smell the dusty earth that mingled with the scent of ripened grapes and snippets of French. She wanted him to tell her more. She wanted him to tell her everything. She could listen to him for hours.

'You paint a vivid picture,' she said, her voice so unusually low and husky that she had to clear her throat to disguise it. 'You have a good imagination.'

He set the bottle down and glanced at her, his eyes dark and glinting with something that made her stomach slowly flip. 'So I've discovered.'

What did *that* mean?

'What if it's turned to vinegar?' she said, forcing herself to focus on the beautiful cut-glass decanter that was now worth a fortune, and not on the hypnotic effect he was having on her.

'It hasn't.'

'How do you know?'

'Smell the cork.'

Twisting round to face her, he held it under her nose and she instinctively inhaled, but all she got was him. Spice, soap, some kind of citrus. An intoxicating combination that muddled her head.

'Delicious,' she murmured, not entirely sure that was a word that could be used to describe the smell of a cork, but then, she wasn't entirely sure either that she actually meant the cork.

'Promising,' he said, and as he turned away to reach forwards and select a couple of glasses she got the strange feeling he wasn't talking entirely about the cork either.

He poured wine into each, watching the flow of liquid intently as he did so, and then nudged one in her direction. 'Here you go.'

'Do you realise there's around forty thousand dollars' worth of wine in that glass?'

'Forget the money.'

'That's easy for you to say.' It was all very well for aristocratic billionaires. For mere mortals, it was a small fortune. 'Forty thousand dollars in pounds would pay off a considerable chunk of my mortgage.'

'A fair point,' he said with a wry smile that flipped her stomach. 'But this is all about the senses.'

Hmm. Well. She didn't know that her senses would be up to much. They were frazzled, completely overwhelmed by him. He was all she could see...his voice was all she could hear. His scent had permeated every cell of her being and she wanted to touch and taste so badly it was becoming a problem. There wasn't a lot of space left for strawberries or compost.

'What do I do?'

'First you look at it, then you smell it, and finally you taste it.'

God, could he read her mind?

'Hold it against this,' he said, handing her a piece of white paper, which she took with fingers that were irritatingly unsteady. 'Tilt the glass. What do you see?'

Getting a grip, Orla did as he instructed and studied the liquid. 'It's a dark sort of reddish brown in the middle,' she said, her voice thankfully not reflecting any of the chaos going on inside her. 'Paler at the rim.'

'Wine browns as it ages and gets hazier.'

'This is very clear. Is that good?'

'It is. Now level it and swirl it around.'

'What does that do?'

'Two things,' he said, demonstrating in a way that bizarrely made her stomach clench. She valued competence. She appreciated it in others. She'd never found it sexy before, but in him, she did.

'First,' he continued, 'when the liquid touches the side of the glass the alcohol evaporates. What remains—the legs—indicates the viscosity or the degree of sweetness. Secondly, it maximises the surface area and releases the aromas.'

If she'd been in a test and had had to say what came second Orla would have been stuck for an answer. All she could think about now were legs. His legs. The long length of his thighs a foot away from hers and how powerful they might be beneath the denim of his jeans.

'What do you see?'

'No legs,' she said a bit breathlessly as she tore her gaze from his thighs and returned it to the glass. 'This must be very dry.'

'You're a fast learner.'

She'd had to be if she'd wanted to claim her place in her family. She'd worked hard and paid attention. The only area that strategy hadn't proven successful had been in the bedroom. She didn't know why. She'd tried her damnedest with her ex-fiancé Matt, yet nothing. It was immensely disappointing and insanely frustrating, and for the benefit of her emotional well-being she tried not to dwell on it much. 'I'm good at listening.'

'Let's see what else you're good at,' said Duarte, his eyes dark and glittering. 'Stick your nose in and sniff it.'

It was hardly the sexiest of instructions, yet she had

an image of burying her nose into his neck, and longing thudded in the pit of her stomach. His nose, she noticed, was gorgeous. Straight. Perfectly proportioned.
Aquiline, even, which wasn't a word she'd ever had
cause to use before.

'What do you smell?'

'Cherries,' she said, the aroma of the wine winding
through her before gradually separating out into individual strands. 'Something herby. Rosemary maybe.
And, weirdly, cheese.'

'You *are* good at this.'

He did the same, only way more expertly than her
and for far longer. He considered, muttered something
in Portuguese and made some notes on a pad on the
table.

'Now taste it,' he said. 'Take a big gulp and swish
it around. You should feel the alcohol at the back of
your throat.'

'And then?'

'Swallow it and breathe in through your mouth and
out through your nose. Note the textures and the astrin-
gency. Then take another gulp. That one you can either
spit out or swallow.'

She would *not* react to that, she told herself firmly.
She wasn't sixteen. But her imagination had other ideas.
Her imagination had her getting up to lock the door
to this room, heading back and then dropping to her
knees before him.

Maybe that bang to the head had done more damage
than she'd assumed to her too. She was dizzy and dis-
combobulated, and when she tried the wine in the way
he'd suggested, knocking it back instead of spitting it

out, she could barely think straight, let alone take note of its textures.

'What do *you* think of it?' she said, struggling for control of her thoughts and setting her glass down before she dropped it.

'It's exceptional. Very vibrant for its age. Long finish. Impressive.'

'How strong is it?'

'Average. Why?'

'I'm feeling very light-headed.'

'That's unlikely to have anything to do with the wine,' he said, putting his own glass down before turning to study her with what looked like concern. 'It could be the heat.'

It was warm in here, that much was true. The sun at this angle bathed the room in abundant evening sunshine. But no, it wasn't the heat. That wouldn't account for the throbbing between her legs. It was him.

Her heart was thundering and her temperature was rocketing, and she could feel it happening inside her again—the strange combination of fire and ice that she'd experienced yesterday when he'd come to an abrupt halt and whipped round in the corridor. Her head was spinning but somehow, in the midst of the chaos, she noticed that he'd gone very still. Very alert. The tension vibrating through him was almost palpable.

As the seconds ticked by the air between them thickened, crackling with electricity. Awareness charged her nerve endings. His gaze dipped to her mouth for a second and her lips tingled. He was so close. All she'd have to do was lean forwards a little and she'd *finally* be able to find out what he felt like, what he tasted like.

'Orla?' he said, his voice very low and gravelly.

'Yes?'

'You need to stop looking at me like that.'

His eyes were blazing and she was dazzled. The rush of adrenalin that was shooting through her was making her feel reckless. 'How am I looking at you?'

'As if you want me to kiss you.'

'I do,' she breathed before she could stop herself, but oh, she *did*. She was going out of her mind. Sex was a problem but kissing would be OK, surely, if he was amenable.

'Well, why didn't you say?' he muttered roughly, clamping one hand to the back of her head to bring her forward and then planting his mouth on hers with a speed that suggested he was very amenable indeed.

She didn't have time or the resources to marvel at that. The inappropriateness of what they were doing didn't cross her mind once. The heat flooding her body and the desire pounding along her veins were wiping her head of rational thought. All she could do was succumb to sensation.

She moaned and wrapped her arms around his neck, and the kiss deepened and intensified. The muscles of his shoulder bunched beneath her fingers as she ran them over him and this time he was the one to groan.

With an urgency that she would have found flattering had she been capable of thought, Duarte disentangled his hands from her hair and moved them to her waist. He lifted and shifted her and then, hardly aware of what was happening, she found herself astride him. He held her hips and tugged her towards him, and when she pressed against him, his erection rubbing her where she so desperately ached for him, she tore her mouth from his and gasped.

But that didn't deter him. He simply set his lips to her neck, lingering on the pulse hammering at its base, while she dropped her head back to give him better access and struggled for breath. With one hand he held her close. He slid the other down her thigh, slipped it beneath the hem of her dress and pushed it up.

Any minute now, she thought dazedly as she burned up with want, her clothes would come off, followed by his, and then there'd be more touching and some body parts would want to be in others and it wouldn't all go wrong for her this time. There'd be no disappointment or despair. There'd be explosions and ecstasy and it would be perfect. More perfect than she could have ever dreamed, and her dreams had been pretty damn good.

But this wasn't a dream, this was reality. The heat and the desire coursing through her were real, which meant that she *could* feel passion, she *wasn't* frigid. She'd always thought she was a failure in the bedroom because she was unable to experience the kind of pleasure she'd heard was possible, but look at what was going on here. Fireworks. Genuine mini-explosions. For the first time ever.

So what if it *hadn't* been her? she thought wildly as he continued to wreak havoc on her skin. She'd only had one lover, her former fiancé, so she had little scope for comparison, but what if the failure had been his? Or maybe it had just been down to simple incompatibility that was nobody's fault.

She hadn't given sex another chance after her engagement had ended because, frankly, if she wasn't going to excel at it, why bother, but could she have missed out on four years of fun and games and even relationships unnecessarily? Need she not have been quite so lonely in all that time?

The questions now ricocheting around her head were huge, breathtaking and utterly overwhelming. On top of the clawing need and delirium, Orla could feel the emotion swelling up inside her, threatening to overspill and quite possibly manifest itself in tears, and that was an outcome she really didn't want to have to explain, so she wrenched herself away and scrambled off him.

'What's wrong?' Duarte muttered hoarsely, breathing hard as he looked at her with eyes that were glazed and burning.

She swallowed down the lump in her throat and tugged at the hem of her dress, as if covering up might provide some kind of defence against the potentially earth-shattering discoveries swirling around her brain. 'I need to go.'

'Do you? Why?'

Because her foundations were rocking and she needed time and space to deal with it. Because the strength of her response to him was scary in its intensity and she was out of her depth here.

'Because this isn't appropriate,' she said desperately, grasping at the only excuse she was willing to give.

'It feels pretty appropriate to me.'

'You're a client.'

'That's irrelevant. I want you,' he said, his eyes dark and compelling. 'Stay.'

'I can't.'

It was one request she couldn't fulfil. Not right now, at least. She couldn't think straight. She didn't know what she was doing. She was totally out of control and it was terrifying.

'Thank you for the wine,' she managed, her head swimming and her heart pounding. 'See you at the conference.'

And then, before she fell completely apart, she fled.

In something of a stupor Duarte listened to the quick, rhythmic tap of Orla's heels on the stone floor of the *adega* fading away and reflected dazedly that if she thought she wouldn't be seeing him again until the conference in three weeks' time, she could think again. Because a kiss like that did not end there.

It had been hot, wild and wholly unexpected. One minute the conversation had been all about the wine, the next, their gazes had collided and the world had stopped. The hunger on her face and the need he'd seen shimmering in her eyes had lit a rocket beneath his pulse and turned him harder than granite.

Once she'd indicated what she wanted, he hadn't thought twice about abandoning the wine and kissing her. He'd acted purely on instinct, and the minute their mouths had met, desire had crashed through him, flooding every inch of his body in seconds. It still lingered, along with the memory of her in his arms, kissing him back with more heat and passion than he could possibly have imagined, as well as utter bewilderment at how suddenly and swiftly she'd backed off.

Was the strength of his response to the kiss down to the fact that it had been such a long time since he'd wanted anyone? It was impossible to tell. And what had spooked her? Again, he had no idea, although he could sympathise if she'd been caught off guard by the explosive nature of the kiss. The impact of it had hit him like a freight train too.

But for all the new questions racing around his head, one he'd had before had definitely been answered. She wanted him just as much as he wanted her.

So what happened next? he wondered as he leapt to his feet and began to pace around the room, repeatedly criss-crossing the lengthening shadows. Once upon a time, he'd have welcomed the obviously mutual attraction, capitalised on the kiss that had given him a rush he hadn't realised he'd been missing, and pursued Orla without hesitation, without doubt. But he was no longer that man. These days, he was battered and bruised and wary. These days, he had the responsibility for a billion-euro business to keep him occupied.

And yet, it wasn't as if he was after a relationship. Thanks to his marriage, from which he still hadn't recovered, he was never having one of those again. In fact, his blood turned to ice at the mere *thought* of it. Love was manipulative and commitment was a prison. And he didn't just have his own experience to base his opinions on. His parents' unpleasant and messy divorce had proved that long ago.

But sex with someone with whom he shared the kind of chemistry that led to unbelievable pleasure? The one-or-two-nights-only sort of thing he'd favoured before he'd married? That he could handle. That would be perfect.

He felt more alive, more energised this evening than he had in months, and he wasn't about to give that up. So he'd put in the groundwork. He'd allay any fears or doubts Orla might have. Seduction had once come to him as naturally as breathing and it wouldn't take too much effort to brush off the dust and fire up his skills. He'd have her in his bed in no time. So, contrary to her parting shot, she wouldn't be seeing him in three weeks' time. She'd be seeing him tomorrow.

CHAPTER FIVE

What a night.

Stifling a yawn and wishing she didn't feel quite so bleary-eyed, Orla climbed into the car and fired up the engine to drive the seven kilometres that lay between her hotel and Duarte's estate.

To say she hadn't slept well was an understatement. Two fitful hours, from three to five, was all she'd managed, and that was on top of the sleepless, stressful night before. She was therefore running on empty, which didn't bode particularly well for a day during which she needed all her wits about her, but at least she was fortified with coffee and the conviction that nothing was going to go wrong.

There was no reason it should, she assured herself as she turned out of the hotel's entrance and onto the road. She was meeting the housekeeping team she'd hired in an hour. She'd confirmed the time and printed off a copy of the instructions she'd already emailed to them, and all other arrangements were on track.

Of course, it would help enormously if she could stop thinking about what had happened yesterday evening. The memories of the kiss she and Duarte had shared had tormented her for most of the night, rendering her so hot and bothered that she'd wondered if she was coming down with something.

The heat and skill of his mouth moving so insistently against hers... The rock-hard muscles of his chest flexing beneath her hands... The glazed look in his eyes and the faint flush slashing across his cheekbones and the heady satisfaction of knowing she'd caused both... And then the abrupt, mortifying way it had ended.

She hadn't had the chance to contemplate the notion that the mediocre sex she'd experienced to date might not be her fault after all or regret the time she'd potentially wasted. She hadn't had the wherewithal to find out how the venue mix-up could have happened. Distressingly, she hadn't had the head space for anything other than the actual kiss itself.

But at least today she'd be so busy concentrating on the job she was here to do she wouldn't have time to dwell on these things. It wasn't as if she and Duarte's paths were going to cross. She'd made it very clear she didn't expect to see him until the conference and there was no earthly reason why someone like him would bother himself with anything as mundane as housekeeping. He had a billion-euro global wine business to run and presumably multiple demands on his time. So there'd be no awkward moments involving stuttering conversation and fierce blushing. No gazing at his mouth and remembering. There was nothing to worry about at all.

Orla swung off the road and onto the wide, sandy drive that led to the Quinta, the awe rippling through her as fresh as it had been when she'd rushed over the day before yesterday, shortly after her initial, monumental mistake had come to light.

As conference venues went, this one was spectacular. The house had been built on the north bank of the
Douro at the beginning of the eighteenth century, the
year the estate was bought by an ancestor of Duarte's
who'd travelled from the UK to try his hand at making
port. Against a cloudless azure sky the white walls of
the three-storey building sparkled in the early morning
sunshine beneath a terracotta tiled roof. Green shutters
were open at the ground-floor windows that stretched
out either side of the huge oak front door, and at those
above on the next floors up.

Behind the facade, the original building had gradually tripled in size and been regularly modernised. It
now boasted ten en-suite bedrooms, countless reception rooms, a dining room that could seat fifty, and a
ballroom, which was where the meetings would be taking place. At the rear, the courtyard that was decorated
with jewel-coloured mosaics featured a fountain in the
shape of a cherub holding aloft a bunch of grapes. And
beyond that, a vine-covered pergola stood over a wide
stone patio that ran the length of the house and had
stunning views of the terraces.

Over the years, the success of that intrepid eigh-
teenth-century winemaker had led to the expansion of
the business and the acquisition of further estates, and
almost all of the winemaking had since moved to Porto.
But, given its size and idyllic setting, this magnificent
building had been used for entertaining for the past
three centuries and still was.

Quite honestly, Orla still couldn't work out how she'd
got it so wrong. The house she'd originally and incor-
rectly identified as the venue for the conference was

lovely—now that it wasn't a complete tip—but it wasn't a patch on this.

She should have questioned the keys that didn't fit, she thought for what had to be the thousandth time. She should have paid more attention to the odd curious glance she'd received over the ten days or so, which she'd attributed to miscommunication as a result of her poor attempts at Portuguese. She shouldn't have been so confident she knew what she was doing that she hadn't triple-checked the instructions.

However, now wasn't the time for unfathomable conundrums. Now was the time to focus on the day ahead, a day free from distractions and lapses in concentration, a day devoid of slip-ups.

Everything was going to go brilliantly, she reminded herself as she pulled up at a wing of the house to the rear, the tradesmen's entrance, got out and bent to retrieve her satchel from the back seat. She had her lists and the order of play. She knew what she was doing, and, more importantly, she knew what everyone else was doing. Everything was under control.

'Bom dia.'

At the sound of the deep voice somewhere behind her, Orla jumped, narrowly avoiding hitting her head on the roof of the car, and whirled round. Her heart gave a great crash against her ribs and then began to race. Duarte was striding her way, his gaze fixed on her, a faint smile hovering at his mouth.

Oh, no, she thought, her heart sinking as the memory of last night's kiss, the wantonness of her response and the way she'd been all over him instantly slammed into her head and flooded her cheeks with heat.

This was bad.

Very bad.

What was he doing here? Why wasn't he doing something brilliant with wine? What had happened to their paths absolutely not crossing? So much for a day free from distraction and loss of focus. Ten seconds in his vicinity and already panic was beginning to flutter inside her. Already she was on edge and wired in a way that had nothing to do with the copious amounts of caffeine she'd consumed earlier. But what could she do? She could hardly order him to leave. It was his estate.

'Good morning,' she replied, hitching her satchel over her shoulder, locking the car and deciding that denial and professionalism while she figured out a way to get rid of him were the way forward here.

'Did you sleep well?'

No. She hadn't. She'd slept appallingly. 'Perfectly well, thank you,' she said, setting off for the back door. 'You?'

'Barely a wink,' he said as he fell into step beside her. 'You kept me up for hours. Literally.'

Her pulse thudded, her mouth went dry and she very nearly stumbled. Why would he say that? How did he expect her to respond? Was she supposed to apologise?

She'd never been in this situation before, working in such physical proximity with a client. She didn't know how to handle it. But she was pretty sure that if he'd decided to start flirting with her it wasn't going to help at all. It wasn't helping much that despite his allegedly rough night he still looked unfairly gorgeous. No washed-out skin or dark, saggy bags under the eyes for him. *He* hadn't had to slather on the concealer or paper over the cracks.

'Did you finish the wine?' she asked as she walked

through the door he held open and into the beautifully cool house.

'I lost the taste for it.'

What a frivolous waste.

Heroically resisting the urge to roll her eyes, Orla started down the long flagstone-floored passageway that led to the kitchen and tried to ignore how near he was. The passageway was as wide as the Douro. There really was no need for his arm to keep brushing against hers. Every time it did, tiny shivers scampered through her body. She even felt them in her toes, for goodness' sake.

'So what are you doing here?' she asked, aiming for politeness and trying not to let her frustration show.

'I thought I could lend a hand.'

With what? What did he think he was going to do? Make up a bed? Did he even know how to? Judging by the mess she'd found at his house, assuming it had been caused by him, it didn't seem likely.

'I have everything under control,' she said, deciding that on balance it was probably better not to be thinking about beds, hands or, in fact, any other body part of his. 'I'm meeting the housekeeping team here in,' she glanced at her watch, 'half an hour.'

'Local?'

'Yes.'

'I'll help translate.'

'The team leader speaks excellent English.' Honestly. Did he really think she wouldn't have thought of that? 'You pay a hefty fee not to have to bother with any of this, Duarte,' she said pointedly while just about managing to retain her smile. 'You really don't need to stick around.'

'I want to.'

But why?

Unless…

Her eyes narrowed as an unwelcome thought occurred to her. 'Do you think I'm going to screw up again?'

'Not at all. But you can answer one question for me,' he said, striding ahead of her into the vast kitchen and taking up a position against an expansive stretch of work surface.

Orla made for the enormous wooden table that stood in the middle of the room and had three centuries of food preparation scored into its surface and sat down. 'What do you want to know?'

'Why are *you* here, seeing to things personally?'

Well, at least *that* was a question she could answer. 'I was let down at the last minute by the team I'd put in place to carry out your instructions,' she said with an inward wince as she laid her satchel on the table and opened the flap. 'They're the best. I use them all the time. Fly them across continents. But they got struck down by a bug. All of them at the same time. It's never happened before. I spent two days trying to fix up a replacement but then decided it would be quicker and simpler to do it myself.'

It had been a frantic, stressful time and in hindsight, *that* was probably why she'd misread his email.

'But why are *you* here?' she asked, wondering if it had really been that simple. 'You weren't due back for another three weeks.'

'I had business in the States. It wrapped up early.'

Which in some ways had been a good thing, she had to admit grudgingly. While his happening upon her taking a nap hadn't been ideal, imagine if her mistake hadn't been uncovered until the day of the conference. There wouldn't have been time to fix things. He'd have been even more furious, and justifiably so. She felt faint at the mere thought of it.

'So when you think about it,' he mused with a nonchalance she didn't trust for a second, 'neither of us is meant to be here. Fate, wouldn't you say?'

She would say nothing of the sort. 'I don't believe in Fate.'

'No, I don't imagine you do,' he said with a quick, dazzling grin. 'You're too practical. But mistakes aside, you're dedicated.'

'*One* mistake,' she corrected, determinedly blinking away the dazzle and reminding herself that practical wasn't boring, practical was good. 'Which is being rectified. And it's my job.'

'Which you love.'

'I do,' she agreed as she began removing her laptop and notebooks from her bag. 'Who wouldn't? It involves opulence. Outlandish, unforgettable, once-in-a-lifetime experiences. VIP events. Unimaginable excess and extravagance.'

It also required stellar organisation, infinite skill when it came to persuasion and negotiating, and the ability to think on her feet. Every single day demanded and expected more from her than the day before, and she was one of the best. Usually.

'Recently, I arranged an engagement proposal on an iceberg,' she said, as much to remind herself of her competence as to prove it to him. 'Once, a client wanted to have a private dinner in front of the Mona Lisa.'

'I ought to up my game.'

Orla reached for her clipboard and thought that Duarte's game was quite high enough. They spoke at least twice a month. His requests ranged from arranging private jets to reserving tables at impossible-to-book restaurants and much more besides, and they were frequent. While most of what he wanted hovered at the bottom of the outrageousness scale, last year he'd asked her to recreate a perfume long since out of production for his mother as a birthday present. That had been a challenge. 'You keep me busy.'

'I could keep you busier.'

Orla froze in the middle of attaching her lists to the clipboard and shot him a startled glance. What did he mean by that? She couldn't work it out. His words were innocent enough but the way he was looking at her was anything but. He was sort of *smouldering* and quite suddenly she was finding it a struggle to breathe. He'd gone very still and his gaze had dropped to her mouth, which went bone-dry, and oh, dear God, was he thinking about last night? Was he planning a repeat?

She was so hopeless at this, she thought desperately, her heart thundering while a wave of heat crashed over her. But *this* shouldn't even be happening. She shouldn't be burning up with the urge to get to her feet, throw herself into his arms and take up where they'd left off. She shouldn't want him to spread her out over the table and feast on her.

The speed and ease with which he could make her lose control was confusing and terrifying. It was as if there were wicked forces at play, luring her into the unknown, over which she had zero control, and if there was one thing she hated, it was that.

But now cool-headed logic battled against hot, mad desire, and she feared it was losing—

And then, relief.

Blessed, blessed relief.

'I think I hear a van.'

By the end of the day, Orla could stand it no longer. Her nerves were in tatters and her stomach was in knots.

As she'd hoped, the work side of things was going splendidly. The house had buzzed with activity. The housekeeping team she'd organised was as efficient and excellent as she'd been assured. Rooms were in the process of being cleaned and laundry pressed. Anything that could be polished shone, and vacuum cleaners had hummed throughout the building all day. Her mistake was well underway to becoming history and her satisfaction on that front was deep.

But, as she'd feared, Duarte was proving to be a menace. While she'd been handing out instructions and emphasising priorities, he'd donned a tool belt. Subsequently, everywhere she'd turned, up he popped, sometimes with a hammer, other times with a screwdriver, and once, when a basin tap was discovered to be leaking, with a wrench. At one point she hadn't seen him for an hour and had dared to hope that he'd gone for good, but unfortunately he'd returned with lunch. For everyone.

There seemed to be no end to the man's talents and it was driving her nuts. She couldn't stop thinking about the smouldering. The tool belt, combined with olive combat shorts and a white polo shirt that hugged his muscles and highlighted his Portuguese heritage, was such a good look on him, she could hardly tear her eyes away. His smile, which he wielded frequently and lethally, laid waste to her reason every time she caught sight of it. So far today she'd knocked over a vase, temporarily mislaid three of her precious lists and spent a good fifteen minutes she could ill afford to spare gazing out of a top-floor window at where he was methodically clearing leaves from the pool, having waved aside protests from the team of gardeners handling the outdoors.

She didn't like it. Any of it. Not the loss of focus, not the weakening of her resolve, and she particularly hated the sinking sensation that if things continued in this vein, a serious slip-up was only a matter of time.

She couldn't allow that to happen, she thought grimly as she stood at the back door and watched the convoy of vans carry off the three dozen housekeeping staff for the night. She was striving for excellence here and for that she needed to stay on the ball. Right now, not only was she *not* on the ball, she wasn't even anywhere near it. She felt as if she was walking a tightrope. One wobble and she'd tumble to the ground, where her insecurities lay waiting to pounce.

So enough was enough. Forget the fact that Duarte was a client who ought to be kept happy at all times. Forget that this was his house. She couldn't carry on like this. She had to find him and get rid of him. Whatever it took.

Beside the pool, Duarte unbuckled the tool belt and dumped it on a lounger. He emptied his pockets of his keys, wallet and phone, then stripped off his polo shirt. After removing his belt and adding it to the mounting pile of belongings, he dived into the cool, fresh water with relish.

The day had been surprisingly enjoyable and unexpectedly revelatory, he reflected as he began to swim lengths, the heat in his body and the tension in his muscles easing with every powerful stroke. He'd already come to the conclusion that, despite initial impressions, Orla was exceptionally capable. Why else would she be joint CEO of her company and how else could she have acquired the elusive wine? But who'd have thought competence would be such a turn-on? She issued crystal-clear instructions, could mentally turn on a sixpence and solved problems with head-spinning speed. She was like a highly efficient, well-oiled dynamo. She demanded excellence and got it, and the longer he'd watched her in action the more insistent the desire drumming through him became.

Whether or not she still wanted him, however, was as clear as mud. She'd spent most of the day trying to avoid him. He strode into a room and she marched out. He'd brought her lunch—since the oat bars she snacked on were hardly the kind of sustenance needed for a long day's work—and she'd responded not with appreciation, as one might have expected, but with a huff of barely concealed disappointment. When avoidance had been impossible, she'd opted for ice-cool professionalism, as if she hadn't melted in his arms and kissed him so passionately last night.

Her frosty attitude towards him didn't bode all that well for his intention to entice her into his bed, Duarte had to admit as he turned and started a length underwater, but he had no intention of giving up. She wasn't the only one with goals. Once he set his mind to something, nothing swayed him. So he'd stick to the plan—perhaps even ramping it up—and she'd succumb soon enough. The women he'd wanted in the past generally had and he didn't see why Orla would be any different.

Coming up for air, he caught sight of her marching across the grass towards him. He swam to the side of the pool, his pulse hammering with an intensity that could have been caused by the exercise but more likely was because of her, and rested his arms on the tiled edge just as she drew to a stop right in front of him.

'Duarte,' she said in the clipped tone he'd become used to over the last twelve or so hours and which, perversely, fanned the embers of desire and sent it streaking through his veins like fire.

'Orla,' he murmured, letting his eyes drift from her fine ankles, up her shapely legs and over her shorts and T-shirt, which were close-fitting enough to make him want to get his hands on the skin beneath and trace her shape.

'We need to talk.'

Oh, dear. That sounded serious. He'd never been a fan of 'talking'. At least, not about anything that mattered, anything that might hurt. Shortly after the deaths of first his son and later his wife, his mother had tentatively suggested therapy. Beleaguered by unimaginable grief and excoriating guilt, he'd instantly shut that conversation down and sensibly she hadn't revisited it. What had happened was his fault, he knew, and he didn't deserve to work through it and come out the other side. He deserved to burn in hell.

'What about?' he drawled, pushing the unwelcome memories down and burying them deep.

'You. More specifically, this...' she waved a hand around '...*situation.*'

Interesting.

What precise situation did she mean?

Assuring himself he could easily deflect the conversation if it headed down a path he'd rather not follow and somewhat relieved that the idea of 'talking' had deflated his desire when his shorts now clung to him like a second skin, Duarte heaved himself out of the pool. He gave himself a shake and strode over to the lounger. He reached for his polo shirt and used it first to rub his hair dry and then to blot the water from his chest. When he was done, he stalked over to the table that could seat twelve and draped it over the back of one chair before dropping himself into another.

'I'm all yours,' he said, leaning back and stretching out to let the evening sun do its thing.

When Orla didn't respond he glanced up at her. She looked dazed. Flushed. She swayed for a second and he briefly wondered if she was about to pass out. Today had been scorching and long. It wasn't beyond the realms of possibility.

'I'm sorry?' she stammered.

'You wanted to talk? About me and a situation.'

She blinked and snapped to. 'Yes. That's right. I do.'

'Fire away.'

'Okay.' She cleared her throat and tucked a lock of wavy golden hair that had escaped her ponytail behind her ear. 'Yes. Good. I just wanted to say thank you for your help today. It was…appreciated.'

She didn't sound as if it was. The moment's hesitation suggested his presence here today had been anything but appreciated, which was intriguing. 'You're welcome.'

'However, there's no need for you to be here tomorrow.'

'It's no trouble.'

'Really. I wouldn't want to put you out.'

'You won't.'

'I'm sure you must have somewhere better to be.'

She was wrong. For once, he had time on his hands, and while there was always something in the business that required his attention, he could afford a few days off to focus on this latest project. He had the feeling that it would be more than worth it. 'I don't.'

Her stunning eyes flashed with annoyance. 'Well, you can't stay here.'

'Why not?'

'You're getting in the way and putting me off my stride.'

'Your stride looks fine to me,' he said, his gaze dropping to her long legs and lingering.

'You're being deliberately obtuse.'

'Then clarify it for me.'

She let out a sigh of exasperation and threw up her hands in what looked like defeat. 'I can't concentrate while you're around,' she said hotly. 'You're too distracting. I need to be able to do my job to the best of my ability and you're preventing me from doing that.'

Her admission jolted through him like lightning, electrifying every nerve ending he possessed. So she *was* affected by him. She was just remarkably adept at hiding how she felt. It was surprisingly satisfying to know. 'I bother you.'

She gave a nod, her jaw tight, as if she was loath to have to admit it. 'Yes.'

'And yet you're still brilliant.'

'I am,' she agreed. 'And I've worked very hard to be. But I won't be brilliant if I keep dropping things and losing lists. You're making me do that. You mess with my head. All day I've been on tenterhooks waiting for some disaster to happen because I'm not paying enough attention, and I can't have it.'

'I think you're overestimating my powers.'

'You couldn't possibly understand.'

'So explain.'

'I have to be in control,' she said, glowering down at him and shoving her hands in the back pockets of her shorts, which did interesting things to her chest. 'I need everything to be perfect. All the time. I can't accept second best. It's just not in me.'

'You're a high achiever,' he replied with a nod. 'I get that. So am I.'

She shook her head. 'It's more than that. For high achievers, the goal is important but mainly it's about the journey. My older brother and younger sister are classic examples of that, so I should know. Nothing fazes them. If something goes wrong they dust themselves off and pick themselves up. They see it as a lesson learned. For me, it's all about the goal, which I have to reach no matter what. It's not about the journey. I couldn't care less about that. I just want results. Failure sends me into a spin. I sink into a pit of self-doubt and despair and it's not a good place for me to be. Ergo, I can't fail.'

So that was why she'd been so desperate to get her job back after he'd fired her. As he'd suspected, rather disappointingly, he found, it had had nothing to do with him. 'That's a lot of pressure.'

'You have no idea,' she muttered vehemently. 'It's fine if I stay on track. Not so much if I don't. Which is what's happening here.'

'I make you panic?'

'Yes.'

'Because I distract you.'

She scowled. 'What do you want? A medal?'

No. He just wanted her. She looked like a goddess standing there in the sun, her hair gleaming beneath the rays, fire in her eyes. A frustrated and annoyed goddess, it was true, but she was magnificent none the less, and desire hammered hard in the pit of his stomach.

'I want you to admit you want me as much as I want you,' he said, focusing every drop of his attention on her so he didn't miss a thing. 'I want you to admit you can't stop thinking about our kiss.'

'Fine,' she snapped, clearly at the end of her tether. 'I *am* attracted to you. I *can't* stop thinking about our kiss. It kept me awake all last night. It's been plaguing me all day. It's—*you're*—driving me nuts.'

'Then I have the perfect solution.'

She frowned at him for one long moment, her expression wary and her body tense. 'What is it?'

'Sleep with me.'

CHAPTER SIX

FOR A SPLIT SECOND, Orla thought she'd misheard. That she'd been so dazzled by the sight of him—his broad, muscled chest, tanned, bare and glistening in the evening sunshine—she'd lost her ability to think.

And to be honest, briefly, she had. Duarte had hauled himself out of the pool and she'd practically combusted on the spot. All she'd been able to do was stare and drool. When he'd lowered his gaze from her face to her legs just now, leisurely perusing the bits in between, she'd been so transfixed that she hadn't even been able to take a breath, let alone summon up a protest at his blatant and outrageous scrutiny.

Her brain had clearly been starved of oxygen by that because she hadn't meant to confess how strongly he affected her. 'Whatever it took' had not meant exposing her vulnerabilities to a man who already wielded far too much power over her. It had not meant admitting to an aspect of her personality that she'd been told, by a therapist she'd seen once when her engagement ended and she spiralled into a pit of self-doubt and hopelessness, was a flaw.

Could she have been subconsciously hoping that he'd sympathise and retreat? If she had—and frankly, she had no idea why that would have been the case when she barely knew him—it had badly backfired. All she'd done was give him ammunition. However, what was said was said and it was too late to take any of it back, and in any case the conversation had taken an unexpected turn.

Surely he couldn't have said what she thought he'd said. And if he *had*, then surely he had to be joking. But he didn't look as though he was joking. His expression was filled with dark, dangerous intent and his voice had dropped an octave, just as it had the evening before when he'd asked her to stay.

'You've lost your mind,' she managed once she'd unglued her tongue from the roof of her mouth and regained the power of speech.

'Not in the slightest,' he said with a cool, even tone that she would have envied had there been space for it amongst all the heat and desire crashing around inside her. 'By your own admission you're distracted because you're attracted to me. That attraction won't go away just because I do. It's too powerful. It will linger. Fester. Swell until it grows out of all proportion, and then you really *will* be distracted. Then you really *will* make mistakes.'

He didn't sound quite so cool now. He sounded like he knew what he was talking about. 'Are you speaking from experience?'

The shrug he gave was careless, but she could practically see the shutters slamming down over his eyes and his guard shooting up, which suggested she was right. Who? When? How fascinating.

'If you want your concentration back, you need to get what's throwing it off course out of your system,' he continued, interestingly leaving her question unanswered. 'Demystify it and it loses its power. We want each other. You're driving me as mad as I apparently drive you. So let's do something about it. Scratch the itch and it goes away.'

Seriously?

No matter how certain Duarte sounded, to Orla that didn't make any sense. Eradicate the attraction by indulging it? She might not have much knowledge on the subject but she didn't think it worked like that. What if it didn't go away? What if it got stronger? *More* distracting? And if sleeping with Duarte was so good that she ended up with further itches that needed scratching, how on earth would *that* help?

'What if it doesn't?' she said, her head fogging at the thought of feeling even more for him than she already did.

'That's never been my experience. Once is generally enough.'

For him, maybe, but what about the women he took to bed? What about her? 'I'm really not sure it's a good idea,' she said with staggering understatement.

'Incredible sex is always a good idea.'

Well, yes, perhaps in *theory*, but she wouldn't know, and the whole idea of sleeping with him felt recklessly dangerous. Not only could she find herself way out of her depth, but also she really didn't fancy making a fool of herself, which was what could well happen if hell froze over and she did throw caution to the wind to take Duarte up on his suggestion.

According to the gossip columns, he'd bedded hundreds of women in the years preceding his marriage. Beautiful women. Experienced women. Imagine if something started between *them* and she got it all wrong. Imagine if her inability to truly enjoy herself in bed hadn't been down to her ex or simple incompatibility but was in fact because of something in *her*. What if the sparks and heat she felt in his vicinity didn't last? What if his effect on her somehow disappeared beneath the pressure to perform, to excel? The humiliation would be unbearable. She'd never be able to work with him again. She wouldn't even be able to look him in the eye.

But on the other hand, insisted a little voice in her head that was becoming increasingly loud, what if it didn't? What if she was overthinking this and quite possibly missing out on not only the opportunity to turn a failure into a success but also some apparently pretty scorching sex in the meantime?

Didn't she owe it to herself to see if she couldn't rectify the situation that had been bugging her for years? She was nearly thirty. How much longer was she going to put it off? And perhaps Duarte was right and just the once *was* the way to get it out of her system. He had vastly more experience than she did, so maybe chemistry *did* work like that. Out of sight, out of mind hadn't exactly been a success. Look at how her night had panned out.

Something had to give here, and she had to at least *try* and find out what she was capable of, she thought, the possibility of it beginning to drum through her. She'd never experienced lust before—which presumably was what all this was—and who knew when the next opportunity might come along? Surely the effect he had on her—so wild and intense—had to mean that anything between them would be better than good.

Deep down, she longed to know whether the reality could live up to her dreams, and what was the worst that could happen? That it didn't? That she felt nothing and had to fake it? Well, that wouldn't be a problem. She excelled at *that*. Her ex hadn't guessed for a moment that her panting and moaning was calculated and strategic rather than spontaneous and instinctive, and if it came to that, nor would Duarte.

'Incredible is a bold claim,' she said, her mouth as dry as the desert and her heart thundering like a steam train.

His dark gaze glittered in the setting sun. 'Incredible is a guarantee.'

Was it? He seemed so sure. Did she dare? To grab the chance to right a wrong and experience some allegedly hot sex with the most attractive man she'd ever met, a man who astonishingly seemed to want her as much as she wanted him, and wasn't really a professional conflict of interest? Why, yes. Despite the potential for failure, apparently she did. 'All right.'

For a big man Duarte moved with impressive speed. Barely before she'd had time to blink he was up and off the seat and closing the distance between them with single-minded intent. He stopped an inch in front of her, planted a hand on the small of her back and drew her in.

'Here?' she managed breathlessly, as her senses swam and her skin beneath his palm burned. 'Now?'

'Do you have a problem with that?'

The heat swirling in the depths of his eyes as he stared down at her took her breath away and her thoughts spun for a second. Ludicrous thoughts, such as when had she last examined her bikini line? What underwear was she wearing? Did it matter? Would he even notice? Given the focus and intensity with which he was looking at her, she doubted he would notice a thousand champagne bottles popping simultaneously behind him. And her body was all right. She kept herself in shape and depilated. It would probably be best to strike while the iron was hot and just get on with it, before she talked herself out of it.

'No,' she said huskily, lowering her gaze to his mouth and feeling a surge of longing so overwhelming she didn't quite know what to do with it. 'No problem at all.'

She put her hands on his bare chest and his hold on her tightened and then he was kissing her, hot and hard. Her heart thundered and fire licked along her veins. She slid her hands up, over warm skin and taut muscles, skimming over his shoulders, until her fingers came into contact with his thick, soft hair. She held his head and he pulled her hips to his, and when she felt the steely length of his erection against her she gasped.

Taking advantage of the break in kissing, Duarte, breathing heavily, removed her T-shirt and, ah, yes, now she remembered. Her underwear was practical and sturdy rather than sexy and feminine, cotton not lace, designed for comfort while at work in the heat. Not that he appeared to mind. He seemed more intent on getting her horizontal. He manoeuvred her round and down and then she was lying back on a double sun lounger, free to ogle him as he reached for his wallet and extracted what she presumed was a condom.

God, he was gorgeous. And he clearly knew his way around a female body. But what would someone like him—former international playboy, looks of a god—expect? Presumably incredible sex required incredible input on her part, but what ought she to be doing? His skills were evidently extensive, while hers were very much limited, and how on earth was she supposed to get an A-plus when she hadn't even revised for the test?

She'd close her eyes and trust her instinct, she told herself firmly. She'd stop thinking and focus on feeling. She was a fast learner. She'd pick up the clues quickly enough. There'd be no problem.

Duarte joined her on the lounger and lowered his mouth to hers, kissing her deeply while she closed her eyes and moaned. Her hand went to the nape of his neck and his moved to her breast. She arched her back, pressing herself against him harder, seeking the tingles she'd experienced the night before, but they remained annoyingly elusive.

Why was that? she wondered frustratedly as he rubbed his thumb over her nipple and she sighed with what she hoped he'd interpret as ecstasy. What was she doing wrong? And, come to think of it, where was the reason-wrecking heat and all-consuming need off to? She could feel it dissipating and she tried to recapture it but to no avail, and no, no, no, no, *no*. This wasn't meant to be happening. She wasn't meant to be panicking that she was going to mess it up. She was meant to be doing *this* and doing it well.

Duarte ran his hand down her body, and in anxious desperation Orla writhed in a way designed to indicate passion, in an attempt to reignite it inside her, but it was as if she were watching the proceedings from somewhere far, far away, and she wanted to cry with despair and frustration.

So much for getting the craziness out of her system. Right now, it wasn't even *in* her system. With all her overthinking, she'd killed the mood. For her at least. But she needn't kill it for him, and who knew, maybe his desire for her would be strong enough for both of them?

Panting hard and frantically hoping to relocate the need that had been tormenting her for days but was now stubbornly absent, she trailed her fingers down his back and round to the button of his shorts. She started undoing it, feeling the hard length of his impressive erection beneath her hand, when he suddenly put his hand over hers and stilled her movements.

'What are you doing?' she said huskily, looking up at him with what she hoped was an encouragingly seductive smile. 'Why are you stopping?'

His eyes were dark and glittering, and a deep frown creased his forehead. 'This isn't doing it for you, is it?'

What? Damn. Why couldn't he have believed her pants and moans, the way her ex had? Why did he have to notice she was struggling to focus? He wasn't helping by putting a halt to things. Couldn't he see that?

'Just carry on,' she murmured, trying to shake his hand off hers so she could continue undoing his fly. 'It'll be fine.'

He stared down at her, as if unable to believe what he was hearing. *'Fine?'*

Oh, dear. Now she'd offended him. 'I meant, I'm sure it'll be incredible,' she said with a batting of her eyelids and a twist of her hips. 'There'll be explosions and ecstasy. Whatever. It's all good.' Or it would be if she could get out of her head. Probably.

'It is far from all good,' Duarte said grimly, disentangling himself from her, sitting up and moving to the edge of the lounger.

Orla missed his heat immediately and inwardly

railed at her inadequacy. There really was no hope for her. 'I'm sorry,' she said, feeling quietly mortified and very exposed.

He looked at her, his eyes stormy and every line of his body rigid. 'You never have to apologise for changing your mind.'

'I haven't changed my mind,' she said, keen to make that clear despite the hopelessness she could feel descending. 'That's not it at all.'

'Then what is it?'

'I started thinking about excellence and expectations and got a bit sidetracked.'

His eyebrows shot up. *'Sidetracked?'*

'Well, yes. You must have slept with lots of women. I, on the other hand, have only slept with one man, not very successfully. You're way more experienced than I am. I have no tricks.'

He retrieved her T-shirt and handed it to her and she put it back on, feeling a little chilly now. So much for hoping her lack of success at sex might have been the fault of her ex or incompatibility. It was clearly neither. It was her. There was something wrong with her.

'What are you doing tomorrow?'

Orla swallowed hard. Right. He was obviously no longer interested and it was back to business. 'The same as today, I expect,' she said, determined not to care. Making sure everything went smoothly and avoiding him, most likely. Only instead of being distracted by memories of the kiss on his sofa, she'd be trying not to think of what had happened here.

'Take the day off.'

What? 'I can't.'

'Everyone here knows what they're doing, right?'

'Well, yes...' Apart from her obviously. She didn't have a clue.

'And you have a phone in case of emergencies.'

'I do, but—'

'Then you can take the day off.'

Why was he so insistent? Why wasn't he simply marching off and going in search of someone who *did* know what they were doing? 'What for?'

'Further research into excellence and expectations,' he said, his deep, hot gaze holding hers so she couldn't look away even if she'd wanted to. 'And tricks.'

Oh.

Oh.

Maybe he was still interested. Orla's pulse skipped a beat and then began to race but she ignored it because she knew now that that translated into precisely nothing. So what would be the point in pursuing things? It would be a disaster again and there was only so much humiliation a person could take.

'There's no need for that,' she said thickly, her throat tight with disappointment and regret.

'There's every need for that,' he countered. 'You're not the only one with goals, Orla. I'm not accustomed to mediocrity either, especially when it comes to sex. So take the day off.'

Orla considered taking the day off a mistake. Duarte knew this because he'd picked her up from her hotel half an hour ago, after she'd done what needed to be done at the Quinta, and she'd already mentioned it half a dozen times. She'd cited professionalism. She'd muttered something about there being a problem with the tablecloths. She'd repeatedly asked herself what she thought she was doing. Out loud.

He, on the other hand, considered it anything other than a mistake. He'd never had a woman in his arms simply going through the motions. He didn't like it. Either his skills were rustier than he'd imagined or Orla required a different approach. Whichever it was, he wanted to get to the bottom of what had sidetracked her. His desire for her was so strong that if something wasn't done about it soon he could suffer permanent damage. His male pride was wounded and demanded satisfaction, and it was more than three long years since he'd last slept with anyone.

So if overthinking was her problem then he had to get inside her head and disrupt from within. He sensed there was a volcano bubbling beneath her surface that needed erupting. He also had the intriguing feeling that the sex she'd previously had, *not very successfully*, was involved, and that, therefore, also merited investigation.

'Where are you taking me?'

With any luck, by the end of the day, to heaven and back. 'The river.'

'Why?'

'Because while you're here you should see more of the local area than just the Quinta. It's beautiful off the beaten track. Nature at its most excellent.' Not to mention far away from work and reality and ideal for his purposes. 'And speaking of excellence, where does your need for it come from?'

'You don't waste time.'

He took his eyes off the road for a split second and cast her a quick glance to find that she was looking at him both shrewdly and suspiciously. 'I don't see the point,' he said, totally unperturbed by this. Orla was skittish and wary and easily spooked by matters of a carnal nature, but she was also trapped in a moving car. He could afford to be direct. 'My badly bruised ego demands answers.'

'I'm a lost cause.'

'How do you know? We've barely even begun.'

'Experience.'

Ah.

'Also, were you not there last night?'

'I was very much there,' he said, remembering how soft and warm she'd been in his arms, how divine she'd smelled and tasted, and feeling a pulse of heat low in his pelvis. 'Even if you weren't.'

'I was to begin with, before getting sidetracked.'

Duarte crushed the pressing yet wildly inappropriate urge to pull over and find out if she still felt that good and reminded himself of his plan to find out what made her tick. 'So back to my question…'

'I'm the middle of three siblings,' she said on a sigh. 'My older sister is an opera singer. A contralto. She's with the Met and lives in New York. My younger brother plays rugby for England. My parents were generally to be found either at a concert hall or on a touchline somewhere. There wasn't a lot of time left for me, you know?'

'No,' he said. 'I wouldn't know. I'm an only child.'

'So you got all the attention.'

He caught a note of wistfulness in her voice, guessed that she was imagining a happy family unit that was all hearts and flowers, and the cynic in him felt compelled to burst that particular bubble.

'Not exactly,' he said flatly, his hands flexing on

the steering wheel. 'My parents divorced when I was twelve. Acrimoniously. They were so busy hurling insults at each other, there wasn't a whole lot of time for me either.'

That hung between them for a moment, then she said softly, 'I didn't know that. I'm sorry.'

'No need,' he replied, really not needing her pity. 'It's been eighteen years and they're civil to each other now. We all rub along well enough. But for a decade I did end up seeking attention elsewhere. Everywhere, actually.'

'You found it. In spades.'

'I did.' And he hadn't regretted a minute of it. Until he'd met Calysta and lost his head.

'I had to work for mine,' she said, putting a stop to his turbulent thoughts before they could head down that dark and twisted path. 'And my only option was school. I studied hard, all the time, making sure I came top of the class every term and acing every test.'

'Did it work?'

'It did. The first time I got a hundred per cent in a maths exam my parents took us all out for a meal to celebrate and *I* was allowed to choose the restaurant. I was eight and it was the best moment of my life, so I didn't stop. I carried on aiming for the top and claiming what snippets of attention I could. Luckily, I really enjoyed studying.'

'What about friends?'

'What friends?' she deadpanned.

She had high expectations of herself. She probably had high expectations of others that were hard to live up to. As he'd thought, the pressure she put on herself must be immense. 'How did you become joint CEO of Hamilton Garrett?'

'I didn't bother with university,' she said. 'There was nothing I was interested in apart from organising and making everything just so, and there isn't a degree for that. After I left school I became an executive assistant at a bank and worked my way up until I became the aide de camp for the bank's president. I left there to start at what was then plain old Hamilton Concierge Services. My aim was always the top and after a lot of blood, sweat and tears I got there last year.'

'Impressive.'

'Just focused and determined.'

'Is there anything you *don't* excel in?'

'Not much. But then, I tend to steer clear of things I know I won't be good at.'

'Such as?'

'Opera singing and rugby,' she said drily.

'That's it?'

A pause. 'There may be other stuff,' she said, hedging in a way that piqued his curiosity.

'Like what?'

'Just stuff.'

'Sex?'

It was an educated guess, based on the last couple of nights, but he could feel her blush from all the way over here and he knew he was right. She was satisfyingly easy to read.

'It's complicated.'

'So it would seem.'

'Anyway,' she said briskly. 'I think that's quite enough about me. What about you? The business press sings your praises almost weekly. You're said to have the Midas touch when it comes to wine and sales and things, and you're good at fixing sinks and fetching lunch. You pursue excellence, too.'

'But not at the expense of all else.' He had friends. He didn't fear failure. Not professionally, at least. On a personal level, it was a different matter altogether. He'd failed his wife and son so badly the guilt and regret still burned through him like boiling oil. But he learned from his mistakes. It wouldn't happen again. Ever.

'You think it's a flaw,' she said, a touch defensively. 'Don't you?'

'No. Why on earth would it be? Why wouldn't you want to be and do the best you can? Besides, the pursuit of perfection keeps me on an even keel and I like feeling good about myself.'

Was it the only thing that made her feel good about herself? That didn't sound healthy, but then, what did he know? He was hardly a role model in matters of self-worth. He'd spent a decade wreaking havoc across Europe trying to find his. Thanks to his unforgivable role in the deaths of Arturo and Calysta, it still remained elusive.

'But you are not alone in thinking it's a problem,' she continued, refocusing his attention before it tumbled down that rabbit hole of pain and guilt. 'I once went to a therapist who suggested the same thing.'

'Why did you need a therapist?'

'I didn't. My mother arranged it and I was in too bad a place to summon up the energy to refuse. My engagement had ended and I was wallowing in a vat of self-doubt and despondency.'

'But not heartbreak?' he said, astonished to hear she'd been engaged when by her own admission she didn't even have friends.

'Well, yes, that too, obviously.'

'What happened?'

'We discovered we weren't suited. My expectations of him were too high apparently, which again I don't see as a problem, even if he did. I mean, what's wrong with wanting and expecting things from people, including the best?'

'Nothing.'

'Quite.'

'As long as what you want and expect isn't beyond what they can give, of course.'

Orla didn't seem to have a response to that. As he swung the Land Rover off the road and onto a bumpy track, Duarte glanced over to see she was looking at him shrewdly, a faint frown creasing her forehead. The memory of their conversation about attraction, the moment she'd asked him if he was speaking from experience in particular, flew into his head and his chest tightened as if gripped by a vice. She was astute. All this talk about therapy and relationship expectations was making him uneasy. If she decided to turn the conversation back to him, asking the kind of questions he'd been asking her, probing into the deeply personal, the roiling of his stomach would get worse and that was hardly the plan for today.

So it was a good thing, then, that, as he pulled up beneath the wide-spreading branches of an acacia tree, they'd reached their destination.

'We're here.'

CHAPTER SEVEN

'HERE' WAS A deserted bend in a stretch of the river that flowed close to the border with Spain but still within the district of Bragança. On both banks, terraces planted with vines were carved into the steep hills that descended to the shore. Just beyond the spot where Duarte had stopped, a golden sandy beach protected by a dense forest shimmered in the hot midday sun. It was secluded and beautiful, quiet and tranquil, and couldn't have reflected Orla's inner state less.

She was just so confused, she thought despairingly, hopping down from the Land Rover and seeking distance and air by wandering down to the shore. By Duarte and his effect on her, but also, more pertinently, by herself. She didn't understand what she was doing. She knew she shouldn't have accepted his invitation to spend the day with him. She had myriad excuses to decline—principally work and the mortification of the evening before—yet she'd found a counter argument to every single one of them.

Why had she done that?

Could it be because she simply wanted to find out more about him? Their interactions over the phone and email were naturally all about him and what he needed from her, but here, so far, the conversation had been all about her. Adept at deflection, he'd largely remained an enigma. So had she accepted it to correct a perceived imbalance that had her constantly on the back foot? Or really, did she just burn with the need to uncover the stories that lay behind the shadows that occasionally flitted across his expression and the guarded wariness that she sometimes caught in his gaze?

If it was the latter, she reflected, lifting her hand to shield her eyes as she gazed at the stunning panoramic view, she wasn't doing a very good job of it, because apart from the brief yet illuminating glimpse he'd given her into his upbringing, the conversation on the way here had hardly corrected any imbalance. On the contrary, it had tipped the scales further in his direction.

What on earth made her want to tell Duarte everything about herself? Why had she brought up the subject of her ex? His way of plain speaking must have rubbed off on her, but whatever had prodded her to mention it, she wished she hadn't. His comment about not expecting more than someone was able to give had stuck in her mind. Was that what she'd done with Matt? Had her expectations been unfairly high? While breaking off their engagement shortly after he'd been made redundant, he'd called her draining, unsupportive and impossible to please. At the time, she'd believed that if he couldn't match up, if he wasn't good enough to get another job, that was his problem, but maybe it wasn't that simple.

Adding to the general chaos filling her head was the suspicion that she'd agreed to today because, despite the disaster of last night, she actually wanted a conversation with Duarte about expectations and tricks. She wanted to know what his goals were, particularly with regards to her. It was entirely possible that deep down, against all the odds, despite all the evidence, she still had hope. Her pulse had skipped a beat when he'd pulled up outside her hotel. Sitting next to him as he drove her here had made her stomach churn and she'd felt as if she couldn't breathe even though the Land Rover had no roof and oxygen abounded.

It was madness, none of it made any sense, and, for someone who always knew what she was doing and where she was going, this flip-flopping of thoughts, the loss of control and her irrational behaviour was a worrying state of affairs. The most sensible, safest thing to do, therefore, would be to tell him she wanted to go back, but that ship had sailed because she didn't.

With a sigh of exasperated helplessness, Orla turned round and walked back to the Land Rover, where Duarte was heaving a cool box out of the boot with impressive ease. Perhaps she'd find some kind of comfort by attempting to rebalance the scales of personal information. Probing into the tragedy of his family might be a step too far, but there were plenty of other things she wanted to know. If *she* was the one asking the questions for a change, perhaps she'd be able to claw back some sense of control.

'How did you find this place?'

'It's part of the estate,' he said, handing her a blanket and taking the cool box and a basket to a flat, grassy, shady spot at the edge of the beach. 'A well-kept secret passed down the generations.'

Part of the estate? Just how big was it? They'd driven for nearly an hour to get here, the road winding up through hill after hill before dropping into the valley. It had to be vast. 'It's spectacular.'

'It's the perfect place for a picnic.'

And what else? Seduction? Who else had he brought here? Lovers? His wife? 'Do you come here often?'

'Not for years. As a university student I brought a girlfriend here once. I haven't been back since.'

With inexplicable relief, Orla laid out the blanket. Duarte dropped to his knees, opened the cool box and began setting out the food, a mouthwatering selection of cold meats and cheeses, tomatoes, olives and rolls. Then from the basket he produced a clear bottle half filled with ruby-coloured liquid, and two glasses.

'What's that?'

'Our wine.'

Their wine? Hmm. She sat down and frowned. 'Is it still drinkable?'

'Should be.' He poured a measure into each glass and handed her one. 'I've been meaning to say thank you.'

'You're welcome.'

'I was impressed.'

It was odd how her pulse gave a little kick at that. 'You didn't look it.'

'You'd succeeded where I'd failed,' he said with a wry smile. 'My pride may have been dented.'

Was that what it had been? With his confidence, he didn't seem the type, and when she recalled how icy he'd become on hearing how she'd acquired it she had the feeling there'd been more to it. 'Is your pride really that fragile?'

'As an eggshell. Hence why we're here.'

Right. Last night. Goals of his own. Research into expectations and tricks… And what had they been discussing again? Ah, yes. The wine.

'Why didn't you finish it the other night?' she asked,

at least ten degrees warmer than she had been a moment before.

'I don't drink alone.'

'Why not? Too great a temptation?'

He gave a slight shrug. 'Something like that.'

Not something like that, Orla decided. Or at least not *just* something like that. Could he have been responsible for the terrible mess she'd found at the house ten days ago? Could drowning his sorrows have been the way he'd handled the deaths of his wife and child? Had he been there, done that? It did seem to be the obvious explanation, and rumour had it he had disappeared for two whole months. However, that was a question she *wasn't* going to ask. That was way too personal.

And in any case *this* glass of wine was making her think of the kiss in his office-slash-sitting room. Of legs. Of tasting and touching and an overwhelming of the senses. She'd let her head get the better of her too then, she thought with a sigh that she stifled with a sip of the wine that was indeed as delicious now as it had been a couple of days ago. Truly, she was her own worst enemy.

With a 'Help yourself' Duarte handed her a plate, and waited for her to take her pick of the smorgasbord before filling his own. Orla sat back and crossed her legs and tried not to ogle as he stretched out on his side and propped himself up on an elbow.

'This is delicious,' she said, nibbling on a chicken leg, then wiping her fingers on a napkin and contemplating what to sample next.

'The cafe in the village is superb.'

'Do you cook?'

It was hardly the most exciting of conversational

topics but she was finding it hard to keep her mind off his hands. She could recall them on her body and, despite the heat of the sun, shivers were skating down her spine. But she'd been here before and wasn't the definition of madness doing something over and over again, expecting different results?

'Occasionally,' he said, breaking open a roll and stuffing it with slices of *presunto*. 'I eat out a lot.'

'For work?'

'Yes. Before I took over as CEO, I was in charge of PR and marketing. It involved a lot of wining and dining.'

'I bet you were good at that.'

He flashed her a quick, dazzling grin. 'I was very good at that.'

He was very good at everything. Except, she rather thought, answering some of her questions truthfully.

'So how did you become CEO?' she asked, popping a piece of soft, creamy cheese into her mouth and almost groaning with delight as the flavour burst on her tongue.

'My father wanted to retire,' he said smoothly. 'The timing was right.'

'Any charges of nepotism?'

'Some.'

'Disproved?'

'I would hope so.'

'I signed you up shortly after.'

He regarded her thoughtfully. 'You're good with dates.'

'I have to be. For my job. So where do you live?' she asked before he could start questioning her about dates of a different kind, which, in her case, were non-existent. He'd once described Casa do São Romão as his home, and maybe it had been for a while, but no one had been living there for a long time.

'I have an apartment in Porto.'

'That's a long way.'

'It is,' he agreed with a nod.

'Do you go there every evening and return every morning?'

'No. I've been staying here. At the Casa. Where I first found you.'

She spun back to the moment this had all begun, remembering how hostile and grim-faced he'd been back then—was it really only four days ago?—and her heart skipped a beat. Was he sleeping in the bed she'd slept in? On the same sheets? For some reason that felt incredibly intimate and her cheeks heated.

'What's the story there?' she asked distractedly, trying to get the fluster and the blush she could feel hitting her face under control.

'What do you mean?'

Oh, no.

Her heart gave a lurch and her gaze flew to his. He'd gone very still, the lazy smile nowhere to be seen, his guard sky high, and she wished she could retract the question because she genuinely hadn't meant to ask. But now she had, she wasn't about to take it back. The curiosity had been killing her. 'The house was a total mess.'

His eyes shadowed for a moment. 'Yes.'

'What happened?'

'The cleaner quit.'

She didn't believe that for a moment. 'You should have asked me to find you another.'

'It must have slipped my mind.'

No, it hadn't. She doubted it had even crossed his

mind, and part of her wanted to press him on it, but his jaw was rigid, his eyes were dark and his expression was filled with…yes, *anguish*.

Her heart turned over and her throat tightened, and she ruthlessly quelled the questions spinning round her head. She couldn't make it worse for him. This time of year had to be awful enough anyway. His son had been stillborn in early May. His wife had died six weeks later. Three years ago next fortnight, in fact. On both occasions her company had sent flowers, a wholly inadequate gesture, she'd thought at the time, if conventionally appropriate.

'I believe we were going to have a discussion about tricks,' she said, now deeply regretting the fact that she'd invaded his privacy and desperately seeking a way to lighten the mood.

As she'd hoped, the anguish faded and a gleam lit the dark, stormy depths of his eyes, and some of the tension gripping her muscles eased.

'I'm intrigued by the ones you think I know.'

'Well, obviously I don't have details,' she said, putting her plate to one side, her appetite gone. 'But I've read the gossip. You've slept with a lot of women.'

'You shouldn't believe everything you read.'

'Do you deny it?'

'No.'

'How many?'

'I've never kept count.'

'That many? You *must* have tricks.'

'I don't,' he said simply. 'What I do have is instinct. I watch, listen and learn. There's no manual and there are no expectations other than that everyone has a great time.'

Everyone? How many women did he have at once? God, the sun really was scorching today. 'Do you really think that the only way to get rid of attraction is by giving in to it?'

'Yes.'

He sounded adamant, but surely his wife had to have been the exception. Presumably in marriage, the continuation of attraction was a bonus rather a hindrance. But then, what did she know? She was hardly an expert. She'd once planned to marry a man to whom she'd only very tepidly been attracted, which boggled the mind because if she compared the effect Matt had had on her with that of Duarte, well, there *was* no comparison.

'As I mentioned,' she said, determinedly ignoring the unacceptable longing to know more about his marriage when she'd already probed far too much, 'my experience is limited.'

He arched one dark eyebrow. 'The ex-fiancé?'

'Yes. And it wasn't all that great.'

'How long were you engaged?'

'Six months. We dated for a year before that.'

'You implied you had no friends.'

Well, no, she didn't. At least, none that she'd call good and none that lasted. Her hours were long, longer since she'd bought into the business and half of it was now her responsibility. She didn't have much time for socialising. And that was fine. 'I work a lot.'

'So how did you meet?'

'Via a dating app.'

She'd been twenty-four and lonely, not to mention still a virgin, thanks to her determination to outperform all her targets at work. She'd wanted to rectify that, since it had somehow felt like failure. Matt had seemed perfect, as driven professionally and personally as she was, and the future had looked so golden she'd forced herself to simply accept the fact that the sex was lukewarm at best.

'How did he propose? On an iceberg?'

As if. 'Over breakfast one morning. He's a tax accountant. He said it would make good fiscal sense to pool our resources, which in hindsight, explains a lot.'

'When did it end?'

'Four years ago. A long time, I will admit,' she said in response to his arch of an eyebrow, 'but crappy sex isn't hard to miss, especially when it was probably all my fault anyway.'

'How the hell would it be your fault?'

'I think I might be frigid.'

'You are far from frigid,' he said, his gaze drifting over her before settling on her mouth. 'You just need to think less and trust in the chemistry. Ours is outstanding, by the way, and that's unusual.'

'What a waste.'

'You also probably need to be in control.'

She stared at him, the ground tilting beneath her for a moment, and said, 'Do you think so?' even as a tiny voice in her head went, Well, *duh*.

'You said so yourself.'

'I was talking about work.'

'Why would it be different in other areas?'

Hmm. Perhaps it wouldn't. She'd never analysed control as an issue before. But, thinking about it, events beyond her control were generally the ones that sent her into a panic, which was why she tried so hard to mitigate them. So maybe he had a point.

'And in light of that,' he continued, his gaze lifting

to hers, the heat blazing in his eyes hitting her like a punch to the gut, 'I should tell you that you can do anything you want to me whenever you want.'

Her mouth went dry and her breath hitched. 'Seriously?'

'Completely. You'd be one hundred per cent in charge. You could decide what you like and what you don't like and you could stop any time.'

'Would that make a difference?'

'You'll only know if you try. Give yourself instructions. Give *me* instructions. You're good at that.'

She was. And it was tempting because she wanted to experience rockets going off and bone-melting bliss. But then, there was the night of the kiss and yesterday, and the possibility that history would repeat itself, at which point she'd have to catch the next plane home with her tail between her legs and hand his account to a colleague, which wasn't an attractive prospect.

'You don't take instructions,' she said.

'No, I don't. But for you, I'm prepared to make an exception.'

'Why?'

'Because I want you. You're stunning and sexy as hell. And passionate, beneath the surface. It seems a shame to let all that go to waste. And I like you.'

For a moment, Orla was speechless. She was too busy gazing at him and melting like butter in the sun to be able to even think straight. He thought her stunning? He liked her? Had he taken another bang to the head?

'But what if you don't like what I do?' she said eventually.

'I very much doubt that would be possible,' he said,

his voice low and so very certain. 'There are no rules. Just do what comes naturally.'

Oh, to have his confidence. But she'd never done anything naturally. She didn't trust in instinct. She studied and planned and practised until everything she did was perfect. She proofread her emails three times before hitting send. When she had to give a presentation she didn't leave anything to the last minute, oh, no. She had it ready weeks in advance, all the better to practise it, practise it and practise it some more. She just didn't understand how instinct—uncontrollable and unpredictable—could be more reliable than careful, considered preparation.

But maybe this wasn't something that could be studied. There was no test, at least, not that she knew of. And what was she going to do? Embrace celibacy, live half a life, in case she continued to fail? That sounded like failure of a different kind. And rather cowardly. So could she change the habit of a lifetime and switch from study to instinct?

Perhaps there was only one way to find out.

Her heart was by now crashing against her ribs so hard she feared one might crack, but Orla drummed up every drop of courage she possessed and said, 'Lie back.'

A muscle in Duarte's jaw jumped and an unholy glint lit his rapidly darkening eyes. 'See?' he said, a wicked grin curving his mouth as he slowly rolled over, using his elbows to prop himself up. 'I told you that you were good at giving orders.'

'Don't talk. I need to concentrate on doing what comes naturally.'

'Ironic.'

'Shh.'

If he wasn't going to be quiet she was going to have to put his mouth to an alternative use. Would that be a good place to start? The right place?

No.

There was no right place. She'd start wherever she wanted to start. And right now, she wanted to explore his body, in detail and at length. Determinedly silencing the hyper-critical voice in her head that was desperate to analyse what she was doing and assess her performance, Orla moved across the blanket, avoiding the remnants of lunch, and knelt beside him, stretched out before her like her own personal banquet.

With her breath in her throat, she leaned forwards and began undoing the buttons of his shirt, taking her time, savouring every inch of gorgeous tanned skin that her movements exposed. But it was awkward at this angle. She felt like a doctor examining a patient—not the ideal scenario to be envisaging—so she shifted, yanked up her skirt, and in one smooth movement she was sitting astride him, and ah, yes, this was better. From here, she could put her hands on his shoulders, and with his help remove the shirt altogether.

As she began to trace the muscles of his chest and then lower, of his abdomen, he tensed and let out a long hiss, and when she lifted her gaze to his face she saw that his eyes were dark and stormy and his jaw was rigid.

He wanted her. A lot. She could feel the hard steel of his erection pressed against her soft centre, and suddenly, unexpectedly, a rush of liquid heat poured through her and settled low in her pelvis. Her head spun and her pulse raced, but she wasn't going to analyse it.

She wasn't going to think about anything. Instead, she was going to kiss him.

Bending forwards and training her gaze on his mouth, Orla planted her hands on the blanket and lowered her head. Her lips settled on his and she tentatively slid her tongue between them to meet his. As she explored him, slowly and thoroughly, her eyes fluttered shut and sparks danced in her head. Her senses took over and it wasn't even a conscious decision that she'd had to make. She was far too drugged for that. He tasted of rich wine and delicious wickedness. His spicy, masculine scent wound through her, intoxicating her further.

She could feel his restraint as he kissed her back, in the rigidity of his body and the curling of his hands into fists at his sides. To know how strongly she was affecting him gave her the biggest of kicks and the confidence to tear her mouth from his and move it along his jaw. The feel of his stubble against her skin made her shiver and his breathing was harsh in her ear. When her mouth closed over the pulse hammering at the base of his throat, he actually growled.

Badly in need of air, Orla drew back dazedly, genuinely panting, and looked down, and somehow, *instinctively* maybe, her hands had made their way to his chest. His heart was thundering beneath her palms, almost as hard and fast as hers, and oh, look, now they were sliding down over hot skin and a light dusting of hair that narrowed down and disappeared beneath the waistband of his shorts.

She was burning up. Her T-shirt was too tight. She was struggling to breathe, and without thought, without a care, she whipped it off and tossed it to one side.

Her bra—lacy today, as if subconsciously she'd *known* that this was a possibility—followed a moment later, leaving her bare from the waist up and exposed to his gaze. But the brush of a breeze made no difference to her temperature, not when Duarte was looking at her with such blazing hunger.

'You're killing me,' he said roughly.

He sounded tortured and for a split-second Orla wondered whether she was doing something wrong, but there *was* no right or wrong, she reminded herself firmly. There was just heat and desire, and to her giddy delight she was still feeling it all.

But she wanted more. Much more.

'Touch me,' she murmured, her voice scratchy and low.

With one swift move, Duarte shifted her down and pushed himself up, one arm sliding round her back to hold her in place. Orla was still catching her breath when his other hand landed on her waist, but she nevertheless felt the sizzle across her skin, as if she'd been branded.

'More,' she gasped, wrapping her hands round his neck and sinking her fingers into his hair while he obliged her by sliding his hand up her side to her breast.

He cupped her there, stroking her feverish flesh, and oh, it was so very different to the night before. Tingles were spreading through her entire body, tiny sparks of electricity that she felt from the top of her head to the ends of her toes and made her tremble. She groaned, she couldn't help it, and this time there was nothing fake or forced about it. This time it had risen up from somewhere deep within her.

She was dizzy with longing. Able to focus on nothing but the sight of his large, tanned hands moving over her skin and the burn they left in their wake. She was growing increasingly desperate to find out what she was capable of, to do something to ease the gnawing ache intensifying inside her. Breathing hard, she reached down. With trembling fingers and a banging heart, she undid his belt then grappled with his fly. Duarte shifted so that she could shove his shorts and underpants down, and then he was in her hand, velvety hot and as hard as iron.

But running her fingers over him wasn't enough. She wanted him in her mouth, to taste him, to find out if he liked that, *how* he liked that, so she planted a hand on his chest and pushed him back. He let out a soft gasp of surprise, but when she scooted down his body and closed her mouth over him, doing to him exactly what she wanted to do, his gasps became harsher, more ragged, and shudders racked his powerful body.

Nature was marvellous, instinct was wonderful, and oh, he *did* like that. He liked every lick, every stroke. And so did she, she liked it a lot, but the clawing ache was relentless now and she badly wanted him inside her. She lifted her head and looked at him. His eyes were dark and dazed and his jaw was clenched, tension gripping every muscle of his body.

'Condom?' she managed, her pulse hammering and her breath coming in sharp, shallow pants.

'Basket.'

The roughness of his voice, almost a growl, scraped over her nerve endings and, about to expire with need, Orla reached over and found it.

'I hope you don't think I'm using you,' she said shakily as she ripped the packet open.

'You aren't but I couldn't care less if you were,' he said through gritted teeth, taking the condom and applying it with impressively swift efficiency while she rid herself of her knickers.

Catching her lower lip with her teeth, she lifted her hips and sank down onto him, her breath hitching at the incredible feel of him, so big and deep inside her. She leaned forwards to kiss him, her hands on his shoulders for support, and began to move. She couldn't help herself. It was as if her body had a mind of its own and she was merely along for the ride.

And what a ride it was becoming. Her blood was on fire. Her bones were melting. Their kisses were generating enough electricity to power a small country and with every wild roll of her hips, sensation blazed through her.

So this was the result when you let things happen naturally, she thought dazedly, as the pressure inside her grew. This was what it was like to moan and groan and sigh without intending to.

Duarte clamped one hand on the small of her back and the other to the back of her neck, pressing her more tightly against him and angling her head to deepen their kisses, as if able to read what she needed and taking care of it. And she found she was all right with that. She was all right with everything. More than all right, in fact.

Her movements were becoming wilder, more uncontrollable. Kissing was impossible and she was unbearably hot. Her body didn't feel like her own. It was being driven by a need that defied analysis—huge, overwhelming, breathtaking. She ached all over, the tension filling her agonising. Her heart was thundering, the pressure was building and she was racing in the direction of something that was barrelling towards her.

And then somewhere in the recesses of her brain, she was aware of Duarte reaching round and pressing his fingers against her with mind-blowing accuracy, and suddenly, with a cry she just couldn't contain, she shattered into a million scorching pieces. Wave after wave of pleasure crashed over her, so intensely she saw stars. Pure ecstasy flooded her entire body and she found she was shaking all over, fighting for breath, for sanity, and convulsing around him.

And when he thrust up one last time, impossibly hard and deep, a great groan tearing from his throat as he pulsed into her over and over again, triggering tiny aftershocks of delight, she knew that it had been perfect. Wonderfully, gloriously, perfect.

CHAPTER EIGHT

UTTERLY SPENT, HIS mind blown and his body boneless, Duarte flopped back, taking Orla, sweat-slicked and limp, with him. He was breathing hard and reeling, scarcely able to believe what had just happened. When he'd suggested she take the initiative and run with it, he'd expected she would need a lot more persuasion. He'd anticipated something resembling a slow burn. Instead, he'd encountered a wildfire.

He couldn't remember the last time he'd come across such enthusiasm. Or experienced such exquisite agony. He'd never had any trouble relinquishing control when it came to sex, but how he'd managed not to touch her at first he had no idea. The thoroughness with which she'd explored him… The torture she'd subjected him to… When her mouth had closed over him he'd nearly jumped out of his skin. When his orgasm had hit, he'd almost passed out.

Orla carefully lifted herself off him, making him wince slightly as she did so, and immediately he missed the soft, warm weight of her body. He was filled with the urge to pull her back into his arms and relight the fire that burned between them, because, despite the fact that he hadn't yet got his breath back from the last quarter of an hour, he wanted more. A lot more.

Which, he thought with a disconcerting jolt as he turned away to deal with the condom with surprisingly shaky hands, was…unexpected.

He hadn't been lying when he'd told Orla that in his pre-marriage experience, one night had generally been enough to satisfy any desire he'd felt. He'd been easily bored and had enjoyed variety, constantly seeking the attention he'd craved in new people. But apparently he'd changed in more ways than one in the last few years, because not only could he take or leave attention these days, he was far from bored with Orla and the thought of variety made him want to recoil in disgust.

Which meant what? What did he want from her? More of this, absolutely, but nothing permanent, that was for sure. So something temporary, then. Sex for as long as she was here, perhaps. That could work. In fact, that would be ideal, because it would both assuage his rampant desire for her until it burned out altogether and provide a much-needed distraction. The anniversary of his wife's death, which never failed to challenge his ability to keep the crushing pain of betrayal and the overwhelming guilt under control, was rapidly approaching. An affair with Orla would be infinitely preferable to seeking solace at the bottom of a bottle, which was how he'd handled both the immediate aftermath of the tragedy and the anniversaries of the last two years.

Wanting more with her was no cause for concern, he assured himself as he rolled back to face her and propped himself up on his elbow while the plan in his head solidified. It wasn't as if he wouldn't be able to send her on her way when it was over.

What *was*, potentially, a worry was whether she'd be on board with the idea. She'd agreed to a one-time thing. That might have been enough for her, a tick in a box, a failure overcome. The control was still in her hands—she could easily turn him down—and that put him faintly on edge, but he'd just have to persuade her to see things his way because this felt like a win-win opportunity to him and he was not going to pass it up.

'So you were right,' she said huskily, still sounding a little breathless.

'About what?'

'I'm not frigid.'

She certainly wasn't. She was the opposite. She was as hot as hell. Volcanic, in fact, just as he'd imagined. So why on earth, when she pursued excellence on all fronts, had she'd chosen to marry a man who'd never been able to tap that? 'There really isn't anything you don't excel at, is there?'

She stretched languidly, tousled and flushed, half naked and stunning, and gave him a wide, satisfied grin. 'Not a lot, no. And anyway, back at you.'

She was wrong. He did not excel at everything. Far from it. He let his emotions cloud his judgement. He had a tendency towards self-absorption. He failed to protect those for whom he was responsible, and the consequences of these weaknesses of his were devastating and irreversible.

But that wasn't what this afternoon was about, so he shoved to one side the memories and the guilt, focusing instead on the gorgeous, pliant woman beside him, and said, 'Just imagine what we could do with more practice.'

'More practice?' Orla echoed softly, staring at him wide-eyed as surprise and delight mingled with the lingering traces of pleasure. 'I thought that once was generally enough.'

'So did I,' Duarte murmured, his gaze dark and hot as it slowly and thoroughly roamed over her. 'But I was wrong.'

'So what are you suggesting?'

'An affair. For the next three weeks, until the conference is over and we both leave. I'm not after a relationship, Orla. I have neither the time nor the inclination. But I do want you and I want more of this. So what do you think?'

Quite frankly, Orla thought that she'd never been so relieved to hear anything in her life. Even Isabelle Baudelaire's *'Oui, bien sûr'* in response to her request for the wine paled in comparison.

Because what had just happened had been the most intense experience of her existence, and she knew with absolute certainty that once wasn't going to be nearly enough. How could it be when it had been so unbelievably good? She wanted him again, right now, and how that was possible when she could still barely feel her toes she had no idea.

That he didn't want a relationship was fine with her. Why would he? He'd had the perfect marriage, which had been tragically cut short. His wife was irreplaceable. Peerless, even. Who could ever compete with a ghost like that?

But she didn't want a relationship either. One was quite enough, and the thought of another, which would inevitably end in deep disappointment and endless self-recrimination, was enough to bring her out in hives, and she too didn't have the time.

But she did want more sex with him, and whether or

not itches were scratched or multiplied she didn't care.
She ought to do more research. What did once prove
anyway? And she needed to know just how excellent
she could be, he could be, they could be together. She
wouldn't get distracted. She excelled at multitasking.
It was only three weeks. It would be hot, intense and
fun, and when the conference was over she'd walk away
with happy memories and no regrets.

'An affair it is.'

For Orla, the next few fabulous days were revelatory,
in both expected and unexpected ways. Having handed
her the key to unlock the secret to spectacular sex, Duarte had unleashed a devil she hadn't even known she'd
been guarding. The first time she'd experienced the
heady heights of earth-shattering bliss by the river had
just been the start of it. He'd taken it upon himself to
prove to her exactly how much pleasure her body could
endure, which had turned out to be a *lot*, and by the end
of the day she'd been completely drained, so lethargic,
her body so boneless, she'd barely been able to move.

Control was a powerful thing, she'd realised as she'd
lain there in the glow of the afternoon sun, catching her
breath yet again, stars dancing in her head. But so was
having the kind of confidence that meant you could temporarily let it go. And that was what he'd given her—
confidence—over and over again.

The realisation that she was capable of excellent sex,
that she'd finally overcome an obstacle that had been
bothering her for years, had been so overwhelming that
at one point during the afternoon she'd had to take a
moment by going for a wander alone along the shore.

Perhaps she should take more risks, she'd thought,

gently kicking at the cool water lapping at her feet. Perhaps she shouldn't simply avoid things she didn't think she'd be any good at. Because maybe, just maybe, she'd turn out to be the opposite. And look what could happen when she *did* take a risk. Yes, there was always the possibility of failure, but should she *not* fail, the results could be astounding.

From that afternoon on, when she wasn't overseeing progress at the Quinta or engaged with other work-related matters, Orla was in Duarte's bed. Or he was in hers. Whichever was closer.

She'd learned that he'd lied about not having tricks. He had plenty, every single one of them astonishing, and in the pursuit of excellence she'd developed a few of her own, one of which she'd tried out in the shower yesterday morning.

In the belief he'd gone off for his habitual early morning swim and she was on her own, she'd switched on the water, lathered herself up and started singing. Terribly. Which was why she generally didn't do it, whatever the genre. But on that occasion, she'd had a song in her head about happiness and rooms without roofs that was driving her nuts and she'd thought, what the hell?

She'd had the fright of her life when a few minutes later Duarte had appeared and asked who was strangling the cat. To cover her mortification, she'd dragged him into the shower with her and then done her very best to wipe the moment from his head, which had only reinforced her newfound belief that the outcome of taking a risk could sometimes be spectacular.

If he had concerns about the beast he'd released, he didn't show it. On the contrary, he was with her every step of the way, as insatiable as she was, as if he,

too, were making up for lost time. And maybe he was.
Whenever he appeared in the press these days he was
conspicuously on his own. If he had had a liaison of any
kind, he'd been exceptionally discreet. If he hadn't, if
she was the first person he'd slept with since his wife,
well, that didn't mean a thing.

'Come for a swim with me,' Duarte said, jolting her
out of her thoughts by tossing the sheet aside, getting
out of bed and distracting her with the view.

A swim? Orla shivered and her pulse skipped a beat.
He'd never invited her along before and she was more
than all right with that. So why the change of plan?

'I should get to work,' she murmured with real regret
because, although it wasn't going to happen, she'd like
nothing more than to mess about in the water with him.

'It's still early.'

'I don't have a costume.'

'No need,' he said, a wicked smile curving his mouth
as he threw her a towel. 'There's no one else here.'

She caught it and set it to one side. 'Another time,
maybe.'

'I'll make it worth your while.'

She frowned. 'Why the insistence?'

'Why the evasion?'

'All right,' she said with an exasperated sigh since
he clearly wasn't going to let this drop and the sight of
him all naked and perfect was robbing her of her wits
anyway. 'I can't swim.'

His dark eyebrows lifted. 'Really?'

'I was never taught. I can't ride a bike either. Overlooked as a child, remember?'

'You could have learned later.'

'Well, yes, I suppose I could have,' she said, instinctively bristling at the faint but definitely implied criticism, 'but by that point it had become another thing to not be able to do and another thing to avoid. I know it's pathetic. I don't need you to judge.'

'It's not pathetic and I'm not judging. I'm just surprised.'

'It's not *that* uncommon.'

'I will teach you.'

No, he wouldn't, was her immediate response to that. There was no way she was getting in a pool and making a complete and utter fool of herself. Especially not naked. And especially not in front of someone like him, who seemed to be brilliant at everything he did. Besides, she'd become so adept at avoiding anything that involved a beach or a pool she barely even thought about her inability to swim any more.

But now she *was*, she found herself wondering, bizarrely, whether it wouldn't be quite nice to be able to go on holiday somewhere hot at some point. Not that she had the time to go on holiday, or, in fact, anyone to go on holiday with, but two weeks in the sun with no way of cooling off had always been her idea of hell. Come to think of it, three weeks out here, working in the relentless heat and constantly covered in a thin film of sweat hadn't been much fun either from that point of view, and if she was being brutally honest she'd longingly eyed up the pools both here and at the Quinta on more than one occasion.

So maybe she ought to accept a lesson or two. Duarte had taught her about wine. He'd taught her about sex. If she was willing to risk it, he could teach her how to swim, she had no doubt. She trusted him, she realised with a warm sort of glow, and interesting things did tend to happen when he took it upon himself to improve her education. So might this not be a golden opportunity to knock another thing off her activities-to-avoid list?

'All right,' she said, gathering up her courage and assuring herself that, quite frankly, nothing could be more embarrassing than being caught singing in the shower. 'Let's go.'

'Are your hands supposed to be where they are?'

At Orla's side in the pool, Duarte watched her paddle her arms and kick her legs and grinned. 'Absolutely.'

'Only I'd have thought one on the stomach and one on the back would make more sense than one on my bottom and the other on my breast. I feel you might be taking advantage.'

There was no might about it. He took advantage of her every time he got the chance, and where his hands were was no accident. He couldn't stop wanting to touch her. Her skin was as soft as silk and her body was warm and lush. Fortunately for the relentless and mind-boggling need he had for her, she was equally as disinclined to pass up such an opportunity. As he'd suspected, beneath the slightly uptight surface bubbled a volcano that erupted with only the tiniest provocation, and he was more than happy to supply that.

The idea of an affair with Orla really had been one of his best and teaching her to swim hadn't been such a bad one either, he thought, removing his hands from her body with some reluctance and letting her go. Not only did it provide ample opportunity for close proximity and direct contact, but it had also occurred to him that by avoiding anything she wasn't good at and deliberately not trying new things, she must have missed out on a lot. For some reason, he hadn't liked the thought of that and it gave him immense satisfaction to be able to do something about it, although for the life of him he couldn't work out why. But then, he didn't know why he'd invited her for a swim in the first place either when generally he used the time to clear his head and restore the order that she so easily destroyed.

'There,' he said, shaking off the profound sense of unease that came with confusion and focusing instead on her progress across the width of the pool. 'You see? You're swimming.'

'Am I?'

At the edge, she stopped and blinked as she looked back, as if only just realising what she'd achieved. 'Oh, my God, I *am*. You're good.'

'It's not me,' he said, feeling something unidentifiable strike him square in the chest and frowning slightly. 'You're the one who had the courage to try and then gave it one hundred per cent.'

The beam she gave him was more blinding than the hot morning sun that was rising above the hills. 'I did, didn't I? How can I ever thank you?'

'There's no need to thank me,' he said as the brilliance of her smile sizzled through him and ignited the ever-present desire, which was something he *did* understand, at least. 'But if you really insist, I can think of something.'

Orla spent the next week overseeing operations that were going so smoothly they didn't require much attention, which was fortunate because her thoughts were becoming increasingly filled with Duarte. She couldn't get enough of him or the conversations they had. They'd

talked about work and travel, family and upbringings—
everything, in fact, apart from past relationships, as if
by unspoken but mutual consent that subject was off
the table.

Yesterday, she'd expressed an interest in the winemaking process and he'd taken her on a tour of the vineyard. This morning she'd swum ten full lengths of the
pool: three breaststroke, three backstroke, four crawl.
Now she was floating about the place, feeling really
rather pleased with herself about everything and unable
to keep the smile off her face, until reality intruded in
the shape of an email from a flower arranger that immediately zapped it.

The ultra-demanding client for whom she'd arranged
the iceberg marriage proposal was celebrating it tomorrow with a huge party in a marquee in the grounds of
her parents' stately home. Requirements had been extremely detailed and uncompromisingly inflexible, so
the news that the ornamental cabbages due to take a
starring role in the thirty floral displays had not turned
up was not ideal, to say the least.

Half an hour later, however, contrary to Orla's hopes
and expectations of an easy fix, 'not ideal' had become
'catastrophic'. Pacing the kitchen, she'd contacted everyone she knew, calling in favours and making prom-
ises in return. She'd tried to beg, borrow or steal, but
all to no avail, and, as she hung up on the last of her
options, panic was beginning to bubble up inside her
and a cold sweat coated her skin.

This was her fault, she thought, swallowing down the
nausea. She'd become so preoccupied with Duarte and
the incredible way he made her feel that she'd taken her
eye off the ball. She should have put in a call to all the

contractors involved in tomorrow night's event and confirmed the arrangements. She shouldn't have assumed that just because everything was going smoothly here, she could rest on her laurels elsewhere.

So what was she going to do? she wondered, anxiety spreading through her veins and burrowing deep. How was she going to fix this? She didn't have a clue. She couldn't think straight. Her head was nothing but white noise. She was useless, a complete waste of space. What on earth had made her think she deserved any kind of success? Her pulse was thundering and her chest was tightening. She couldn't breathe. *She couldn't breathe.*

'Orla? Are you all right?'

Duarte's voice filtered through the thick, swirling fog and she was dimly aware of him stalking towards her, vaguely wondering what he was doing there when he'd told her he'd be working at the house today, but mainly thinking, no. She wasn't all right. She wasn't all right at all. The room was spinning and she was hot and dizzy and quite possibly about to pass out.

But she didn't. Seconds before she toppled like a ninepin, a pair of large hands landed on her upper arms, keeping her vertical and holding her steady.

'Look at me.'

Like that was going to help. Looking at him would just make her dizzier. It always did. But sitting was good, she thought woozily as he pushed her down into a chair. Sitting would definitely stop her crumpling into a heap on the floor.

'Breathe.'

'I can't,' she croaked. Her throat was too tight and, because he'd dropped to his knees in front of her and was leaning in close, he was stealing all the air.

'Breathe with me.'

He placed her clammy hand in the centre of his chest and held it there, covering it with his warm, dry one, and she didn't even have to think about focusing on the rise and fall she could feel beneath her palm. All her senses narrowed in on that one thing, the warm solidity of his body acting like a sort of anchor, calming the chaos whirling around inside her as she instinctively followed his lead until eventually her heart rate slowed and the panic subsided.

'Thank you,' she murmured shakily, faintly mortified and not quite able to look him in the eye as she reluctantly took her hand back.

'What happened?'

'I had a panic attack.'

'Why?'

'There's a national shortage of ornamental cabbages.'

'What on earth are ornamental cabbages?'

'Bedding plants,' she said, lifting her eyes to his and seeing the fierce concern in his expression turn to puzzlement. 'For an engagement party tomorrow night. The iceberg proposal. But there aren't any. Anywhere.'

Duarte sat back on his heels and rested his forearms on his knees, his frown deepening, as if he couldn't see the problem. 'So use something else.'

If only it was that simple. 'Nothing else will do,' she said. 'The bride-to-be was very specific. It's a disaster. A complete and utter disaster.'

At the thought of it, tendrils of renewed panic began to unfurl inside her and her breath caught, making the dizziness return.

'It doesn't have to be,' he said with enviable calm. 'If you can persuade Isabelle Baudelaire to part with a two-hundred-and-fifty-thousand-dollar bottle of wine, you can persuade this bride-to-be to accept an alternative to ornamental cabbages.'

She stared at him, holding his gaze and taking strength from his steadiness until her head cleared and she could breathe once again. Well, when he put it like that, she probably could. Cardoons had been suggested by one of her contacts. They were as bold as ornamental cabbages, if not bolder, stunning in their own way, and supply wasn't an issue. 'Cardoons might work.'

'And no one will ever know.'

But that wasn't really the point. '*I* will,' she said, swallowing hard. 'I'll always know I screwed up.'

'*You* didn't,' he countered. 'This is not your fault.'

Debatable, but irrelevant. 'I'm still responsible. The buck stops with me.'

'It's a hiccup. Which you will fix. And everything will be fine.'

'It won't be fine,' she said. 'It won't be what the client wanted. It won't be perfect.'

'It will be almost perfect.'

She shook her head in denial. 'Almost perfect is not good enough.'

'It's more than enough.'

It wasn't. It never had been. Second-best wasn't in her mindset. 'That'll do' was not a phrase she'd ever used. She could understand why he didn't get it. No one ever did.

'You are exceptional at what you do, Orla,' Duarte continued in the same steady vein while she continued to resist. 'I've seen you at work here and watched how you've managed people and handled problems. Focus on the many things you've achieved and trust yourself.'

That was easy for him to say, and it gave her a kick to know that he thought her work exceptional, but she doubted his entire life imploded when he made a mistake. She'd bet he didn't live with a super-critical inner voice that constantly drove him to achieve more and be better. That battered him with insinuations of worthlessness when he was down and made him feel he *deserved* to be overlooked.

He was impossible to overlook. He just had to walk into a room and all heads swivelled in his direction. He came across as supremely confident in who he was and what he did. He was out to prove nothing.

Whereas she was out to prove...

Well, she wasn't quite sure what she was out to prove. Which was odd when she'd always known exactly what drove her. But right now, suddenly, she wasn't sure of anything. Because to her shock and confusion, as everything he'd said spun around her brain like a demented, out-of-control top, she was wondering whether she oughtn't ease up on herself a little. As he'd once pointed out, she did put an immense amount of pressure on herself. She always set herself goals that were slightly out of reach, forever needing more to silence the judgemental devil that lived in her head.

Announcing she'd acquire for Duarte the bottle of Chateau Lafite 1869 was a case in point. It had been a nigh on impossible task. She hadn't slept. She'd been too wired, too focused on the goal. She'd felt no great sense of triumph at having achieved the inconceivable in itself, only at what it had meant for her job and her emotional well-being.

She'd lived like this for the best part of twenty years. She'd never considered perfectionism a flaw—despite what that therapist she'd seen once had insinuated—but maybe he'd been right after all and it was. She knew from experience that it wasn't an irritating little personality quirk. At times it could be hellish. But maybe true perfection was impossible anyway, and if it was, then the pursuit of it was not only wildly unrealistic but also incredibly unhealthy.

How much longer could she go on like this? she wondered, her stomach and her thoughts spinning. She had no time for friends or hobbies. Her to-do lists were out of control. She was heading for burnout. Her doctor would certainly be pleased if she took her foot off the pedal. Her cortisol levels were stratospheric.

And mightn't it be nice to live in the moment for a change instead of either analysing her performance on tasks gone by or thinking about everything she had to do next? Happiness and contentment weren't things she'd ever really thought about, but could she honestly say she was happy? No. She couldn't. Not in the way her siblings were. They were far more sorted than she was. They took setbacks in their stride. They didn't wallow in recrimination and self-doubt when things went wrong. *And* they had the whole relationship thing nailed. Her sister was married and her brother had a long-term girlfriend. She, on the other hand, had been planning to marry a man with whom she had less-than-mediocre sex simply because she refused to admit defeat. She hadn't been jealous of them for years. She found she was now.

So could she unravel two decades' worth of perfectionist traits and allow that good enough *was* good enough? The thought of it made her feel even more nauseous than before, and every cell of her body was quivering with resistance, but something had to change. She couldn't carry on like this. So perhaps she could try it and see how it went, however terrifying.

'You're right,' she said, taking a deep breath and bracing herself for a giant leap into the unknown. 'Cardoons will have to do.'

Noting that the colour had returned to Orla's cheeks and the strength to her voice, Duarte got to his feet and took a surprisingly unsteady step back before turning on his heel, shoving his hands in his pockets and stalking out. He needed air, the more of it he could get and the fresher it was, the better.

Thank God he'd been around to stop her falling, he thought grimly as he emerged into the bright afternoon sunshine and inhaled raggedly, his pulse still hammering at the memory of the sight of her standing there about to swoon. Why he'd changed his mind and opted to work from here instead of staying at the house he hadn't a clue. It wasn't as if he couldn't stay away from her. He wasn't *that* desperate. He was totally in control of the effect she had on him. He didn't *need* to know where she was or what she was doing. He'd decided to head to the kitchen because he was thirsty and felt like an ice-cold beer, not because he'd caught sight of her through the window pacing up and down the flagstones with such a wretched expression on her face that his heart had almost stopped.

But none of that mattered. All that *did* matter was that he'd been in the right place at the right time and a good thing too because if she'd cracked her head on the stone floor she could have hurt herself badly. She could have lain there in pain—or worse—for hours.

Orla evidently wasn't as indestructible as she liked

to make out. She had insecurities and vulnerabilities and that meant that he was keeping an eye on her. He wasn't ignoring another woman's emotional well-being. He'd learned that lesson. So from now on, he was sticking to her like glue.

CHAPTER NINE

ORLA SAT ON the terrace at the Casa, nursing a cup of steaming coffee in the early morning sunshine and contemplating the idea that Duarte was about as ideal a man as it was possible to get. He inspired trust. He could read her body as if he'd studied her for an exam and her mind as if he could see into it. And he was good company.

When she thought about how patient he'd been while she'd freaked out about ornamental cabbages, she melted. He hadn't scoffed about the triviality of bedding plants. He hadn't diminished what to her were very real, very significant concerns. He'd handled her with care and perception and talked her off the ledge, and every time the memory of it slid into her head, she found herself grinning like a fool.

And he might have had a point about the whole 'good enough' thing, she'd grudgingly come to admit. Her demanding bride-to-be had raved about the cardoons, deeming them infinitely superior to the apparently rather lacklustre ornamental cabbage. A minor problem with the drains here had been swiftly, if imperfectly and only temporarily, resolved—which was… well, not too bad, actually. She'd spent years believing that her sense of self-worth was tied up in excelling at everything, but perhaps it didn't have to be that way. Perhaps she could find it in something else. Or even, maybe, someone else...

But Duarte was wrong about one thing. The chemistry that sizzled between them was far from fading. It burned like a living flame inside her, growing stronger every day. Colours were brighter. Smells were more intense. She knew when he was around even if she couldn't see him. Her skin would break out in goosebumps and then, a moment or two later, there he'd be.

In fact, all her senses appeared to be heightened and she felt on top of the world. Her swimming was improving in leaps and bounds. Work was going brilliantly. Progress at the Quinta was steaming ahead and she'd just signed up another ultra-high net worth client, who, happily for her company's bottom line, showed every indication of being all for opulence and extravagance.

Everything was perfect.

Her skin prickled and she couldn't help grinning when a moment later she felt Duarte sweep her hair to one side and drop a hot kiss at the base of her neck.

'I need to go to Porto this evening,' he murmured against her skin, making her shiver and wonder whether there was time for a quickie. 'I have a meeting first thing tomorrow.'

Well, maybe not quite that perfect, she amended, her spirits taking a sudden dip as the blood in her veins chilled. He'd been extremely attentive lately, ever since the ornamental cabbage incident, in fact, and she'd got used to having him around. She didn't like the idea of eating supper on her own. But it would be fine. It wasn't as if she'd miss him or anything. She'd only known him a couple of weeks, and she was hardly addicted to the sex. Honestly. She'd spent innumerable evenings alone. She'd occupy herself with work, just as she usually did.

'OK,' she said, feigning nonchalance with a casual shrug. 'No problem.'

He moved round her and dropped into the seat opposite. 'Come with me.'

At that, those spirits of hers bounced right back and her heart gave a little skip.

Well.

She *could* decline, she told herself, battling the rising urge to grin like an idiot. To prove to herself that she could take or leave him, that she *wasn't* addicted, perhaps. But God, she didn't want to. She wanted to spend the night with him in Porto. She wanted to see where he lived and what he did outside this lovely bubble they currently existed in. The world wouldn't collapse if a problem arose and she wasn't there. She had her phone and she'd keep it on.

So the hyper-critical voice in her head warning her she was straying into dangerous territory could pipe down. This *wasn't* one of those risks she'd contemplated while paddling at the edge of the river. She was still leaving once the conference was over. She wasn't going to develop any unwise ideas about what this affair of theirs either was or wasn't. But nor was she going to waste a single minute of it.

'I'd love to.'

That evening, Duarte flew her to Porto by helicopter, a forty-five-minute journey that was, in equal parts, terrifying and thrilling.

Terrifying because, despite having organised more such trips than she could count, she'd never actually taken one herself and it was alarming to be hurtling through the air in what amounted to little more than a tin can. And thrilling, because she recalled his asking her to research helicopter options and arrange the lease shortly after he'd signed up to her company's services but never in a million years had she imagined she'd one day occupy the passenger seat.

From the airport they travelled straight to his apartment on the coast, which could not be more different to the properties on the wine estate. It stretched across the entire top floor of a fifteen-storey modern block of what she supposed was cutting-edge design. Light flooded in through acres of glass and bounced off the many reflective surfaces. Rich, gleaming wood and cream marble abounded, and the views of the sea from virtually every angle were stunning. While Orla was a fan of a perfectly positioned cushion or six and the occasional colour-coded bookcase, she could see how this décor would suit Duarte. It was warm, unfussy and unashamedly masculine.

'Nice place,' she said as she walked out onto the vast, lushly planted terrace and joined him at the balcony.

'Thank you.'

He handed her a glass of *vinho verde* and the brush of his fingers against hers sent shivers scuttling down her spine in a way that really she ought to be used to by now but which still caught her by surprise.

'Have you lived here long?'

'Two and a half years.'

He must have moved here soon after his wife had died, she mused, taking a sip and feeling the deliciously cool white wine slip down her throat. It was on the tip of her tongue to ask, because increasingly she found herself wondering about the woman he'd married. What had she been like? The press had painted her as great a party animal as he'd been, but she longed to know more. And what of the overdose? Had that been an accident or deliberate?

However, she couldn't ask. The subject was still far too personal for a brief affair, however intense. Besides, it would ruin the mood of a beautiful evening, so she crushed the curiosity, turned away from the pink-and-gold-streaked sky, and instead focused on the table that sat beneath the pergola strung with fairy lights.

'What's all this?'

'Dinner.'

Well, yes, she could see that, but as she moved closer to peruse the dishes set out on the table her heart began to thud so hard she could feel it in her ears. It was more than dinner. A couple of days ago she and Duarte had had a conversation about culinary loves and hates. And here she could see a platter of langoustines and a dish of plump black olives. A bowl of vibrant guacamole, a basket of ridge-cut crisps and, on a wooden board, sliced impossibly thinly, medium rare steak. All her favourite things.

Her mouth went dry and her head spun for a second. She could totally see how he'd bedded so many women back in the day when he'd lived fast and played hard. Being the object of his attention was like standing for too long in the midday sun—dazzling and dizzying.

'God, you're good at this,' she said, wondering if it would be rude to delay dinner by dragging him off to one of the three bedrooms so she could show him her appreciation properly.

He glanced up from the candle he was in the process

of lighting and shot her a wicked grin. 'What, specifically, are you referring to?'

'The whole seduction thing.'

He went still and something flickered in the depths
of his eyes, gone before Orla could even begin to work
out what it was.

'Well, as you know, practice makes perfect,' he
drawled with a shrug, but she noticed that his smile
had hardened a fraction and suddenly, inexplicably, she
felt a bit sick.

Could she have offended him? she wondered, the
wine in her stomach turning to vinegar. Impossible. His
past was no great secret. For years his exploits had been
plastered all over the front covers of the more salacious
global press. She was merely stating a fact. There was
no need to feel bad.

'Right,' she said, her throat nevertheless strangely
tight.

'Take a seat.'

'Thank you.'

'What would you like to do tomorrow while I'm in
my meeting?' he asked, his gaze cool, his expression
unreadable.

'I'm not sure.'

'Have a think and let me know.'

While Orla slumbered peacefully in his bed, Duarte sat
on the balcony in the warm, still dark of the night, staring out into the distance, feeling anything but peaceful.

Dinner had turned out to be unexpectedly awkward.
Conversation, for once, had flowed like concrete. And
it was all because of that comment of hers about his seduction techniques.

It had stung, he thought, vaguely rubbing his chest. He didn't know why. When applied to his exploits prior to his marriage, it was nothing less than the truth. He'd revelled in the chase and honed his skills to razor-sharp perfection. Yet there'd been no calculation in his decision to have delivered to his apartment all Orla's favourite food tonight. No ulterior motive. They had to eat and it had simply seemed the easiest option. Besides, their affair was blazing. Seduction was unnecessary.

Perhaps, with hindsight, inviting her here had been a bad idea. At the time, he hadn't even had to convince himself that he needed to keep her close so he could keep an eye on her. He'd acted purely on instinct. The last two weeks had been a heady rush of lazy conversation and endless pleasure. As he'd confessed by the river, he liked her, even more so now than he had done then. She was clever and perceptive, self-aware and quick to learn. She had a smile that he wanted to bottle so he could take it out whenever he needed a moment of sunshine, and he found her scent on his pillows so soothing that staying at the Casa didn't bother him any more. Thanks to her original mistake it was unrecognisable anyway, and besides, the new memories they were creating there were doing an excellent job of erasing the old.

Missing even a second of that when she'd soon be gone for good had been deeply unappealing, and he hadn't thought twice about issuing that invitation. But he should have, because it had been rash and reckless and smacked of a man with a shaky grip on his control.

What he'd been thinking over the last fortnight he had no idea. He didn't need to know what made her tick. Her innermost thoughts and opinions were of no importance. She didn't need to know anything about the city of his birth or the place where he lived. And God knew why he'd taken her on a tour of the vineyard the day before yesterday. It wasn't as if he'd wanted her to be impressed by the changes and innovations he'd brought to the business, even though she had been.

He'd come to suspect that the stab to the chest he'd felt when she'd swum a width of his pool on her own had been one of pride. The way she'd handled the cabbage crisis had filled him with admiration, and none of that was necessary. It suggested emotional intimacy, and, unlike intimacy of the physical kind, that played no part in anything. He had no business taking it upon himself to make her see what she was missing out on, living her life the way she did. Instead of ordering all her favourite food last night they should have just eaten out. This was sex without strings and that was it.

But as long as he remembered that there was no need for concern, he told himself, ruthlessly silencing the little voice in his head trying to protest that it might have become more than that. Tonight had been a mistake and some of the things he'd said and done over the last couple of weeks had been dangerously unwise, but there was no point in overanalysing anything or attaching to it a greater significance than it warranted. What was done was done and regrets were pointless. The swimming lessons and conversation could stop easily enough. It was just a question of control.

Tomorrow he'd be in a meeting most of the morning, and when he was done he'd take Orla back to the Quinta. Once there, he'd spend the days they had left proving to her and himself exactly what this fling of theirs was. He'd keep his distance by day and make up for it by night, until she was gone, and everything would be fine.

The following morning Orla was taken on a private tour of Duarte's port house, where she discovered a taste for dry white port and a fascination for the history of his family.

The original founder, Duarte's ancestor, might have come from a humble background, but flushed with vinicultural success, he'd married into the local aristocracy, and ever since then the family's wealth and connections had multiplied. Offspring attended the world's finest schools and best universities, before generally taking up a position in the business.

Judging by the oil paintings that hung on the walls of a gallery built specifically for that purpose, Duarte's looks had been passed down the generations along with his staggering personal wealth. And he'd definitely ended up with the best of them, she'd thought dreamily as she'd stood and stared at his portrait for so long someone had asked her if she'd wanted a seat.

In comparison, she felt rather inadequate and insignificant, so to counter that she visited the most beautiful book shop she'd ever seen, followed by a *pasteleria* famed for its custard tarts, and the exquisite perfection she'd found in each had made her feel a whole lot better.

At first, Orla had been relieved to be on her own. That awkward moment before dinner last night had been followed by some horribly stilted conversation and then some mind-blowing yet strangely soulless sex. This morning, just before Duarte had left for his meeting, she'd tried to apologise, although she wasn't quite sure what she was apologising for, but he'd looked at her as if he hadn't a clue what she was referring to before kissing her senseless and telling her his car was at her disposal. It was all baffling, not least the switch from soulless to smouldering, and because she felt as though she was suddenly on shaky ground she'd welcomed the breathing space his meeting gave her.

But by the time she arrived back at the airport, she was unexpectedly sorry he hadn't been there to share the experiences with her. At the port house, she'd kept turning to ask him something about one ancestor of his or another, but of course he wasn't there. In the Livraria Lello she'd come across a book about the history of seventeenth-century winemaking in south-west Spain and had wanted to know if he already had it and, if not, whether he might like it. She'd missed him, which was ridiculous when they'd only been apart for a handful of hours and the morning had started off rather oddly, but it was what it was.

She was also filled to the brim with a warm sort of glow that she just couldn't seem to contain. For the best part of a decade she'd organised the lives of other people and, while she loved her job, when it came to things like marriage proposals on icebergs, she couldn't help but feel the occasional pang of envy. This was the first time ever that someone had arranged something solely for her. From the moment they'd taken off yesterday evening she'd barely had to lift a finger. She'd been sublimely fed, luxuriously chauffeured around and, despite the odd uncomfortable moment, been taken care of most excellently. Duarte had made all that happen— for her—and as a result she felt ever so slightly giddy.

'How was your meeting?' she asked when he joined

her in the private lounge at the airport, her heart banging against her ribs at the sight of him because the man in a beautifully cut charcoal-grey suit really was something else.

'Productive,' he said, shrugging off his jacket and rolling up his shirtsleeves with an efficiency that left her weak-kneed and breathless. 'I signed a new contract to supply the biggest department store chain in the States.'

'We should celebrate.'

His ebony gaze collided with hers, glittering with a sudden heat that stole the breath from her lungs, and everything fell away, the noise, the lights, the people, everything. 'Hold that thought.'

She held that thought all the way back to the Quinta. She couldn't have shaken it even if she'd wanted to. Forget the landscape. She'd admired it on the journey out. All she could admire now were his hands. His forearms. His profile, complete with the sexiest pair of sunglasses she'd ever seen on a man.

When not occupied with flying the helicopter, his hand was on her thigh, skin on skin, just high enough for her to wish it was higher, covering her where she needed him. She felt increasingly feverish, hot and trembling as if she were on fire. Her stomach was fluttering and her head was buzzing. The pressure in her chest matched in intensity the throbbing between her legs. She was burning up with wanting him and her heart felt too big for her chest. If she didn't have him inside her soon she was going to explode.

The minute they'd touched down on the estate and Duarte had switched off the engine, Orla unclipped her seatbelt, her hands shaking. He took off his headset and unbuckled himself, but before he could jump out she launched herself across the gap and planted herself on his lap. She smothered his gasp of shock with her mouth and started kissing him with all the wild, unidentifiable tangle of emotions swirling about inside her, until he put his hands on her head and drew her back, his eyes blazing.

'Stop.'

'No,' she breathed raggedly. She didn't want to stop, ever.

'We can't do this.'

What? 'We can.'

'You'll snap the lever.'

'Who cares?'

'I do,' he growled, nudging her off. 'It's my helicopter and I need it functional. Get in the back.'

Orla didn't have to be told twice. With less dignity than she'd have ideally liked, she scrambled between the seats and into the small utilitarian space designed not for passengers but luggage. She landed on the rubberised floor, and a second later Duarte was on top of her, pressing her down with his warm, hard weight and kissing her with a fierce, desperate need that matched her own.

She didn't want finesse. She had no idea what he was muttering in her ear, her Portuguese just not up to that, but she caught the urgency in his voice and guessed that he had no time for it either. While she yanked his shirt from the waistband of his trousers, he shoved her skirt up, dispensed with her knickers and grabbed her knees. He clamped his hands on her hips and shifted, and then his head was between her legs, his mouth on her, hot and skilled.

At the electrifying sensations that lanced through

her like lightning, a groan tore from her throat and her chest heaved. Her hands found their way to his head, and her back arched and then, suddenly, she was crying out as spasms of white-hot pleasure racked her body.

She was only dimly aware of Duarte moving to rummage around in his overnight case. She was limp. Blitzed. She'd never shattered so fast and hard that she'd very nearly passed out. Yet, unbelievably, when he lifted her hips and slid into her with one powerful thrust, it triggered a fresh wave of ecstasy that detonated the aftershocks and had her shuddering and shaking all over again.

She wrapped her arms around his neck and her legs around his waist, her heart filled to bursting, and when he hurled them both over the edge into a bright, dazzling shower of stars she wondered how, when the conference was over, she was ever going to let him go.

That was more like it, thought Duarte, rearranging his clothes while his heart rate slowed and his breathing steadied. Frantic and desperate and unexpectedly intense, but, at the end of the day, just sex.

He helped a flushed and dazed Orla off the helicopter, grabbed his bag, and then, with the intention of implementing his plan to avoid her by day at the forefront of his mind, without looking back, strode away.

'Wait.'

He instinctively stopped and spun round. 'What?' he snapped, irritated beyond belief that he didn't even seem to be able to resist her voice and determined more than ever to keep his distance the minute he'd dealt with this.

'I bought these for you.'

She held out a bag, and for a moment he just stared at it as though it were about to explode.

'Little custard tarts,' she said with a warm smile. 'Your favourite, you said.'

Yes, well, he'd said too much lately. Given away too much. But that stopped now. *'Obrigado.'*

'You're welcome. And thank you for taking me to Porto and arranging everything. No one's ever done anything like that for me before.'

Her eyes were shining and his stomach clenched with even greater unease. What was going on? Why was she looking at him so...*tenderly*? She'd better not be getting any ideas.

'It was hardly a proposal on an iceberg or dinner in front of the Mona Lisa.'

'Doesn't matter. I don't need grand gestures that are frequently style over substance. I had a really great time.'

'Good,' he said bluntly, mentally adding to his plan the need to figure out how he was going to pulverise any potential yet very much misguided expectations she may have. 'I'm returning to the house. I'll see you tonight.'

CHAPTER TEN

THREE DAYS LATER, after weeks of azure skies and glorious sunshine, the weather changed. As a result of a front moving in from the west, the pressure plummeted and a thick layer of cloud lay heavily over the estate.

All morning, Orla had felt on edge, her stomach with a strange sense of foreboding that had nothing to do with anything on the professional front.

Everything for the conference, which was now in four days' time, was either ready or about to be. Guests had been assigned rooms and arrival details had been finalised. The wine had been retrieved from the cellars and food and staff were arriving, including Mariana Valdez, who thankfully defied the stereotype of the illustrious yet temperamental uber-chef by being utterly charming.

On a personal level, however, it was an entirely different matter. Ever since they'd arrived back from Porto, Duarte had been distant and brooding and worryingly monosyllabic. Citing work, he'd been around less during the day and she found that, as in Porto, she missed him. He'd continued to rock her world at night, more so than before, in fact, which was definitely *not* a cause for complaint, but, while he was at least physically present then, emotionally, she sensed, he was always miles away.

But at least the reason for that wasn't hard to figure out. Today was the anniversary of his wife's death, and if the weight of that knowledge sat like a lump of lead on her chest she couldn't imagine what he must be going through.

She'd woken early this morning, the date flashing in her head like a beacon, and lain there next to him, listening to the gentle rumble of his breathing, her mind racing and her heart aching. How was he going to handle it? Would he want to be on his own? Would he accept her support? Should she brace herself for rejection? Silence? Should she even mention anything?

They weren't exactly friends, and she supposed a brief affair—however intense—wasn't designed to encourage that kind of intimacy. But at the same time, he'd be hurting. How could he not? He might look like a god but at the end of the day he was only human. The whirlwind fairy-tale romance had ended in tragedy. The love of his life was gone for ever. It had to be agony, and if it was solely up to her she'd be there for him. But what would he want?

In the end she'd decided to play it by ear. Whatever Duarte wanted, whatever he needed to get through the day, whether it be space, silence or sex, she'd provide it. She'd be sympathetic and supportive. She could do that, despite her ex once having told her otherwise as their engagement limped to an end. This wasn't someone who'd lost his job due to a corporate restructure and then endlessly moaned about not being able to find a new one without actually putting in all that much effort to facilitate that. This was a man who'd lost his son and beloved wife within six weeks of each other. While it was possible that perhaps she'd been a little harsh on Matt, Duarte's situation could not be more different.

Yet now, tonight, with the rain hammering down outside and the window of opportunity rapidly closing, Orla couldn't stand it any longer. Of all the scenarios that had played out in her head, the status quo had not been one of them. However, all day Duarte had acted as if nothing was different. He'd woken up and she'd braced herself for whatever might be coming her way, but he'd merely reached for her and rolled her beneath him. Then, after grabbing a coffee and a croissant, he'd opened up his laptop and got to work, just as he had yesterday, the day before and the day before that.

Perhaps denial was his coping mechanism. Perhaps he didn't need comforting or to talk about it. The trouble was, because she was aching for him, she *wanted* to talk about it. She *longed* to comfort him. The urge to bring it up had been clamouring inside her all day, swelling and intensifying to an unbearable degree, and if she didn't ask him about it now, when they were at her hotel and privacy was plentiful, then when?

'So how are you feeling?' she said, pulling the sheet over her naked, still languid body, shifting onto her side and propping herself up on her elbow as Duarte emerged from the shower room in a white towel wrapped round his hips and a cloud of steam.

He headed for the window and closed the shutters, treating her to a lovely view of his bare back in the meantime.

'That's the fifth time you've asked me that this evening,' he said tersely. 'And I'm still fine.'

But was he? Really? How could he be?

'You haven't been fine since we got back from Porto,'

she said, forcing herself to focus on the mystery of his attitude lately and not his near nakedness. 'You've been distracted and distant.'

'I've been right here.'

'I mean emotionally.'

'What do emotions have to do with anything?'

Right. Well, for him, nothing, obviously. Unfortunately, she was riddled with the things, and they were demanding attention with increasing insistence, which meant that she couldn't let this go.

'You know, if you wanted to talk to me about anything, anything at all, I'd listen,' she said. 'Like you listened to me when I was going on about plants.'

He turned, his expression puzzled. 'What on Earth would I want to talk to you about?'

For a moment, she couldn't breathe. Her lungs had frozen and her throat had closed up. OK, so that hurt, she thought, forcing out a breath. That stabbed at her heart and then sliced right through the rest of her. But she had to persevere because he was clearly in denial and that couldn't be healthy. 'I understand it might be difficult.'

'What might be?'

'Well, today.'

'Why? What's so special about today?'

Surely it didn't need to be said. Surely he didn't need to be reminded. 'It's the anniversary of your wife's death.'

Duarte went very still. His brows snapped together in the deepest frown she'd ever seen on him and he seemed to pale beneath his tan. Shock jolted through her and her eyes widened. The air thickened, the only sound in the room the sound of rain hitting the window like gunshot.

Had he forgotten? No. Impossible. It had only been three

years. He wasn't the sort of man to let the anniversary of the death of a much-loved wife slip by unnoticed. He couldn't be. She had to be mistaken. It had to be denial, after all.

But the tiny seed of doubt that had taken root in her head was growing a foot a second, and before she could stop herself she said, 'Did you forget?'

'Apparently I did,' he muttered, his jaw so tight it looked as though it was about to shatter.

She gasped and clapped a hand to her mouth. 'Why? How?'

'What business is it of yours?'

His tone was flat, brutal, and hit her like a blow to the gut, even though she knew that the answer to his question was none, no matter how much she might wish otherwise. They weren't in a relationship. They were just having an affair, and one that would soon be over. She had no right to pry. No right to feel eviscerated by the fact that he didn't want to share anything of meaning with her when she'd shared so much. She had no right to anything, but he was toppling off the pedestal she'd had him on, and suddenly that mattered. She wanted to know why. 'How could you?'

'We can't all be perfect.'

'But she was your soulmate,' she said, too agitated and distressed by the notion that he might not be the man she'd thought he was to heed the warning note in his voice. 'The love of your life. I don't understand.'

'Leave it, Orla.'

'But—'

'I said, leave it.'

Still reeling with the shock that had nearly taken out his knees, Duarte grabbed his T-shirt off the bed and yanked it on as if it might provide some kind of protection against the detonation of his world.

Orla's reminder of the date had landed like a grenade that had then gone off. He couldn't believe he'd forgotten. How the hell had it happened? He had no idea, but it did make sense of a lot of the things that had been baffling the life out of him today. Such as the curious glances she'd been casting his way. The bizarre tiptoeing around him and the constant questions about how he was feeling. The concern in her expression and the sympathy in her eyes, which he hadn't been able to fathom and which had only added to the unease that had been gripping him for the last forty-eight hours.

Around lunchtime he'd wondered if she'd started to regret their affair. If she wanted to put a stop to it for some reason that may or may not have had something to do with his strategy of keeping his distance, and had been trying to figure out a way to let him down gently.

The idea that she regretted anything about what they'd been doing had left a strangely sour taste in his mouth, and he'd recoiled in denial at the thought of their affair ending early. But he needn't have worried about that because he'd been wrong. She'd simply remembered the date, that was all, and why wouldn't she? At the time, her company had sent flowers. She'd handwritten him a personal message of condolence. And being good with dates was part of the job, she'd once told him.

He needed to get out of here, he thought grimly as he discarded the towel and pulled on his shorts and jeans. He'd already revealed too much. When, too stunned to exercise his customary caution, he'd admitted he had indeed forgotten the significance of today's date, Orla had been horrified. She'd looked at him as if he'd told her he drowned kittens for fun. She clearly found him severely lacking and he needed no judgement, from anyone, least of all from her. That was precisely what he'd been trying to avoid by allowing the myth of his marriage to perpetuate and the truth to remain buried.

So he ought to leave, pack up his things at the Casa and fly straight to Porto. Before he said or did something he'd *really* regret. Like telling her the truth. He'd have to be insane to do anything as stupid as that. He'd never uttered a word of it to anyone. If he did, to her, if he gave her even half an inch, she'd take a mile. She'd bulldoze her way through his fractured defences and poke around at the exposed weaknesses they were designed to protect. She'd uncover the man he was behind the facade, and she would find him weak. Shameful. Abhorrent.

And yet he was so sick of the secrets, the lies and the guilt. Not even his parents knew the whole truth of what had gone on during the course of his relationship with Calysta. He carried the burden alone, and because he wasn't as good at shouldering it as he liked to tell himself, it was crippling.

He didn't know how much longer he could hold it together. For weeks now, he'd been fraying at the edges, the gruelling schedule he'd adopted to keep a lid on his emotions and get through the days taking its toll. His mother was worried. He'd become short with his staff. It couldn't continue.

So what if he *did* tell Orla what had really happened? Could he trust her to listen without judgement? The feeling that somehow he'd let her down curdled his stomach. He wanted to set the record straight. He wanted to be able to let go of the guilt.

After she'd spilled the truth about her pregnancy Calysta had regularly tried to get him to talk, to no avail, and he was all too aware that if only he had, if only he'd listened, things could have turned out differently.

Might that be the case here? Could shedding the crushing load somehow be cathartic? And what if Orla *wasn't* sickened by the real him? What if somehow she understood? What if she was able to shed some light on the quagmire of his soul?

'I'm sorry,' she said hoarsely, jolting him out of his thoughts as she slid off the bed, still wrapped in the sheet, and reached for her clothes. 'I should never have brought it up. How you choose to handle this is entirely up to you. I should go.'

'No.'

Her gaze snapped to his, her eyes wide with surprise. 'What?'

'Stay.'

'Why?'

He silenced the voice in his head insisting he had to be insane to be considering doing this. The NDA Orla had signed still held. He had nothing to lose and possibly everything to gain. It would be fine.

'Because I want to tell you what really happened.'

At that, Orla went still, a shiver of apprehension rippling through her as Duarte stalked into the bathroom to hang up his towel.

She had never seen him look so serious, she thought, her heart thudding heavily as she slipped on her T-shirt and the pair of knickers she'd discarded earlier. So haunted and desolate. So completely the opposite of the former playboy she'd caught the occasional glimpse of over the last couple of weeks. She had the unsettling feeling that whatever he wanted to tell her was momentous. It was going to turn everything she thought she knew about him on its head, and that was happening already. Already his halo was shining a little less brightly than before.

Was she ready for that?

God only knew.

But she had told him she'd listen, and this *was* what she'd wanted. To discover the real man behind the image, whoever that might be. The curiosity about his wife and the marriage they'd had, not to mention the shameful jealousy she'd failed to overcome, had become unbearable. And who knew, if he wasn't dealing with everything as stoically as the world believed, maybe she could try to help him in the way he'd helped her to make a start at overcoming her issues? All she had to do was keep calm in the face of any seismic revelation, which would be a challenge when she was gripped with trepidation, but she'd just have to handle it.

'All right,' she said, settling back against the pillows as Duarte sat down in the armchair that stood in the shadows in a corner of the softly lit room. 'I'm listening.'

He rubbed his hands over his face and then shoved them through his hair. 'Calysta was far from my soulmate,' he said grimly. 'And I didn't love her. In fact, I loathed her.'

Right. Orla swallowed hard, trying to absorb the shock of that when every cell of her body wanted to resist what she was hearing.

'But what about the fairy tale?' she asked, thinking of the pictures she'd seen spread across the pages of *Hello* that March. The bride, beaming, beautiful in white. Duarte looking darkly—although, come to think of it, unsmilingly—handsome in his navy suit as they stood side by side on the battlements of a castle just outside Sintra.

'There was no fairy tale,' he said flatly. 'It ended up being more of a nightmare. We'd been dating for a month when she told me she was pregnant. I married her out of a sense of duty. I felt responsible for her and the baby. That was it.'

No. She didn't want to believe it. She wanted to clap her hands over her ears and screw her eyes tight shut. Yet why would he lie? 'And what about Calysta?' she asked, faintly dreading an answer that would make a mockery of the photos and destroy further an already tarnished image of perfection. 'Did she marry out of duty too?'

He let out a harsh laugh that chilled her to the bone instead. 'Oh, no,' he said, his voice tinged with bitterness. 'She claimed to love me.'

Her throat tightened. 'Claimed?'

A shadow flitted across his face. 'As I said, we'd only known each other a month.'

So what? She'd known him less than that and—

Well.

No.

Her feelings, whatever they might be, weren't important right now.

'What happened to make you hate her?' she said, determinedly stamping out the emotions hurtling around her system, and focusing.

'We got married when she was twelve weeks into the pregnancy. A couple of months after that we had a discussion about the future. I wanted to focus on building a secure, stable life for our son, she hadn't let up socialising and wanted to carry on. Things got increasingly heated. I told her in no uncertain terms that the partying was to stop and she told me that she'd got pregnant on purpose but really wished she'd chosen someone else.'

And there went another piece of the lovely fantasy, crashing to the ground and shattering. 'What sort of woman *does* that?'

'One who's all alone in the world and desperately wants a family,' he said. 'Her parents died when she was young. She was very insecure.'

'She was very beautiful.'

'Yes,' he said with a frown. 'She was. I wanted her and I pursued her. But she was clever. She held out.'

'Was she the mistake you referred to when you were telling me about the dangers of letting desire go unaddressed?'

He gave a brief nod. 'It made me want her more. It made me dull-witted and blind.'

'What did you do when you found out?'

He sat back, closed his eyes and pinched the bridge of his nose. 'Lost it,' he said gruffly. 'I realised I'd been trapped. I felt like a fool. I felt somehow betrayed. We had a monumental argument. Two days later I took her to the hospital because she hadn't felt any movement for a while and Arturo had previously been very active. A scan showed that he no longer had a heartbeat.'

That hung between them for a moment during which Orla's eyes began to sting and her heart ached so badly it hurt. 'You don't believe the two events were linked,' she said, barely able to get the words past the lump in her throat.

'Why not?' he said bleakly.

'Is there any evidence for that?'

He shrugged. 'There's no evidence to the contrary. And Calysta certainly blamed me.'

Whatever the truth, the grief and the guilt must have been unbearable. On top of the betrayal he'd already been feeling, he had to have been torn apart. She couldn't *begin* to imagine what it must have been like. 'What happened after that?'

'We buried him and I went back to work, but it was all a blur. We stopped speaking and she was out every night and eventually I told her I wanted a divorce. A week later she took an overdose and died.'

'Deliberately?' she asked, and held her breath.

'I don't know,' he said on a shaky exhale. 'The inquest was inconclusive. All I do know is that I should have noticed what was going on. However I felt about her, she was my responsibility. If I hadn't been so wrapped up in bitterness and resentment, I'd have been able to help. But I was a wreck on all fronts and my judgement was screwed.'

'You were young.'

'I was twenty-seven,' he said with a slow shake of his head. 'Not that young.'

'She can't have been well.'

He regarded her thoughtfully for a moment, his brow creased, then he gave a shrug. 'You're probably right about that. She was very volatile. One minute she was the life and soul of the party, the next she was under the covers with the blinds closed to shut out the light. And she had to deliver Arturo, which must have been hell.'

'She could have been depressed.'

'Or she could have decided that if I was never going to love her then life wasn't worth living.'

Her heart stopped for a second. Did he truly believe that? If he did, no wonder he was still so affected by what had happened. 'Did she see anyone afterwards? A doctor? A counsellor?'

'Not to my knowledge.'

'That's a shame.'

'Believe me, I know,' he said bitterly. 'I live with the guilt of it every single day.'

'I'm not judging.'

His eyebrows lifted. 'Aren't you?'

'No. Of course not.'

'You have impossibly high expectations of people.'

'Well, yes. But—'

His mouth twisted. 'But this is only sex, so you have no expectations of me at all.'

What? Where on earth had *that* come from?

'That wasn't what I was going to say,' she said, utterly bewildered by his observation, which was so very wrong. 'I was going to say, I've never been in a position like that, so how could I possibly judge? How could anyone? But I do know that what happened wasn't your fault.' Everything else might be up in the air right now, she knew *that* down to her bones.

'Everything points to the fact that it was,' he said roughly. 'It *feels* like it was.'

A strangely fierce need to protect surged up inside her. 'No. You're wrong. It was just an impossibly tragic set of circumstances, initiated by a woman who might have had issues, but was also selfish and manipulative,' she said, wishing she could rewind time and rewrite his history. 'I'm not surprised you're angry.'

'I'm not angry. I'm guilty.'

'You are guilty of nothing.'

'I refuse to believe that.'

'You have to.'

'I can't.'

He suddenly looked devastated, as if the weight of the world was crushing him, and the backs of her eyes stung.

'What do your parents say about it all?' she said, swallowing down the boulder in her throat.

'They believe the myth.'

So he'd been handling this all on his own? It made her heart ache for him even more. 'How did that come about?'

'Assumptions were made from the moment Calysta and I got together,' he said. 'In the aftermath they continued, and I was in no fit state to correct them. I was too busy drowning my grief and guilt in wine.'

'Here.'

He nodded. 'The villa where we'd lived on the outskirts of Porto held too many memories. I spent two full months here—you saw the evidence—and then returned to work, coming back only when I needed to escape. There were enough people waiting for me to screw the business up without me giving them more ammunition. It was easier to accept the pity and the sympathy than to explain. I'm not proud of that.'

No, that much was clear. He was tortured by all of it. He blamed himself, and she could see why, but he shouldn't. He'd done what he'd thought was the right thing and been punished for it. He hadn't had the ideal marriage. He'd had a terrible one.

She'd been right to suspect that her view of him

would be turned upside down by what he had to say but she hadn't expected the truth to be quite so gritty. Her perceptions of perfection, of him, were shattering all around her. It was huge, overwhelming, and she didn't quite know what to do with it all.

'Do you want to carry on talking about this?' she asked, taking refuge in something that thanks to him she *did* now know how to handle.

His eyes glittered. 'No.'

'Then come back to bed.'

CHAPTER ELEVEN

CONTRARY TO HIS EXPECTATIONS, Duarte didn't feel better after telling Orla the truth and he didn't feel lighter. After a fitful night, he flew to Lisbon first thing for a meeting with his lawyer about the acquisition of a vineyard in California, an exciting opportunity that would open up new markets and at any other time would have given him immense satisfaction. But there was no sense of triumph. The catharsis he'd hoped for didn't materialise. Instead, all day his stomach churned with a strange sense of dread.

There was no point pretending he didn't know the source of his apprehension. He'd had ample time to figure it out. Instead of returning to the Quinta immediately after the meeting had finished, as had been his original plan, he'd headed to the beach, where he'd spent the afternoon surfing the angry waves of the Atlantic beneath a bruised sky the colour of the Douro's slate-based soil in an effort to unravel the chaos swirling around inside him.

He'd allowed their affair to spiral out of control, he knew now with unassailable certainty. From the moment he'd threatened Orla with scuppering the agreement she'd made with Isabelle Baudelaire, he'd arrogantly assumed that he was in charge, and that that was where he'd remain. But he'd been wrong. Somehow, without his even being aware of it, the power had been gradually slipping away from him until she held it all, and he hadn't even considered that a possibility. Once again, he'd been so consumed with the present that he'd been blind to the danger of the future.

She'd sneaked through his defences and stolen control of his thoughts. She'd had him changing his plans on a whim and behaving in a way that he simply didn't recognise and certainly couldn't explain. Such as teaching her to swim or encouraging her to believe that life didn't have to be perfect, that it was all right to fail. What business of his was any of that?

Things between them had become too intense. He'd wanted a distraction, sure, but he'd never expected to it to take over so completely. He'd never anticipated the attraction intensifying instead of dissipating. Somewhere along the line their affair had turned into something that was more than just sex, despite his efforts to convince himself otherwise. He'd told her the truth about his marriage because he felt he could trust her with it, which was stupidly rash and beyond dangerous. It was true that they'd been working well together for several years now and she'd signed an NDA, so she couldn't do anything with the information, but that didn't mean it was all right to be sharing with her something so intensely personal, something that no one else knew.

And when had wanting to live up to her expectations become so important? He had no idea about that either. All he knew was that the moment she'd told him to come back to bed last night was the moment he'd realised how petrified he'd been of her judgement. How badly he *hadn't* wanted her to find him shameful and abhorrent. The relief that had flooded through him when it had become clear that she didn't had nearly had him weeping with gratitude.

He'd sworn he would never again allow a woman to hold all the power, he reminded himself grimly as he angled the helicopter and the Quinta came into view far below, and he had no intention of breaking that vow. He would not allow emotion to cloud his judgement and he would not end up in a position where he could be held accountable for someone else's well-being and destroy that someone along the way.

So he had to end things with Orla before he was in so deep that happened and he couldn't get out. She represented too great a threat to the way he wanted to live his life, free from the responsibility and commitment that experience had proven he couldn't handle. It wouldn't be fair to her, either, to let things carry on. He'd caught the way she looked at him sometimes, with stars in her eyes and a dreamy smile on her face. He didn't deserve stars and dreams. He'd never deserve her, so there was no pointing in wanting her any more.

All was set for the conference. There was no need for her to remain in Portugal. He'd told himself to back off once before and been too damn weak to follow it through, but this time it would be different. This time, the minute he landed, he'd track her down. He'd tell her it was over and send her home, whatever it took, and absolutely nothing was going to stop him.

Finally.

As the familiar rumble of the Land Rover cut through the still of the night, Orla jumped off the bed and ran to the window. Headlights lit up the road to the hotel but she could just about make out the shape of Duarte in the driving seat, and God, it was good to see him. He'd been gone *such* a long time. Because he'd been due back mid-afternoon and her texts had gone unanswered, she'd been going out of her mind with worry. She'd been on the point of calling the police when she'd received a reply from him asking where she was.

Waiting for him to return had been agonising. She'd done a lot of thinking while he'd been away and come to a number of conclusions that she ached to share with him. Given the lull in activity at the Quinta, the calm before the storm as it were, she'd had to do *something* to fill the time and it was inevitable that her thoughts would be filled with him, with herself, with them.

Especially after last night.

She understood him so much better now, she thought, her heart thundering as he got out of the car and slammed the door behind him. He was racked with guilt that in her opinion was very much misplaced. No wonder he'd flipped out so badly when he'd found her asleep in his bed the day they'd met. She'd invaded his privacy and caught a glimpse into his carefully guarded soul. She'd dug up the truth he'd kept buried and he'd resented that.

Every time she recalled what he'd been through, she wanted to weep. No one deserved to suffer such torment and it broke her heart that he'd had to deal with it alone. Had she been able to help him last night? God, she hoped so, but who knew? He'd been quiet this morning before he'd left for Lisbon.

She'd been so wrong to place him on a pedestal, she'd realised over a cup of tea this afternoon. He'd never claimed to be perfect. That had been all on her. She'd taken the bits of him he'd allowed her to see and judged him accordingly. But she'd been foolish to do so. No one was perfect. And what on earth gave her any right to judge anyone anyway?

Her ex had been right all along. She hadn't been particularly supportive or sympathetic when he'd needed it. The minute he'd told her he'd been axed as part of a strategy to reduce headcount, he'd plummeted in her estimation because she'd thought he clearly hadn't been good enough to be retained. But that had been grossly unfair of her. The loss of his job hadn't been his fault and she should have recognised the massive collapse of confidence he'd suffered because she experienced the same on the rare occasion she failed.

She *did* have expectations of people that were unjustly high, she'd thought, accepting the guilt washing over her that was nothing less than she deserved. She did judge. And because of it, she subconsciously pushed people away. Colleagues, potential friends, the occasional fiancé… She'd always told herself that she didn't have time for relationships of any kind, but in reality she'd always been pretty unforgiving of other people's foibles, and no one needed that kind of pressure. As a result, she was always on her own, which had never bothered her before, but now, she found, did. A lot. She hadn't realised how lonely she'd become until she'd met Duarte and embarked on an affair during which she was with him pretty much all day every day.

Most things in life, she'd discovered in the course of her soul-searching, weren't as black and white as she'd always assumed. They lay somewhere in the grey, the middle ground. And, while this was uncharted territory for her, it was territory that she was determined to explore because she was beginning to think that, contrary to the beliefs she'd held for so long, there was actually little good about perfectionism and having impossibly high expectations. Both made for isolation and loneliness. Both inevitably led to wholly unnecessary disappointment.

If she was being brutally honest, to discover that Duarte had feet of clay, that he was as flawed and fallible as she'd learned she was, was something of a relief. Now that she'd allowed 'good enough' into her way of thinking she'd been worrying about being able to match up to him. But now she felt that perhaps she *could* match up. At least she hoped so. Because she didn't want this to end. She wanted him. For far more than an affair. She wanted him for ever, because she was head over heels in love with him.

From the moment she'd taken his call and signed him up shortly after his marriage three and a half years ago, she'd been fascinated by him. Every time his name had popped up on her phone her heart beat that little bit faster. For every request he'd made she put in that little bit more effort. The reality of the man far outclassed any dream she'd ever had. He was patient. Thoughtful. Not to mention hot as hell and able to make her come in under thirty seconds. And he'd shone a light on some of her deepest, darkest fears and reduced them to the faintest of shadows.

But how did he feel about her?

Their affair wasn't just about sex. It never really had been. Right from the beginning he'd looked out for her. He'd taught her how to swim and shown her another, better, way to live her life. He'd given her belief in her-

self that didn't come from the pursuit of perfection, and
he'd told her the truth about his marriage. All that had
to mean something, but what?

Did she dare to find out?

It would be a massive risk, she thought, her heart
hammering even harder as she heard footsteps thud
along the corridor outside her room. They hadn't known
each other long. They both had issues that needed working through. But perhaps it was a risk she ought to take,
because they could be so good for one another. And
now she knew there was no ghost to compete with,
what was stopping them from carrying on and seeing
where things went?

At the sharp rap on the door, Orla practically jumped
a foot in the air. She spun round from the window and
headed to open it, her feet barely touching the floor.
Her heart was fit to burst with hope and anticipation,
her smile wide and giddy as she flung back the door,
but at the sight of the expression on Duarte's handsome
face, she froze.

His jaw was tight and his eyes were dark. He looked
tense, on edge, and something about the way he was
standing sent a bundle of nerves skittering through her.
He seemed braced for something, something unpleasant.

A cold sweat broke out all over her skin and her
pulse began to race. Had something happened? What?
She couldn't tell. His face was completely unreadable.

'Come in,' she said, instinct warning her to proceed
with caution as she stood to one side to let him pass.

But he didn't move an inch. 'I won't, thanks.'

What? Why not? 'Bad meeting?'

'The meeting was fine.'

'So what's wrong?' Because something was definitely up. Could it be a delayed reaction to last night's conversation? If it was, whatever he needed from her, she'd give it to him. She'd give him everything. Especially if he actually came into her room.

'Nothing's wrong,' he said, thrusting his hands into the pockets of his trousers. 'How was your day?'

'Professionally uneventful, personally illuminating.'

He frowned at that, just for a moment. 'Everything ready for Friday?'

'Yes.'

'Good. Then your services are no longer required.'

Oh? What did that mean? 'Well, I wouldn't put it quite like that,' she said with the hint of a knowing grin despite the faint ribbon of anxiety beginning to wind through her. 'My...*services*...are available until Sunday.' Hopefully even beyond.

'I'm serious,' he said. 'You should go home. Tomorrow.'

The smile slid from her face. Tomorrow was Wednesday. The conference started on Friday. What was going on? 'I should be here in case things go wrong.'

'They won't.'

'When did you become the expert?'

'I'll call if there's a problem.'

Her pulse sounded in her head. Her mouth dried, and as the truth dawned, her stomach rolled. 'You're not joking, are you?' she said with difficulty. 'You really want me to go.'

'Do I look like I'm joking?'

No. She'd never seen anyone appear to be joking less. His jaw was so tight it looked as if it were about to crack. He was pale beneath his tan, but there was no mistaking the intent behind his words. He was resolute, impenetrable. He was batting away every point, every protest she made, and would continue to do so.

And then it hit her like a blow to the head that *she* was the unpleasant business. While she'd been carefully picking up the pieces of her shattered foundations and putting them back together in a different, better way so that she could dream of a future with him, he'd been revving up to tell her to leave.

'Why?' she managed, her throat impossibly tight.

'Your work here is done.'

'And what about us?'

'There is no us.'

His face was utterly unreadable and it was horrible. Who *was* this? Where was the man she'd fallen in love with? She didn't recognise the ice-cold stranger before her.

She swallowed hard, feeling nauseous and faint. 'There could be.'

A muscle hammered in his jaw. 'There won't be.'

'Does this have anything to do with last night?'

'No,' he said with the barest of shrugs. 'I've simply had time to reflect on things and come to the realisation I've had enough.'

While she'd come to the realisation that she hadn't had nearly enough.

The pain that shot though her at that was swift and harsh. It pulverised reason and made her desperate. It made her reckless. 'I'm in love with you.'

The only indication he even heard her was a flicker of something in the depths of his eyes, but it was gone before she could identify it. 'I regret that happened.'

Orla stared at him, frozen in shock, the air trapped in her lungs while the world about her collapsed. And then, charging through the rubble, came fury. He *regretted that happened*? What the *hell*? How dared he dismiss her feelings like that, as if nothing they'd shared mattered, as if *she* didn't matter? How could he be so brutal? After everything? The hot, wild tangle of emotions swirling through her coalesced into one cold, hard lump and settled in her chest, and then, blessedly, she could feel absolutely nothing.

Up until this very moment, despite how this little chat had developed, she would have given him the benefit of the doubt. She'd have slept on it, tracked him down in the morning and tried to figure out what was behind all this. But not now. Now he'd drawn an indelible line in the sand and obliterated both what they'd had and what they could have had. Which meant that she wasn't going to hang around when she was very obviously not needed. So, contrary to his instructions—instructions! As if *he* had the right to dictate what she was to do when this was her *job*—she wouldn't be here tomorrow. She'd leave tonight. He and his bloody conference didn't deserve even a second's more consideration.

'Well, that seems to say it all, doesn't it?' she said numbly.

He gave a curt nod. 'I believe so.'

'Goodnight, then.'

'Goodnight.'

And with that, he turned round and strode down the corridor, leaving her standing there, stock still, chilled to the bone and wondering what the hell had just happened.

Duarte didn't recall getting to his car and driving back to the Casa. It was only when he switched off the engine and killed the headlights that he realised that his palms were sweating and his entire body was trembling.

With relief.

That was what it had to be, he told himself as he shakily stepped down from the Land Rover and inhaled great gulps of air.

Because he'd done what he'd set out to do and he hadn't faltered. He hadn't been blown away by the dazzling smile she'd greeted him with. He'd ruthlessly ignored the tsunami of pleasure that had rushed through him at the sight of her, and he'd resisted the fierce urge to push her back, slam the door and tumble her to the bed. When she'd told him she was in love with him he'd steeled himself so successfully that the overwhelming desire to sweep her into his arms and never let her go hadn't even made it into his head. He'd remained strong and in control at all times, even in the face of her evident shock and anger once she'd finally got the message.

As a result, he'd avoided a highly dangerous liaison that would have inevitably ended up in pieces. He didn't want to hold Orla's emotions in his hands. He couldn't be responsible for them. He didn't want her love. He wasn't capable of returning it. He'd only destroy it.

But disaster had been averted, he thought grimly as he stalked into the dark, quiet house. Tomorrow she'd leave. He was safe. More importantly, *she* was safe. So it was all good.

Thanks to the savage anger coursing through her veins like fire, Orla held it together as she packed up her things, checked out and then drove the two hundred and fifty kilometres from the hotel to the airport in the early hours of the morning. She spent the entire duration of the first flight back to London grimly thanking her lucky stars that she'd discovered Duarte's true colours before humiliating herself by begging him to let her stay. He wasn't at all the man she'd thought he was and she'd had a narrow escape, she'd told herself over and over again in the taxi from Heathrow to her flat. Such a narrow escape.

It was only when she walked over her threshold and closed the door on the world outside that she fell apart. Exhausted, miserable and wretched, her armour falling away and vanishing into thin air, she dumped her bags in the hall and sank to the floor.

The pain that lanced through her then was unlike any she'd felt before. It sliced open her chest and tore her heart to shreds. It whipped the breath from her lungs and put a sting in her eyes. She thought she'd been devastated when Matt had broken up with her, but that was a scratch compared to this. This was true agony.

How had things gone so badly wrong? she wondered as the sting became tears that seeped out of her eyes and flowed down her cheeks. They'd been going so well. She'd had no sign that anything was amiss. Apart from the strangely charged moment she'd handed him the custard tarts on their return from Porto, perhaps. At the time, she hadn't paid it much attention. She'd been too starry-eyed from the scorching encounter in the helicopter and too overwhelmed with emotion for nuance. But now she thought about it, his jaw had been rigidly tight then too. Perhaps she'd gone too far, overstepped a line.

And she'd done it again by pressing him on his marriage. Deep down he couldn't have wanted to talk about it. It was a harrowing tale. She should never have indulged her curiosity. She should never have forced him to relive it. Yes, she'd tried to backtrack and leave him in peace at the time, but she wouldn't have been able to for long. It would have festered until the belief that she was right would have pushed her to demand the truth anyway.

What had she been thinking? What on earth had made her believe that she could possibly help? She knew nothing of what he'd been through. Nothing. She wasn't right. About anything.

She'd been so stupid to allow herself to fall in love with him, she thought on a heaving, painful sob. She'd been swept away by the romance of the location and the situation and read too much into everything. Despite the intensity of their affair, the conversation and the thoughtfulness, they hadn't had a real relationship. They'd barely stepped off the estate. It had been a one-scene fantasy. The perfect fantasy, in fact, until reality had intruded and smashed it to bits.

She'd been a fool to believe in it and as deluded as Isabelle Baudelaire to assume that she could be the one to bring him back to life and teach him to love. She wasn't that person. She wouldn't ever be that person. It was truly over. There was no coming back from this. So what on earth was she going to do now?

CHAPTER TWELVE

AT EIGHT O'CLOCK in the morning Duarte addressed the team Orla had been working with and updated them on her departure. The news that she'd left without so much as a goodbye was greeted with looks of surprise and expressions of disappointment. He, however, did not share either sentiment. He'd have only been surprised if she'd defied his order to go, and all he felt was relief.

Everything had turned out exactly as he'd planned and, as he stalked into the bustling kitchen of the Quinta in search of the coffee that he needed to get through the day after a largely sleepless night, he felt as if he could breathe for the first time in weeks. He was free. Of commitment, of responsibility, and, more importantly, of all the emotions he'd felt whenever he'd been with her.

He'd definitely done the right thing in sending her away, he told himself as he retrieved two cups from the cupboard, frowned, and returned one. He'd soon get used to being on his own again. He'd only known her properly for three weeks. By Monday he'd be back in Porto, back to work, and what had happened here would fade until it became nothing more than a distant memory.

Besides, it wasn't as if he couldn't manage this coming weekend. He ran a billion-euro business. He could handle a two-day conference. How hard could it be? He didn't need Orla and her unsettling insights. He wasn't going to miss her in the slightest. He was perfectly all right. Couldn't be better, in fact, and everything was going to be fine.

But it wasn't fine. It wasn't fine at all.

Thanks to Orla's meticulous planning and preparations, the conference itself went off without a hitch. The weather had improved and the Quinta looked spectacular. The food and drink had been exceptional, issues had been discussed and problems had been solved. Any doubts anyone may have had about his ability to run his company had been well and truly squashed.

However, this boat trip up the Douro, to round off the weekend, was proving problematic.

Duarte hadn't given much thought to the route. He'd left the logistics up to the crew. But he should have insisted on knowing the plan, because they were heading for the spot where he'd taken Orla for a picnic and now, no matter how busy he'd been over the last couple of days, no matter how hard he forced himself to focus on the tour and entertain his guests this afternoon, she was all he could think about.

Despite his intentions to the contrary, he had missed her. The Casa was quiet and empty without her vibrant, dazzling presence, yet filled with the memories that they'd created together, which fractured his sleep. To his intense frustration, he'd been seeking her out all weekend. Every time it hit him that she wasn't there, bleak disappointment struck him in the chest, as confusing as it was unwelcome. And increasingly, when he thought of the way he'd sent her home, he didn't feel relief. His stomach invariably knotted and a weight sat on his chest, the regret so intense it made his head spin. His appetite had disappeared and a dull heaviness had seeped into every cell of his body.

Yesterday evening, after his guests had retired for the night and the staff had returned to the village, he'd headed for the vines, hoping that the peace and tranquillity of the hills and the warm scent of the earth would soothe the chaos swirling around inside him as it so often did. But he'd found no solace there. In fact, with no guests to distract him, his unsettled thoughts had turned to Orla even more and she'd become a burr, sticking to his skin, impossible to remove.

Today, the creeping restlessness had expanded and spread, its tendrils reaching into every inch of him, and it was now crushing him on all sides. He stood at the polished wood railing that ran around the bow of the cruiser, staring at the bend in the river around which lay the beach, breathing in deep lungsfuls of air while inside his guests helped themselves to a sumptuous buffet. But nothing he did seemed to relieve the pressure. It was in his head. In his chest. Everywhere.

His knees shook and he gripped the railing so tightly his knuckles went white, but it was too much, and suddenly, unexpectedly, something inside him snapped. His defences splintered and a wild rush of emotions, thoughts and realisations rained down on him.

He missed her, he loved her, and he'd been the biggest of fools to have taken this long to realise it. He'd been thinking about her for months, long before he'd actually met her. Making spurious requests to fill in the time between the genuine ones, just so he could hear her voice. That was how he'd ended up with the helicopter. He could have easily told his secretary to liaise with her. He hadn't had to get personally involved. But their conversations had triggered fantasies that had become addictive, fantasies that he knew now had come nowhere close to the reality, and he hadn't wanted to let that go.

For three years he'd been petrified of a relationship. Of commitment. Of letting anyone get too close and then destroying them with his staggering self-absorption and emotional obstinacy. But there was nothing terrifying about what he'd been doing with Orla. He *liked* the way he'd behaved with her—before he'd screwed everything up—*and* the fact that traces of the man he used to be had returned. She was not Calysta and this was not the same.

For days he'd been resisting and denying the points she'd made about his marriage with every bone in his body because he was too afraid of the possibility of a relationship opening up and him wrecking it. But perhaps Orla was right. Perhaps none of what had happened had been his fault. The terrible day of the scan, the obstetrician had talked about a heart defect as the most likely cause of Arturo's death in the womb, but he'd barely listened. He'd just recalled the savage argument two nights earlier, and the link between the events had seemed so damn obvious. He'd held himself to blame ever since, but maybe he had to accept that it had simply been nature at its most cruel.

And as for Calysta, after Arturo's funeral he should have been around more instead of immersing himself in work. However much he'd despised her at that point, however much he'd been grieving for the son he'd badly wanted despite the circumstances of his conception, he should have considered what she'd been going through. But he would never have loved her the way she'd needed him to, whatever the circumstances, and she would never have been able to accept that.

So could he let go of the guilt? He wanted to. God, how he wanted to. Because he wanted Orla back. He wanted her trust and her love. He wanted it all.

But whether she'd even agree to see him was anyone's guess. The look of devastation on her face when he'd told her he was sorry she'd fallen in love with him still haunted his dreams. Out of sheer fear, he'd been cruel and callous. He felt sick and his chest ached to think of it.

Could he fix the godawful mess he'd made of things? He'd do his damnedest to try. As he'd once told Orla, he too had goals, and this was his biggest, most important one ever. So he'd do whatever it took, however long it took, and this time he would not screw it up.

Releasing his white-knuckled grip on the rail, Duarte turned on his heel and stalked into the cockpit to address the captain.

'The trip is over,' he said, his jaw set and his entire body filling with resolve. 'Turn the boat around.'

'Orla!'

Orla had barely stepped out of the lift when Sam Hamilton, her co-CEO for the time being, accosted her in the lobby of their fifth-floor offices in London's West End.

At his expression, the little hairs at the back of her neck shot up and her pulse skipped a beat. The last time he'd looked this serious, three days ago, in fact, he'd told her he planned to retire within the next twelve months, and if she wanted it the business would be hers. The news should have had her punching the air in triumph. Instead, she'd just about managed to muster up a weak smile and mutter a half-hearted 'thank you', but that had been it. Despite the endless talking-tos she'd given herself recently, she was still so damn sad about Duarte.

But enough was enough. A weekend of moping about, immersed in self-pity and misery, was plenty. Any more ice cream and she'd turn into a pistachio. Who needed a relationship anyway? How many of them failed? She didn't know the statistics, but she knew it was a lot, and she wanted none of it.

No. Instead, she'd decided it was time for change. She was going to focus on her issues. She'd figured her insecurities and fears would exist whether she failed or succeeded, so she'd start with them. She'd always associated her sense of self-worth with a need to achieve, but why did it have to be that way? Why couldn't she find it elsewhere? Say, from her job? From friends? From who she was, which wasn't *so* bad really? So she was going to be less unforgiving. Of herself and other people. She'd learn to accept criticism without getting all defensive about it and start to build some proper, healthy relationships.

She'd forget about Duarte and the bittersweet memories soon enough. Just because she thought about him constantly didn't mean that she would for eternity. She'd talk herself out of it eventually. She talked herself out of things all the time. And, quite honestly, so what if she had fallen in love with him? It was nothing to be ashamed of, although it was regrettable that she'd told him. Unfortunately, you couldn't choose whom you loved and you couldn't make them love you in return.

You just had to accept things as they were, and try to avoid the chaos, mess and misery that was love for a very long time.

At least the super-loud, super-critical voice in her head had gone. She wasn't perfect, nothing in life was, and that was OK. She *was*, however, utterly drained by all this self-analysis on top of everything that had transpired before and, quite frankly, she could do without the hassle of whatever it was that had Sam in such a state so early. But she was a professional, so she'd take it in her supremely capable stride.

'Sam,' she said, plastering a smile to her face and hoisting her satchel higher onto her shoulder as they set off across the lobby. 'Is there a problem?'

'We've had a complaint.'

Oh? Her heart plummeted. No wonder he was agitated. Complaints were unwelcome, and, thankfully, rare. 'What is it?'

'It's more a case of who.'

Her eyebrows lifted. 'Who?'

'Yes. He's in your office.'

'Who is?'

'Duarte de Castro e Bragança.'

Orla froze mid-step, her head spinning and her heart suddenly pounding. No. That couldn't be the case. What did he have to complain about? Sam had informed her that the conference had been a success from start to finish, although apparently the river cruise had ended rather abruptly and ahead of schedule. And why was he in *her* office anyway?

'Can't you deal with it?' she said, her stomach clenching at the thought of him in her space, breathing her air and looking around her things. 'He's your client now.'

'I believe that's the complaint.'

What? He was the one who'd necessitated the switch with his brutal dismissal of her. So how dared he saunter in here and turn her world on its head again? This was *her* space. Her *sanctuary*.

Well.

Whatever.

Duarte didn't bother her any longer. Did Not Bother Her. She had no need to be distressed by this latest turn of events. She was immune to his charms now. She'd handle him with polite professionalism, get to the bottom of his so-called complaint and then she'd send him on his way.

'Fine,' she said flatly, setting her jaw and straightening her spine. 'Leave it with me.'

At the sound of the door to Orla's office opening, Duarte, who'd been pacing up and down in front of the window, oblivious to the view, oblivious to anything other than the drumming of his pulse and the desperate need to put things right, spun round.

Orla closed the door behind her and then turned to him, and a wave of longing crashed over him. He'd missed her. He'd missed her immeasurably. How on earth could he have sent her away? What had he been thinking?

'Good morning,' she said with a practised smile that didn't reach anywhere near her eyes, and which he hated, but then, he hadn't expected an easy ride. He deserved the ice and the bristling even if it did chill him to the bone and fill him with shame.

'Good morning.'

She strode over to the desk and sat down, so cool, so professional, so hard to read now. 'Have you been offered coffee?'

'I have,' he said, seating himself in a chair on the other side of her desk and linking his hands to stop them shaking.

'Good. So. I understand you have a complaint.'

'I do.'

'What is it?'

'I called to speak to you and was told that you'd given my account to someone else.'

'Yes,' she said with a brisk nod. 'To Sam. My co-CEO.'

He swallowed with difficulty. 'Why?'

'Because he's excellent.'

'That's not what I meant and you know it.'

'We crossed a line, Duarte,' she said bluntly, her voice completely devoid of expression. 'Do you honestly think we could have carried on working together after what happened at the Quinta?'

'Which part in particular are you referring to?'

'All of it.' She swivelled round to switch on her computer. 'It was a mistake from start to finish.'

'You don't make mistakes.'

'I do. And I've discovered recently that that's fine.'

He frowned. They'd been many things, but a mistake was not one of them. Did she really think that? Had he done that to her with his cowardice and fear?

'Was there anything else?'

Oh, yes. He wasn't done. Not by a long shot. He'd prepared a speech. He'd been practising. 'I've barely begun.'

'Well, I have a meeting in,' she glanced at her watch, 'ten minutes. So I can give you five.'

Then he didn't have a second to waste. This was the most important moment of his life. His entire future happiness depended on it. He took a deep breath and focused. 'I wanted to apologise for our last conversation,' he said gruffly, regret pouring through him at the memory of it. 'For the way I behaved. It was appalling and unnecessary, and when I think of it I am deeply ashamed.'

'Accepted,' she said with a dismissive wave of her hand.

'I wanted to explain.'

'No explanation necessary.'

His heart began to pound. 'You were right about everything.'

'Not any more, I'm not. I'm through with all that.'

What did that mean? Was she through with him too? A bolt of pure panic shot through him. 'I'm in love with you.'

She stared at her monitor, utterly still for a moment, and then she clicked her mouse and adjusted her keyboard. 'That's...regrettable,' she said, and typed in what could have been her password.

Not that he was capable of that level of logic. He was reeling with the shattering realisation that he'd blown it. For good. The flatness of her tone... The way she couldn't look at him... Her choice of words, which was no coincidence... One mad, terrible conversation that had been driven by the demons that he'd foolishly allowed to override everything else and he'd ruined the best thing that had ever happened to him.

Suddenly Duarte couldn't breathe. The shock of what

he'd done and the realisation that it was undoable had winded him. His vision blurred. His chest was tight. He couldn't speak for the pain scything through him.

'You'll be in good hands with Sam' came her voice through the fog. 'And now, if you'll excuse me, I really am very busy.'

Yes, he could see that. Whatever it was that she was looking at was demanding her full attention. She was scrolling and typing, scrolling and typing, while his world was splintering into a million tiny pieces.

'Right,' he said gruffly, his throat sore, his entire body trembling. 'I see. In that case, I won't waste another second of your time.'

He got up in a daze. Turned to leave, grateful for the fact that his legs would get him out of here. But then at the door, his hand on the handle, he stopped. No, dammit. That *wasn't* it. He wasn't having this. He'd come here for a reason. He had things to say and they needed saying. He'd vowed on the boat to do whatever it took and that was precisely what he *would* do.

Squaring his shoulders and taking strength from the determination and adrenalin rocketing around his system, Duarte spun back, and froze at the raw, naked misery that crumpled Orla's face for a split second before it disappeared and her expression was once again unreadable.

But he'd caught a glimpse behind the mask, thank *God*, and, while it killed him to see, it also had hope and relief roaring through him because she wasn't as indifferent to him as she was trying to make out. She wasn't indifferent at all.

Why, oh, why couldn't Duarte have left? Orla thought desperately, her heart racing as he slowly stalked back towards her. She'd been doing so well, holding the emotions raging through her at bay and clinging on to her dignity even though it had taken every drop of strength she possessed. So well to steel herself against his declaration of love, which meant nothing when the memory of Tuesday night was still so raw.

Why had he had to turn around at that precise moment when the pain of what she'd lost had become too much? There was no chance he hadn't caught the brief slip of her deliberately icy facade. Gone were the nerves she thought she'd detected in him a moment ago. He was all steely purpose, his jaw set and his eyes glinting darkly as he bypassed the chair he'd earlier vacated and came to perch on her desk, so close she could reach out and touch him if she wanted to.

'I still have four minutes,' he said, gripping the edge tightly as he gazed down at her.

Orla pushed her chair back, out of his mind-scrambling orbit, and sat on her hands. 'Three and a half actually.'

And that was three and a half too many. How long would her strength hold out? Already, his proximity was battering away at her defences. Already she could feel herself weakening.

'I'm so, so sorry,' he said gruffly. 'For everything that I said on Tuesday night. I was terrified of my feelings for you. I wasn't ready to let go of the past. Ever since Calysta died I've been wrapped up in the idea that because what happened to her was my fault, I can't be responsible for someone else's emotions. But you were right. About so much. Especially the guilt and the blame. And if I've been wrong about that, then I'm wrong about the rest of it. I love you, Orla.

I think I've been falling in love with you ever since I asked you to research helicopters for me when I didn't even need one.'

Her heart thundered in her ears, and, with her armour suffering blow after blow, she simply couldn't keep the icy front up any longer. 'I offered you everything,' she said hoarsely as all the hurt and pain broke through to batter her from every angle.

'I know.'

'You were cruel.'

His expression twisted and the sigh he gave was tortured. 'I know.'

'You hurt me.'

'Irrevocably?'

'I don't know.'

He stared at her, regret and sorrow filling his gaze, and then he swallowed hard and gave a nod. 'I understand,' he said roughly. 'Right. Well. That was all I wanted to say. I should go.'

He pushed himself off the desk and, in a split second that seemed to last a year, Orla's brain spun. Was she really going to let him leave? After everything he'd told her? When it had to have cost him so much to say? Despite everything she still loved him madly and she wanted nothing more than to throw herself into his arms and never let go.

But was she brave enough to do it? Just because he'd recognised his hang-ups didn't mean they were going to disappear overnight. But then, she thought, her heart hammering wildly, nor were hers. Was this one of those risks worth taking? Yes, it absolutely was.

'No. Wait,' she said before he could take a further step.

He stilled, his gaze snapping to hers, so wary, so hopeful it made her chest ache.

'I'm sorry too.'

He shook his head and frowned. 'You have nothing to apologise for.'

'I do. I should never have pushed you into talking about something you weren't ready to face.'

'I might never have been ready and I needed to face it.'

'There are things I've also had to face. Things that you've helped me to deal with.'

His jaw clenched, the tiny muscle there on the right pounding away. 'What are you saying?'

She took a deep breath and rose from her chair. 'We could continue to face them together.'

He nodded slowly, once, and her pulse skipped a beat. 'We could.'

'I've missed you.'

'Not nearly as much as I've missed you.'

He opened his arms then and whether she threw herself or he pulled her into them she didn't know. All she knew was that he was kissing her as if his life depended on it, and all her doubts and fears were being swept away on the wave of hot desire and delirious joy that was rushing through her.

'I love you,' he muttered against her mouth as his hold on her loosened. 'Very much.'

'I love you, too.'

'I've been so blind. So stupid. I'm so sorry I hurt you.' He pulled back slightly and the remorse on his face tore at her heart. 'I'll never forgive myself. How can I ever make it up to you?'

'You can start by locking the door.'

'What?'

'Lock the door,' she said again softly as she started to undo the buttons of his shirt just in case there was any lingering confusion. 'And then, my darling, you can show me exactly how sorry you are.'

'Ah, I see,' he said, a glint appearing in his eye as he did as she instructed and then took her in his arms and sat her on her desk. 'I thought you had a meeting.'

Back on the buttons, her whole body vibrating with love and happiness, Orla smiled up at him, leaned forwards and murmured in his ear, 'I lied.'

EPILOGUE

The South of France, three months later

THE LATE SEPTEMBER evening sunshine bathed the privately-owned chateau on the outskirts of Nice in warm golden sunshine. The air was heady with the scent of the lavender that was planted all around, and in the vast, lavishly appointed ballroom five hundred guests had dined on lobster and lamb before parting with millions in the wildly extravagant auction. Ten minutes ago, a band had taken to the stage and the dance floor was filling with men in tuxedos and women in silk.

Out on the terrace that overlooked the city and the sparkling azure Mediterranean beyond, Orla was wrapped in Duarte's arms, eyes closed, smiling softly and swaying to the sultry beat that was drifting out through half a dozen pairs of French doors.

Champagne had been flowing for hours, but she hadn't needed any of it. She was bubbling with happiness and overflowing with love enough as it was.

The last three months had been unbelievably brilliant. Four weeks after Duarte had made all her dreams come true that horrible then fabulous morning in her office, she'd packed up her flat and moved to Porto.

She could do her job from anywhere and his apartment needed a cushion or two. When not travelling for work, they spent the weeks in the city and the weekends at the Casa do São Romão.

Today, at lunchtime, they'd flown to Nice for Isabelle Baudelaire's charity ball and checked in to the finest hotel in the city, where they'd idled away most of the afternoon in bed before getting ready.

'One evening of your time,' she murmured against the warm skin of his neck. 'Worth the sacrifice, do you think?'

'Most definitely.'

'Isabelle told me that because of you she sold double the number of tickets she'd expected to and increased the auction donations by half.'

'I'm not sure that was anything to do with me,' he said, the vibrations of his voice sending shivers rippling through her. 'She rivals you for tenacity and skill.'

It was *all* to do with him, she thought dreamily. When he smiled, which he did frequently these days, he was irresistible. 'I wonder who won the trip to the Arctic.'

'I did.'

She leaned back and stared up at him in shock. 'Heavens, why?'

'For the icebergs.'

At the look in his eye, the expression on his face, she went very still and her breath caught. 'What?'

'The Arctic has icebergs,' he said, then frowned. 'But now I think about it, I seem to recall you saying you didn't care much for style-over-substance grand gestures, so that might have been a bad idea. And in any case the trip's in December, and I don't think I can wait that long.'

Her heart thundered and the ground beneath her feet tilted. 'Wait that long to do what?'

'To give you this. I've been carrying it around for days. You should have it before it gets lost.'

'This' was a diamond the shape and size of an almond in a ring of platinum. It sparkled in the setting sun, and when he slid it onto the third finger of her left hand her vision blurred and her throat tightened.

'I love you, Orla,' he said, softly, tenderly. 'More and more each day. Will you marry me?'

She swallowed back the lump in her throat and threw her arms round his neck. 'Yes, of course I will,' she said in between kisses. 'I love you, too. So much.'

'Sorry about the Arctic,' he murmured when they finally broke for air.

'Don't be,' she said, her heart swelling with joy and love. 'It's perfect.'

* * * * *

COMING SOON!

We really hope you enjoyed reading this book. If you're looking for more romance, be sure to head to the shops when new books are available on

Thursday 21st July

MILLS & BOON®

Coming next month

HIS DESERT BRIDE BY DEMAND
Lela May Wright

"Can you explain what happened?" Akeem asked. "The intensity?"

Could she? Nine years had passed between them—a lifetime and still... No, she couldn't.

"My father had a lifetime of being reckless for his own amusement—"

"And you wanted a taste of it?"

"No," he denied, his voice a harsh rasp.

"Then what did you want?" Charlotte pushed.

"A night—"

"You risked your reputation for a night?" She cut him off, her insides twisting. "And so far, it's been a disaster, and we haven't even got to bed." She blew out a puff of agitated air.

"Make no mistake," he warned, "things have changed."

"Changed?"

"My bed is off limits."

She laughed, a throaty gurgle. "How dare you pull me from my life—fly me who knows how many miles into a kingdom I've never heard of and turn my words back on me?" She fixed him with an exasperated glare. "How dare you try to turn the tables on me?"

"If the tables have turned on anyone," he corrected, "it is me because you will be my wife."

Continue reading
HIS DESERT BRIDE BY DEMAND
Lela May Wright

Available next month
www.millsandboon.co.uk